All But Impossible

Books by Edward D. Hoch
Crippen & Landru, Publishers

Diagnosis: Impossible, The Problems of Dr. Sam Hawthorne. Available as a print book and as a Kindle e-book

The Ripper of Storyville and Other Ben Snow Tales. Available as a Kindle e-book

The Velvet Touch. Available as a Kindle e-book

The Old Spies Club and Other Intrigues of Rand. Available as a Kindle e-book

The Iron Angel and Other Tales of the Gypsy Sleuth. Available as a Kindle e-book

More Things Impossible, The Second Casebook of Dr. Sam Hawthorne. Available as a print book and as a Kindle e-book

Nothing Is Impossible, Further Problems of Dr. Sam Hawthorne. Available as a print book and as a Kindle e-book

All But Impossible, The Impossible Files of Dr. Sam Hawthorne. Available as a print book and (forthcoming) as a Kindle e-book

All But Impossible

EDWARD D. HOCH

*With a Memory of Ed Hoch
by Douglas G. Greene*

Crippen & Landru Publishers
Norfolk, Virginia
2017

Cover Design by Gail Cross

ISBN (limited clothbound edition): 978-1-936363-21-6
ISBN (trade softcover edition): 978-1-936363-22-3

FIRST EDITION

Printed in the United States of America
on recycled acid-free paper

Crippen & Landru Publishers
P.O. Box 9315
Norfolk, VA 23505
USA

e-mail: crippenlandru@earthlink.net
web: www.crippenlandru.com

CONTENTS

ED HOCH: SOME MEMORIES

It was during the early 1970s that I first started reading *Ellery Queen's Mystery Magazine* regularly. Copies were always for sale at grocery checkout counters for 75 cents—this was, after all, more than forty years ago. I would turn first to stories by Edward D. Hoch. They were always well told, they had interesting characters and settings, and they were usually fairplay detective stories with all the clues given to the reader. During 1971 the issues also contained stories written by the pseudonymous "Mr. X." Under the series title "The Will-o'- the-Wisp-Mystery," each of the six stories was complete in itself but each ended in a cliffhanger leading to the next story. This, I said to myself, was the way a mystery story should be told. It was only later that I learned the "Mr. X' was actually Edward D. Hoch, and the idea behind the series was the brainchild of Ellery Queen himself.

Later that year, I found on a newsstand a paperback book, in the same format as *Ellery Queen's Mystery Magazine*, with the title *The Spy and the Thief*, and its author was (I was delighted to discover) Edward D. Hoch. The book featured two of Hoch's series characters, Jeffery Rand and Nick Velvet, and the introduction was by Ellery Queen. The introduction mentioned in passing that Hoch had written another short story collection—one that I had never heard of (*The Judges of Hades*) about a character about whom I was also unfamiliar (Simon Ark). I looked and looked but couldn't find a copy anywhere—this was long before the Internet.

With some trepidation, I decided to screw my courage to the sticking post (whatever Shakespeare might have meant by that phrase) and wrote to Hoch himself in care of the magazine. A short while later, a parcel arrived from the author enclosing not only a copy of the book (warmly inscribed) but also a second Simon Ark collection, *City of Brass*. All of which is a long way of saying that I discovered that Ed Hoch was not only a wonderful writer but a heck of a nice guy as well.

Ed Hoch was a rare writer, probably a unique one, in that he made a living as the author of short stories. Decades ago, in the heyday of the pulp magazines (like *Black Mask* and *Dime Detective*) and the mass market "slicks" (like *The Saturday Evening Post* and *Collier's*), a writer could be a short-story specialist, but today's market doesn't allow such specialization—unless you happen to be Ed Hoch. He eventually wrote about 960 short stories in various genres—science fiction, Westerns, historicals, young adult, and several very fine ghost stories—which are collected in *The Future Is Ours, 32 Tales of the Fantastic*, edited by Steven Steinbock—but he quickly emphasized mysteries and detective stories. He tried writing novels. One, *The Shattered Raven*, featured the Mystery Writers of America. He also wrote a series of three novels, beginning with *The Transvection Machine*, about the Computer Cops investigating future crimes. He even became a ghost writer for one of the paperback original novels that was credited to "Ellery Queen" —*The Blue Movie Murders*. But he said a week or two after he started on a novel, he wanted to work on other ideas that were always bubbling up inside his brain.

And in many ways that was the key to Ed's genius. An idea would come to him—a way of murdering someone in a locked room, a crime committed in a cabin surrounded by unmarked snow, a person who jumps from a window and vanishes—and it would percolate in his head; he would ponder it, manipulate it, come up with an original way of handling it, and a compact story would emerge. Ed loved a challenge. Friends would dare him to come up with a solution to an ingenious situation—and almost nothing would stump him for long, When he was challenged to devise a murder within the rotating door of a department store, he, of course, solved it. I was with him when he began to think about a plot device as he got on an escalator and had it worked out by the time he got off. I suggested that he write a story based on a famous plot device, the "Paris Exposition" story, a late-19th, early 20th century legend of a mother and daughter who arrive at a hotel at the Paris Exposition in 1889. The girl leaves the hotel for an hour or two, but when she returns her mother has vanished and the hotel denies that she was ever there. In some versions, even the room in the hotel has vanished. Mystery writers from Anna Katharine Green to Cornell Woolrich to John Dickson Carr adapted various parts of this story, and such movies as *Bunny Lake Is Missing* and the television series *Monk* also used it. Ed, of course, had little trouble devising an original variant in "The Problem of the Leather Man," and he slyly used my name in it for a character who, in fact, doesn't actually appear.

Ed's first published story was "Village of the Dead" about Simon Ark; it was published in 1955 in *Famous Detective*, one of the last of the pulp magazines. Ark was Hoch's tribute to the long tradition of detectives who investigate the occult. Ark spoke an ancient Coptic tongue and he implied that he had been alive for 2000 years. The cases he solved had to do with weird religious rituals and witchcraft and vampires. Soon Hoch was inventing series character after series character: Father David Noone, who combined Catholic theology with crime solving; Captain Jules Leopold of a city very much like Hoch's hometown of Rochester, New York; Ben Snow, a cowboy detective in the old West who is often confused with Billy the Kid. In 1962, he broke into *Ellery Queen's Mystery Magazine* and *Alfred Hitchcock's Mystery Magazine*, then as now the two premier magazines in the field. By the time I was a regular reader of EQMM in 1971, he was in almost every issue, and beginning in May 1973 he began an unbroken record of being in every issue for the next thirty-five years. Eventually, he was pictured six times on the cover of EQMM, a record surpassed only by Sherlock Holmes.

And he continued to devise series characters, some of the most imaginative ever to come from the pen of a mystery monger. Nick Velvet became a perennial favorite—a choosy crook who would steal only something that was considered worthless—a bald man's comb, water from a swimming pool, a birthday cake, a cigar, a balloon, a cobweb. The mystery was why anyone would pay to steal such items, and often Nick would also have to solve a crime along the way in order to avoid being arrested. Another favorite was Jeffery Rand, who began during the height of the James Bond spy craze as an expert on "concealed communications," and whose adventures continued to involve international intrigue. And Michael Vlado, a Gypsy King who solves crimes mainly in eastern Europe during the collapse of the Soviet empire. And con-man Ulysses S. Bird. And spy for George Washington, Alexander Swift, in an evocative historical series. Unlike many male authors, whose attempts to see matters through the eyes of women were, at best, embarrassing, Hoch created several persuasive female sleuths, including policewoman Annie Sears and department-store buyer Susan Holt, whose business life took her around the world. Hoch also created a youthful pair of crime-solving couriers, Juliet Ives and Walt Stanton.

For many readers—myself included—Hoch's finest creation was Dr. Sam Hawthorne, a New England country doctor from the first half of the last century who is faced with a series of impossible crimes—a wagon that enters a covered bridge and vanishes, a man murdered in a voting booth, a child who disappears from a swing, another child who vanishes from a bicycle, even one that seems to re-create Charlotte Perkins Gilman's famous tale of the yellow wallpaper as an impossible crime.

As wonderful as these stories are in their ingenuity and superb storytelling, I remember Ed Hoch mainly for himself. After he sent me those two books in 1971, Ed and I corresponded and spoke on the phone frequently until we met in person in 1986 at a Bouchercon in Baltimore. From then on, we saw each other at every Bouchercon and almost every Malice Domestic convention. Joined by our close friend Steve Steinbock—who now writes the book review column for EQMM—Ed and Ed's wife Pat and I would have dinner together and debate whose turn it was to be the host. Ed would always order the same dinner—filet mignon cooked well-done (to the consistency of a hockey puck) and french fries, with vanilla ice cream for dessert—except at the Bouchercon in Denver in 2000 when we went to a Western restaurant which not only had a young woman in tights and a feather boa on a trapeze overhead but also Western meats on the menu. I can't recall whether we persuaded him to have buffalo or elk, but it was one or the other. He survived.

Ed had an encyclopedic knowledge of mystery and detective fiction, and he knew everyone worth knowing in the field. It is often said of people that he or she "never had a bad word to say about anyone," and then someone will smirk knowingly and (wink, wink, nudge, nudge) recall when he or she did in fact have some bad words—but that was never true about Ed. I cannot recall when he ever said anything unkind or ungenerous.

Like Anthony Boucher before him, Ed was a devout Roman Catholic with a strong concern for social justice. Often we would talk about religion. On one occasion at a Bouchercon, Steve Steinbock and I were at a bar (where else?) discussing some point or other about religious doctrine, he from a Jewish viewpoint, I from a Christian (Episcopalian) perspective, when we saw Ed coming down the stairs across the lobby. Steve and I remember differently which one of us yelled, "Ed! Come here; we need a Catholic!" Ed, of course, came over. I am sure we never resolved anything, but friends don't need to.

On January 18, 2008, Janet Hutchings, the Editor of EQMM, called me to say that Ed had died suddenly that morning. I was in shock. The mystery community had lost a great writer; the world had lost a great and good human being; but personally—and this was uppermost in my mind, and still is—I had lost a close friend.

Douglas G. Greene

THE PROBLEM OF
THE COUNTRY CHURCH

T his was in November of '36 [Dr. Sam Hawthorne told his visitor, filling their glasses with the usual small libation]—just after President Roosevelt's re-election. My former nurse April had been happily married for nearly two years to Andre Mulhone, owner of the Greenbush Inn, a popular Maine resort hotel. They'd recently had their first child, a boy they named Sam after me, and I'd been asked to be his godfather. It was an honor I couldn't refuse.

So it was that I drove up to southern Maine on that second week-end in November, leaving Mary Best to handle things at the office, referring patients to Dr. Potter, a friend who'd agreed to handle any emergencies. By this time of year the trees were bare in Maine, and I was surprised not to find any trace of snow on the ground. It had been a warm autumn, but Friday had turned cold and rainy and I half expected the rain to become snow as I drove north. Instead there was sunshine, and I reached the Greenbush Inn before dinnertime.

Andre came out from behind the registration desk to shake hands. "It's great to see you again, Dr. Sam! April and I are overjoyed you're going to be Sam's godfather." Mulhone came from a French-Irish background. His first wife had died in an auto accident. He was a handsome man, older than April, and his cosmopolitan interests had opened a whole new world to her. I was happy for them both.

April appeared a moment later, coming through the swinging door from the kitchen. "Sam, how are you? It's so good of you to come."

"You know I wouldn't miss the baptism. Where's it to be held?"

"At a little country church near here called St. George in the Woods. The minister comes here for dinner once a week and we've grown quite friendly." She glanced into the dining room and took my arm. "Come meet your namesake's godmother."

Ivy Preston was one of the waitresses at the inn, a sleek brunette whose brown eyes fixed me with an open stare. "So you're the unmarried doctor."

"Ivy!" April pretended shock.

"Pleased to meet you, Ivy," I said, extending my hand.

"Forgive me, Dr. Hawthorne. April is always trying to find me a boy friend and I like to kid her about it."

"Call me Sam," I told her. "I won't take it as being too personal."

Andre walked over to join us. "Are the women ganging up on you, Sam?"

"I can handle it," I reassured him.

"Have you seen little Sam yet?" Ivy asked.

"I just got here."

"He's adorable! Let's have a peek at him, April."

Sam Mulhone, barely a month old, was in a blue bassinet on a side table in the kitchen. The cook, a middle-aged Frenchman named Henri, was taking time out from his pre-dinner chores to tickle the baby gently under the chin. I smiled and said, "He looks just like you, April."

"Don't let his father hear you say that. He has baby pictures to prove Sam is a Mulhone through and through."

The baby was chubby and good-natured, with a wisp of brownish hair. "Does he keep you awake at night?"

"He hasn't been bad at all. Once he goes to sleep, nothing seems to bother him. If we're lucky, he'll sleep right through his christening tomorrow."

As we left the kitchen, I said, "Tell me about yourself, April. Do you work here in the kitchen?"

"I help out sometimes, but mostly I handle the registrations and the accounts books. Our business has really grown in the past two years, Sam. We're a popular resort and also a fine dining place. The summer people even drive up from New Hampshire to have dinner here. Andre's been very successful."

"Do you ever miss nursing?"

"Yes. But working for you in the office wasn't the same as hospital nursing. I was taking care of your books, doing many of the same things I'm doing here. I like it. Of course, now that Sam's on the scene, I'll be looking after him a good share of the time."

Ivy went back to work as the first dinner customers arrived. So showed a couple to a table by the window and presented them with menus. "That used to be another of my jobs," April said, "but I think Ivy will be taking it over now."

"She seems very agreeable."

"I hope you didn't mind being kidded about your bachelorhood. Actually, Ivy *has* a boy friend, a young man who does odd jobs around here, Joe Curtiss. He picks up guests at the train station and fixes things. He shovels snow in the winter. He even rigged up a snowplow that the horse can pull."

"No need for that yet."

She laughed. "Remember all the snow the first time we came here when I met Andre?"

"How could I forget?"

"How's your new nurse doing?"

"Mary's doing fine—she's a great help to me. That doesn't mean I don't miss you, though."

A sandy-haired young man came through the front door carrying a pile of firewood. "Just in case it turns chilly tonight," he told April. "I'll leave it by the fireplace."

"Thanks, Joe. Dr. Sam, this is Joe Curtiss. Meet Dr. Sam Hawthorne, Joe. He's going to be Sam's godfather tomorrow."

The young man grinned in response. "I wish I could be there. But I have to take some people to the train. Nice to meet you, Dr. Hawthorne."

He added the wood to a stack next to the fireplace, then went off to speak with Ivy.

"How many employees do you have here in all?" I asked April.

"Well, if you count Andre and me there are twelve full-time people and another six who come in part-time when we need them."

Andre joined us again. "Remember, Dr. Sam, we talked once about skiing becoming a popular American sport? I may not live to see it but my son will. There'll be a day when this area has trails blazed through the woods and down the sides of the mountains. People will come from all over the Northeast to ski in a New England winter, the way Europeans go to Switzerland now."

"You certainly have a perfect location for it," I said, remembering the hills on the way up.

"Come, I'll show you your room," April said. "You're dining with us tonight—in an hour?"

"Fine."

"The Reverend Dr. Lawrence is joining us. He'll be performing the christening in the morning."

* * *

Howard Lawrence was white-haired and nearsighted. "I am not St. Lawrence," he assured me on our first meeting, blinking from behind thick glasses, "though my name is spelled the same way." I was certain he'd used that line many times before.

"It's a pleasure to meet you, sir."

"Please call me Howard," he said, shaking my hand.

We sat with April and Andre at a window table. Though it had been dark for some time, a few spotlights on the roof of the inn illuminated the grounds nearby. "It's a lovely place," the minister commented. "I envy the lad growing up in these surroundings."

The meal was delicious, much better than those I remembered from my visit two years earlier. Maybe it was April's influence, or a new chef. I couldn't remember if Henri had been there on my earlier visit.

It being the off-season, there were only about a dozen other guests at the inn. "And the Depression doesn't help any," Andre said. "But we did very well this summer and we have good bookings over the holidays."

I was aware of a man seated alone at a table across the dining room from us. "Is that man here alone?" I asked April.

Howard Lawrence peered in the direction I indicated and shrugged. "I can't see that far, even with these glasses. Is it anyone I know, April?"

"I doubt it. His name's Frederick Winter. His family owns Winter's Department Store in Boston. He's not the churchgoing sort."

"He comes here a couple of times a year," Andre explained. "Generally he has some young woman with him, but he's here alone this time."

Winter finished his dinner a short time later and stopped at the table on his way out, greeting Andre and April with a smile and some small talk. He was dark-haired and probably in his mid-thirties, running slightly overweight. "Would you like to join us for dessert?" Andre asked him.

"No, go on with your meal. I just stopped by to say hello."

I could see from his disarming smile that he could be the sort to attract women for the wrong reasons. He shook hands firmly when April introduced me and told him about the christening. "Let me know when you bring the boy down to Boston for a shopping spree" he told April.

She laughed. "That won't be for a few years yet."

After Winter had gone, Andre remarked, "I hope he has enough money to cover his bill."

"What's that?" the minister asked.

"Nothing—I probably shouldn't have mentioned it. Last time there was a little trouble with his check, but he made good on it."

Dr. Lawrence sighed. "I don't envy you your job, Andre. At least I know the money I receive on the collection plate is real."

"What time do you want us there tomorrow?" April asked.

"Let's make it at eleven," he said, "if that's convenient for you."

* * *

Saturday dawned with a warming breeze coming up from the south. By ten-thirty, Andre had pulled his car around to the detached log house behind the inn that served as the family's comfortable living quarters. I was waiting there with Ivy Preston, who looked stylish in her camel coat and cloche hat. April came out the front door carrying the bassinet with Sam inside.

"He's sleeping peacefully," she told us. "I think we're going to be lucky." I could just glimpse his closed eyes surrounded by the baby bunting.

I climbed in the front seat with Andre, while the women got in back with the baby. The Church of St. George in the Woods was on the main highway about two miles past the turnoff for the Greenbush Inn. Andre's late-model Nash rode smoothly, and he handled it with ease. We reached the church almost before I realized it. "Here we are," he said, parking in the cinder driveway next to the old stone building. The double oak doors were unlocked and we entered a medium-sized church with about twenty-five or thirty pews facing the altar. It was dimly lit by a few flickering candles, but I could make out a small choir loft extending over the last few pews and an organ up front to the right of the altar. A wooden board listed the numbers of the Sunday hymns.

Ivy was carrying the bassinet and she slipped into the third pew from the rear. I stepped in next to her while Andre and April walked to the front of the church. Dr. Lawrence appeared almost at once and turned on a small spotlight that bathed the altar in a subdued pink glow. He shook their hands and called a greeting back to us. I could see the baptismal font now, a carved marble pedestal whose concave top held a few inches of holy water for administering the blessing. The minister fell in deep conversation with the parents, impressing upon them in low tones the importance of bringing up the boy as a good Christian.

Then he called back to Ivy and me, "You can bring the baby now." Andre and April turned to watch.

I stood and stepped out of the pew while Ivy reached to her other side and carefully lifted the bay in its blue bunting from the bassinet. Then she joined me and we walked down the aisle together. At the altar, April reached out for her son. I was watching her face—and saw the radiance of her expression suddenly freeze into a bewildered stare.

"What is this? Where—?"

She pulled back the hood of the bunting and we all saw it. The baby was gone. In its place was a curly-haired Shirley Temple doll.

"Is this some sort of terrible joke?" Andre asked Ivy angrily.

Then I noticed the little piece of paper pinned to the doll's dress. "What's this?" I said, removing it, trying to suppress my sense of alarm.

It was a block of type cut from a magazine:

> Have fifty thousand dollars ready, 25,000 in twenty-dollar bills, 15,000 in ten-dollar bills, and 10,000 in five-dollar bills. In 4–5 hours we will inform you where to deliver the money.

* * *

We searched every pew of the church and then I hurried outside to see if anyone was getting away. I even checked Andre's Nash, though there was no rational reason why the baby should have been there. When I came back inside, Ivy Preston was close to tears. "I should have known right away that something was wrong. This doll wasn't as heavy as the baby."

"It's not your fault," April tried to comfort her, somehow managing to keep control of her own emotions.

"But this thing is impossible!" Andre said. "There are only four of us here—five counting Dr. Lawrence. None of us did it and no one else could have entered the church without being seen."

He turned to me for confirmation and I was glad to give it. "There are only dim lights in here but it's bright outdoors. See how it brightens up when these big oak doors are opened? Surely we'd have noticed that. There's no one hiding between or beneath the pews, but I'll check the rest of the building just to be sure."

Dr. Lawrence had been struggling to read the message pinned to the doll. "Does this mean the baby has been kidnaped?" he asked.

"No!" April insisted. "It must be a joke of some sort!" She turned to me. "Sam?"

"I don't know, April. Let me search the rest of the place."

With Dr. Lawrence guiding me, we checked the vestry behind the altar and any likely hiding places by the altar itself. I went up the few steps to the pulpit, but it was empty. We went up to the choir loft and examined a small side door the minister said the choir used on special occasions like Christmas. "It's kept locked most of the time," he said. "The congregation uses the front door."

An ordinary skeleton key would probably have opened it, but that was the least of our problems. No one could have approached Ivy and me without being noticed. Certainly no one could have removed the baby and substituted a doll while standing only inches away from us. I went back and checked the bassinet again. There was nothing else in it, no false bottom or secret compartment.

Andrew watched me search. When I came up empty-handed, he put his arm tenderly around April and said quietly, "I think it's time to call the police."

* * *

A State Police car was on the scene within a half hour. The officer was probably still in his twenties, a blond young man named Corporal Jenkins. After listening to our story, he examined the message that had been cut from the magazine and pinned to the doll.

"Notice this word 'hours,'" he said, pointing to it. "That's been changed with a pencil. You can see underneath it the printing says 'days.' Whoever did this didn't want to wait that long, so he changed it. This was cut from some magazine account of the Lindbergh kidnaping. It's the first half of the ransom note left when Lindbergh's baby son was taken."

"They found him dead!" April said with a gasp. Her shaky composure showed signs of cracking.

"This looks like the work of an amateur to me," Corporal Jenkins told her gently.

Andre hugged April tighter as she began to cry. "If he's such an amateur, how did he manage to take the baby in the first place?" he asked Jenkins.

"I don't know," the officer admitted. "But I can have fifty men up here by the end of the day. We'll search these woods—"

I checked my pocketwatch and said, "Sam's been gone for over an hour. I think we should all get back to the inn. If the kidnaper does try to contact you, Andre, that's where he'll call."

* * *

We drove back together, with the State Police car following. Dr. Lawrence promised to follow shortly. There was little activity at the inn when we reached it, though I saw Frederick Winter walking toward it from the nearby woods. We headed immediately for Andre's office and he told the desk clerk he wasn't to be disturbed for routine business but that any incoming phone calls should be put right through.

Henri, the chef I'd met the previous day, was waiting in Andre's office. "We have a problem in the kitchen, Mr. Mulhone."

"I'm sorry, Henri, I can't handle it now. Do the best you can and I'll try to check with you later."

The Frenchman seemed a bit surprised, but like a good employee he said, "Very well, sir," and retreated from the room.

We settled down in the office to wait. "As soon as there's some contact from the kidnapers," Jenkins said, "I'll feel justified in contacting the F.B.I."

"Why not now?" April wanted to know. Her nerves were dangerously on edge and I considered getting a sedative from my bag upstairs.

"Well, the whole thing just seems so impossible—" He hesitated, then continued, "It *could* be a joke of some sort."

"A joke!" Andrew growled. "Our *baby is missing!*"

* * *

I excused myself and headed for my room, but I encountered Joe Curtiss, carrying some guests' bags in from his car. "Dr. Hawthorne, wait up a minute, will you?" He left the bags at the reception desk and hurried over. "What's the trouble? I just got back from the station and I saw everyone trooping into the office with glum faces. How'd the christening go?"

"It was postponed," I told him shortly, hurrying on upstairs.

In my room I opened the medical pouch I always carried in my suitcase and took out some powders for possible administration to April and her husband. I had no intention of using them unless it became absolutely necessary, because they could be faced with some terrible decisions during the next few hours.

I returned to the office and waited with them. Corporal Jenkins had made some local calls, putting out a missing-persons alarm for an infant boy. He also asked that the railroad station be checked in case someone tried to leave with the baby.

For his part, Andre was on the phone with his banker, making arrangements about the money, should the situation come to that April sat on the big leather sofa with Ivy Preston, listening to it all as if in a daze.

"How are you doing?" I asked her, coming over to join them.

"I don't understand any of this, Dr. Sam," she said. "Why is Andre calling his bank? We don't have that kind of money in ready cash."

I'd understood enough of the conversation to answer her. "I believe he's putting up the inn as collateral on a loan."

"No!" She hurried to her husband's side. "Andre, you can't—it's all you have!"

"He's my son, too, April. Getting him back is all that matters."

Ivy went to try to comfort her and Andre must have seen that the strain of waiting for the phone to ring was becoming too much. "April," he suggested, "why don't you and Dr. Sam go to the kitchen and see what was bothering Henri earlier. Whatever happened, we have our guests to consider."

She didn't answer for a moment. Then she straightened up and wiped her eyes. "Will you come with me, Sam?"

"Of course."

We found Henri issuing orders to his assistant, who was cleaning the big old wood-burning stove. He seemed relieved to see April and immediately launched into his tale of woe. "When we stack cordwood against the wall outside, it is for use in the stove."

"Of course," April agreed. "Everyone here knows that."

"But one of your guests has been stealing it and taking it away in the rumble seat of his car."

"Are you sure?"

"Positive. I noticed some logs missing yesterday and this morning I saw what was happening. I watched him for fifteen minutes but I did not feel it was my place to confront him."

"Who are you talking about?"

"Mr. Winter. I know he has been a valued guest here for years."

"Fred Winter stealing our firewood? I can't believe it!"

"Please tell your husband. He must take some action."

April promised and we went out to look at the woodpile. "The entire *pile* would hardly bring five dollars," she said. "Firewood's so easy to come by in Maine!"

"Henri seems truly concerned, though."

"The woodpile's his territory. He feels as if he's being personally challenged." April turned and headed across the lot toward the house. I didn't know if I wanted to follow her, but I knew I had to. "April—"

"What is it, Dr. Sam?"

"I have to ask you something. It's a terrible question for me to ask, but I have to know. Is little Sam dead?"

"What! What are you talking about?"

"There's no possible way that doll could have been substituted for the baby in church, April. I was seated next to Ivy the entire time and no one approached us. The only explanation is that the doll and note were already in the bassinet when you brought it out to the car. If little Sam somehow died accidentally and you wanted to—"

"*No!*" she screamed. "My God, Dr. Sam!"

I got her into the house somehow and sat with her until her sobbing let up, then I tried to explain. "It was just that none of us got a good look at the baby in the car. And until now you've remained relatively calm about the kidnaping. It's as if you know he'll be found."

"Of course I know he'll be found! You're here, aren't you, Sam? If there's anyone in the world who can find him, it's you!"

"Yes," I said and stared bleakly out the window. My solution to the problem had seemed perfectly logical, except that this was April. She could never have done the thing I'd suggested.

* * *

We sat for the better part of an hour, talking very little, leaving only for a brief look at the baby's nursery. The sight of the crib and the small toys brought tears to her eyes again. "Sam, you should have known your idea was wrong—logically. You imagined my baby dying accidentally and me substituting the doll to fake a kidnaping and hide the fact of his death—a spur-of-the-moment crime. But on the spur of the moment, where would I have gotten the Shirley Temple doll? Certainly it wasn't a gift my son would have received."

I was starting to agree with her when there was a quick knock and the nursery door opened. Corporal Jenkins stuck his head in. "We've heard from the kidnaper, ma'am . . ."

We hurried across the yard to the inn and found Andre on the phone to his bank once more. "The kidnaper called," Ivy told us excitedly. "He wants the money packed in a small suitcase and brought to the train station. Andre's to put it on board the four-thirty train to Boston."

"Just the suitcase?" I asked.

"That's all."

I turned to Jenkins. "Where does that train originate?"

"Bangor."

"Can you have men on it?"

"Sure."

"No!" April said sharply. "First we get Sam back! Then we worry about the kidnaper."

"She's right," Andre insisted. "Nothing must jeopardize the return of our son. We'll deliver the money as instructed."

"What did the kidnaper say?" I asked him.

"Just that he has Sam, and no harm will come to him if we follow orders about the money and the train."

"That's all?"

He glanced at April and then away. "Oh, there were the usual threats one expects from this sort of person."

"We'll get Sam back," I told his parents.

"I'm driving to the bank now to pick up the money," Andre said.

"You can't drive in the state you're in," Ivy told him reasonably. "Joe will drive you."

April agreed. "Do you want me to come along?"

Andre shook his head. "Stay here, sweetheart. Once the money is paid, he might call again to tell us where Sam is."

I think the fate of the Lindbergh baby was in all our minds just then. Nobody wanted to look at April. "I have an old suitcase you can use," Ivy said, trying to cover the awkward moment of silence. "It's in the kitchen."

I went with her while she emptied the small tan suitcase of a couple of dirty uniforms.

"Tell me something, Ivy," I said. "Have you ever been to a christening before at St. George in the Woods?"

"Oh yes. A lot of my friends are having babies—in spite of the Depression."

"Was there anything about this morning that Dr. Lawrence did differently?"

"No, it was exactly like the others I've seen as far as it went. Of course, the baby doesn't usually disappear."

"No." I picked up the empty suitcase and we headed back to Andre's office.

"Do you think they'll find him, Sam?" she asked me.

"If Andre's willing to pay the money, I see no reason for the kidnaper to harm the baby."

"The Lindbergh baby was killed, and Corporal Jenkins said it was the same ransom note. I don't know what I'll do if April doesn't get Sam back."

I slipped my arm around her shoulders to comfort her. "Once the money's delivered, I'm sure—" I stopped in midsentence, spotting something by the side of the inn that interested me: Frederick Winter, the young man from the wealthy Boston family, was stooped over the woodpile.

"What is it?" Ivy asked.

I handed her the suitcase. "Take this inside. I have something to do."

As I approached the woodpile, Winter straightened up. "Hello, there," he said with an innocent smile.

"What are you doing?"

"I dropped my cigarette lighter. I was just looking for it."

"Interesting. I understand you've been out here a few times lately. Is it the same lighter each time?"

His smile faded. "Say, who are you?"

"Sam Hawthorne. We met in the dining room last night. I'm a friend of the Mulhones."

"Well, I'm not harming anything."

"You've been taking wood from this pile—Henri, the chef, saw you."

"A few pieces of firewood for back home! Is that a crime?"

"You're taking the wood to burn it?" I asked.

"Why else would I take it?"

"To make space in the pile."

"For what?"

"A missing baby."

His forehead wrinkled into a quizzical frown. "You're crazy, you know that?" He turned and walked away.

I went through the pile and found nothing but wood. Maybe the man was right, I thought. Maybe I *was* becoming a little crazy . . .

* * *

Joe Curtiss stowed the empty suitcase in the rumble seat of his car and a subdued Andre Mulhone got into the roadster with him. I followed along at a distance in Corporal Jenkins' car. We waited while they stopped at the bank for the money and then headed for the station.

"We shouldn't get too close," I cautioned. "The kidnaper could be watching."

"Don't worry, Doctor."

"I'm sorry, but I'm worried about that baby. We can't do anything to frighten the kidnaper into killing him."

"We have to face the fact that he may be dead already."

My mouth went dry. "Yes," I replied.

"By nightfall I'll have fifty men here. The F.B.I. is on its way from Boston."

"What about the four-thirty train?"

"I called the station and told them to flag it down."

"Flag it down?"

"We're a small town. Usually the train doesn't stop unless there's a passenger getting off or the stationmaster flags it."

"Could the kidnaper have boarded it this morning and simply be riding it back and forth, making his phone call from a station along the route?"

"He didn't board it here. The morning train went through without stopping."

I thought about that, keeping my eyes on the roadster ahead of us. Presently it turned off the road and stopped at the wooden station house with the sign GREENBUSH in place above the door. Joe got the suitcase from the rumble seat and Andre carried it out to the platform alone. We all waited in silence.

It was ten minutes before we heard the steam whistle on the 4:30 train to Boston. The engineer saw the flag and slowed to a stop at the station. Andre lifted the suitcase and placed it on board, apparently telling the conductor that someone would claim it. "That's it," Jenkins said. "We'll head back to the inn."

"Where does Ivy Preston live?" I asked him.

"Ivy? She has a little cottage just down the road from the inn."

"I'd appreciate it if you'll drop me there on our way past," I told him.

* * *

Ivy answered the door and asked anxiously, "Is something wrong? Did the money get put on the train?"

"Everything's fine. The kidnaper should have it by now. The others have gone back to the inn, but I thought I'd stop here. Is April with you?" Though she hadn't invited me in, I stepped past her into a modestly furnished living room.

"She's back at the inn. I left her with Dr. Lawrence while I came home for a few minutes."

I nodded and sat down on the sofa. "I wanted to tell you that the mystery's been solved. The kidnaper has the money but Corporal Jenkins has him—he was arrested a few minutes ago."

Her mouth dropped open. "What?"

"I'm afraid he's your boy friend, Joe Curtiss."

She sank into the chair opposite me, the color draining from her face. "But how is that possible?"

"I've worked it all out—the only way it could have been done. You see, Joe slipped up when he said he couldn't attend the christening because he was taking people to the train. After the kidnaping, we saw him arriving with some luggage. But there were no passengers getting on or off the train this morning. Corporal Jenkins said it didn't even stop. If Joe was lying, what had he been up to at the time? It seems obvious the kidnaper had to be someone connected with the inn—most likely an employee or friend who knew about the christening and about Dr. Lawrence's routine at these events."

"Joe wasn't even there!" Ivy insisted. "No one entered the church after us, and you searched all the pews yourself!"

"No one entered the church after us because Joe was already hidden there. No one approached the pew, and little Sam certainly didn't drop through the floor. There's only one other place he could have gone."

"Where?"

"Up," I told her.

"Up?"

"The choir loft overhangs the last few pews, and we were seated in the third pew from the rear. Joe Curtiss, hidden there, lowered a stout cord with a hook on the end, snagged the handles of the bassinet, raised it to the choir loft, and substituted the Shirley Temple doll for little Sam. Then he lowered it down the same way."

"And nobody *saw* it?"

"The church was dimly lit, especially toward the rear. You and I were facing the altar, as were April and Andre. Only Dr. Lawrence, with his notoriously poor eyesight, was facing the rear. No one saw a thing. The baby's a good sleeper, and there was a better than even chance the ascent to the choir loft wouldn't disturb him. It didn't. While we searched the pews, Joe slipped out the side door with the baby, unlocking it with a skeleton key."

"Then *he* called about the ransom?"

"Yes."

"But how did he hope to recover the ransom money after Andre put it on the train?"

"Simple. Andre didn't put it on the train. Joe Curtiss had an identical suitcase filled with old newspapers hidden in the rumble seat of his roadster. That's what he gave Andre to put on the train. The suitcase with the money remained in his rumble seat. By the time we discovered the money was gone, anyone on the train might have made the substitution."

Ivy stood up and walked to the front window. "I think I'd better get back to the inn—Joe will need me."

"You'll be seeing him soon enough, Ivy. There's one other thing. The kidnaping at the church would only have worked if we were seated where we were, just under the choir loft. He knew we'd be there."

"Yes?"

"You picked the pew, Ivy. Just as you shielded the bassinet from me with your body. Just as you produced a suitcase for the ransom money. The two of you had to be in it together. You probably hooked the cord around the bassinet handles so there'd be no delay. And you produced the two identical suitcases for the substitution and suggested that *Joe* drive Andre to the station. I figured I'd find you here because one of you had to keep checking on the baby."

"No! You're crazy if you think I had anything to do—"

As if on cue, there came the sound of a baby crying in the next room.

* * *

April saw me walking across the front yard of the Greenbush Inn with little Sam held carefully in my arms. She came running to meet me and there were tears in her eyes.

"He's fine," I told her as I handed the baby over.

"I knew he would be, Sam, with you as his godfather."

THE PROBLEM OF
THE GRANGE HALL

D R. Lincoln Jones, Northmont's first black physician, joined the staff of Pilgrim Memorial Hospital in March of 1929 [Dr. Sam Hawthorne reminisced as he poured two glasses of wine]. The hospital opened that month, and I've already told you about the Pilgrims Windmill affair and the trouble we had at the time with ghostly figures, a terrible fire, and threats from the Ku Klux Klan.

Happily for us all, the next eight years passed uneventfully for Lincoln Jones—if you can call marriage and the birth of two children uneventful. I wasn't on the hospital staff myself, but my office was in the physicians' wing of the building and I usually saw Linc a couple of times a week. He was a tall, handsome man on the verge of forty like myself, specializing in children's illnesses. In the city he would have been called a pediatrician, but in Northmont we weren't nearly so fancy.

It was decided that the hospital would celebrate its eighth anniversary that March with a community dinner and a dance at the Grange Hall. Eighth anniversaries aren't usually worth noting, but the Depression had been hard on Pilgrim Memorial along with every other facet of American life. The hospital needed money for new equipment, and the celebration was a perfect opportunity to raise some of it. The committee was bringing in a big New York band, Sweeney Lamb and his All-Stars, for the dance.

"Are you and your wife going to the dance on Saturday?" I asked Linc Jones one day when I encountered him in the hospital corridor.

"Do we have any choice?" he answered with a grin. It had been made clear that all of the staff physicians and doctors with offices in the building were expected to purchase a pair of tickets. "Who are you taking?"

"My nurse Mary Best," I told him. "She deserves a treat for putting up with me."

"Well, it should be fun. I went to high school with Sweeney Lamb's trumpet player, a fellow named Bix Blake. Haven't seen him in years."

The Grange Hall was out beyond the hospital, almost to the edge of town. I felt a bit like a high school kid myself on Friday night, calling for Mary Best at the small house she rented, going up to the door with a corsage to go with her dress.

"How nice of you, Sam!" she told me as she pinned it on. "This is just like a date." She may have been gently mocking my bachelor status but I couldn't be sure.

"It's not every week we have a dance with a big city orchestra here in Northmont."

The month of March had started out cold that year but there'd been very little snow. By the weekend of the dance it was feeling almost like spring. As I parked my car and helped Mary out, taking care that her long gown didn't drag on the ground, the first arrivals we saw were Sheriff Lens and his wife. We exchanged warm greetings and walked into the hall together. The sheriff and I had worn blue suits, and I was surprised to see some of the hospital and town officials in tuxedos. "It's sure a big night," the sheriff said. We went in and found a table together, with me sitting between Vera Lens and Mary.

"A little excitement in this town at last!" Vera Lens said. She was younger than the sheriff and they'd been married about ten years. "I hope it'll liven things up. We haven't even had a good murder since last summer."

"And let's hope we *don't* have one," the sheriff told her, "at least not tonight."

I spotted Linc Jones and his wife Charlene at another table. "Let's go say hello," I suggested to Mary.

The tables were arranged in a horseshoe shape around the dance floor, with the bandstand at the front of the hall. Linc and his wife were opposite us, on the other side of the horseshoe. "Well, Sam! Good to see you here. You remember my wife Charlene, don't you?"

"I certainly do!" She'd be hard to forget, a lovely dark-skinned woman who knew how to use just the right amount of make-up. It had been the talk of Pilgrim Memorial when he returned from vacation that first year with a new wife

"Hello, Sam," she said with a smile. "Good to see you again. You too, Mary."

Sweeney Lamb's musicians were beginning to take the stage. Until then I hadn't thought much about Linc's high school chum, and the fact that the Sweeney Lamb orchestra had always been white. There was an audible murmur from a few tables as two black musicians joined the fifteen others on stage. One of them carried a trumpet and Linc Jones waved to him.

"That's my old buddy," he said. "Come on up, Sam, and I'll introduce you."

Bix Blake was darker than Linc, with a pushed-in nose that may have been broken at one time. I saw him frown as we approached, and his eyes seemed to go beyond our heads to the table where we'd been seated. "Lincoln Jones," he said with a trace of resignation. "I forgot this was your town."

"It's not really mine, Bix. This here's Sam Hawthorne, one of the doctors I work with."

I held out my hand. "How are you, Bix? Welcome to Northmont. We've all been looking forward to this affair."

Blake's handshake was firm. "It's a bit different from playin' in New York."

"Can we get together after?" Linc asked. "We've got a lot of catching up to do."

Bix Blake worked the valves of his trumpet. "Our bus is leavin' right after the show, but I'll be back in that little dressing room during the break, after the first hour. Come back then."

"I'll do that."

Sweeney Lamb himself had appeared by that time, fronting the band as he murmured instructions to some of his people. He was fairly well known and I recognized him at once from his pictures—handsome, broad-shouldered, with traces of grey in his hair. In person his eyeglasses were thicker than I'd expected but otherwise he was just like his photographs. "Nice to meet you, Mr. Lamb," I said. "I'm Dr. Sam Hawthorne from the hospital. Dr. Jones here went to school with your trumpeter."

He glanced at Linc, and then over at Bix. "Nice town you got here," he said, not offering to shake either of our hands. He started adjusting the microphone and we took the hint that the music was about to begin.

Back at the table Charlene asked, "Did he remember you?"

"Oh, sure," Linc answered. "We're getting together during the break."

"Did he ask about me?"

"No."

I glanced from one to the other. "You knew him too, Charlene?"

She glanced down without replying and Line answered for her. "They were engaged once, briefly, but that was a long time ago."

"Bix said I picked Line instead of him because I wanted to marry a doctor and have lots of money."

Mary Best placed her hand on Charlene's and tried to say something comforting but just then Sweeney Lamb's voice boomed through the Grange Hall.

"Good evening, ladies and gentlemen! It's a pleasure to be here in Northmont to help you folks celebrate the eighth anniversary of Pilgrim

Memorial Hospital. I'm Sweeney Lamb, but I guess you all knew that." He paused for the applause and then continued, "Before we strike up the band for an evening of fabulous music, we're going to hear just a few words from the director of Pilgrim Memorial, Dr. Robert Yale."

Bob Yale had been part of Pilgrim Memorial since its beginning, and when the previous director retired he'd been the logical successor. He was bright, articulate, and willing to try new things. "I won't keep you long," he told the audience. "I know we're all anxious to get out on the dance floor. Just remember why we're here. Pilgrim Memorial needs your help. We need money. Northmont may be a small community, but the hospital is known and respected in this state. I want it to stay that way. I want us to grow as the community grows, to be ready for tomorrow's challenges. The medical problems of today, whether TB or polio or cancer, cannot be met with yesterday's equipment. You know our goal—help us to reach it! And now, without further ado, it's back to Sweeney Lamb and his All-Stars!"

Lamb's band opened with a jazzy theme and then switched to something slower for dancing. *Pennies From Heaven* and *Red Sails in the Sunset* had even some of the older townspeople out on the floor. "Your friend Bix is mighty good with that trumpet," I told Lincoln Jones.

"I'm glad to see some black faces up there. It's been a big problem, especially for a band that tours. In most cities the Negro musicians have to stay at separate hotels. But some of the big New York bands are starting to integrate their players now."

After another jazz tune Sweeney Lamb took the microphone to announce, "Now, as a special treat, the song stylings of Miss Helen McDonald, with Spider Downs on saxophone."

A blonde young woman in a long pink dress came on stage and bowed, then started a dreamy rendition of *It's a Sin to Tell a Lie*. Mary stirred and stood up. "Aren't you ever going to ask me to dance, Sam?"

"Sorry," I said, perhaps blushing a bit. "I'd been enjoying the music so much that I'd almost forgotten she was my date for the evening. I certainly owed her a dance or two. Linc and Charlene quickly joined us to cover my awkwardness.

"She's good," Mary Best decided, fitting comfortably into my arms. "I think I've heard her on the radio."

Helen McDonald was indeed good. There was a swinging beat to the way she delivered the lyrics that really put them across. On the next number, *The Way You Look Tonight*, Bix Blake contributed a trumpet bit and then Spider

Downs, the other black musician, did a saxophone solo. Sweeney passed around some sheet music for the next selection. Helen and Spider Downs each took one. She folded hers and passed it on to Bix, then stood on the sidelines while the band played an instrumental version of *I'm Putting All My Eggs in One Basket*. After that they took a break.

I stopped to say a few words to Bob Yale, the hospital director. "Great evening, Bob! This should encourage a few donations."

"I certainly hope so."

Linc Jones had walked on ahead, crossing the dance floor to intercept Bix. Watching them from a distance, I wondered just how friendly they were. Bix's face, at that moment, was twisted into an expression like pain or anger. I walked close enough to hear Linc compliment him on his playing, and Bix reply, "I'll be better next set." Bix led the way to a door behind the stage, apparently the dressing room he'd mentioned earlier.

I saw that Mary was at the table alone. "Where's Charlene?"

"Ladies' room. I didn't feel like battling the crowd."

I kept an eye on the dressing room door as we spoke. After several minutes, they still hadn't emerged and, feeling a concern I couldn't quite express, I headed back in that direction. Sweeney Lamb appeared at that moment, glancing around the floor. "Seen Bix?" he asked me.

"I believe he's in there, chatting with an old high-school friend."

Lamb walked to the door I'd indicated, and the other black musician, Spider Downs, joined us. The bandleader knocked and tried the knob. "It's locked."

I tried knocking and called out, "Linc! It's Sam Hawthorne. Open up!"

A voice beyond the door distinctly said, "Sam!" I didn't know whether it was a cry for help or only one of recognition, but I felt I had to get in there. I rattled the knob uselessly. "Who's got the key to this?"

"No key," Lamb said. "There's a bolt on the other side. We used it as a dressing room earlier."

"Help me with this," I asked the black musician. We hit the door together with our shoulders and the bolt pulled from the wooden frame. The door sprang open.

Lincoln Jones was kneeling next to the body of his old school chum. In one hand he held a hypodermic needle. "What's happened here, Linc?"

"I—I don't know."

I knelt on the other side of Bix Blake and felt for a pulse. Behind me I heard the voice of Sheriff Lens. "What's goin' on here? Let me through, please. I'm the sheriff. What is it, Doc?"

I looked up at him. "Bix Blake. He's dead."

Sheriff Lens took in the rest of the scene in an instant. He wasn't the smartest man in the world but he knew his job. "Doc Jones," he said, reaching out his hand, "you'd best give me that hypodermic."

* * *

Word of the tragedy spread quickly through the large room, becoming as distorted as one might expect under the tense circumstances. As I headed back to the table to tell Mary, the first person I encountered was Charlene Jones. "What in God's name has happened?" she demanded, close to hysteria. "Someone just told me Linc stabbed a man!"

"Nothing like that," I assured her. "Bix Blake is dead and no one knows what happened. There was no knife. Linc had a hypodermic needle—"

"What for? What does it mean?"

"He may have been trying to save Bix's life. We don't know yet."

"I have to see Linc," she insisted, pushing past me toward the crowded doorway.

Finally I reached our table and told Mary Best what had happened. "Do you think Linc killed him?" she asked, getting right to the point.

"I don't know. We have to find out what killed him first."

Dr. Bob Yale came hurrying over. "What do you know about this, Sam?"

"Very little. One of the black musicians, the trumpet player, is dead. Linc Jones was with him when he died."

"My God! Does this mean they won't be finishing the dance?"

"You'll have to ask Sweeney Lamb that." At the moment a man's death seemed more important to me.

But Bob Yale did get to Lamb, and I saw the two of them off in a corner a few minutes later. When Yale returned to me he was all smiles. "They don't have another job for three nights. He's willing to stay in Northmont and do the whole thing again tomorrow night. How does that sound?"

"For the same price?" I asked skeptically.

"He's donating it. Do you think everyone will come back, Sam?"

"Bix Blake won't."

I walked away from him as an ambulance arrived from Pilgrim Memorial. The person I really wanted to see was Sheriff Lens, but it was another half-hour before I found him alone, looking decidedly unhappy. By that time the word had spread that the dance had been postponed until the following night, and some people were beginning to depart.

"How does it look, Sheriff?"

"Not good for Lincoln Jones, Doc. I want you to sit in while I go over his story in detail."

"Glad to. Want to do it now?"

"I'm just waiting for a preliminary report from the hospital. There's a slight chance it was a natural death, but I doubt it. Looks to me like he was injected with some fast-acting poison."

"Surely not by Linc!"

"I don't know, Doc. The room has no windows and the only door was bolted from inside. No one else was in there."

"Can I take a look at it? I just had a glimpse when we broke in."

He led the way to the broken door, which he'd secured with a length of twine. I entered behind him and stared at the walls. Its main function was obviously as a storeroom, and cardboard boxes were stacked along the left wall. I looked inside one and found extra tablecloths, apparently on loan for tonight's function. The room was about fifteen feet square, with a line of mirrors fastened to the wall opposite the door. Chairs and small tables were placed in front of the mirrors, the best the Grange could offer in the way of dressing room facilities. Along the right wall was a pipe with wooden coat-hangers holding the band members' outerwear, a variety of coats and jackets.

"Someone could have been hiding behind these coats," I suggested.

"That's pretty doubtful, Doc, but let's see what Jones has to say."

They were beginning to clear the tables in the hall now, and Sweeney Lamb was standing with the girl singer, Helen McDonald. Both of them seemed to be in a daze.

"He was such a nice man," the blonde girl said. I doubted if she was much over twenty. "Do they think it was a heart attack?"

"We're waiting for word from the hospital," I told her. Then, turning to the bandleader, I asked, "Did Bix have any health problems?"

"He's only been with me a few months but he seemed healthy enough. Let me ask Spider." He called to the black musician who'd helped me break in the door earlier. "This is Spider Downs, a damn fine saxophone man. He and Bix joined the band together. Spider, you knew him longer than I did. Were there any health problems?"

Spider was a short, bald man who was built like a barrel. He was probably no older than me and his chest and shoulders were those of a weight lifter or piano mover. "Nothing to kill him," Spider assured us. "His lip gave him some trouble once in a while, but that's not unusual for horn men. We live with it."

I spotted Bob Yale hurrying into the hall, bound for Sheriff Lens, and I wanted to hear his report. I joined them just as he was saying, "The preliminary result is that death was due to respiratory failure caused by an intravenous injection of methylmorphine."

Sheriff Lens looked blank. "Methylmorphine?"

"Better known as codeine," I explained.

"I take that stuff in cough medicine," the sheriff said.

Dr. Yale nodded. "This would have been a purer version, quite fatal even in small doses."

"The hypodermic needle?" I asked.

Yale nodded. "Full of it. There was a puncture mark in his thigh."

"Then he was murdered," the sheriff said.

I liked to caution against jumping to conclusions. "Suicide is always a possibility."

"Come on, Doc. Let's go talk to Lincoln Jones."

Linc had been sitting with his wife back at the table, and when the sheriff asked him to accompany us she started to come too. "What's this all about, Sheriff? What are you trying to say Linc did?"

"Nothing, yet. I just want to ask him some questions about what happened."

"He didn't do a thing! Bix Blake was always a trouble-maker. Alive or dead, he's a trouble-maker."

"Hush now!" Linc told her, rising to follow us.

The sheriff led us back to the death scene, as I knew he would. We pulled out three of the chairs facing the mirrors and Linc asked, right away, "What killed him?"

"The needle was full of codeine," I said quietly. "It was injected into his thigh."

Linc didn't seem too surprised. "He acted like he couldn't breathe."

"Tell us exactly what happened," the sheriff suggested.

"Well, I knew Bix from our high school days. Before the dance began I even took Sam up to meet him. We decided to catch up on things during the break between sets. We came in here together to talk."

"Who bolted the door?" I asked.

"Bix did. He said if anyone wanted a smoke he could go outside."

"Did you argue?" Sheriff Lens asked.

Linc averted his eyes. "We had nothing to argue about."

"Did you argue?" he repeated.

"Not really. He mentioned Charlene."

"Your wife?"

"He was engaged to her once, but that was long ago, in the old neighborhood."

"What did he say about Charlene?" I prodded.

"He said I'd stolen her away because I went to college. She wanted to marry a doctor and be wealthy. It was nothing new. He told Charlene the same thing twelve years ago."

"Did you fight?"

"Physically? Of course not! By that time I could see he was having trouble breathing."

"What about the needle?" the sheriff wanted to know.

"There was no needle. Not then."

"You'd better explain yourself."

Linc shifted on his chair. For the first time he appeared nervous. "Well, his breathing kept getting worse and I asked what was wrong. I just thought he was overwrought, but then I saw it was more than that. Suddenly he just collapsed—right about there, in the center of the room. Right where you found him. I dropped to my knees to examine him, then started giving artificial respiration. That was when I noticed the needle, lying near his foot. I picked it up to examine it just as you broke down the door."

"Is it possible that he injected the poison himself, that he meant to commit suicide?"

"No, no. That would have been impossible. His hands were in full view at all times. I'll tell you I was watching them because I feared he might take a punch at me."

"Refresh my memory," I said. "What happened to that needle after we burst into the room."

"The sheriff asked me for it and I handed it to him."

Sheriff Lens nodded. "Wrapped it real careful in a clean handkerchief and turned it over to the ambulance people when they came for the body. Should have gotten some pictures of the scene, but we weren't sure it was murder then."

"You're not sure now," I reminded him.

"I'm sure. Dr. Jones, I'm goin' to have to hold you for further questioning, on suspicion of murder."

Linc sighed and stood up. "Let me speak with my wife. Then I'll come with you."

We went back to the hall and he crossed the floor to the table where Charlene sat with Mary Best. "You're making a big mistake, Sheriff."

"Tell me how else it could have been, Doc."

"I'm not ready to do that yet."

Charlene listened to Linc's quiet words and then started to cry. "They can't do this to you! That damned Bix Blake! You never killed him."

"I know that, darlin'. Just see what you can do about getting me a good lawyer. And take care of the kids till I get back."

The dance had been on a Friday night, and the next morning everyone in town was talking about it. Bob Yale was talking about squeezing in a few more tables for that evening because so many people wanted to come. "It's going to make more money for us, Sam."

I'd walked down the hall to his office in the hospital wing, wanting to clarify a few things. "Some would consider it blood money," I pointed out. "You know Linc is innocent."

"I'd like to think he is. There's pretty nasty talk around town, though. They know Lincoln would never harm a hair on their heads, but this Bix was someone from his past—another Negro—and they were arguing about a black woman."

"She happens to be Linc's wife, and I hardly think he killed someone over her after all these years. Bix Blake was certainly no threat to their marriage."

"How do you know?"

I walked out in disgust, deciding I'd rather talk to Linc down at the jail. When I arrived, Charlene was with him. I decided to talk with Sheriff Lens instead.

"He'll be taken before the judge on Monday, Doc, and probably held for the grand jury. He's got motive: the fight about his wife. He's got opportunity, the only one with opportunity. And he's got method. I figure the codeine is available at the hospital."

"Yes," I admitted.

"How long does it take to kill someone with it?"

"If you swallow it in that strength you'd get sleepy and have trouble breath-ing within twenty minutes. Injected into the bloodstream, the effects are immediate."

"It kills instantly?"

"Theoretically, yes. In practice, the victim's size, health, and drug toler-ance would he factors that could slow the action for several minutes."

"Did you get a look at the needle, Doc?"

"Briefly, yes."

"I understand from Dr. Yale it's the sort used at Pilgrim Memorial."

"It's the sort used just about everywhere, the most popular brand. Anyone who's diabetic probably has one at home."

Sheriff Lens chewed on his lower lip. He was holding Linc Jones for a judge but I could see he wasn't happy about it. "Let's look at the possibilities, Doc. Did Blake kill himself? No, because Lincoln Jones never saw the needle in his hand. Did someone else hide in the room and jab him with the needle? No, because there was no hiding place."

"I haven't quite agreed to that yet. I'll want another look at the room."

"Was he jabbed after you burst into the room? No, because Jones was already holding the needle and Blake was dead."

"Agreed."

"If he didn't kill himself, and Lincoln Jones was the only person with him, then Lincoln Jones must have killed him. It's as simple as that, Doc."

"It's not that simple because he didn't do it. You don't go to a dance with a hypodermic needle full of poison because you might encounter someone you disagreed with twelve years earlier. Linc approached him as an old friend, not an enemy."

"Maybe Bix Blake brought the poison to kill Jones, they struggled and he got jabbed in the leg."

"Same argument, Sheriff. Would he have brought poison to use on Linc, after all those years? Linc, at least, didn't even realize there was still animos-ity over his marriage to Charlene. Besides, if it happened that way, in self-defense, Linc would have no reason to lie about what occurred."

Sheriff Lens sighed. "Then it's another one of your locked-room puzzles, Doc."

"Maybe." I glanced at my watch. It was after noon and I wanted to speak with Sweeney Lamb. "I'm going to shove off now. Tell Linc I didn't want to interrupt his visit with Charlene. I'll be back to see him later."

Most of the band was at Northmont's only hotel, but Helen McDonald told me Sweeney was out at the bus. "I'll take you there if you'd like," she offered.

"That would be helpful."

It was parked about a block from the hotel in an undeveloped field. "I feel terrible about Bix," she said as we walked. "I'd gotten to be real friendly with him in the months since he joined the band."

"Was he at the hotel with the rest of you?"

"Oh, sure. Spider's there too. We don't have much trouble in New England."

"What happens when there is trouble?"

"Bix and Spider have been known to sleep on the bus."

I could see it was a vehicle with many miles on it, in need of a paint job. Sweeney Lamb was seated inside, going over some sheet music arrangements for the evening performance. "Gotta make it a bit different from last night's selection," he explained. "And someone else has to play Bix's part."

"Who'll that be?"

"Probably Spider. He doubles on the trumpet."

I thought about that. "Is it a job to kill for?"

Lamb and Helen both laughed. "Not hardly," the bandleader replied. "They pay the same, and the trumpet and sax both get solos in different numbers."

I picked up a scrapbook that was lying on the seat next to him. There were newspaper ads for the band, and pictures of their performances. One from last summer showed them playing in short-sleeved shirts at a Coney Island jazz festival. "You play all sorts of music," I said.

"Well, jazz and pop."

I flipped over a few more pages and found a two-year-old photo of Helen McDonald in a sexy strapless gown. I smiled at her. "I thought you were just out of high school."

"Don't I wish!"

"Did either of you ever see Bix with a hypodermic needle?" I asked.

Sweeney Lamb frowned. "I don't allow no drugs in my band. Any needles, they're out! I had a drummer die of a heroin overdose just last summer."

"Have the police been on you about it?"

"They don't bother us," Helen replied. "Sweeney runs a clean crew."

I decided there was nothing more to be learned there. "We'll be looking forward to tonight."

He nodded. "A fresh start. I'll open with a little tribute to Bix and then we take off with a new beginning."

I left Helen on the bus and headed back to my office at Pilgrim Memorial. I had no patients scheduled that Saturday, but Mary was in the office and there was always the possibility of an emergency.

"Not a thing," she told me, "except Charlene Jones. She stopped by after visiting Linc at the jail."

"Where is she now?"

She nodded toward my inner office, where the door was standing open. I could see Charlene in the patients' chair by my desk. I walked in and asked, "How's Linc doing?"

"Not bad. He knows he's innocent. It's just some terrible mistake."

"Tell me about you and Bix. Did you break your engagement to him?"

"That was right out of high school. We were all awfully young. He admitted it was the right thing."

"Might he have killed himself and tried to frame Linc?"

"I hadn't seen him in maybe twelve years. Neither grudges nor romances last that long without a little fuel. Whatever happened to Bix had nothing to do with either Linc or me."

I pressed my lips together, thinking. "Could you come down to the Grange Hall with me, Charlene? Right now?"

"What for?"

"I want to try something."

"All right."

The place was already open for the evening's dance and I led the way at once to the makeshift dressing room. "This is where it happened," I told her. "The men changed their clothes here."

"What about the girl singer?"

"She used it later, during their first few instrumentals."

Charlene was a small woman, but I could see at once that my first theory was a loser. She was far too large to have hidden in one of the boxes of tablecloths. "Would you stand behind that rack of coats, please?"

She didn't move. She just stood there staring at me. "My God, Sam, you think I killed him somehow!"

"No, no—"

"Yes, you do! What motive could I have had? Even if I'd done it, do you think I'd let Linc go to jail in my place?"

"Please, Charlene, just stand behind the coats."

This time she did as I asked, but I could clearly see her feet beneath the coats. "Could you grab the pipe and pull yourself up?" She gamely tried it and the pipe almost pulled free from the wall. Surely there'd been no one hiding in the room either before or after Bix's death.

"Satisfied?" she asked.

"I just had to check all the possibilities. You were away from the table during the crucial period."

She left the room without another word and I feared that I may have lost a friend.

* * *

I went back to the hospital next, and found Sheriff Lens with Bob Yale outside the latter's office. "Hi, Doc. Just stopped by to pick up the dead man's clothes." He held up a paper bag.

"Stop in my office before you leave, Sheriff."

A couple of minutes later he appeared in my door. "What's up, Doc?"

"I just had an idea. I'd like to see the clothes Bix was wearing."

The sheriff opened the bag and dumped them on my examining table. "I went over them quick and didn't find anything."

I started checking the pockets and the sheriff chuckled. "Nothin' in that one but a hole."

There was indeed a small hole in the side pants pocket. I stuck my finger through it and wondered about the workings of fate. "Where's Bix's body, Sheriff?"

"Still here at the hospital, waitin' for instructions from the next of kin."

"Let's go take a look at it."

I'd never gotten used to examining day-old corpses, but it took me only a moment to find what I was looking for. "See this, Sheriff? And *this?*"

"What does it mean?"

"Tonight we're going to catch ourselves a murderer."

* * *

The dance that evening might have been a replica of the previous night's affair. Most everyone was dressed in the same clothes, and before the music started I asked Sweeney Lamb to duplicate everything he'd done on Friday night. "You mean play the same tunes?"

"Exactly," I said. "They'll get new music in the second set."

People looked around at each other as Sweeney Lamb and Dr. Yale made their opening remarks again, then really began to feel spooked when the band opened with their theme and then switched into *Pennies From Heaven.*

"Is this your idea?" Mary Best asked.

"It is," I admitted. "We'll see if it's a good one."

Spider Downs was playing Bix's part on the trumpet, and his own chair was empty. Otherwise everything was the same. Helen McDonald appeared on cue wearing the same pink gown and launched into *It's a Sin to Tell a Lie.*

A number of couples were on the dance floor, but others remained at their tables as if waiting to see what would happen. As the set drew near its concluding number I caught the eye of Sheriff Lens. Sweeney Lamb was on the bandstand, passing out the sheet music for the final arrangement, just as he had the night before. Helen McDonald hesitated, then took one and passed it on to Spider, seated in Bix's place.

"Come on!" I told the sheriff.

She turned pale as she saw us coming, and tried to leave the bandstand. But I had one arm and Sheriff Lens had the other. "You'd better come with us, Miss McDonald," he told her. "We want to ask you about the murder of Bix Blake."

"I didn't—"

"Yes, you did," I told her. "You killed him and we're going to prove it."

News of the killing had reached New York, and by the time the second night's dance ended there were big-city reporters waiting with their questions. I was glad we had a few answers.

With Bob Yale from the hospital and Sweeney Lamb both standing nearby, Sheriff Lens began. "We expect a full statement from Miss McDonald shortly, and Dr. Lincoln Jones will be released from jail within the hour. For the rest of it, I'm going to turn you over to Dr. Sam Hawthorne who played an important part in assisting with my investigations."

I stood to address the gathering.

"It appeared at first that Bix Blake had been murdered by an injection of codeine while in a locked room with only Lincoln Jones present," I began, capturing their attention from the start. "However, further investigation suggested another possibility. Bix may have been injected with the poison before he entered the room and locked the door."

Bob Yale interrupted. "Codeine injected in that strong of a dosage usually takes effect immediately."

I nodded. "But its symptoms can be delayed a few minutes or longer by a drug tolerance, which is exactly what Bix Blake had. It's not unheard-of among musicians these days. I believe he was a heroin addict. He injected the hypodermic needle into his own thigh at the end of the first set, through a hole in his pants pocket. A close examination of the body this afternoon revealed previous needle marks in the thighs. They'd been missed on the initial examination because of his dark skin."

"You're saying he committed suicide?"

"Hardly. A hypo full of an almost clear codeine solution could easily be mistaken for white heroin. Bix wouldn't have chosen to kill himself in front of his old friend Linc, at least not without telling him the reason. I think Bix was murdered by his drug supplier, who gave him a needle full of codeine instead of heroin. That's why I wanted a repeat performance tonight that followed last evening's events exactly.

"I thought I remembered something from last night, but I had to see it again to be sure. When Sweeney here passed out the sheet music arrangements for the final song of the set, Helen McDonald took one, even though it was an instrumental in which she had no part. She then folded the sheet music and passed it to Bix. Tonight I saw her take the sheet music but she didn't fold it when she passed it to Spider in Bix's chair. Last night she passed Bix the deadly hypo in the fold of that sheet music. I noticed the pain on his face as he left the bandstand to meet Linc, immediately after injecting himself. And he told Linc he'd be better next set, meaning when the drug took effect. But there was no next set for Bix. As he grew weaker and died in that dressing room, the needle slipped through the hole in his pocket and fell to the floor next to his feet, where Lincoln Jones found it."

Lamb could only shake his head. "Why was he injecting it into his thigh rather than his arm?"

"Because your band wears short-sleeved shirts in the summer, I saw the picture in your scrapbook."

"But even if she was supplying Bix with drugs, why would Helen kill him?"

Sheriff Lens answered that one. "Her initial statement indicates he'd been blackmailing her for free drugs, threatening to tell you that she was responsible for the heroin death of your drummer last year. They both knew how you felt about drugs in the band."

Lamb seemed crushed by what had happened. Perhaps the tragedy of it, for Bix and Helen and his drummer, was only now sinking in. I left him and went down to the jail, so I'd be there when Linc was released. Charlene saw me coming and even managed a smile.

"Thank you," she said. "Thank you for getting him out."

THE PROBLEM OF
THE VANISHING SALESMAN

W ELL, we had a lot of strange crimes during my younger days in Northmont [old Dr. Sam Hawthorne told his visitor as he reached for the brandy], but none was stranger than the disappearance of Mr. James Philby, a man who vanished but kept insisting he hadn't. Let me pour you a small libation, then settle back in your chair while I tell you about it.

It was early May of '37, a busy month that would see the Hindenburg dirigible disaster and the crowning of George VI as king of England. Such worldshaking events had little impact on Northmont, however, where the talk was more likely to run to the weather and spring planting. It was the season when traveling salesmen were most likely to begin their annual rounds.

James Philby was a relatively young man in his early thirties who'd been driving through southern New England the previous summer selling everything from lightning rods to butter churns. I'd chatted with him a couple of times when his route through town happened to coincide with my house calls. I hadn't thought about him all winter, but now it was May and here he was back again.

Philby drove a green four-door Nash whose back seat and trunk were loaded with his samples. He carried some of the smaller products with him and sold them right from the car. but for the bigger things there were only samples—or more likely a photograph in one of the catalogues stuffed into the trunk. He was a handsome sort, with black hair that he wore slicked back, and a thin mustache like Clark Gable had in the movies. The farm wives often greeted him with a friendly cup of coffee while their husbands and sons were out plowing in the fields.

I encountered him at the widow Gaines's place on the highroad, just coming out of the driveway. Her name was Abby Gaines and she wasn't yet fifty, but since her husband's death she'd become the widow Gaines to the community. The farm had been sold off to Douglas Crawford, her neighbor to the north, and she lived alone in the little farmhouse with a white picket fence. Philby stopped the Nash and leaned out the window. "Hello, Doc. Remember me?"

"James Philby, isn't it?"

"Right you are," he answered with a grin. "I'm back on my spring route. Just sold the lady a new lightning rod for her barn and–" He smacked the side of his head. "Forgot my samples!"

He was out of the car and trotting back to the farmhouse, leaving me sitting there in my car. "Hey, Philby! You've got me blocked. I can't get in." It was true. The Nash had stopped right in the middle of the narrow gravel driveway, and the white picket fence prevented me from driving around it on the grass.

"I'll only be a second, Doc," he assured me over his shoulder.

I sighed and tapped my fingers impatiently on the steering wheel. I'd already started my turn when I paused to let him out, and then he stopped to speak to me, blocking my entrance. Now I watched him return to the side porch, knock, and open the big storm door that was left over from winter. It was solid wood, with even its little window covered by cardboard, so I could see nothing of him from my angle.

As the seconds lengthened into minutes, my patience began to run out. True, my house call on Abby Gaines wasn't a medical emergency. I was merely checking on an infection for which I'd previously treated her. But after another two minutes I left my car and went up to the door I'd seen Philby enter. I pulled open the storm door, and called through the doorway. "Philby! Are you in there? Come and move your car."

Abby Gaines appeared from the kitchen at once, holding a wooden spoon. "Dr. Hawthorne–I didn't know you were here!"

"That salesman Philby has me blocked in your driveway. Where is he?"

"Philby? He left about ten minutes ago."

"I know, but he came back. He said he forgot the samples of the lightning rods he was showing you."

She looked baffled for just an instant. "That's right–he left them leaning against the wall by the front door and they're gone now. But I didn't hear him come back. The floor would have squeaked."

"Could he be somewhere in the house?" I glanced at the stairway to the second floor.

"I know I'd have heard him if he came in, but we can take a look." She led me quickly through the first-floor rooms–a front parlor, sitting room, kitchen, and an inside bathroom that was a recent addition. At the back of the house, off the kitchen, was a large woodshed that served as a general storage area. There were two other doors to it, from outside. One at the back, facing the barn, stood slightly ajar. The other was bolted from the inside. I opened it and saw that I was on the far end of the side porch, some ten feet from the door Philby had entered. We went upstairs next, inspecting each of the four bedrooms and a storage area that served in place of an attic.

"You can see he's nowhere in here," Abby Gaines said, opening the last of the closet doors. "You must have been mistaken."

I pulled the curtain aside and pointed down at the driveway. "You can see his car's still there. He came back for his lightning rods and vanished."

"Oh, surely not! You've been reading too many of those thrillers, Doctor."

"What about the basement?"

"There's no access to it from the house. You have to go through the outside doors. I had the stairway blocked when I added the inside bathroom, after Jesse died." Jesse Gaines had been her husband for more than twenty years.

We went back downstairs and I decided to ignore the missing salesman for the moment while I tended to my patient. I got my bag from the car and examined Mrs. Gaines. The infection was much improved and I instructed her to continue with the medication for another week.

As she walked out on the porch with me, I motioned toward the cars at the beginning of her driveway and said, "I don't know what you're going to do with Philby's car. I can't imagine what happened to him."

"Oh, I'm sure he'll turn up."

I wasn't nearly so sure, having seen the man vanish before my own eyes, but I got into my own car, waved to her, and backed onto the road. Later in the day, when I was back in the office, I told my nurse Mary Best about the strange occurrence.

"There must be some explanation," she said, busy at her desk.

"I think I'll give Abby Gaines a call and see if he turned up."

She answered on the second ring, and when I asked about James Philby she replied, "Well, I guess he came back because the car is gone."

"But you didn't see him?"

"No. I was lying down for a few minutes. I may have dozed off."

I hung up and told Mary, "I guess he came back."

"Of course he did, Sam! Not everybody who drops out of sight for a few minutes simply vanishes."

Her voice was firm and her words sensible. But I was the one who'd sat in the car and watched him step onto Abby Gaines's porch.

* * *

It was two days later that I was driving out the highroad past the Gaines house when I noticed a car in the driveway. It wasn't the green Nash but, a black Ford belonging to Douglas Crawford, the neighbor who'd bought the Gaines farmland after Jesse's death. I hadn't seen Crawford to speak to recently and I decided to stop. This time, to keep from blocking anyone, I pulled onto the shoulder of the road and left my car outside the white picket fence.

Douglas Crawford was a big sandy-haired man who smiled a lot. His eyes always seemed to be squinting against the sun, and his handsome wife Eileen was constantly after him to wear sunglasses. "Looks like you got something to hide," Crawford would respond, and in truth he seemed one of the most open men in Northmont.

Right now he was carrying two large cans of maple syrup up to the porch. He held one under his arm while he rang the doorbell, but he didn't wait for a reply. He opened the woodshed door and placed the cans inside.

"Hello, Douglas," Abby Gaines said as she opened the door.

"Brought you some maple syrup. Put it in the woodshed."

"I do thank you. That's very thoughtful." At that moment she saw me coming up the driveway. "Oh, hello, Dr. Hawthorne. I wasn't expecting you."

Crawford turned and we shook hands. "Howdy, Doc. Haven't seen you around lately."

"It was a bad winter for the flu. Things are better now. Maybe I can relax a bit."

"Ever play any golf? They've opened a nice new course over in Shinn Corners."

"I'll have to take it up."

He came down the porch steps, waving back at Abby Gaines. "Enjoy the maple syrup."

"I will! Thank you again."

He went off in his car and I turned my attention to Abby. "I was driving by and I thought I'd see how you're feeling."

"Much better, thank you."

"Good, good!" I edged into the real reason for my visit. "Have you seen any more of that salesman, Philby?"

"Not yet. I ordered a pair of his lightning rods for the roof but he hasn't delivered them yet."

"That's odd."

"He said it might take a week. I'm in no hurry."

"I don't know that anyone has seen him since the other day out here."

"I'm sure he'll turn up."

I left her standing on the porch, after suggesting she lock her door. The storm door was still in place, and I supposed she had to find someone who would take it down for her. Being a widow all alone is never easy.

The following day was Saturday, and I'd agreed to accompany Mary Best on an outing with some convalescent children from a hospital in the adjoining county. We spent an enjoyable afternoon among them, and I marveled at Mary's skill in mingling with the children as an equal.

Watching her playing with them, I almost missed the green Nash as it drove by on the dirt road, fast enough to trail a cloud of dust. "That's Philby's car," I told her. "I'm going after him."

She was too busy with the children to give it more than a glance, but she offered a "Be careful!" as I sprinted off toward my car. In the old days, when I'd owned a succession of high-powered sports cars, I might have caught him at the first hill despite the dust, but I'd turned more conservative with my most recent car purchase, settling comfortably into a Buick sedan. I closed the windows tight and set off after the Nash, plowing into the dust cloud as I gained on it. There was one advantage to all the dust—he couldn't see me coming until I was right on top of him. I honked my horn repeatedly and he pulled to the side of the road.

In that instant, as I emerged from my car and strode over to the Nash, I had a sudden doubt as to who I would find there. Somehow I still considered James Philby as one of the missing.

The door opened on the driver's side and Philby got out. "What's going on, Doc?" he asked with his customary grin. "You nearly ran me off the road."

He was the same man, short and handsome with his slick black hair and Clark Gable mustache. He had vanished and now he was back, acting like nothing had happened. "You disappeared up at the Gaines place. I was worried about you. No one has seen you."

"Lots of people have seen me. I've been around the towns selling my lightning rods and things. Spring is the best time to sell lightning rods. The old ones might have been damaged by winter storms."

"What happened to you the other day at the Gaines house? You walked up on her porch and disappeared."

"I went after my lightning rod samples. Then I walked back to the barn to check the rods out there. She doesn't use the barn anymore, but it could still be hit by lightning."

"I was watching that porch every minute, Philby. You never left it, and Abby Gaines says you didn't enter the house."

"You blinked, Doc. Or maybe you dozed off for a moment."

"I never took my eyes off the porch because I was waiting for you to come back and move your car out of my way."

He shrugged and changed the subject. "Want to buy a lightning rod, Doc? I've got a popular model here with a weather vane on it, tells you which way the wind's blowing."

"Not today, thanks," I responded, though in truth I could have used something that told me which way the wind was blowing. I seemed to have a mystery without a crime, but I had a chilly feeling that those circumstances were about to change. I returned to my car and drove back to join Mary and the children.

* * *

Douglas Crawford's wife Eileen was a big-boned woman with shoulders as broad as a man's. She was handsome rather than attractive, and I was used to seeing her in town two or three times a week, shopping and picking up supplies for the farm. On Monday morning when I spotted her lifting sacks of fertilizer into the back of her small truck, I crossed the street and asked if I could help.

"Thank you, Dr. Hawthorne. I have it under control." She heaved the final bag into the truck.

"I wonder if you could help me with something. Do you know a traveling salesman named James Philby?"

She squinted at me, the sun in her eyes, and replied, "I know him. He was around late last summer, even helped Douglas with the harvest once or twice. Peeled off his shirt and worked right along with the rest of the men. My husband liked him better than I did."

"Seen much of him this spring?"

"He stopped by once with his lightning rods, but we didn't need any."

"What sort of man is he? I've met him only briefly a few times."

"He's all right, I suppose. I thought he forced his friendship on us a bit suddenly. I'd watch him working with Douglas in the field last summer and wonder what he was trying to sell us."

"Did you ever find out?"

She shook her head. "We bought a sundial from him, that was all. I gave him supper and he spilled a bowl of soup."

"A sundial," I repeated. "An odd item for him to be selling."

"What's odd about it?"

"No one relies on sundials any more. They're merely decorative. Everything else that Philby sells is useful."

She smiled at my reasoning. "I doubt that Philby bothers to make the distinction." She closed the back of her truck and slid behind the steering wheel. "Stop in and see us when you're out our way."

"I'll do that," I promised.

But the whole affair continued to prey on my mind. I'd seen James Philby disappear on the porch of the Gaines farmhouse, even though he denied it. In a way, the denial was as much a mystery as the disappearance itself. Back at the office, Mary Best could see I was still troubled.

"You should forget about it, Sam," she advised. "Maybe you're starting to see mysteries where there aren't any."

Luckily, that Monday afternoon had a crowded schedule of office calls and I had little time to ponder the comings and goings of James Philby. It was the following afternoon, when I was free of appointments for a few hours, that I decided to drive over to Sheriff Lens's office at the jail.

The sheriff and I had been friends for years, ever since my arrival in Northmont in the 1920s. I occasionally saw him and his wife socially, and considered him my closest friend in the town, even with the difference in our ages. This day the jail was empty of prisoners and he'd just sent his deputy out for coffee.

"It's a slow time of year and I'm grateful for it. What's on your mind, Doc?"

I told him about the incident with James Philby. "It's been bothering me ever since it happened."

"Lettin' your imagination get the best of you, Doc. It don't sound like an impossible crime to me. There's no crime at all, and if you glanced away for a few seconds it wasn't impossible."

"You sound like Philby. I know what I saw."

"Maybe—" He was interrupted by the ringing of the telephone, and I got up to leave. "Sheriff Lens here," he said into the mouth-piece. He listened to a few words and his eyes went to mine. Something had happened. "Try to stay calm, Mrs. Crawford. Which way did he go?" Then, "All right, we're on our way. Doc Hawthorne is with me."

"What is it?" I asked as he hung up.

"That was Eileen Crawford. Her husband's just been shot by your salesman friend, Philby. She thinks he's dead."

* * *

We found Mrs. Crawford on the verge of hysteria, and I quickly gave her a capsule to calm her down. Douglas was sprawled on the floor near the front door, his chest torn by a bullet that had come out his back. It must have killed him instantly. "What happened?" Sheriff Lens asked. "Try to tell us exactly what happened."

"He—he pulled up in the driveway and got out. I could see him coming, carrying one of his lightning rods. I called to Douglas in the kitchen and asked if he'd ordered anything from Philby. He came in to see what I was talking about. Then he went to the screen door and opened it. He asked the salesman what he wanted, and then I heard the shot. Philby was carrying a rifle along with that lightning rod." She started to sob again, and I decided a stronger sleeping capsule might be the best thing for her now.

As I reached for her glass, the sheriff stayed my hand. "Just a minute, Doc. Mrs. Crawford, you said on the phone that he headed down the road in his car. Which way did he go?"

"Toward the Gaines place."

Another car pulled up in the driveway, and the sheriff's deputy hurried in. The town ambulance was right behind him. Lens motioned for them to keep back for a moment. "Mrs. Crawford, do you know of any reason for him to have shot Douglas? Was there hard feeling between them?"

She shook her head. "Nothing. I remember once last year he mentioned that his father had known Douglas several years ago, but Douglas told me he didn't remember it."

"Stay with her," Lens told his deputy.

I gave her a capsule to help her sleep and then hurried after the sheriff. "Where do you think he went?" I asked.

"Hard to tell. If we'd have come by the Gaines place we might have seen him."

We turned down that way now, and as soon as we cleared a thick stand of pine trees I spotted the green Nash. "There he is! In the Gaines driveway!" He was parked just by the picket fence, blocking access as he had once before. As the sheriff's car approached, we saw him leave the vehicle and head for the side porch of Abby Gaines's house. He was carrying a lightning rod in one hand.

Sheriff Lens skidded to a stop behind the Nash and climbed out as fast as he could, drawing his revolver. "Stop right there, Philby!" he shouted. "You're under arrest." The little salesman turned toward us with a sort of smile, then pulled open the storm door, obscuring our view of him.

"Come on!" I yelled to the sheriff, breaking into a run.

The storm door had swung shut, revealing the empty porch, only this time the door to the house was locked. I rang the bell and then checked the woodshed door at the far end of the porch. It was locked too, just like the first time.

"What's all this?" Abby Gaines asked, opening the door to face the revolver in Sheriff Lens's hand.

"We want James Philby," the sheriff told her. "He just ran in here."

She seemed as baffled as the first time. "No one ran in here. The door was locked the whole while. I took Dr. Hawthorne's advice."

"I'll have to search," Sheriff Lens said, keeping his gun raised and ready.

"Of course, if you don't believe me." She turned to me for support. "Why would I lie about such a thing?"

"Douglas Crawford's been murdered," I explained somberly. "Eileen says Philby did it."

"My God!" She sat down in the nearest chair. "What's this world coming to?"

I stayed with her while the sheriff completed his search. The feeling was growing inside me that he'd find nothing, just as I'd found nothing on the previous occasion. He searched both floors of the house, the woodshed, and even the basement which could be reached only from outside. He walked through the grass and weeds to the unused barn, but a quick look around turned up nothing but a family of small grass snakes beneath a toppled door.

"He's nowhere, Doc," the sheriff concluded, slipping his pistol back in its holster.

"Just like the first time. It's as if he stepped into another dimension."

"Why would he kill Douglas?" Abby asked.

"We don't quite know," Sheriff Lens replied. "I'm goin' to look over his car."

The green Nash yielded nothing but a salesman's samples. Among them I found one of the sundials the Crawfords had purchased from Philby last fall. It was only the metal top, really, without the supporting base. The gnomon that cast the shadow seemed sharp and just a bit dangerous. "I'd hate to fall against that," I told the sheriff.

"Not too likely." There were a couple more lightning rods in the car, laid across the back of the front passenger seat so they'd fit. The sheriff was especially interested in them, and finally on the floor beneath them he came up with what he wanted, partly hidden from sight by a reel of ground wire for the lightning rods. "Here's the rifle," he announced with a tone of triumph. "Been fired recently too. I'm surprised he left it."

"Maybe he didn't need it in that other dimension," I suggested.

I walked completely around the house, studying it from all angles. If Philby hadn't entered the house he'd gone somewhere else. The big storm door with its cardboard-covered window effectively obscured everything behind it when it was fully opened. Even the woodshed door couldn't be seen from out on the road, though it was locked and too far away to have helped Philby in his disappearance. Only the two doors led onto the porch, with a kitchen window between them. I tried to open it and couldn't.

"Nailed shut," Abby Gaines informed me. "My husband did it years ago because we get a terrible draft from the west wind. He packed insulating strips around it and nailed the whole thing."

She stood in the doorway and watched as I got down on my knees and tested the wooden boards of the porch. One seemed loose, but I could only lift it an inch or so. "He didn't go that way," I decided.

"You think I'm lying, don't you?"

I stared up at her. "No, I don't. But perhaps you're not telling us the correct version of the truth. James Philby vanished twice, both times on this porch. Assuming he did so voluntarily, he must have chosen this place for a reason. He must have felt you'd protect him somehow."

"That's rubbish!" She was angry now, not liking what I might be implying.

"Were you ever more than casual friends?"

"He's a salesman, for God's sake!"

"And you're a lonely widow."

"I resent your implication, Dr. Hawthorne."

It was best for us both that Sheriff Lens joined us at that moment, before I added to the words I was already regretting. I had no reason to accuse her of improprieties with James Philby. Perhaps it was only a sign of my growing frustration with the day's events. "I'm impounding the car," Lens announced as he joined us on the porch. "I'll have someone tow it into town. And I'd advise you to keep your doors and windows locked until we find him, Mrs. Gaines."

"You can be sure I'll do that."

The sheriff used her telephone to call his deputy up at the Crawford place, then we headed back into town. "This looks like another one of your locked rooms," he suggested on the way.

"Hardly that. It may be a locked house, but Philby was outside when he disappeared, not inside."

"How do you figure he did it?"

"I haven't the faintest idea," I admitted.

I'd left my car at the jail, and the sheriff dropped me off there, promising to keep me advised of developments. I drove back to my office in a wing of Pilgrim Memorial Hospital and checked my appointment schedule with Mary Best. It had been a quiet afternoon and the only scheduled patient had called to cancel. I told her about Douglas Crawford.

"It never stops, does it?"

"Doesn't seem to."

"Have they found Philby yet?"

"Sheriff Lens and I spotted him going into Abby Gaines's house."

She looked at my face, guessing what I was about to say. "Not again?"

"Yep. Opened the storm door and disappeared."

"She must have let him in."

"She says not. The sheriff searched the place and found nothing, just like I did last time."

Mary picked up a pad of paper and sat down at my desk. She was wearing her blonde hair short that season, and it gave her a studious, intense look. "What does this porch look like?"

I described it to her in detail as she made some notes and drew a few lines of a rough sketch. "Floor?" she asked.

"I checked it out. One loose board, but it only moved a few inches. Not room enough for him to slip under, anyway."

"You said he's a small man."

"Not that small. He's about five-five."

"Roof?"

"I'd have seen him above the storm door. There's nothing up there anyway. It's just a covering for the porch."

"How about this woodshed door?"

I shook my head. "That's out for two reasons. It was bolted from the inside and it was ten feet away. The storm door would have swung shut if Philby wasn't holding it, and then we would have seen him going toward the other door."

"So it gets down to Mrs. Gaines letting him into the house."

"Seems like it. But I searched the place the first time and the sheriff searched it today. It's not that big a house."

The sheriff himself came by a little later in the afternoon, looking perplexed. "No sign of him anywhere. I've got the state police watching the roads in case he had another vehicle waiting, but that don't seem too likely."

"Why not?" I asked.

"Well, he was very deliberate about leavin' his car at the Gaines house, Doc. It was almost as if he sat in the driveway waitin' till he saw us coming."

I'd considered the same possibility, even though it didn't make a great deal of sense. Philby couldn't have known I'd be in the car, but maybe he was just waiting for the sheriff.

"Maybe he's hiding in the house waiting for dark," Mary Best suggested. "Waiting for Abby Gaines to drive him across the state line."

Sheriff Lens grunted. "And maybe he ran around the house and hid in the trunk of my patrol car while we were in the house. But I doubt it."

Mary was not about to be put off by his banter. "Have you looked in your trunk, Sheriff?"

"Hell, no!"

She insisted on taking his keys, marching out to the parking lot, and opening the trunk while we watched through my office window. She seemed disappointed when she lifted the lid to reveal a spare tire and some tools. "All right," she told us when she returned, handing him back his keys, "So Philby wasn't in there. But he has to be somewhere. And I'm going to figure out where."

We went over everything again, mainly for her benefit, though I knew from my own experience that it never hurts to talk over these things. Mary was quick to begin analyzing the problem. "You both saw him walk up on the porch?"

"That's right."

"And he couldn't have come off it without your seeing that too. He couldn't have gone through the woodshed door, or the floor, or the roof of the porch. He could only have gone into that house while the storm door was open, obscuring your view."

"And either Mrs. Gaines knew about it or she didn't," the sheriff chimed in. "But where did he hide?"

"He might have slipped out a window or something," Mary suggested.

"Not without her seeing him, aiding him," I said. "Remember, we were only an instant behind him, and she let us in at once. She wouldn't have had time to wait at a window and close it after him, and when I circled the house myself a few minutes later all the windows were closed."

Mary's face suddenly glowed with triumph. "All right, how's this? Philby had to enter that house. He couldn't have gone anywhere else. Yet he had vanished a moment later. Keep in mind two things. First, Abby Gaines had business dealings with the murdered man, sold him a good share of the farm after her husband died. Maybe he cheated her or she thought he had. Second, you've described James Philby several times as a small or short man. His mustache and slicked-back hair could easily have been fake."

"What are you trying to say, Mary?"

"I forget whether it was you or Sherlock Holmes who first said that when you've excluded the impossible, whatever remains, however improbable, must be the truth. The missing James Philby and the widowed Abby Gaines are the same person."

* * *

Sheriff Lens and I stared at each other. "Well, I don't know," he muttered. "That seems awfully far-fetched. But it might be worth another drive out to her place. What do you say, Doc?"

I stood up. "Let's go."

"I'm coming too!" Mary Best decided. "We can shut the office, can't we?"

It was only ten minutes to closing time. "Sure, come along."

On the way out the highroad, Mary sat in the back seat and continued to build her case. "You never saw the two of them together, did you? And Philby never came around until after Jesse Gaines died. He wasn't needed then. He wasn't needed until Abby was alone and plotting her revenge on the man she felt had stolen her property."

"You might have something," Sheriff Lens said grimly. "We'll see."

"There's more. I mentioned Sherlock Holmes before. Didn't either of you notice the similarity between James Philby's name and that of James Phillimore, in one of Holmes's unrecorded cases? Phillimore was said to have gone back into his house for an umbrella and vanished. James Philby went back to Abby Gaines's house for a lightning rod that first time, and vanished."

I had to chuckle at that, at the weird twists that fate sometimes played. But we were almost at the Gaines house, and I couldn't let the game go on any longer. "Mary, Mary—James Philby and Abby Gaines are not the same person. They could never have been the same person. I've been treating Abby Gaines for a year—"

"I know that but—"

"—and Eileen Crawford told me Philby helped out with the harvest last year, working alongside the other men with his shirt off."

"Oh. Then how—?"

"Let me off here by the driveway. You two wait in the car."

I avoided the house and went directly to the barn at the rear of the property. Though it was almost suppertime, there was still plenty of daylight left. I entered the old barn through the big sliding door and looked around, taking in the hayloft and the empty stanchions where cows had once been confined for milking. Sheriff Lens had been out here, I knew, but only briefly. I lit a match and dropped it onto a small pile of straw at my feet.

It took about five minutes for the barn to fill with the aroma of burning straw. I was about to stamp out the fire and give up when there was a slight movement in the hayloft directly above me. A figure emerged and started down the rickety wooden ladder. It was the missing salesman, James Philby.

"I'm glad to see you back with us again," I said.

"Put out that fire before you burn the place down!"

I stamped it out and followed him from the barn. "The sheriff's waiting at the end of the driveway," I pointed out, in case he was thinking about running away. "Why did you kill Douglas Crawford?"

"It's a long story."

"I've got plenty of time." I saw that Abby Gaines had come out on her porch to see what was going on.

"He had some business dealings with my father years ago. My father killed himself and I always blamed it on Crawford. It was the biggest thing in my life, and when I mentioned it to him he didn't even remember it."

"So you killed him." We were walking slowly out past the house. The sheriff and Mary had gotten out of the car to meet us.

"Yes. I tried twice last year and failed both times. I sold him a sundial with a particularly sharp pointed gnomon, hoping I could trip him so he'd fall onto it. That didn't work at all. I helped with the harvest and was invited to supper, and I poisoned his soup, but he and his wife changed places at the last minute and I had to tip over the bowl to keep her from being poisoned. She must have thought I was awfully clumsy. This time I decided I'd waited long enough. I shot him with my rifle and gambled on making a getaway. After dark tonight I'd have headed across country."

"After arranging to disappear at the Gaines's front door."

"I tried it with you and the trick worked fine. I figured it would work just as well with Sheriff Lens."

"Both times your car was just off the road, so we couldn't get around it. We had to watch your little drama from the road, where the storm door provided the perfect shield."

Sheriff Lens had come up with his handcuffs. "Perfect shield for what, Doc? Was Abby Gaines involved after all? Was she hiding him?"

"No, no. The poor woman is completely innocent. I imagine he chose this place simply because it had a barn that wasn't being used. There are lots of good hiding places in an old barn. But he had to focus our attention on the house, not the barn."

"How'd you do it, Philby?" the sheriff asked.

"Let Dr. Hawthorne tell you. He seems to know everything."

"My big mistake was in assuming that woodshed door was always locked," I continued. "Of course it wasn't. I stood right here and watched Crawford open it to put some cans of maple syrup inside. In truth it was usually unlocked, like the Gaines front door. You simply stepped through the woodshed door and bolted it behind you, both times. Then, while the house was being searched, you ran out the back door to the barn and hid there. The first time, you probably found just the hiding place you needed."

"Wait a minute!" Mary Best objected. "You said yourself, Sam, that he couldn't reach the woodshed door while still holding the storm door open to block our view. They're ten feet apart."

"We all forgot one important fact. Both times he worked the trick, Philby was holding a six-foot-long lightning rod in his hand. He'd left it next to the front door the first time. He held the storm door open with the lightning rod until he reached and opened the woodshed door. Then, as he pulled the lightning rod into the woodshed after him, the storm door swung shut on its spring."

"I'll be damned!" Sheriff Lens said.

"That reminds me," Philby told us suddenly, "I left my lightning rod in the hayloft. Can I go back to the barn for it?"

"Get in the car," the sheriff ordered. "Your disappearin' days are over."

THE PROBLEM OF
THE LEATHER MAN

Ever since I'd moved to southern New England in the early 1920s [Dr. Sam Hawthorne told his guest, lifting the glass for a sip of brandy], I'd heard occasional stories about the Leather Man. At first I thought it was a mere legend to frighten the children at night, but later I learned that there really was such a person—a laconic wanderer dressed in a homemade leather suit who toured Connecticut and eastern New York State for some thirty years until his death in 1889.

The summer of 1937 was when the Leather Man returned, and in Northmont we weren't ready for him.

It was Sheriff Lens who roused me with a phone call at three in the morning on the first day of August.

"Hawthorne," I mumbled into the bedside phone.

"Doc, I got a bad accident out on Turk Hill Road, near Putnam. You were the closest one to call."

"I'll be there," I answered shortly and hung up. My head was back on the pillow when I jerked myself awake and clambered out of bed. I wiped my face with a wet washcloth, dressed quickly, and hurried out to my car. Except for an occasional patient in labor, it was rare for me to be called out at that hour. Although automobiles had become more numerous on the roads around Northmont, accidents were infrequent.

I reached the scene of this one within fifteen minutes of the sheriff's summons. A black Ford had run off the road and turned over in a ditch. Sheriff Lens's car was on the road about ten feet away and the sheriff himself was doing the best he could with the badly injured driver. A woman from a nearby farmhouse stood watching from a safe distance.

"How bad is it?" I asked the sheriff.

"Bleedin' from the head, Doc," he answered quietly, standing up to greet me in the glare of his car's headlights, "It's March Gilman."

I knew Gilman from the Rotary meetings, though he'd never been a patient or close friend. He was a man around forty with a successful feed grain business in town, and a reputation of chasing after ladies.

"Bad wound," I said, dropping to my knees beside him. "Have you called the ambulance?"

"Right away, but they were having some engine trouble. That's when I phoned you."

I leaned closer to the bleeding man. "March! March, can you hear me?"

His eyes flickered open for just an instant. "What—?"

"You've had an accident, March."

"Leather . . . the Leather Man—"

"What's that?" I asked. I'd heard him clearly enough but I didn't under-stand the words.

"Leather Man . . . in the road. Tried to avoid him and . . . went into ditch."

"What Leather Man, March? Who was he?"

But that was all he said, and in the distance I could hear the clanging of the ambulance bell along the dark dirt road. I tried to stanch the flow of blood from his head until it arrived, but I knew the life was draining out of him.

As they were loading him into the ambulance, the woman who'd been watching moved closer. When she stepped into the light I recognized her as one of the teachers from the Northmont grammar school. "Miss Whycliff—I didn't realize it was you."

"I still live here in the homestead," she replied, arms folded across her breasts as if to protect herself from the mild night air. She was an attractive but plain woman in her late thirties, unmarried and carrying on with life after the death of her parents. There were women like her in most rural communities.

"What happened here?" I asked as Sheriff Lens saw the ambulance on its way.

"I don't really know. He must have been driving fast. I heard the car go by the house and then skid and go into the ditch. I think it woke me up. I threw on some clothes and when I saw he was injured I phoned the sheriff at once."

"Did you see anyone else?" Sheriff Lens asked as he joined us. "This Leather Man he mentioned?"

"No one. But of course the road was dark." She hesitated. "There was a Leather Man in these parts long ago. I don't know much of the legend, but our local historian could tell you."

"I don't believe in ghosts," the sheriff told her. "The fella you're talkin' about's been dead nearly fifty years."

"Some people have seen him this summer," she replied. "I've heard talk that he's back."

"Rubbish!" Sheriff Lens told her. He was not one to believe in things he hadn't seen for himself.

Hannah Whycliff shrugged. "Will you send someone to tow this car out of my front yard?"

"First thing in the morning," he promised.

He drove to Pilgrim Memorial Hospital then, and I followed in my car. March Gilman was dead by the time we arrived.

Mary Best was busy with her office chores, getting out the August first billing, when I arrived a little before ten. "I just phoned you, Sam. I was worried when you weren't here at nine."

"I had a three A.M. emergency, so I decided to sleep an extra hour."

"The accident that killed March Gilman?"

I nodded. "I suppose the news is all over town."

"Pretty much. I gather he was someone important."

"Small-town important," I told her. Mary had taken over as my nurse after April married and moved to Maine. Sometimes I forgot she'd only been in Northmont two years and didn't yet know everyone. "What's my schedule for today?"

"It's pretty slow. Mrs. Ritter at ten-thirty and Douglas Greene at eleven, and then you're free for the day."

At noon I drove over to see Sheriff Lens. "Just looking at the hospital report on March Gilman,'" he said. "Died of massive head injuries. No surprise there. He had a bad bleeding wound and a lesser one that probably caused a mild concussion."

"I'm sorry I couldn't do anything to save him." I sat down by his desk. "But this business about the Leather Man still bothers me. Hannah Whycliff said the town historian would have information about the legend. Would that be Spencer Cobb?"

"Only one I know, and he's sorta unofficial."

Spencer Cobb had an office in our little library building on the far side of the town square. I found him on a short stepladder, checking an atlas of old New England maps in a leather-bound volume with a scuffed and disintegrating cover. "Hello, Sam," he greeted me. "What can I do for you?" He was white-haired, though barely fifty, and smoked a pipe almost constantly.

"I've got a historical question for you, Spencer. Ever hear of the Leather Man?"

"You're really going way back now. Come—sit down while I dig out some old references." He was actually the county surveyor, but since the job only occupied a small part of his time he'd taken on the additional duties of Northmont's historian.

Presently he laid an old photograph before me on the desk. It showed a scruffy man in his fifties seated on a wooden bench eating a piece of bread or a bun. He was clad entirely in a bulky, shiny garment with crude stitching plainly visible. The pants and coat seemed to be made of the same patchwork material—leather scraps held together by thongs. He wore a visored cap and boots that seemed to have wooden soles. Resting next to him was a leather bag perhaps two feet square.

"This was the Leather Man," Spencer Cobb said. "The photograph was taken not long before his death in 1889."

"Tell me about him."

Cobb struck a match and relit his pipe. "He first appeared in this area in the late 1850s, dressed as you see him here. For the next thirty years, summer and winter, he followed a particular route, walking along country roads from the Hudson River on the west to the Connecticut River on the east. It took him about thirty-four days to complete each circuit of three hundred sixty-five miles. He came as regularly as the full moon, though every thirty-four days instead of the moon's twenty-nine or thirty days. Once they established his route, some thought it had a mystic significance, with the three hundred sixty-five miles standing for the days of the year."

"Who was he? Did anyone know?"

"He rarely spoke—only a few words in broken English. Though he had his regular stops, if anyone questioned him too closely would abandon that stop in the future. People were frightened of him at first, but they came to know him as a peaceful man who wanted no trouble. It was believed from his accent that he was French."

"What happened to him?"

"In December of 1888 someone noticed a sore on his lip that appeared to be cancerous. He was taken to a hospital in Hartford, but promptly ran away. The press identified him as a Frenchman named Jules Bourglay who'd fled his homeland following business losses and a tragic love affair. However, none of this was ever proven, and when the Leather Man died of cancer the following March, his meager belongings offered no clue to his identity."

"A fascinating story," I agreed, "But there have been recent reports—"

Spencer Cobb nodded. "I know. The Leather Man is back. I've been hearing stories all summer. Since I don't believe it ghosts I can only assume that someone is retracing the old route, for reasons of his own."

"I have a road map in the car. If I bring it in, could you outline the route for me?"

"Certainly, I have it in one of these old newspaper clippings. There's a great deal of material available because so many people at the time kept scrapbooks of his comings and goings."

I watched while he carefully copied the route of the Leather Man. If this new traveler was retracing the old route, I figured I should be able to locate him without too much difficulty. I'd become fascinated by the story, and curious about what he knew regarding the accident that killed March Gilman.

"Thanks, Spencer," I told him. "You've been a big help."

I went back to the office and plotted the distances on the map. "Why are you doing all this?" Mary Best asked, "What happens if you find him? Are you going to walk with him?"

"Maybe."

"That's the funniest thing I've heard!"

"Look, he's covering three hundred sixty-five miles every thirty-four days. That works out to better than ten and a half miles a day, every day. Why should anyone in his right mind do such a thing?"

"The original Leather Man did it. Maybe this is his grandson or something."

I could see she was laughing at me, but I wanted to find him. With the unfolded map beside me on the seat, I set off in my car along his route. Hannah Whycliff's house was as good a starting point as any, and I drove up there to begin my search. Her car was gone, and Gilman's wrecked vehicle had been towed away as promised. I parked in the drive and walked back to the road, looking for traces of the accident. The gravel in front of her house was unmarked, and only a broken piece of bumper remained in the ditch as evidence of the accident.

I tried to imagine where the Leather Man might have been crossing, then decided he'd have stuck to the road, especially at that hour of the night. But why had he been walking at all? Apparently he slept overnight with people, or in fields in good weather. What was he doing up at three in the morning?

I got back into my car and started driving.

* * *

After twenty miles of slow and careful searching over the next hour, I came to the conclusion that the Leather Man was nowhere to be found. Perhaps he'd given up his trek, if he'd ever begun it. Maybe the whole thing had been a myth. I stopped in a filling station that had a public telephone and called Mary back at the office.

"I can't find him," I told her. "I've covered the twenty miles between Northmont and Shinn Corners and he's nowhere on the road. Any emergencies back there?"

"All quiet."

"I guess I'll give up and head back in."

"Maybe you've been going the wrong way," she suggested.

"What?"

"You've been driving in a counterclockwise direction around his route. Maybe he walks in a clockwise direction."

"Damn!" I tried to think why I'd driven the way I did, and decided it was because March Gilman had been going in this direction when he went into the ditch and killed himself. Of course that proved nothing. If there had been a man in leather on the road last night he might have been walking in either direction. "Thanks, Mary. You could be right."

Next I phoned Spencer Cobb and asked him the crucial question. "You never told me which way the original Leather Man walked. Was it clockwise or counterclockwise?"

"Let's see—clockwise, I believe. It's not stated as such in the papers I have, but that seems to have been the case."

"Thanks, Spencer."

"Have you found him?"

"I'm on the trail."

I retraced my route and then kept on going past the Whycliff house, skirting Northmont and heading back east. I took it especially show this time, and before I'd gone three miles I spotted a slim, brown-clad figure walking ahead of me in the road. He moved to one side as I drew up next to him, but I didn't drive past.

"Want a ride?" I called out the open window.

"No, mate. I'm walking."

He spoke with a strange accent, not quite British, and there was no arguing with his words. I made a quick decision and pulled up behind him, parking my car off the road. I hurried to catch up with him and asked, "Don't mind if I walk with you, do you?"

"Suit yourself, mate."

I fell into step beside him. Up close, I could see that he was indeed wearing a leather suit, not made of separate pieces held together by thongs like the original Leather Man, but one that fit him quite well and reminded me a bit of the buckskin garments one associated with Daniel Boone and other frontiersmen. He carried a knapsack of the same material, with a few possessions bundled into the bottom of it.

"Headed anywhere in particular?" I asked.

"I'm on a trek."

"That's a nice leather suit you're wearing. I hear people call you the Leather Man."

He turned his head in my direction and I got my first good view of his sandy hair and weathered face. He was probably in his forties, but I could have been off by ten years either way. His eyes were the palest blue I'd ever seen. He looked nothing like the picture of the old Leather Man that Spencer Cobb had shown me. A car appeared over the hill ahead, traveling at a good speed, raising a small cloud of dust behind it. "Who calls me that?" the man asked.

"People who've seen you on your route."

The car slowed to pass us and I saw Hannah Whycliff behind the wheel, heading home. I waved and she waved back. "Haven't seen many people," he muttered. "Just when I stop occasionally for food or a night's rest."

"That woman who just passed us—you were in front of her house at three this morning."

"Might have been," he acknowledged. "When there's a moon I like to walk for part of the night and sleep through the morning. It's cooler that way."

"What's your name? Mine's Sam Hawthorne."

"Zach Taylor." He extended a bronzed hand and we shook.

"Zach as in Zachary?"

"That's right."

"We had a president by that name. Long ago."

"So they tell me."

We were sitting a steady pace, a bit faster than I liked to walk. "You're not from around here. Are you British?"

"Australian, mate. Ever hear of a place called Alice Springs?"

"Vaguely. I might have seen it on a map once."

"It's real outback country there. Nothing but desert."

"What brought you to New England?"

"Just decided to see the world. Got this far and thought it was nice enough to stay a while. I spent the spring in New York and then came up here."

It was getting late in the day, almost dinnertime, but we kept walking. "Your trek is following the route of the original Leather Man, more than fifty years ago," I observed. "That's more than coincidence."

"Well, I was wearing this leather outfit and someone mentioned your Leather Man up in these parts. I looked up his route at the library and decided to follow it."

"You've been doing this all summer?"

"Yes."

"If you were out at three this morning you must have seen an automobile accident. A Ford tried to avoid you and went into a ditch."

Now he eyed me with open suspicion. "Is that what this is all about? Are you a policeman, Sam Hawthorne?"

"No, I'm a doctor."

We were approaching a railway crossing where I knew the crossing guard. He was an elderly squinty-eyed man named Seth Howlings, and as we approached he came out of his shed to lower the gate across the grade crossing. "Hello, Seth," I called out.

He turned toward me. "Dr. Sam! Haven't seen you in a long time. And on foot, too! What happened to your car?"

"I'm getting some exercise today. Is there a train coming?"

"Sure is! Can't you hear it?"

I could then. It sounded a distant whistle and in another moment it came into view. It wa a twenty-car freight train, traveling at moderate speed. "You've got good ears to hear it coming that far away," I told Seth after the train had passed.

"Best there are," he said with a toothless grin as he raised the gate. "I could hear a cow mooing in the next county."

I chuckled and fell into step beside Zach Taylor. "How late you working tonight, Seth?"

"Till my wife picks me up. She keeps track of my hours."

"See you later."

We crossed the tracks and set off down the highway again. "You know a lot of people in this area?" Zach asked.

"Quite a few. I've been a doctor here for fifteen years."

"You hungry? I've got some sourdough bread in my sack here, and a little whiskey to wash it down."

"You're tempting me."

The whiskey burned going down, but the bread had a nice original taste. We paused only about ten minutes before we were off again. Another car passed us, but the driver was no one I knew. Traffic was sparse on this section of the road.

"I was asking you about that accident with the Ford," I reminded him after a time of walking in silence.

"Yes. You were, weren't you?"

"You saw it?"

"I never saw the car until it was on top of me. Don't know where he came from. I dove to one side and he ran off the road. I could see he was dazed but he didn't seem badly hurt, and I'm not one to get involved in those things."

"So you just kept going."

"Sure. I walked for another half-hour and then found a haystack to sleep in. How's the bloke in the car?"

"He's dead."

"God, I'm sorry to hear that."

"You should have stopped to help him, Zach."

He took out the whiskey again and downed another healthy shot, passing the bottle to me. "Last time I stopped to help someone at an accident, I spent a couple nights in jail. Damned cops thought I was a hobo."

"Aren't you, in a way?"

"Not a chance, mate! I've got money on me. Sometimes I even pay for my lodging and food, when I can't get it free."

"But you're wandering the back roads of New England."

"Man, I'm on walkabout!"

"What?"

"Walkabout. I don't suppose you know the word. It's an Australian custom—an Australian Aborigine custom, really—meaning an informal leave from work during which the person returns to native life and wanders the bush, sometimes visiting relatives."

"So this is your walkabout."

"Exactly."

"What is it you've left back home?"

"A wife and family, actually. I hope to return to them someday."

We walked on as night fell, and I realized that it must be after eight-thirty. Where had the day gone, and how far had I walked with this man? More important, how many shots of his whiskey had I drunk? "Won't you be stopping for the night?"

"Soon," he agreed. "Soon."

He told me more about his wife and children as we walked, and about life in Australia. He recounted exploits of the legendary bandit Ned Kelly, who wore a suit of homemade armor in his battles with police. After a time the whiskey bottle was empty and he hurled it into the brush along the road.

"I am too tired to go further," he finally admitted. Up ahead, a lighted sign announced a house that offered beds and breakfast for travelers. "I'll stay here for the night," he told me.

"Then I'll be leaving you and going back to my car." As soon as the words were out of my mouth I realized how foolish they were. We'd been walking for hours. It would take me half the night to return to my car.

"That's too far. Stay the night with me, mate."

I thought about phoning Sheriff Lens for a ride, but I'd drunk more whiskey than expected and I didn't want him to see me wavering a bit as I walked. Maybe it would be best to sleep for a few hours.

A fat, middle-aged woman agreed us at the door of the big house. "Welcome, travelers," she greeted us. "I'm Mrs. Pomroy. Looking for a place to spend the night?"

"That we are," Zach Taylor told her. "Can you accommodate us?"

"I've got two nice beds right at the top of the stairs. Ten dollars each and that includes a sturdy breakfast in the morning."

"We'll take them," I agreed, feeling sleepier by the minute.

"Glen!" she called out, and almost at once a small man with grey hair and a slight limp appeared. "This is my husband, Glen. He'll show you to your room. Glen—number two, top of the stairs."

He smiled at us halfheartedly. "Good to have you folks stop. Any bags?"

"No, mate," Zach told him. "Just us."

He led us up the stairs and his wife called out, "You can pay in the morning. I'll wake you at eight for breakfast if you're not up yet."

The room was large and cheerful, even by the uncertain light from a single floor lamp. There were two beds covered with flowery spreads, and a water pitcher and bowl. "Bathroom's down the hall," Pomroy told us. "We leave a little light on all night."

I shed my outer clothes and fell into bed, exhausted. The combination of all that walking and the shots of whiskey had proven to be too much for me. I had a glimpse of Zach climbing into the other bed, and then I was asleep.

It was daylight when at last I opened my eyes. I was aware that someone was knocking on my door and I looked at the pocket watch I'd left on the table next to the bed. It was five minutes after eight. Then I noticed that Zach's bed was empty, the spread pulled neatly into place. It looked undisturbed.

"Just a minute!" I called to the knocker, pulling on my pants.

I opened the door to find Mrs. Pomroy standing there. "Time for breakfast, if you want it."

"I'll be right down. Where's the other man?"

She looked blank. "What other man?"

"Zach Taylor, the fellow who was with me."

Mrs. Pomroy stared me straight in the eye. "You were alone, mister. There was no one with you."

* * *

Sheriff Lens arrived within a half-hour of my call. Mrs. Pomroy's place was across the county line, so he was officially outside jurisdiction, but that didn't stop him from asking Mrs. Pomroy a few questions.

"Doc here says he came in last night with another man. You say he came alone."

She glared at me and then back at the sheriff. "Alone he was."

Then why'd you give me a room with two beds?"

She shrugged. "It was empty. You were the only guest we had."

Sheriff Lens shifted uneasily. "I've known Doc a good many years, Mrs. Pomroy. If he says he came here with someone—"

"It was obvious he'd been drinking heavily, Sheriff. He couldn't even walk straight. Maybe he was with someone else, but not here."

The sheriff glanced at me inquiringly. "Is that true, Doc?"

"This fellow, the Leather Man, had a bottle of whiskey. We had a few shots while we walked."

The woman's husband came in from outside and she immediately lined up his support. "Tell them, Glen. Tell them this man was alone.

The short man glanced at me. "Sure was! I was glad to see he wasn't drivin', the shape he was in."

I sighed and started over again, "There was a man with me. He went to sleep in the other bed. His name is Zach Taylor and he's wearing a leather suit, almost like buckskin."

They both shook their heads, unwilling to budge from their story. Maybe they killed him for his few meager possessions, I thought, but then why wouldn't they have killed me too? "Come on, Doc," the sheriff said, his arm on my shoulder. "I'll give you a ride back to your car."

As I turned to leave, Mrs. Pomroy reminded me, "That'll be ten dollars for the room."

Back in his car, Sheriff Lens was silent until I spoke. "I found this so-called Leather Man, and when he wouldn't stop to talk with me, I parked my car and walked with him. He's Australian, on something called a walkabout. Trying to find himself, I guess. He saw the accident but didn't think Gilman was seriously hurt. He was afraid of getting involved so he kept on walking."

"What about the drinkin', Doc? Is that part true?"

"He had a bottle with him. After a while I took a couple of swigs from it. I'll admit it hit me harder than I'd expected, but I knew what was going on at all times. Zach Taylor was with me when we took the room at Mrs. Pomroy's place."

"Did you sign a register or anything?"

"No. She rents rooms and gives you breakfast, that's all. She's not operating a hotel."

You think they killed him or something?"

"I don't know what to think. The last I saw of him, he was climbing into the bed next to mine."

"But the bed was made this morning."

"I slept so soundly Mrs. Pomroy could have brought a parade of elephants in there and I wouldn't have known it. She could easily have come in and made the bed."

"The door wasn't locked?"

I tried to remember. "I don't think so. I'm sure we had no key."

He stared hard at the highway ahead. "I don't know what to think, Doc."

"Well, I can at least prove he was with me. When we get to the railroad crossing back across the county line, stop the car."

We reached it in another ten minutes, and I saw old Seth Howlings upcoming out of the crossing guard's little shed. "Hello, Seth."

"It's Dr. Sam again! But in a car this time."

"Howdy, Seth," Sheriff Lens said, getting out to join me.

"Hello, Sheriff. Beautiful day, isn't it?"

"Sure is!"

I walked closer to him. "Remember when I came by yesterday afternoon, Seth?"

"Sure do! Just as the five thirty-five was passing through."

"Remember the man who was with me?"

He looked blank. "You was alone, Dr. Sam. Are you trying to trick me?"

"Alone?" the sheriff repeated. "Are you certain of that?"

"Certain as I can be. Dr. Sam walked up and we chatted some while the train passed. Then he crossed the tracks and went on his way."

"Alone?"

"Alone."

I was in the middle of a nightmare from which there was no awakening.

* * *

Sheriff Lens and I drove on. "I'm not crazy, Sheriff."

"I know that, Doc."

"And I wasn't drunk enough to have imagined the whole thing. In fact, I never would have had any whiskey at all if Zach Taylor hadn't given it to me."

"Still, that old coot would have no reason to lie. You can't think he's in some sort of conspiracy with the Pomroys! They probably don't even know each other."

"I don't know what to think at this point. But I'm damned if I'm going to let it rest! I have to prove I wasn't imagining this Leather Man."

Sheriff Lens thought about it. "Someone must have seen you on the road together."

"There were only a few cars, and no one I knew except—"

"What is it?"

"Hannah Whycliff. She passed us in her car and waved. I'd forgotten about her."

We drove on to the Whycliff house, where the image of the Leather Man had made its first appearance in March Gilman's headlights. Hannah Whycliff's car was in the driveway and she came to the door when the sheriff rang the bell. She greeted us both and then asked, "Is this more questions about the accident?"

"Not exactly, Miss Whycliff," the sheriff said. "Doc here has a problem. He was with this so-called Leather Man yesterday, but now the man has disappeared and two different people deny seeing him with Doc."

"I remember you passed and waved when I was walking with him. It was late yesterday afternoon."

She turned to look at me. "I remember seeing you, Dr. Sam. I wondered what had happened to your car, but I was in a hurry and couldn't stop."

"Then you saw the Leather Man?" Sheriff Lens prompted.

"No, Dr. Sam was alone. I saw no one else."

The thing was so fantastic I simply shook my head and gave a humorless chuckle. It defied the laws of logic. "Tell me, do you know Seth Howlings, the railroad crossing guard? He's just this side of the county line."

"I may have seen him but I'm sure I've never spoken to him. Why do you ask?"

"And how about a couple named Mr. and Mrs. Glen Pomroy, over in the next county? They rent out rooms in their house for overnight guests."

"I never heard of them. What are all these questions for?"

"We're tryin' to find witnesses who saw Doc with this Leather Man," the sheriff told her. "The man might have been responsible for that accident in front of your house."

"I never saw any Leather Man. The doctor was alone."

"Thank you, Miss Whycliff," the sheriff said. We walked back to the car.

I settled into the front seat and said, "She's lying."

"Sure, and so are the Pomroys and old Seth. But why, Doc? These people don't even know each other."

"I don't know," I admitted. "I only know they're lying."

"Do you think the Leather Man could have hypnotized them so they didn't remember seeing him?"

I snorted at that suggestion. "Hannah Whycliff drove past us in a car. The best hypnotist in the world couldn't have done it that fast."

"Then there's only one other explanation, Doc. Do you believe in ghosts?"

* * *

When I told Mary Best about it the next morning, she saw things a bit more clearly than I did. "We have to find the Leather Man, Sam. We have to locate this Zach Taylor and learn the truth."

"He's probably dead and buried somewhere out behind the Pomroy place."

"But maybe he isn't! Maybe he just went away!"

"Then why are they all lying about it? The sheriff even raised the possibility he was the ghost of the original Leather Man, but that one was French, not Australian."

"Can you get along without me today? I'm going out looking for him."

"You're wasting your time, Mary. Even if you find him, that won't explain why everyone lied."

"Everyone didn't lie. Only three people lied—four, if you count Mrs. Pomroy's husband. There has to be a reason."

I let her go. There were patients to be seen, but I handled them all without her. I spent most of the day thinking about Zach Taylor and my walk with him. He'd appeared there on the road, and then he'd disappeared. Maybe I'd never walked with him at all. Maybe I'd imagined the whole thing.

It was only later, toward the end of the day, that I realized what I'd done. March Gilman had been alive in that ditch after the car went off the road. After causing the accident, Zach Taylor had killed and robbed him. Deciding I might be suspicious of him, he bribed the Pomroys to deny his existence. Then he walked back and bribed old Seth and Hannah Whycliff too. That was the only answer.

And I'd let Mary Best go out alone in search of a murderer.

It took me less than a minute to realize that I was getting foolish in my middle age. If Zach had killed Gilman and thought I suspected him, he had more than enough opportunity during our walk to leave me dead in a ditch too. There'd be no need to try bribing four people who might later blackmail him.

I thought about it some more, and remembered something I'd read not too long before. I reached into the bookcase in my waiting room and selected a volume of essays, *While Rome Burns*, by Alexander Woollcott. One of them, "The Vanishing Lady," deals with the legend of a young Englishwoman and her frail mother, recently returned from India, who visit the Paris Exposition in 1889 on their way back to England. The mother vanishes, and the hotel staff denies she ever existed. Their room has different furnishings and wallpaper. All traces of the mother are gone. In the end, a young man from the British Embassy establishes that her mother died suddenly of the black plague, contracted in India. The conspiracy of silence was necessary to prevent panic from driving visitors out of Paris and ruining the Exposition. In a footnote at the end, Woollcott says that he traced the original story to a column in the *Detroit Free Press*, published during the 1889 Paris Exposition. But the author of the column could no longer remember whether he had invented the story or heard it somewhere.

All right, was there any possibility the Australian had suffered from some illness? Had he died during the night and his death been hushed up by the Pomroys, who'd then bribed the others?

But Zach Taylor hadn't appeared ill at all. He was the picture of health, in fact. And the Pomroys would have had no way of knowing that Seth Howlings and Hannah were the only persons who'd seen us. Old Seth hardly seemed the sort to be bribed, anyhow.

By late afternoon I'd had no word from Mary and I was beginning to worry about her. I went out to my car after the departure of my last patient, thinking I should begin searching for her. Just then I saw the familiar little roadster pull into the parking lot. The Leather Man was next to her in the front seat.

"I thought you were dead," I told him. "Where'd you find him, Mary?"

"On his route, just where he was supposed to be. If he wasn't dead, I knew he'd be there."

"Good to see you again, mate," Zach said as he got out of the car. "Your little girl here is certainly persuasive. Once she found me she insisted I had to come back with her. This disrupts my whole route."

"We'll drive you back to where she picked you up," I assured him. "Or anywhere else you want to go. Just tell me what happened at the Pomroys' place last night."

"You mean where we stayed? Nothing happened. I got up early and left. I wanted to be on the road, and you were still sound asleep. Sorry I didn't say goodbye."

"Did you talk to Mrs. Pomroy?"

"It was too early for breakfast so I just paid her and left."

A small, sharp idea was gnawing at my brain. "How much did you pay her?"

"Twenty dollars, mate. I paid for your bed too!"

I went back inside and called Sheriff Lens.

When we returned to the Pomroy house, Glen Pomroy was on the front porch, scrubbing the steps. He looked up expectantly as we approached, but his expression soured when he recognized me. "Is your wife around?" I asked.

"We don't want trouble."

"Neither do I. We just want to see Mrs. Pomroy."

She appeared at the screen door then, pushing it open slowly. "I'm here," she said.

"We found the Leather Man," I told her. "He paid you for both our beds."

"Yeah, I forgot that," she answered glumly. "Guess we owe you ten dollars." The denials had gone out of her.

"You figured I was too drunk to remember clearly, so you made up the bed after he left and lied about his ever being here. That way you got an extra ten dollars out of me. It may have seemed like a minor swindle to you, but it caused me a great deal of trouble."

"I'll be contacting your sheriff to keep an eye on you," Sheriff Lens told them. "If there are any more complaints from your guests you'll both be makin' your beds at the county jail."

When we were back in the car he turned to me and said, "That takes care of the Pomroys, but it doesn't explain the other two. They both claimed you were alone too."

"Seth Howlings is our next stop. When we get there, don't say anything at first. Let me do all the talking."

Seth was seated in the crossing guard's little shack, dozing, but he came awake instantly as I approached. "How are you, Seth?"

"Back again, Dr. Sam? I've seen more of you the past two days than I usually do in a month."

"I doubt that, Seth. I doubt if you've seen me at all. Who's this standing with me now?"

My question seemed to unnerve him, and lie shifted his gaze from my face to a point just to the left of me where no one stood. Then he seemed to look in the other direction, but his eyes skipped quickly past Sheriff Lens.

"Seth," I said quietly, "you're blind, aren't you?"

His hands began to shake. "I don't need eyes for this job. I can hear them trains comin' from the next county! The sound travels along the rails, and their steam whistles can be heard for miles."

"How did it happen, Seth? Why didn't you go to a doctor?"

"I never had no pain, just halos around the lights, and my vision kept narrowing down till it was just like looking into a tunnel. After a while even that was gone. I figured at my age it didn't make no difference. My wife drove me to work here every day, and picked me up. So long as I could hear the trains comin' and lower and raise the gate, what difference did it make?" His face wore an expression of utter sadness. "Will they take my job away from me, Dr. Sam?"

I knew it was glaucoma, and there was nothing anyone could do for him. "Probably, Seth. I'm sure you're good at it, but you wouldn't want to cause an accident, would you? Suppose some little child wandered onto the tracks and you didn't hear him."

" I wouldn't want that," he agreed.

"This is Sheriff Lens with me. He'll see about getting a replacement for you right away."

The sheriff put a reassuring hand on Seth's shoulder. "I'll have someone out here within an hour, and we'll arrange with your wife to pick you up."

Back in the car, I shook my head in wonder. "To think we had a blind man guarding that railroad crossing—"

"How'd you know, Doc?"

"He answered people when they talked to him, but he never spoke first to someone. When I asked about the man who was with me, his immediate reaction was that I was trying to trick him. What did he mean by that? It was an odd choice of words if he had seen me alone at the crossing. And both times I saw him he mentioned my coming on foot or in a car, as if to convince me he could see. Then I remembered Zach never spoke while we were there. And Seth emphasized hearing the train, not seeing it. With his wife to pick him up, and relying on his ears, he could do the job."

"Blind people's hearing is supposed to be very sensitive," Sheriff Lens pointed out. "He must have heard the footsteps of two people if he knew you arrived on foot."

"We approached just as a train was coming, and that distracted him. Only I spoke, and after the train passed I remember falling into step with Zach Taylor. If he listened then, he'd have heard only one set of departing footsteps. When we questioned him, he feared I suspected something about his blindness so he stuck to the story he thought was true—that I was alone."

"So Seth Howlings and the Pomroys had their own entirely different reasons for denying the existence of the Leather Man. But what about Hannah Whycliff? Isn't it stretching coincidence a bit far to have a third person who didn't see him for some reason?"

"We'll call on Miss Whycliff next," I answered grimly.

It was almost evening when we turned into her driveway once more. This time it took her a while to answer the ring. "I hope we're not interrupting your dinner," I said.

"No, no. What is it this time?"

"I'm afraid it's still about the Leather Man. We've located him at last."

"How does that concern me?"

"You lied about not seeing him with me on the road yesterday. You see, the sheriff here started out his questioning by telling you that two other people had already denied seeing the Leather Man with me. That was a mistake. You quickly decided it was to your advantage to agree with them, to tell the same lie. You wanted the Leather Man to be gone, to never have existed."

"Why would I want that?" she asked.

"Because you were afraid he saw you murder March Gilman."

Her gaze shifted from me to the sheriff and back again. "Whatever gave you that idea?"

"Zach—the Leather Man—saw the accident and didn't think Gilman had been hurt badly at all. He hadn't seen the car coming until it was almost upon him. You told me you heard the car skid on the road as Gilman tried to apply the brakes, yet when I examined the road yesterday morning, just hours after the accident, the gravel was unmarked by any trace of skidding. Zach didn't see the car coming because it came out of your driveway, Miss Whycliff. It didn't skid. It wasn't going fast at all, but it went off the road to avoid the Leather Man. March Gilman was thrown clear and dazed. Before he became fully conscious you saw your chance. You came down to the road and hit him with something—perhaps a hammer. He was barely able to speak by the time I arrived, and he died soon after. There was evidence of two blows to the head."

"Why would I kill March Gilman?" she asked.

"I don't know. He had a reputation as a ladies' man. What went on between the two of you—"

"Get out of here, both of you! Get out this instant!"

I turned back toward the driveway, just as Mary pulled her car in behind the sheriffs. "We have a witness," I said softly.

Her eyes widened as she saw the Leather Man step out of the car and walk toward us. "No! No, keep him away from me!"

"He really exists, much as you wanted him not to. He's going to tell us what he saw."

"Keep him away!" she shouted. "I'll tell you! I killed March Gilman. And I'll tell you what he did to deserve it!"

"What's the matter with her, mate?" Zach asked as the sheriff led her away.

"She thought you were someone else," I told him. "She thought you were the avenging angel."

"No," he said with a grin. "I'm just a chap on walkabout."

THE PROBLEM OF
THE PHANTOM PARLOR

N OW let me tell you [Dr. Sam Hawthorne began, barely waiting until his wife had filled the visitor's glass], it was a week like nothing I ever knew in Northmont. That week was the closest I ever came to believing in the supernatural. But I'd better start with Josephine Grady, the twelve-year-old girl who'd come up from Stamford to spend the last week in August with her Aunt Min before returning to school after Labor Day.

This was late summer of '37, not long after that business with the Leather Man, and I was hoping for a little peace and quiet for a change. I wouldn't be getting it that week. Min Grady brought her niece into the office shortly before noon on Monday and that was the beginning of it. Josephine's medical problem was simple, and not uncommon for girls her age. My main problem was gaining her confidence and talking with her about things her mother should have told her already. "Didn't your Aunt Min talk to you?" I asked casually. Aunt Min, a solidly built woman in her late forties, was waiting in the outer office, so I kept my voice down.

"Oh, Aunt Min is sort of spooky sometimes," she confided, twisting the hem of her blue dress nervously. "That whole house is spooky. After last summer, I hated to come back again."

"What, happened last summer?"

"Weird things. She finally told me the house was haunted. I begged Mom not to send me back this year, but she said it was all my imagination. She said a week with Aunt Min wouldn't kill me, but look at me now!"

I had to chuckle a bit at that. "Josephine—is that what your friends call you, Josephine?"

"Well. Josie."

"Josie, this would have happened whether you were here or at home. It's part of growing up. Now tell me about the weird things at the house. It's a lovely old mansion, really, and I never thought of it as being weird."

She looked down at her bare knees. "My grandfather died there."

"That was long ago, back after the war. Lots of old people die at home. From what I hear, he'd been sick for years. But he built a beautiful house."

"It's got a ghost room," she said suddenly, blurting it out. "And sometimes there are sounds in the night when I'm trying to sleep."

"The wind and a little imagination can do wonders in the middle of the night," I tried to assure her. "I'll tell you what—how would it be if I looked in on you in a day or two, just to see how you're doing in your haunted house?"

She seemed to take heart in that. "Will you come tomorrow?"

I smiled. "All right, tomorrow afternoon. I have a call to make out that way, and I'll come to see you on the way back."

Min Grady was seated in the waiting room, and I delivered Josie into her hands. Min was an unmarried—still called a "maiden lady" in those quaint days—who wore cotton print housedresses and carried a furled umbrella with her on all her visits into town. When I told her of my promise to stop by the house the following afternoon she frowned and asked, "This won't cost extra, will it?"

"No, no. It's included in my regular fee for an office call. It's just a follow-up."

That seemed to satisfy her. "Then we'll be expecting you tomorrow."

After she'd gone I stayed in the waiting room and sat down across from Mary Best's desk. Mary was my nurse and receptionist and confidant. There were days when I thought I was in love with her. "Can you imagine that poor girl? Neither her mother nor her aunt said a word to her. Min Grady just brought her to me instead."

"It's a small town, Sam. It always will be. You've lived here long enough to know that."

"Josie's at a very impressionable age. You often read of hauntings and psychic phenomena involving a child of her age."

"You don't believe in such things, do you?"

"Of course not. But the girl may need help."

"You're not the one to give it if she does," Mary pointed out. "You heal the body, not the mind."

"I'll just stop by the house. It'll be an excuse to see it, if nothing else. I've never been inside."

"That big old place always reminds me of a castle."

"Actually it's not as old as it looks. Min Grady's father built it in nineteen ten, just twenty-seven years ago. From what I've heard, it was a really tragic story. Carson Grady was a railroad baron, worth millions by the time he turned fifty. He and his family chose to settle here in Northmont, and he planned this house like an English country home. But they'd barely dug the foundation when Grady was terribly injured in a train wreck on his line out in Iowa. He lived, but was completely paralyzed from the neck down. In due time, the house was finished and the family moved in, but Carlson Grady never left his bed for the rest of his life. Of course his every need was tended to, and his wife and two daughters remained with him until his death in nineteen twenty-one. Joephine's mother moved away then and married a man named Scarcross—"

"But she uses the Grady name," Mary pointed out.

"I'm not clear what happened to Scarcross. He either died or abandoned them. Anyway, Josephine's mother reverted to her maiden name. It was a money name, and still is. Min Grady remained here with her mother, who died a few years later. The house has been Min's ever since. I suppose she and her sister received the bulk of the estate."

"Does the house have a reputation for being haunted?"

"Not that I've ever heard. I think it's something Min Grady made up to add excitement to Josie's stay."

"It seems to have done that."

* * *

I reached the Grady house around three on Tuesday afternoon. The house itself was stone, with a wooden garage and toolshed in back. It was a sunny summer day and I could see Josie walking alone across the big side lawn. A gardener was working among the rose-bushes, cutting back some dead blossoms.

"Hello there!" I called to her, getting out of the car. I left my black bag on the seat, knowing I wouldn't be needing it.

"I thought you were never coming!" she exclaimed as she came to meet me. "It's after three."

"I had another stop to make first. How are we feeling today?"

"Better," she admitted. "Come on in the house."

The three-story stone building had a wide porch stretched across the entire facade. There were a half-dozen rocking chairs lined up here, and one with a small table beside it might have been Min Grady's favorite. On the table rested an open pack of cigarettes and an ashtray, together with a copy of Margaret Mitchell's popular novel *Gone With the Wind*.

"Hello, Dr. Hawthorne," Min Grady said, opening the screen door to come out and greet me. Her dress was a bit better than the one she'd worn to my office, and I could see she was wearing some makeup. I wondered if this was for my benefit or if some other visitor was expected.

"Good afternoon, Miss Grady. Are you enjoying the book?"

"Yes, indeed, though it's quite long. I hope to finish it by Labor Day." She dropped her voice a bit. "There was really no need for you to come. My niece is fine today."

"I just thought I'd look in."

"Let me get you some lemonade. It's very refreshing on a warm day like this."

Though she hadn't actually invited me inside, Josie ran onto the porch and held open the screen door. I took this as a sort of invitation and followed Min into the big house. The inside seemed to be decorated much as it must have been at the time it was built. Heavily brocaded drapes framed the windows, and the furniture had a massive turn-of-the-century look to it. After the darkness of the front part of the house, it was almost a treat when Min Grady led me down a wide hall past closed double doors and into a larger room with a great semicircular window that looked out on the rolling hills beyond the back lawn. A single giant oak towered above all the others, standing guard as it might have done fifty years earlier, long before the house was built.

"We call it the guardian oak," Min said as if reading my thoughts. "It was one of the reasons my father chose this spot to build the house. And this is the recital room."

The room was large and airy, obviously meant for entertaining, with a grand piano nestled in one corner. I could picture the power barons of New England gathered here, dressed in formal evening clothes, listening to a piano recital following a dinner of several courses. Apparently it had never happened. Carson Grady's dream had died in that train wreck.

She showed me the dining room and the large kitchen, then took me upstairs to the great master bedroom where her father had lived and died, "This is my room now," she said simply, It overlooked the front of the house, commanding a view of approaching cars.

"Was he able to sit in a wheelchair?" I asked, more from a clinical interest than for any other reason.

"No. He was in his bed until the day he died. Sometimes it took my mother and the nurse and my sister and me to make the bed with him in it. It was a hospital-type bed and I suppose he was reasonably comfortable, but it was a terrible way to spend the last eleven years of his life. Today perhaps some sort of surgery might have helped him. Back then there was no hope."

"Did he suffer from depression?"

"Not generally. We tried to keep his spirits up, and he made a pretense of running the railroad from his bed. Men would come to the house with all sorts of documents for him to study. I would read them to him, and he would dictate letters for me to send. Sometimes in the evening he would dictate notes for a journal, but he soon abandoned that. With the coming of the war, the visits to the house became less frequent. The railroad needed to be run by someone on the scene, in the office."

"Is it possible that Josie believes Carson Grady still haunts this house?"

"I don't know what's wrong with that girl at times. She was barely here when she was imagining all sorts of things."

Josie came up to join us and we changed the subject. She showed me her little room down at the end of the hall. "This was where my mother slept when she was a child. I wish I could see the oak from here."

After that we went downstairs again, and as soon as we were out of earshot the girl whispered, "Come here! I want to show you something."

I followed along as she led me to the closed double doors I'd noticed earlier, along the wide hall leading to the big recital room. She turned the knob and pulled the doors open. "Look at this!"

It was a large, elaborate china closet, its shelves filled with costly gilt-edged china that looked clean and shiny. "What lovely dishes!" I remarked.

"It's not always here, Doctor," she told me in a conspiratorial whisper. "Sometimes at night there's a little parlor here, with a sofa and chairs and pictures on the wall."

"I'm sure you imagined—"

"I *don't* imagine it! That's what she said too, when I asked her about it. I saw it last summer and again Sunday night. I can describe every piece of furniture in the room!"

"Sometimes the mind plays strange tricks. A dream can seem very real."

She closed the door, obviously disgusted with me. "This place is haunted! I think his ghost is in that room."

"Whose ghost?"

"My grandfather's."

I reached for one of my cards. "Look, here's my telephone number at home. If anything strange happens the rest of the week while you're here, phone me at home and I'll come at once. How's that?"

"You don't believe me, do you?"

I smiled down at her. "No, but I'm willing to be convinced."

On the way back to my car I encountered Min Grady talking with the gardener. He was a man in his forties named Bill Herkimer who did odd jobs around town. I hadn't realized he'd been working for Min. "How's my niece, Doctor?" she asked.

"Fine. I don't think she'll have any more trouble."

Herkimer removed a toothpick from between his lips. "She's a cute little girl. The place brightens right up when she comes to visit."

Josie's aunt walked back toward the big house and I lingered with the gardener. "Ever do any work inside the house, Bill?" I asked casually. "It's a great-looking place."

"The grounds keep me busy enough in the summer. She's got close to thirty acres."

"Do you live here?"

"No, I just come out three days a week. I still try to keep up some of my other customers."

"Good seeing you again, Bill," I said as I continued back to my car. He nodded and returned to the roses.

* * *

I thought little about Min Grady and her niece on Wednesday. It was an unusually busy day for me, with some hospital calls and a couple of new patients. When I got home that evening the last thing I wanted to hear was the ringing of the telephone.

I picked it up and heard Josephine Grady's terrified voice. "Doctor, come quick! Something's happened to Aunt Min! I think she's dead!"

"Hold on, Josie. Try to talk slower. Are you at the house?"

"She's on the floor in that parlor I told you about! It's really there. She's got blood all over her head!"

"I'll be right out, Josie. Don't touch anything."

I paused only long enough to phone Sheriff Lens and repeat the conversation. "You'd better meet me out there. Sheriff. I don't think she's imagining it."

"I'll be there, Doe."

I reached the big Grady house just seconds before Sheriff Lens. He ran up to my car, puffing from the exertion, and we saw a white-faced Josephine Grady awaiting us in one of the porch rocking chairs. "Josie—"

"I was afraid to stay in the house after I called," she told us. Her hands were gripping the arms of the rocking chair and I could see she was on the verge of panic.

"Calm down now," I told her gently, unobtrusively feeling her pulse. "We're here. Everything will be all right. This is Sheriff Lens."

"Hello there, Josie. Suppose you wait out here with Doc while I take a look inside."

He opened the screen door and I could feel her starting to shake again. "I was upstairs and I heard a noise like a loud voice and the start of a scream. I ran into Aunt Min's bedroom but she wasn't there. Then I went downstairs and the double doors were standing open. It wasn't a china closet, it was a parlor like before, with dark red walls and heavy drapes over the window. Aunt Min was on the floor, all bloody, right in front of the sofa with its chintz covering and red tassels. I screamed and ran out to call you. I didn't know what else to do!"

"Everything will be all—"

Sheriff Lens appeared in the doorway. "Doc, can you look in here? I need an official declaration of death."

"I'm coming, too," Josephine said. "I'll be all right."

I kept her behind me as we entered, trying to shield her eyes from the sight that had already terrified her. Min Grady was sprawled across the hall floor, just outside the closed double doors. It appeared she'd suffered a blow to the head, with a fair amount of bleeding. I knew before I knelt down beside her that she was dead.

"That's not where she was!" Josie gasped behind me. "She was in the parlor!"

Before I could stop her she ran around me and yanked open the big double doors. Behind them was the china cabinet, looking exactly as it had the previous day. Josie fell fainting to the floor before I could grab her.

* * *

Josie's mother, Katherine Grady, arrived by car the following morning. I'd phoned her in Stamford the previous night and she'd made the ninety-minute drive shortly after dawn. She seemed slightly younger than Min, with blond hair and a slim figure. We'd arranged for Josie to stay with Sheriff Lens and his wife overnight, and when I met her at the Grady house her daughter and the sheriff had not yet arrived.

"Tell me what happened," she pleaded. "I could barely believe your call last night."

"I was sorry to phone you so late, Mrs. Scarcross—"

"It's Grady. I use my maiden name. But please call me Kate." She glanced up at the house. "We were always Min and Kate."

"—but when I called earlier your line was busy,"

"I was on the phone all evening with teachers at my daughter's school. I'm president of our Parent-Teacher Association and school opens next week."

"It must be difficult, raising Josie without her father."

She gave me a smile. "We manage. Josie is a fine girl."

"A young woman now. Your sister brought her to see me Monday, before this terrible tragedy."

Kate nodded. "Josie phoned me Monday night and told me about it.

"Did she tell you about this phantom room, too?"

The woman hesitated. "Yes, she did. Josie has always been very imaginative."

"It might be just a phase she's going through, but obviously it's upset her a great deal. The killing of her aunt, coupled with these fantasies of hers, could have a lasting effect."

"I think I know the origin of this story of the phantom parlor. When she was younger—"

At that moment Sheriff Lens drove up with Josie in the ear with him. She jumped out as soon as he'd stopped and ran to her mother's arms. "It was terrible," the girl sobbed. "Aunt Min was dead in that awful room!"

"There, there, darling. Everything will be all right."

"But the room is gone again and nobody believes me!"

We went inside then and walked through the main floor. The bloodstain was still on the hall carpet and when we opened the double doors the china closet was still on view. Sheriff Lens tapped the wooden sides and back inconclusively, searching for a secret panel, but found nothing. We continued on into the large recital room with its lovely view of the guardian oak.

"I hate to relive the painful moment for you, Josie," Sheriff Lens began, "but you must tell us again about finding the body. You must describe this room for us. How large was it?"

She thought for a moment, holding tight to her mother's arm. "I think it was about twice as long as me, lying down."

"Nine or ten feet?"

"Maybe. And sort of square, but probably deeper than it was wide. About seven feet by nine feet? I'm really not certain."

"What about the furnishings?"

"Well, I think I told you about the sofa with its red tassels. The walls were red too, but a darker red, and the closed drapes over the window were dark too. There were two chairs and they were more brown."

"What about the floor?"

"There was a bright oriental rug. And one lamp, but it was very dim. It stood next to the sofa."

"It doesn't sound like a very inviting room," I commented.

"Oh, it wasn't. It was scary!"

"How many times have you seen it, all together?"

"There were two times last summer. And then I saw it Sunday night after I got here. And last night when I found Aunt Min's body."

"Did you ever ask your aunt about it?" her mother wanted to know.

"The first time she just denied it was there. She showed me the china closet and said I must have imagined the little parlor. But I knew I didn't."

Kate Grady just shook her head. "I can't understand any of it."

Sheriff Lens cleared his throat. "As the next of kin I'm afraid I'll need to have you formally identify the body, Miz Grady. And the undertaker will need a dress to bury her in."

Kate Grady nodded. "I'll go up now and pick one out. Josie, was your aunt still sleeping in the big bedroom?"

The girl nodded. "I'll go with you," she said, as if not wanting to leave her mother's side.

Sheriff Lens sighed. "What do you think, Doc? Is it just a child with an overactive imagination, or is the place haunted?"

"I don't know. But I doubt if it was a ghost that killed Min Grady."

I drove back to my office in one wing of Pilgrim Memorial Hospital. At that time Northmont had no regular coroner and autopsies were assigned to which-ever resident happened to be free. Lincoln Jones, our only black physician, had drawn this one. I found him in his office and asked about Min Grady.

"A blunt instrument, Sam. Something fairly heavy, like a candlestick or even a hammer. It was only one blow, but a hard one." He took an envelope out of his desk. "I thought you and the sheriff might be interested in this. It was clutched in her left hand, as if she grabbed it as she fell."

I stared down at the red tassel in the envelope, remembering Josie's descrip-tion of the tasseled sofa in the room that didn't exist.

* * *

Later that day, when I returned to the Grady house, Kate and her daughter were going through the clothes in Min's bedroom. "This is a hopeless task," Kate admitted "With all the things in this house it'll take a month to clean it out."

"The body's been released to the undertaker," I told her, "You can go ahead with the funeral arrangements now."

She nodded. "I'd like to have her laid out tomorrow, Saturday, and Sunday, with the funeral Labor Day morning."

"I'm sure that can be arranged."

Josie came in from the hall. "We need a key for that storeroom."

Her mother nodded. "It's probably here someplace. Help me with these bedclothes. We'll take them down to the basement for washing."

I decided it was a good thing to keep Josie busy, taking her mind off the shock of finding the body. When I was alone with Kate Grady I asked, "Do you know anything about this room your daughter described? You started to tell me something earlier."

"It was about the story," She gazed out the bedroom window at the road, remembering her father. "Even after he was confined to this room, he was always a good and kind man. When he was growing up, he once met a woman named Madeline Yale Wynne, whose father invented the Yale lock. She had a minor writing career and my father became fascinated with one of her stories that appeared in *Harper's* magazine. It was called 'The Little Room,' and dealt with a girl visiting her aunts at a New England farmhouse. She remembered a little room where she had played, but when she went back years later the little room had vanished, replaced by a shallow china closet, and the aunts denied it had ever existed. Years later, when the woman visited again with her own daughter, she found the little room was back and the aunts denied the existence of the china closet. After her mother's death the daughter returned to the house, and the china closet was there. She felt she must somehow learn the truth, and asked two close friends to visit the place together. But they became separated and on their individual visits one found a little room while the other found a china closet. Finally they determined to return to the house together." She paused.

"And what did they find?" I urged.

"The house had burned to the ground during the night. That was the end of the story."

"And you told this story to Josephine?"

"My father told it to me many times, and in later years I repeated it to her. In her imagination the little room of fantasy became this phantom parlor. The china closet downstairs has always existed, but her visits to her aunt became like those in the story."

I put my hand in my pocket and fingered the red tassel. "Do you mind if I look around outside?"

"Not at all."

I went out the front door and walked around to the rear of the house. There was only one large window there, the magnificent half-circle in the big downstairs recital room. Next to it, where Josie's parlor should have been, the stones of the wall were unbroken.

"Lookin' over the house?" a nearby voice asked.

I turned and saw Bill Herkimer, the gardener, walking toward me. "Hello, Bill. I didn't know you were working today."

"I'm not. Just came by to pick up my tools. Won't be any more work for me here now that Min Grady's dead."

"It was a terrible thing. Any idea who might have killed her?"

Herkimer shrugged. "A hobo, probably, looking for food. They come off the freight trains down at the junction."

"I know." I'd always suspected that Herkimer himself came to Northmont last summer by exactly that route. "How's the girl taking it?"

"Josie? She found the body, which was quite a shock. I think she'll be all right, though." I started to turn away and then asked, "Bill, you've been in the house, haven't you?"

"A few times," he admitted.

"Were you ever in the little parlor on the main floor? The one with the red wails and the tasseled sofa?"

"Can't say that I was. Don't remember it, anyhow."

"Thanks anyway." I had a final thought. "You might ask Kate Grady, Min's sister, if she wants you to keep on working through the rest of the summer."

"Don't think I will," he decided. "Never met the woman."

"I could introduce you. She's inside now."

"Another time, maybe," He walked off across the back lawn, leaving me alone. I noticed he wasn't carrying any tools.

* * *

When I returned to the front of the house, Mrs. Russell from down the road had appeared with a wicker basket of fresh fruit for Kate and her daughter. They were standing in conversation on the big front porch and she waved when she saw me. "Hello, Dr. Hawthorne!"

"Good day, Mrs. Russell." She was a large jolly woman about Kate Grady's age, an infrequent patient of mine.

"Isn't this a shocking thing, what happened to poor Minnie? I won't feel safe in my house until the murderer is caught."

"None of us will," I assured her.

"To think that I was in this house talking to her just last Sunday!"

My interest stirred. "Did she ever have you into the parlor—the red room with the tasseled sofa?"

Mrs. Russell frowned. "I never saw any parlor like that. She always entertained visitors in that big room with the wonderful view."

After she'd gone I asked Kate Grady if I could examine the china closet again. "Of course," she told me. "Josie and I have work to do upstairs."

I opened the white double doors and stared grimly at the shelves of china. Then I went into the large room next door. I was busy tapping the wall adjoining the china closet when I realized that Josie had slipped back downstairs to watch me. "What are you doing?" she asked.

"Looking for secret panels."

"Are there any?"

"If I knew that, they wouldn't be secret."

"You believe me about the room, don't you?"

"There certainly is space for such a room, and it doesn't seem to be used for anything else. Are there any tools around? I need some sort of drill."

"Mr. Herkimer keeps a few tools in the basement."

I followed her down the cellar stairs, fearing he might have returned for them, but they were still there. I chose a drill and a small flashlight and went upstairs. Working together, we cleared the china from me of the shelves and I turned the crank to drill several small holes in the wooden backing. Then I put my eye to one or them and shined the flashlight through the others.

If I'd expected to find the phantom parlor, I was in for a disappointment, The flashlight's beam revealed only a big window with cobwebs draped from the rafters and walls.

"What's this?" Kate Grady asked from behind me. "What are you doing in the china closet?"

"I'm sorry I should have asked permission. There seems to be too much space unaccounted for, and I drilled some holes in the wood to see what was back there."

"It was to be my father's private study," she explained. "His smoking room. After the accident he decided there was no need for it, so it remained unfinished. My mother had a china closet installed in part of it."

"Did your father leave any blueprints or papers concerning the house?"

"There might be some things in the Northmont library. I believe Min gave them some papers after Mother died and I moved away and married. She was so furious about not meeting my husband or being invited to the wedding that she acted as if I'd abandoned the family. She told me I was cut off from the house and everything that had belonged to my father. I'd already received an inheritance, of course, but she said the house and all his belongings were hers. I was pregnant by then and I didn't fight her, though I resented her attitude. Father left a trust fund for his first grandchild, and that always upset her."

"And then your husband left you."

She gave a warning glance toward Josie, who'd drifted into the big room to gaze out the window but was still within earshot. "Mr. Scarcross did not want the responsibility of children," she said simply. "He was gone by the time she was born and he's never returned."

I took the red tassel from my pocket. It was time for her to see it. "Your sister was clutching this in her hand when she died."

The color drained from her face. "The parlor—"

"Yes, just as Josie described it. Is there any other tasseled red sofa in the house?"

"No." She took a deep breath. "If the parlor exists, does that mean my father—?"

"I don't tseheve in ghosts, Mrs. Grady. This house exists in the here and new, not in some parallel universe where it's still nineteen ten and your father is alive and well." I headed for the door.

"Where are you going?"

"I want to stop by the library before it closes."

* * *

The Northmont library occupied one wing of the courthouse, with a separate entrance onto the side street. Miss Isaacs, the elderly librarian who'd run the place during my entire fifteen-year residence in the town, was moving about the room with the help of her cane when I entered just before the six o'clock closing hour.

"Well, Dr. Hawthorne, this is an odd time for you to acquire a yen for reading."

"It's something special, Miss Isaacs."

"I'm just closing," she announced through thin lips.

"I understand that Min Grady donated her father's papers to this library some years back."

"Don't know why she did it," Miss Isaacs sniffed. "They were just personal papers from his years as an invalid. All the important things had already gone to Yale."

"Would it be possible to see what you have?"

"Tomorrow morning. We're closed now, Dr, Hawthorne"

"Miss Isaacs—"

She stared at me grimly. "The time is six o'clock. We're closed now."

There was no arguing with her.

In the morning I was back there at ten when she opened the door. If she was surprised at my persistence she gave no sign of it. "If I remember correctly, you wanted the Carson Grady papers."

"That's correct, Miss Isaacs."

She brought me a large cardboard file. "This is everything. I told you there wasn't much."

I saw at once that there were no plans or drawings of the house. The file contained only unimportant letters and a journal he'd tried dictating to his daughters over the years. Even this seemed to have been a failure, with gaps of six months or longer not uncommon. Mostly it commented on the changing seasons. One entry, dated just after the end of the Great War, seemed typical: *My lovely daughter Kate is transcribing this as I lie on my sickbed. Finally the world is at peace and we can only hope that it will last. It is mid-November now and the trees are bare. I stare out the window at the great old guardian oak and even if is devoid of leaves. Winter is a depressing time for many people, but to someone confined to his bed, unable move, summer can be even more depressing.*

"It was a hard life for him," I commented, closing the journal.

Miss Isaacs nodded, helping me put everything back in the cardboard file. "He used to come in here sometimes. After the accident I visited him out there just once, up in his room. I brought him some books and I know the family appreciated it."

"Thanks for your help," I told her. It wasn't her fault that I'd found nothing useful.

That afternoon I went to the funeral parlor. It seemed as if half the town was there, drawn perhaps by the violence of Min Grady's death rather than by any special fondness for her. Kate Grady stayed close to the casket, greeting each new arrival, but I noticed that Josephine drifted away. Sheriff Lens was there, of course, and I asked him how the investigation was going.

"Not very well, Doc," he admitted. "No sign of forced entry at the house, but she could have opened the door to her killer. People do it all the time."

"The missing room is what bothers me, Sheriff. If Josie is telling the truth, what happened to it? Is the place haunted?"

"And if she's not telling the truth?"

"I hate to even think about that."

Josie walked past us and went outside. I left the sheriff and followed her out, but she'd disappeared around the corner of the building toward the parking lot. I saw Bill Herkimer lingering nearby. "Hello, Bill. Going inside?"

"I—no, I don't think so. I came to pay my respects, but I'm not much at wakes. I like to remember people the way they were."

Josie came back then, having retrieved something from the car. "Hello, Mr. Herkimer."

He smiled broadly. "Hello, Josie. How are you today?"

"Okay," she answered with a shrug.

"Will you be going back with your mother after the funeral?"

"Sure. I can't stay here."

I turned to see Kate Grady sticking her head out the door, apparently seeking her daughter. She saw us talking and suddenly she came running down the steps and along the sidewalk, her face a study in fury. "Josie! Get back inside!"

"I just—"

"*Get back inside!* Do what you're told!"

I tried to calm her down. "Mrs. Grady, we were just talking. Josie wasn't here more than a minute. This is your sister's gardener, Bill Herkimer."

She turned on me then. "It's been twelve years but I'd still know him anywhere. This is Bill Scarcross, my ex-husband!"

* * *

I walked with him after that, just the two of us, threading our way between the cars and out to the highway where we started toward the town square a few blocks away. "What brought you to Northmont?" I asked.

"I don't know. I'd never seen the house or met Kate's sister. My own life was sort of a mess and this seemed a way to bring back happier times. I only came to look, but then I met her gardener in a bar one night. Min Grady's gardener. He told me he was moving out west because of his health. He'd developed an allergy to all those flowers. More important, he told me that Min's niece visited for a week each summer, and on some holidays, too. After all those years I wanted to see my daughter."

"So you applied for his job."

The man I now knew as Bill Scarcross nodded. "I had no great skill but I read books at the library. Soon Miss Grady was complimenting me on my gardening ability. And my daughter came to visit. A week with her, even at a distance, made it all worthwhile. Min had never met. me, of course, and I managed to stay out of sight when Kate delivered her and picked her up. I saw Josie briefly at Easter and again this week. She seems to be turning into a young woman before my very eyes."

"She is that," I agreed. "Do you want to get back with Kate?"

He gave a snort, "You saw her just now. There's no chance of that! I left her and she'll never forgive me,"

I took a deep breath. "I have to ask you this, Bill. Did you kill Man Grady?"

"Min? Of course not! Why should I ruin my only chance to see my daughter, even for one week a year?"

"You were at the house a lot. Did you ever see anyone else hanging around? Did you see or hear anything strange while you were inside?"

"I told you, I was only in there a few times. I kept some tools in the basement. Once I heard a strange noise, but big houses are always making noises, aren't they?"

"Your daughter mentioned noises, too. Was it a sort of howling, like someone imitating a ghost?"

He shook his head. "Nothing like that. It was more of a faint whining, and it didn't last long."

"An animal?"

"It could have been," he answered doubtfully.

"I have to go back for my car," I told him. "I'll see you later, Bill. Will you be at the funeral?"

"No need to stay away, now that she's seen me.

* * *

Sheriff Lens and his wife had invited Kate and Josie to their house for an early dinner before the calling hours resumed at the funeral parlor. It was a nice gesture and I was especially thankful, because I'd decided I needed another look at that china closet. There was still plenty of daylight left when I reached the house, and I parked the ear around back, entering through the cellar door. It was easy to unlatch from outside, using only a stick, and I knew a killer could have done the same thing. I mounted the steps to the main floor, moving quietly, and then stopped dead.

One door of the china closet stood slightly ajar.

I moved down the hall, barely able to breathe, somehow knowing what I would find. I opened the door further and there was Josie's parlor. Red walls, heavy drapes over the window, sofa with red tassels—all just as she'd described it. I could even see the stain from Min's blood still on the oriental rug.

I stepped into the little room as if in a dream.

And then I heard her behind me, and turned to see the hammer in her hand.

"I left Josie with the sheriff and came home to do some cleaning up," Kate Grady said. "You should have stayed away."

"No, but I should have checked the garage for your car."

"So you found the phantom room at last."

I shook my head. "It's not a room. It's an elevator."

That was when she swung the hammer.

* * *

It was much later, after the evening visiting hours, before I finally got a chance to explain it all to Sheriff Lens. By that time Kate Grady was locked up and things were starting to settle down. "I never bought you'd hit a lady, Doc," he said with a trace of a smile.

"She was coming at me with a hammer, Sheriff. I didn't have much choice. I think you'll find it's the same weapon she used to kill her sister. It came from Bill's toolbox in the basement."

"You'd better start at the beginning, with this phantom parlor."

"I read something this morning at the library. It was a journal that Carson Grady tried to keep, dictating to his daughters from his sickbed. He mentioned looking out the window at the guardian oak, but the only window from which it could be seen is the big semicircle in the recital room on the main floor. Carson Grady's bedroom faced the front of the house. This baffled me at first, but then Bill Scarcross mentioned hearing a whining noise in the house once. Josie had heard some sort of noise too. I remembered that construction on the Grady house was just beginning when Carson Grady was in the train wreck that crippled him, and suddenly it was all clear to me. Grady had altered the plans of his house to include an elevator. Moreover, it was an elevator large enough to accommodate his hospital bed. Early elevators were often decorated to look like little rooms, with chairs and lamps. This one even had drapes covering an imaginary window. When it was running it made the noise that Scarcross and Josie heard, but a hole in the china closet revealed only the empty shaft."

"But Kate Grady wasn't even here the night her sister was killed, Doc."

"So we thought at the time. But her home is only ninety minutes away by car, and remember, her telephone line was busy for some time when I tried to call her that night. She'd simply left the phone off the hook while she was gone. I assume what brought her here was Josie's Monday night phone conversation, in which she told her mother about the phantom parlor. Kate knew about the elevator, of course. She'd lived in the house while growing up, and even took dictation from her father while he enjoyed the view from the downstairs window. She knew also that Min kept the elevator a secret. Josie had no doubt mentioned seeing the mysterious parlor last summer as well, and when it happened again Kate must have realized it was deliberate. Min was trying to frighten the girl, perhaps even worse. Josie's share of her grandfather's inheritance was held in a trust fund, remember. If anything happened to her, I imagine that money would have gone to Kate and Min. She came up here Tuesday night to accuse Min of threatening her daughter, frightening her with that vanishing room. They argued and Kate accidentally killed her."

But Sheriff Lens shook his head. "She left her phone off the hook, Doc. Remember that. She was establishing an alibi, and that means premeditation. Min was unmarried, and with her dead the money and the house would probably go to Kate. If she was innocent she'd have told us about the elevator and the parlor right away."

"I suppose you're right," I agreed. "Kate went back there tonight to clean the blood from the elevator floor. In case it was discovered, she couldn't have evidence like that to back up her daughter's story."

"Someone must have known the elevator was there."

"Just Min and Kate and their dead parents. The workmen who built it probably weren't from town, and after twenty-five years they'd be dead or scattered by now. It was a secret the sisters had, all the time they were growing up—a secret linked to their father's helplessness, Each of them treasured it, perhaps for those moments when they'd been alone with Carson Grady in the little moving room."

"What about the china closet?"

"It was attached below the elevator, of course. It appeared behind those doors when the elevator rose to the second floor. When the elevator was on the first floor, the china closet was in the basement. Grady no doubt got the idea from that story by Madeline Yale Wynne that he was always recounting. Tonight Kate brought the elevator to the first floor so she could bring water from the kitchen to clean up the blood, and that's when I found it. She was hiding in the house when Josie found the body Tuesday night, and rolled it out of the elevator while her daughter was phoning for help. Then she slipped out the back and ran to where she'd hidden her car, for the drive back home."

Sheriff Lens stroked his chin. "Why didn't we notice the parlor when it was on the second floor?"

"There was mention of a locked storeroom on that floor, but we never connected it with the phantom parlor. The elevator buttons were well hidden, of course."

"What's going to happen to Josie now that her mother is in jail?"

I thought about it. "Well, she's just discovered a father who loves her very much. I think Bill Scarcross just might make a difference."

THE PROBLEM OF
THE POISONED POOL

THE summer of '37 had been a busy one for me [old Dr. Sam Hawthorne told his visitor, pausing to lift the glass to his lips] and I was almost relieved when September finally rolled around. The schools were open again and the quiet agricultural pace of a Northmont summer shifted into the increased social activity of autumn. The late-summer county fair had come and gone, but we still had Ernest Holland's clambake to look forward to.

Holland was the publisher of the *Northmont Blade*, the more successful of our two weekly newspapers. He'd moved to the area five or six years back and built himself a fancy house complete with swimming pool. I was hardly in his social circle, but in a town our size few people were. I was his regular doctor, and that was enough to get me invited to the clambake.

"Clambake's next Saturday," he reminded my nurse Mary Best on his way out of the office one mid-September day. "The pool's open, so bring your bathing suit."

"Is he serious about inviting me?" Mary asked after he'd gone.

"Of course he is. I just stopped by briefly at last year's affair but everyone seemed to be having a good time. He had about twenty people there, counting employees."

That was how I ended up driving Mary to the Holland house for the traditional clambake on the last Saturday in September. The *Blade* was published on Friday, and she was reading it in the car. The single column of world news contained little except an item reporting that Mussolini had arrived in Berlin for a four-day visit. "What's he doing there?" Mary wondered. "Getting cozy with Hitler, I'll bet!"

"Could be," I replied. "Anything in the local news?"

"No," she answered hesitantly as she turned the pages. "Oh, here's something in Lydia Mayer's social column. Did you know that Ernest Holland's brother Philip is visiting from California?"

"Never knew he had a brother," I admitted. "But then there's no reason I should have known."

"We'll probably meet him at the clambake."

"The day was a bit cool for swimming and Mary hadn't brought her bathing suit after all. I had my trunks in the car but doubted that I'd try the water either. We parked in a roped-off area where Mark Towers was directing new arrivals. Mark was a fellow around forty, about my age, who'd worked at the paper ever since Holland lured him away from the rival weekly. He looked younger, probably because he exercised regularly and kept his weight down. Mary informed me that he was one of the town's most eligible bachelors.

"Just a plain old Buick, Doc?" he greeted me. "You used to drive some pretty sporty roadsters."

"That was in my younger days, Mark. I'm all settled down now."

"Go on! You're a bachelor just like me. We know where the fun is." He glanced knowingly at Mary Best and I came close to punching him. Instead I blushed and walked away.

She hurried after me as I strode purposefully toward the front door. "Don't mind him," she told me. "I don't."

"The trouble with Mark Towers is that he thinks everyone is like him."

Holland's wife Sue greeted us at the door. She was dark-haired and lovely, with the sort of cheerful good looks that come with money, a leisurely life, and monthly trips to a Boston beauty salon. "Good to see you, Sam. We're glad you could make it."

She glanced at Mary and I quickly introduced them. Sue Holland had her own doctor over in Shinn Corners, so they'd never met on a professional basis. "So nice to meet you, Mary. Ernest thinks you're great! He's always talking about how efficient you are."

"I just make it seem that way," Mary replied with a smile. "It's easy with a boss like Sam."

"Come on in and grab a drink. We'll be eating around five o'clock. In the meantime there's the pool if the cool weather hasn't put you off."

The first person we encountered was wearing bathing trunks and carrying a glass of beer. He looked like a younger version of Ernest Holland, and I guessed correctly that this was his visiting brother from California. "You must be Philip," I said, extending my hand, "I'm Dr. Sam Hawthorne, and this is my nurse Mary Best."

He gave my hand a firm shake. Up close, his skin was tanned and a bit weathered, betrayed by too many hours exposed to the California sun. "Nice meeting you, Doctor. My brother has mentioned you."

"Isn't it too cold to go swimming?" Mary asked.

"Not for me. Back home I'm in the water virtually every day of the year. Slip into your suit and join me."

"I left it home," she admitted.

A silver-haired woman appeared and I recognized Lydia Mayer, the paper's social editor. I'd always thought it a bit presumptuous of a weekly the size of the *Blade* to even have a society column, but people in Northmont liked it and the column was credited with boosting the paper's circulation. "Hello, Phil," she said, snapping his picture with a box camera. "Showing off your body again?"

"For you, doll, anytime!" He grinned and went off with his beer. Lydia shrugged. "One of life's little tribulations. The boss's brother. She was one of those women whose age was always a mystery. She might have been thirty or fifty, but I'd have bet on the latter. "Come on, let's get a drink."

Ernest Holland was at the catered bar with his wife, drinking whiskey on the rocks while she sipped a tall Tom Collins through a straw. "Sue told me you were here," he said. "What'll you have?"

Lydia settled for a martini while Mary, who rarely drank, took a plain ginger ale. I had a little bourbon and followed the others outside. Mark Towers had come up from the parking area to join the guests, so I assumed everyone had arrived. It was a mixed crowd consisting of Holland's employees plus some friends and acquaintances like myself. He'd never been on awfully good terms with the town fathers, though I noticed that his minister, white-haired Dr. Fredricks, was in attendance.

Some of the younger guests were playing croquet on the lawn, but Mary and I stuck close to our host and hostess. That was how we ended up, a half-hour later, in a semicircle of metal chairs about ten feet from the edge of the pool. Ernest and Sue were there, along with Lydia Mayer and Mark Towers. There was no sign of Ernest's brother.

"What do you think about the German situation?" Holland asked me. "Some people think Hitler is leading the country into war."

"Oh, it's hard to say. I can't believe he'd repeat the kaiser's mistakes so soon."

"Mussolini has gone to Berlin to meet with him, wearing a uniform created especially for the occasion. They say Hitler will turn out a million people next week to hear the two of them speak"

"Men must always talk of war," Sue Holland objected, sipping her drink, but the men ignored her.

Mark Towers lit a Cuban cigar. "I don't think we have much to worry about. The British should be able to keep Hitler in line."

"You should be editing a big-city paper, Mark," Lydia told him. "It's all right for me to be doing my little social column in a town like Northmont, but you need to be writing about the world scene." Towers was nominally the editor of the *Northmont Blade*, though it was well known that Holland himself made virtually all the editorial decisions.

Sue went off to see how the food was coming while the others launched into a discussion of the relative merits of small-town and big-city newspaper publishing. I got up and walked over to gaze at the placid surface of the empty pool. Ernest Holland once told me that he'd wanted a swimming pool ever since reading *The Great Gatsby* back in the mid-1920s. It was a large pool, probably forty feet long by twenty feet wide, with a diving board at the deep end and steps at the shallow end. The edge of the pool was covered in tile like a bathroom floor, with a lip that extended out a couple of inches over the water. It was placid now with barely a breeze blowing, and I had a distorted view of the bottom, painted a tempting blue-green like some Caribbean sky. It was almost all I needed to lure me in, but I was careful to remain far enough back from the edge.

I returned to the others to find Mary Best looking bored and Ernest Holland expounding on the ambiance of a big-city newsroom. Apparently he'd worked briefly at the New York *Herald-Tribune* his younger days. "Of course this was in the twenties, and it was like something out of the play *The Front Page*.

"People hiding in roll-top desks?" Lydia murmured.

"I remember one time," Ernest began, and suddenly Mary pointed toward the pool.

"Look there! It's your brother!"

Everyone looked, and saw a dripping Philip Holland boosting himself out of the swimming pool. "Howdy, everyone."

Ernest Holland frowned at his brother. "How in hell did you get in there?"

"The usual way. I dove in." He picked up a towel and started to dry himself.

"That pool was empty," Mark Towers said.

I had to agree. "I just walked over there. No one was in it"

Phil Holland smiled and winked at us. "Then I guess it's my secret, isn't it?" He went off in search of another beer.

"You're his brother," Lydia addressed Ernest. "How'd he do it?"

Holland shrugged. "*Why* is a better question, and I can answer that. He's been trying to top me all his life. I was the older brother and whenever I had something, growing up, he would always try to better it. Sibling rivalry, I suppose. He saw the pool and since he couldn't have one of his own he decided to top me by performing some foolish magic trick. I thought he was over that phase of his adolescence by now."

"Calm down, Ernest," his wife urged. "The food will be ready in ten minutes."

I reached a sudden decision. "That gives me time enough for a quick swim."

Mary was the most surprised of all. "You're going in the pool?"

"Why not? Philip just came out of it."

* * *

Sue Holland showed me to a dressing room just inside the house, and I changed quickly into the black bathing trunks I'd brought along. I didn't feel like a swim so much as I felt like solving a mystery. I'd tackled dozens of strange crimes and impossibilities since coming to Northmont fifteen years earlier, but never one involving a swimming pool. Even my memory of a Philo Vance novel from a few years back offered no help, since the method of disappearing from a pool would not fit the present circumstances. There had to be some sort of opening under the water, and I was intent on finding it.

"Don't stay in too long, Mary cautioned. "The air is still a bit chilly."

I stuck a toe in and decided it wasn't too bad. Then I walked in the shallow end and started swimming, using a conventional breast stroke. The water was about a foot below the tile edge of the pool, and I saw nothing unusual there. Some of the others had come over to watch me as I did a quick dive under water and inspected the sides and bottom. Never good at holding my breath under water, I surfaced in less than a minute and waved to Mary. With a deep breath I went down again, but still I found nothing. The painted walls of the swimming pool betrayed not a crack. There was no secret entrance to Holland's swimming pool.

I swam to the shallow end and walked up the steps to join the others. Mary handed me a fresh towel to dry myself. "Find anything?"

"Not a thing."

"He must have been there all the time. You couldn't see him because the water distorted your view."

I shook my head. "We were all seated out here, facing the pool, for twenty minutes or more. There was no turbulence. No one was swimming. His head never broke the surface. And he certainly wasn't wearing a diving suit. In fact he was wearing nothing but bathing trunks. Either he can breathe under water or he materialized in this pool by magic."

Inside, the word of Phil Holland's swimming pool trick—if it was a trick—had spread to the others. Still in his bathing trunks, with a towel wrapped around his middle, he stood sipping his beer and turning aside all questions. "Do it again so we can all see it," Rose Innes suggested. She was the newspaper's cooking expert, a jolly overweight woman who shared an office with Lydia Mayer.

Phil Holland smirked slightly, enjoying his moment of glory, and asked, "What do you think, big brother—should I do it again?"

"Why don't you do the reverse?" Ernest suggested. "Dive into the pool and disappear." There was a touch of nastiness in his tone.

"Well, I could do that too."

Everyone started talking at once, believing Ernest's challenge had been sincere. I walked over to Sue Holland who was making herself another Tom Collins. "I think you'd better rescue your husband. This swimming pool business with Phil seems to be getting out of hand."

"Things with my brother-in-law always get out of hand," she agreed. Then, raising her voice for all to hear, she announced. "It's clambake time! Everybody outside!"

The caterers had set up tables for the twenty guests out beyond the pool. As we strolled out, Sue Holland explained that two hundred soft-shell clams had been baked on hot rocks in a sand pit, along with four dozen ears of corn, five broiling chickens, ten sweet potatoes, and twenty lobsters. They had been layered with four bushels of wet seaweed supplied by the chef. As soon as the clams had opened they were ready to serve.

I sat with Mary, something of a clam expert, who immediately announced, "These are great!" The others seemed to be enjoying the feast as well, though I noticed that Phil Holland had not yet sat down. In fact he had removed his towel and was strolling around in his bathing trunks, chatting with people while he finished his been.

"Going swimming again?" Towers asked him.

"You bet your life! That's why I'm not eating. Brother Ernest has challenged me to jump into the pool and disappear, and that's just what I'm going to do."

"It wasn't exactly a challenge," Ernest called out from his table. Next to him, Sue raised her glass to her lips and tried to ignore the whole thing. A waiter was serving beer from a pitcher but she waved him away, preferring to stick with her Tom Collins.

The beer tasted good to me. I was about to comment that the entire clambake was one of the best meals I'd had in years where Phil finished his beer and set down the empty glass. Then he strode deliberately to the edge of the swimming pool and dove into the deep end.

For a moment no one moved, waiting for him to resurface.

Holland kept eating, trying to ignore his brother's scene-stealing performance, but after about two minutes Sue grew restless at his side. The water in the pool was completely still and from our limited vantage point at the tables no head had broken the surface. She stood up, and I followed suit. That was the signal for a half-dozen others to start for the pool, and in a moment only Ernest Holland remained at the tables.

Sue was still carrying her drink as she approached the pool, perhaps trying to appear as nonchalant as possible. I was by her side and Rose Innes was right behind us, leading the others. They all wanted to see if Holland's brother had performed a miracle before their eyes and vanished from the pool.

I took a deep breath and peered over the edge.

Philip Holland hadn't vanished.

He was lying at the bottom of the pool, face down, arms and legs stretched out like some giant starfish.

* * *

Sue Holland dropped her glass and would have fallen after it into the pool if I hadn't caught her. "Mary!" I shouted. "Take care of her. She's fainted."

I was still in my swimsuit and I knew it was my job to go in after him. I dove off the side and went straight to the bottom, trying to get an arm around him. He'd been in the water about four minutes by my estimation and I knew there was a tiny chance he still might live if I could get him to the surface in time. His body weighed less under water, but I was still having trouble getting him up when Mark Towers joined me. He'd doffed his shoes and shirt and followed me into the pool. Between us, we managed to lift Phil Holland's limp body to the tiles. Several people immediately started working on him, to no avail.

I climbed out of the pool and went to find Mary. "You'd better phone for an ambulance. There may be some hope."

"I just did. And I called Sheriff Lens too."

We went back to the pool where Ernest Holland, ashen-faced, had finally joined the group around his brother. Mark Towers was in the pool retrieving a shoe that he'd dropped, along with the glass and straw that had fallen from Sue Holland's hand as she went into a faint. Sue herself was seated on one of the chairs, holding her head in her hands.

I went up to her and asked, "Are you all right? I have some smelling salts in my bag."

"I just can't think," she responded, shaking her head to clear it. "What happened? Is Phil–?"

"They're working on him. It doesn't look good."

"Oh my God!"

Finally I went over and knelt by the body, checking for pulse and breathing. There was nothing. He was dead.

"Do you think it was a heart attack?" Mary Best asked. "What else would have been that sudden?"

"I don't know. We'll have to wait for the autopsy."

Sheriff Lens arrived just after the ambulance. He'd been at home when the call came in, and pinned his badge to a blue sport shirt he'd been wearing. "Hello, Doc," he greeted me. "Are you a guest or did they call you?"

"A guest. I'm Ernest Holland's physician. The dead man is his younger brother Philip who's been visiting from California. He dove into the pool as part of a stunt and never came up. We had him out within minutes but he was already dead."

The sheriff glanced over at the tables heaped with food. "You think it was cramps after eating?"

"He had nothing but a beer or two. And it was too fast for cramps. He didn't struggle or thrash around at all."

Ernest Holland came over to where we were standing. "I don't understand any of this, Sheriff. My brother was in perfect health." He seemed more annoyed than despondent over his brother's death, as if Phil had managed to top him one last time.

"We'll get to the bottom of it," Sheriff Lens assured him. "I'll be talking to you shortly." As he walked away from Holland he said, "Fill me in, Doc. Who's here and what happened?"

"His annual clambake. Twenty guests in all. There's Holland and his wife Sue, Mary and me, three of his people from the newspaper—Mark Towers, Rose Innes, and Lydia Mayer—and the victim of course. The other twelve are a couple more employees plus people like me that he deals with in town. You probably know the minister. There are a half-dozen catering people, including the chef. That's it."

"Think he might have been poisoned?"

"I don't see how. It looks like a drowning to me, except that it happened so fast." I quickly ran over all that had happened since Mary and I arrived.

"Sounds like there was no love lost between the brothers."

"Don't read too much into that, Sheriff," I advised. "Certainly there was sibling rivalry, but that's nothing unusual."

Since the death appeared to be natural or accidental, the sheriff limited himself to talking with Holland and his wife, along with Mark Towers and myself because we were the ones who'd gone in after the body. The clambake itself had come to an abrupt end and the others were departing as quickly as they could.

"You can give me a complete guest list if I need it?" Sheriff Lens asked Sue Holland.

"Certainly, but why would you need it?"

"We won't know till after the autopsy," he answered. It was not a reply designed to make anyone sleep better that night.

Before I left I walked over to the swimming pool and stared into its glistening water. How had Phil Holland planned to disappear from there? The same way that he'd appeared earlier? And what had kept him from it? What had been waiting there, invisible, just beneath the surface?

* * *

I'd expected to sleep late on Sunday morning, but it was not to be. After assuring me it would be Monday before he had the autopsy results, Sheriff Lens was at my door before ten o'clock. "Sorry to bother you this early on a Sunday, Doc, but I need you to come along to the Hollands' house. We're pretty certain Philip Holland died from potassium cyanide poisoning."

"That's impossible!" was my first reaction. "If the poison was in the beer he'd have been dead before he reached the pool. It kills within a minute or so. I've handled enough poisoning cases to know that."

"Hell, Doc, maybe the whole pool was poisoned."

I knew he wasn't serious, but I still had to point out that Towers and I had both been in it immediately after Holland was stricken. "There was nothing wrong with the water."

"Why don't you get dressed and come along with me to the Holland home? I need you, Doc."

"Let me grab a quick breakfast and I will."

Sheriff Lens nodded. "Pour some coffee for me too."

We arrived there shortly after eleven to find that the minister, Dr. Fredricks, had driven over to visit them following his Sunday morning service. Fredricks was a kindly white-haired man who looked more at home in his preacher's black suit than he had in his more casual clambake wear the previous day.

He greeted us as we entered and shook our hands. "I came over to help with the funeral arrangements. It's a very trying time for everyone. Such a terrible accident—"

The sheriff interrupted him. "I'm afraid it wasn't an accident. The preliminary autopsy results indicate Mr. Holland died of potassium cyanide poisoning."

The dead man's brother frowned at the news. "How is that possible?"

"We don't know."

"There must be some mistake," Sue Holland suggested. She wore a green housecoat wrapped around her trim figure. Obviously the minister had surprised them with his visit. "Isn't that the poison you can smell?"

"The odor of bitter almonds, usually," the sheriff agreed, "but being in the water like that might have washed away some of the odor."

"Was there any water in my brother's lungs?" Ernest asked.

"A small amount. He might have been gasping for breath as he died."

"God!" Sue Holland said, looking away.

"I'm sorry, ma'am. I know it's hard news to accept."

"We've decided the funeral will be Tuesday morning," Ernest announced. "Dr. Fredricks will hold the service at his church." By concentrating on the funeral he seemed to be avoiding the fact as his brother's death.

Sheriff Lens looked uncomfortable. "I'll need to speak with you in private, Mr. Holland. And Mrs. Holland as well."

Ernest stood up and started to pace. He was wearing a white shirt and trousers, further along in dressing than his wife, but still in bedroom slippers. "There's no need for an extensive investigation, Sheriff. It's obvious my brother poisoned himself."

"Suicide?" I said. Somehow I hadn't considered the possibility.

"He spent his life trying to top me. I was always the older brother he needed to best in one way or another. I was almost glad when he put a continent between us and moved to California. This visit was a disaster from the beginning." He turned to his wife for her agreement. "Wasn't it, Sue?"

"It wasn't good," she admitted quietly.

"He'd become even more of an ass than I remembered. Everything about my success was reason for a sarcastic remark—the newspaper, this house, even my swimming pool. He remembered that I'd always wanted one since I read *Gatsby*."

"The swimming pool," I repeated. "Tell us about the swimming pool."

Dr. Fredricks had gotten to his feet. "If there's nothing more for me to do, I really must be going. Again, Ernest and Sue, my sincere sympathy in your time of sorrow. I'll be at the funeral parlor tomorrow evening, and we've scheduled the service for Tuesday." He needed to the sheriff and me as he left.

"It was nice of him to come over," Sue Holland observed. "We don't attend church that often, but of course he was at the clambake when it happened."

I took up the conversation again. "That's what we're trying to determine—exactly what happened at the swimming pool." I held up a finger. "First, a group of us was sitting there chatting, talking about Hitler and Mussolini as I remember it. I'd even walked over to look at the pool. There was no movement in the water, no one breaking the surface to breathe, and I saw no one under the water. The pool was empty. A few minutes later, Phil Holland emerged from the water, virtually challenging us to figure out where he'd come from. I even went for a swim myself to examine the walls of the pool. There was no hiding place, no secret entrance."

"Of course not!" Holland agreed. "It's just a swimming pool!"

I held up another finger. "Second, your brother is challenged by you to reverse the trick, to jump into the pool and disappear."

"I wanted him to disappear, all right—all the way back to California!"

"Ernest—" Sue rested a calming hand on his arm.

"He was willing to do that. Our problem is, how did he work the first trick and how did he plan to work the second one?"

"He could jump in the pool and disappear by dying," Ernest Holland said. "I think that's just what he did. He topped me one last time by killing himself at my clambake."

"Ernest, that's insane!" Sue objected.

"Maybe he was insane."

"I don't mean him, I mean you, for even thinking such a thing."

Sheriff Lens shifted nervously in his chair. "Mr. Holland, if your brother killed himself, how do you figure he pulled it off? Potassium cyanide kills within a minute or two. He had nothing but the beer and it couldn't have been that or you'd have seen the symptoms before he dove in."

"He might have had a capsule of some sort in his mouth," Holland speculated. "Something he could bite into once he was in the water."

Sheriff Lens turned to me. "Are there such things, Doc?"

"Gelatin capsules aren't widely used, but they can be made up. I suppose someone could put poison inside. But he would have had to plan in advance and bring it with him. Somehow he didn't seem like a man planning suicide."

"It's either suicide or the entire pool was poisoned," Ernest Holland said. "What other possibility is there?"

"I don't know," I admitted.

* * *

The idea of a poisoned pool was ridiculous, of course. A small amount of poison, or even a gallon of it, would be diluted so much as to be harmless. Also there was the undeniable fact that Towers and I had suffered no ill effects from our time in the pool. I explained all this to the sheriff as we drove back to my modest house.

"Then what do you think, Doc? Suicide?"

"I don't know. Suicide doesn't explain how Phil Holland could magically appear in the empty pool earlier."

Sheriff Lens had followed my reasoning for too many years to be left behind now. "You think the two things are connected, don't you Doc? He was going to vanish from the pool the same way he got into it in the first place. Only something or someone stopped him."

"Maybe."

"You've solved tougher cases than this. You'll figure it out."

But after the sheriff had dropped me back home and I'd had time to think about it, I wondered if I had ever solved a tougher case than this.

Holland had been hoping his brother's body would be released early Sunday afternoon so there'd be time to embalm it for viewing Sunday evening. But it wasn't to be, and Monday afternoon and evening would be the only calling times. It didn't really matter Sue told me later when I phoned, because Phil had no friends in Northmont. As for his life in California, he'd been something of a playboy, working around the fringes of the film industry and romancing a few starlets, but never settling down. She'd phoned his most recent female friend, who'd shed a few tears at the news of his death but suggested he be buried back East.

"I'd like to speak with some of the people on the *Blade*," I told Sue. "Will they be getting out an issue this week?"

"Certainly," she assured me. "Ernest won't be in the office until after Tuesday's funeral, but Mark Towers will get out the issue. It'll go to press Thursday evening just as it always does."

"I noticed Lydia Mayer taking some photographs at the clambake. Were those for the paper?"

"I think she plans to use one or two in her column."

"If I stopped by the office tomorrow morning, would she have prints of them yet?"

"Oh yes. We have our own darkroom and Lydia develops all her own things right in the office."

"I'd like to see them, in case she caught something I missed."

"Of course," Sue Holland said. "Does this mean you don't believe my husband's suicide theory?"

"I don't know what to believe, frankly. How's he taking it?"

"He's resting right now. For all his bluster, it's still a shock to see a brother die before your eyes."

I believed her.

* * *

I phoned Mary at the office Monday morning and told her I'd be late. I knew there were no patients due until eleven. Then I went over to the town square, where the *Blade* office was right next to Dr. Fredrick's church. The small staff was bustling around like, I supposed, any other Monday. Mark Towers was all business now, and with the telephone cradled between chin and shoulder as he wrote furiously he bore little resemblance to the man who'd been directing us where to park on Saturday. The only reminder was the Cuban cigar smoldering in his ashtray.

He hung up the phone as I passed his desk. "Hello, Doc. I hear Phil was poisoned."

"That's what the autopsy says."

"Is this one of these impossible crimes you like to solve?"

"I like to solve them," I agreed. "It's too soon to tell just what this is. I came in to look at the pictures Lydia Mayer took on Saturday."

"Lydia!" he called out.

She appeared from the back room, carrying a stack of papers, and I explained what I wanted. "Sure, Dr. Sam. I have the pictures back on my desk. Because of what happened we decided not to run a social column on the party. We're just reporting Philip Holland's death as a news item."

I followed her into the little office she shared with Rose Innes. Each of them had a big Underwood typewriter by her desk, and Rose was in the process of cutting a piece from a large chocolate cake. "You're just in time to help test this recipe," she told me. "It's kirsch-flavored Black Forest cake with cream filling and sour cherries."

"Sounds much too rich for my diet," I told her. "Thanks anyway."

Lydia snorted. "Can you imagine sharing an office with Rose and her recipes all day?" She rummaged through the papers on her desk and came up with a folder of the pictures she'd taken on Saturday.

They were the usual black-and-white prints of passable quality, showing groups of people, drinks in hand, standing and seated. Some had been taken in the pool area and there was the one of Philip Holland in his bathing suit that she'd taken just after she arrived. None of the snapshots told me anything new. I put them back in the folder and returned it to her.

Rose took her cake to pass around to Towers and the other employees, and I used the opportunity to ask Lydia a few questions. "You've been here a long time, haven't you?"

"Ever since Ernest started the paper. I was one of his first employees."

"Wasn't Philip living back East then?"

She nodded. "In Boston. He never had quite the resolve of Ernest. Too busy being a playboy. I suppose it happened to lots of people who came of age during prohibition. Phil was the one with the hip flask and the girl on his arm. He watched big brother marry a perfect woman and start a weekly newspaper. I think when Ernest started building the big house and fancy pool that was more than his brother could stomach. He headed for California."

"Why did he come back?"

Lydia Mayer shrugged. "A visit. I know Mark thought he was angling to become editor of the paper, somehow talking his brother into replacing Mark with him, but that would never have happened I told Mark that Ernest would never hire his brother for anything."

"No love lost between the two."

"No," she agreed, then looked sharply at me. "Ernest wouldn't kill him, if that's what you're thinking. Not his own brother."

"The thought never crossed my mind. How long had Phil been staying with them?"

"Since around Labor Day. He spoke of going back, but I don't think he ever mentioned a date."

Rose Innes came back with her cake. Only one piece remained. "Just enough for you, Dr. Sam."

I smiled at her. "No thanks, Rose."

"Well, I guess I'll have to eat it myself."

* * *

I didn't go to the funeral parlor that evening, but I was in church with Sheriff Lens the following morning for Dr. Fredricks's service A number of business people, advertisers in the *Blade*, were in attendance, as well as the newspaper staff who had come from the office next door. After the service we followed along to the cemetery and stood back a ways as Ernest Holland's brother was buried.

"What do you think, Doc?" the sheriff asked as we strode back to the car. "Do you know how he was killed?"

"The first trick is the key to the mystery. If we knew how he managed to emerge from that empty pool, we'd know the rest." I was silent, deep in my own thoughts, until we reached the center of town. "I want to go out there later today, Sheriff. I want to see the pool one more time."

"Take a swim," he suggested. "It's warm enough for it."

"I've had my swim."

"The poisoned pool," he mused. "Do you think he had some chemical on his skin that reacted with the water?"

I chuckled. "That's not too likely. For one thing, it would have killed him the first time he was in the water. Nothing was rubbed on his skin after he came out except a towel. Any sort of chemical on his skin would more likely have been washed away."

"Could someone have injected him with a hypodermic just before he jumped in?"

"The autopsy didn't find any needle marks. Besides, Holland would certainly have reacted to being stuck with a hypodermic needle before diving into the pool. No, the poison was almost certainly ingested. As soon as it hit the stomach acids he was a dead man."

"He'd only been here a few weeks. That's awfully soon to make an enemy who would kill him."

"Most of the people at the party had known him earlier, and some of them might have had reason to fear his return."

"I think I'd better go out there with you later," Sheriff Lens decided.

We arrived in mid-afternoon and found Sue Holland swimming in the pool. As she climbed out, clad in a dark green bathing suit that showed off her perfect legs, she greeted us and said, "Nobody's been in since it happened Saturday. Ernest wouldn't come near it. I figured somebody had to go in, just to prove it wasn't jinxed or something."

"Is your husband around?"

She glanced from Sheriff Lens to me. "He's in the living room with Mark. Come on, I'll take you in."

We entered through the side door, and I was surprised how big the place looked when not crowded with guests and caterers. Holland and his editor were bent over a coffee table studying typed stories for the week's paper. Even on the day of his brother's funeral, Ernest Holland was still in charge at the *Blade*.

"Sorry to interrupt," I told them. The sheriff and I wanted another look at the pool area."

"Go right ahead. Sue will take care of you." Holland's gaze returned to the pages before him as he made a point with Mark Towers.

His wife was making herself a drink behind the bar. "He doesn't seem too concerned about his brother," the sheriff commented.

"They weren't close," she remarked, lifting the glass to her lips. "But you already know that."

I turned suddenly and walked out to the pool. It had come to me so quickly that I couldn't completely trust my intuition. I had to think it out. I had to be sure. Staring down at the barely moving water of the swimming pool, I knew I was right.

I walked back into the living room and Sue Holland was staring at me. "What's wrong? You look so strange."

I moistened my lips slightly. "I know how Phil Holland was killed. And I know who did it."

"You can't mean that."

"Yes I can. It came to me just now when I saw you lift that glass to your lips. I remembered you doing that at the clambake while we were eating, sipping the Tom Collins you'd been drinking through a straw earlier."

Towers and her husband had stopped talking and were turned in our direction. Sheriff Lens shifted uncomfortably, not knowing what to expect. "After Philip died, Mark retrieved your glass and straw from the pool. But you weren't using a straw at dinner, so where did it come from? How did it get into the pool?"

She grabbed for something beneath the bar and ran for the back door. I was after her in an instant. I caught her around the waist as she reached the edge of the pool, twisting the tiny vial of white powder from her grasp.

"Not that way," I gasped, yanking her back. "That's the way you murdered Philip Holland."

* * *

All the time it took me to explain it, Ernest Holland's expression never changed. He sat there on the sofa, staring straight ahead. Perhaps he was remembering the pain he had caused Philip as a child, or the pain Philip had caused him as an adult.

"You see, it all hinged on how Philip pulled off that pool trick in the first place. When I realized Sue wasn't using a straw any longer when she dropped the glass in the pool, I asked myself—as I asked her just now—where it came from. We saw Mark retrieve the glass and straw, so they were floating on the surface before he dove in. I certainly didn't have a straw when I dove after Philip, so he must have had the straw with him all the time. When he died it floated to the surface. And what does a straw suggest if you're in the water? Any boy can tell you it's a breathing device. You can remain submerged and breathe through the straw without being seen. That's just what Philip did. When we came out to sit around the pool he was already in it, standing near the shallow end so his head was just below the surface of the water. He was up against the near side of the pool, breathing through the straw that just broke the surface of the water. We couldn't see him from where we sat, and even when I walked over to look in I didn't see him. He was flat against the pool wall, and with that little lip of tile going out a couple of inches over the water, it helped to hide him. I would have had to lean over and look straight down into the water, which I had no reason to do. In fact, I remember standing back from the edge."

"He was only wearing bathing trunks," Mark Towers pointed out. "Why didn't we see the straw?"

"He slipped it under the waistband of his trunks, I imagine. It might have gotten flattened a little but it was still usable for his purpose."

Sheriff Lens had been waiting while Sue Holland dressed. Now he brought her out. Ernest was shocked to see her in handcuffs, and he half rose from his seat. "Is that necessary, Sheriff?"

"She just tried to kill herself at the pool, Mr. Holland. We don't want that, do we?"

"Of course not," he agreed. He didn't meet his wife's eyes.

"This was all to steal attention from his brother," I went on. "A childish thing, but perhaps all this has its roots in childhood. Certainly when Philip was challenged to vanish from the pool he had to try it, even though he knew his method would be revealed. It's one thing to step out of a swimming pool believed to be empty, which hasn't been thoroughly examined. It's something else to dive into a pool and try to remain hidden, breathing through a straw. One of us would surely have peered over the edge, or walked around to the other side and spotted him at once. He'd lose that round, but he was prepared to top his brother in another way, wasn't he, Sue?"

She turned toward me. "You seem to know it all."

"He asked you for a second straw to hide in the waistband of his trunks. Only this time you gave him one containing potassium cyanide, the water-soluble powder moistened just enough to make it stick inside the straw. He dove into the pool, stood against the near side under water, poked the straw above the surface, a deep breath. He was dead within a minute"

"Why would she do it, Doc?" Sheriff Lens asked.

"Why would he ask her for a straw to do a trick that would steal the spotlight from her husband's party? Why did she fear what be was going to do next? I believe she and Philip had an affair years ago when he was living here, and he was about to gloat about this to Ernest. Sue couldn't risk losing everything because Philip wanted to embarrass her husband. She was willing to kill him rather than lose Ernest and this house and everything else. Isn't that right Sue?"

She stared at me and at the sheriff. She didn't look at her husband. "I won't talk here. I'll make a statement at your office, Sheriff."

"The drinking straw was the key to it," I finished up. "If the straw was found floating in the pool with his body, she knew the truth might come out. That's why she faked a near-faint and dropped her glass in the water. We'd assume the straw had been in the glass as it was earlier."

Mark Towers spoke for the first time. "Where'd she get the poison?"

"Potassium cyanide is used in photography. Your darkroom at the newspaper probably has some. She just needed to transfer a little to that vial she had. That could have been done sometime when she dropped in to see her husband. I don't know why she took it originally, but she found a use for it."

Her story, when she finally told it to Sheriff Lens, was that she'd taken the poison to kill some moles that had been digging up the yard. She'd placed it in the straws for this purpose, and when Philip Holland asked her for a straw to perform his pool trick she'd accidentally given him a poisoned one.

I doubted if there was a jury in the entire state that would buy this explanation, even from a woman as attractive as Sue Holland.

THE PROBLEM OF
THE MISSING ROADHOUSE

I T might never happened if the clouds from an approaching cold front had not moved in to obscure the full moon on that pleasant August evening in 1938. Jack and Becky Tober were driving home from the Friday night square dance at the Grange Hall in Northmont. It was just after eleven o'clock and Becky was pleading with her husband to surrender the wheel of the Dodge to her.

"You've had too much to drink, Jack. Let me drive."

He turned on her gruffly, pushing her hand from the wheel. "I could drive us home in my sleep. Just watch for the road sign."

The sign, on the right side of the dirt road, would show an arrow indicating a left turn with the words Turk Hill Road. It was a tricky stretch to maneuver after dark on a cloudy night, and Jack Tober had to keep his attention on the rutted roadway every inch of the way. "You sure we haven't passed it, Becky?"

"No, it's still ahead. Are you all right?"

"Fine."

"You didn't sound it when you were arguing with Foster over that last beer, and then going out to the parking lot with him."

"All he wants to talk about is the Spanish Civil War. What in hell do I care if Franco captured Vinaroz? All he—"

"There's the sign, Jack. Turn here!"

"Damn! Almost missed it." He turned left onto the narrow dirt road and started up the gentle hill toward their farm. It was not a big place by local standards—less than forty acres—and after buying it a few years back they'd converted it into an apple orchard, with some vegetables and a few chickens as sidelines.

"Watch where you're driving, Jack. You'll have us in a ditch."

"Damn road gets narrower every time I drive it!"

They topped a slight grade and suddenly he saw lights ahead. They were on the left, almost across from where their farm should be. There should be nothing but woods there, not the low building and the tiny parking lot that were coming into view. "What is this, Becky? We're on the wrong road."

He slowed and peered out the window on his side of the car. It seemed to be a roadhouse, with music and voices coming from inside. There was a tall man standing by one of the six or eight cars and Jack called to him. "Where am I? What is this place?"

The man motioned toward the neon sign on the side of the building. "The Apple Orchard. Come on in."

Jack Tober was shaking his head. "The apple orchard is where we live. We own it."

"You must mean the orchard across the road. That's where the place got its name."

Jack saw nothing but darkness across the road. "My farm's nowhere near a roadhouse. I must have the wrong place."

The man stepped closer. His face was rough and weathered, and he wore a peaked nautical cap. "If you've never been here you should come in for a beer."

Becky spoke up. "You've had enough, Jack. I just want to go home. Back up and we'll turn around."

He shifted the car into reverse and started backing up. Almost at once there was a thud as he hit something. "What was that?"

"God, you've hit Lenny!" the man in the cap shouted. "Go forward!"

"Lenny who?" Jack grumbled, but he and Becky were out of the car instantly, hurrying to the rear where the man stood over a crumpled body.

"Is he breathing?" Becky said.

"Can't tell," the man said. "We'd better get him in to the hospital right away."

Jack's hand came away from the body covered with blood. The sight of it sobered him instantly. "Somebody call an ambulance."

"It would be faster if you could drive him to the hospital," the man said.

"In my car?" Jack was thinking of the stranger's blood on his upholstery.

But Becky quickly overcame his obvious reluctance. "Help get him in the backseat, Jack. I'll get the lap robe from the trunk."

"All right."

The injured man was around thirty, with brown hair. He was dressed in a suit and tie, and the marks of Jack Tober's tires were obvious across his head and body. They got him into the backseat, wrapped in the robe, and Becky said, "I think he's dead."

"Drive him to Pilgrim Memorial Hospital," the man in the cap said. "I'll get my car and follow behind you."

Jack shifted gears and they turned around in the nearly empty parking lot. "Do you want me to drive?" Becky asked, the tension obvious in her voice.

"I'm fine. That sobered me up in a hurry."

They headed back down the road with the unconscious man, not waiting for the man who was following. Jack realized suddenly that he didn't even know that person's name. In ten minutes they were at the hospital, pulling up at the emergency room entrance.

"Accident victim," Jack told the nurse on duty.

She hurried out to the car with stretcher-bearers. "What happened to him?" she asked, searching for a pulse.

"I backed into him with my car."

"I believe this man is beyond help."

"You mean he's dead?" Becky asked. "I was afraid of that."

A few moments later, when a young doctor had verified the fact of death, he told Jack and Becky, "We'll have to notify Sheriff Lens about the accident. I'd suggest you remain here until he arrives."

* * *

I heard all this from Jack Tober later [old Dr. Sam Hawthorne reminisced] but the following morning when Sheriff Lens showed up at my office I knew nothing about it. "You free right now, Doc?" he asked, poking his head in at the door while I was going over the past due accounts with my nurse, Mary Best.

"For fifteen minutes," I answered, glancing at the clock. "Come on in. What's up?"

"Man named Lenny Blue was killed in an auto accident last night. There's something not quite right about it."

"What would that be?"

Sheriff Lens was all the way into the office now, tipping his cap to Mary. "Sorry to interrupt. Did either of you ever hear of a roadhouse called the Apple Orchard?"

We both shook our heads. "Is it near here?" Mary asked.

"Somewhere around Turk Hill Road, or at least that's where the Tobers say it is."

"Jack Tober?"

The sheriff nodded. "He a patient of yours, Doc?"

"I treated him once for the flu when Dr. Webster was away. Exactly what happened?"

"They tell a strange story. Jack and Becky were driving home from the square dance last night when they took a wrong turn or something. They ended up at this roadhouse, the Apple Orchard. A man in the parking lot spoke to them but they didn't get his name. Tober was backing up when he hit something. He'd run over Lenny Blue, who was apparently standing behind the car."

"Lenny Blue." Mary repeated the name. "I believe he was brought into the hospital once before with some sort of mental problem."

"Tall, gangly fellow in his twenties. Nobody knows much about him, except that he was a bit crazy."

"Is he from Northmont?" I asked.

"He was rooming with Mrs. Goutski over on Cedar Street. Been there about a year. Worked as a hired hand picking apples and things in season."

"The Apple Orchard."

"Yeah, it fits," Sheriff Lens said sadly. "Only trouble is, there's no such place anyone can find."

I glanced at the office clock. "There's a patient due in a few minutes, and two more after that. Then I'll be free for the rest of the day. There are no house calls scheduled after lunch, are there, Mary?"

She checked the appointment book. "Not today."

"Then I'll have a talk with Tober and his wife."

That was how I finally heard the story of what happened the previous night. Just after lunch, Jack Tober sat across from me in my office and narrated it in detail, as if discussing a particularly vivid motion picture he'd just seen down at the Northmont Cinema. From time to time he'd turn to his wife Becky for verification and she would nod or correct him on a minor point.

"What about this man who followed you to the hospital?" I asked when he'd finished.

Tober simply shook his head. "He never showed up. I suppose he didn't want to get involved."

"You didn't get his name?"

"No."

It was then that Sheriff Lens entered the office and handed me a note. I read it quickly and said, "It seems that you have a problem, Mr. Tober."

"Why? Because the man died?"

"More than that. The autopsy shows a bullet wound in the head. Lenny Blue was murdered."

* * *

While the sheriff went off to question Mrs. Goutski, the woman who'd been renting the apartment to Lenny, I decided it might be worth my time to retrace the Tobers' route of the previous night while it was still fresh in their minds. Sheriff Lens had impounded their Dodge, looking for evidence of the accident, so we took my Buick and headed to the Grange Hall where their adventure had begun.

"Do you come here often?" I asked as we drove up and parked in front of the Grange Hall. I knew they had frequent dances, often with out-of-town bands, and the previous year I'd been involved in a murder investigation there.

"Sometimes on Wednesdays," Becky explained. "They have square dancing on Wednesdays." She patted her husband on the shoulder. "But this guy has too many beers and has trouble driving home."

"I was all right," Jack Tober mumbled, perhaps a bit embarrassed by her words.

"So you were driving?"

"Yes."

"You pulled out of the parking lot and headed—where?"

"Toward home. Our farm and orchard are on Turk Hill Road."

I started the Buick and headed that way, turning right on Fairfax. It was a dirt road with three dirt roads off to the left before one encountered the first right turn. The second of these was Turk Hill Road. "You're sure this is where you turned?" I asked.

"I saw the sign," Becky confirmed.

It was the only one of the three roads with a sign, probably because the Tobers and other families lived on it. Except for an occasional fruit stand and one or two farms, I knew of nothing on the other roads. Certainly I had no patients on either of them. Turk Hill Road, on the other hand, was a bit wider and smoother, a tribute to the heavier traffic generated by the several orchards that lined it.

Driving along it now, I tried to imagine what it might have been like the previous night, shrouded in darkness with even the moon hidden by clouds. Both sides of the road were lined with fruit trees. Even the farmhouses were set far back, connected to Turk Hill Road only by dirt or cinder driveways. "It wasn't this far," Tober said suddenly. "We're almost to our place on the right."

"I'll keep going. You might have been fooled by the darkness."

Before long we came to the next crossroads and I had to admit they were right. Not only was there no roadhouse—there was not even space for a road-house. I turned around and headed back along Turk Hill Road, driving more slowly this time. Still there was nothing.

"We'd better try the other roads," Becky Tober suggested half-heartedly. "It's got to be somewhere."

The next road to the north, called simply North Road, was even worse, with only one driveway to a distant farmhouse. We pulled in at a large fruit stand, its front opened to reveal boxes of newly picked plums, cherries, peaches, corn, and tomatoes.

"Any melons yet?" I asked the stout woman who came out to wait on us.

"Should have some tomorrow. Try us in the afternoon."

I glanced up and down the road. There were no other cars in sight, though the stand was probably large enough to accommodate a dozen drive-in customers at one time. "Not much traffic on this road, I guess."

"They know we're here. Aunt Peachy's. I been open ten summers now."

"I guess I don't come on the North Road much. Is there a roadhouse around here? A place called the Apple Orchard?"

"Roadhouse?" she said with a snort. "Ain't one o' them in the whole county, is there?"

"Not that I know of."

The Tobers had gotten out of the car and when she recognized them Aunt Peachy called out, "you gonna have some of them good apples for me soon?"

"A few more weeks," Jack Tober promised. "I'll be over with a few baskets."

As they drove on along North Road, I said, "I didn't know you knew her."

"She sells some of our apples," Becky explained. "All the farms and orchards around here supply her."

There was nothing on the rest of North Road, not even a driveway. On the way back we waved to Aunt Peachy.

* * *

I was driving back to town when I remembered we hadn't tried South Road, the first left turn off Fairfax Road. We didn't expect to find anything there, but we were wrong. We hadn't gone a half-mile before we came upon the still-smoldering ruins of a barn fire. It was on the left, but Tober insisted it wasn't far enough along the road.

"Even if we took the wrong turn somehow, we drove farther than this. I'm sure of it!"

I pulled the car to a stop in the tall grass along the road. A man in overalls was inspecting the remains of the barn, and I recognized Sy Holden. "What happened, Sy? This your barn?"

He walked over to the car. "It *was* my barn, Doc. Burned down sometime toward dawn. By the time I got the volunteers up here there was nothing left."

Sy had been farming the area for as long as I'd lived in Northmont, and though he'd never been a patient of mine I knew him from town meetings and the like. His farm fronted on the main road, but he'd acquired the Sawyer place when the old man died and kept this barn as an auxiliary. It was a mile or more from his farmhouse, which was why he hadn't discovered the blaze sooner.

"There was no lightning last night," I observed, "though it was cloudy."

"It could have been kids, or hobos camped out in there. I'm just glad I didn't keep any animals out here. All I lost was the barn and some hay."

"Did you see or hear anything unusual earlier—before midnight?"

"Like what?"

"Maybe a gunshot."

"Nothing like that. This road is so desolate that any car late at night attracts attention, but we're too far away for it to bother us. Once I came out here after dark searching for a stray calf and heard voices, but I didn't bother to investigate. You catch people doing something they shouldn't be doing and sometimes they get angry."

"True enough," I agreed. "Ever hear of a roadhouse on these back roads, a place with drinks and music called the Apple Orchard?"

Sy Holden shook his head. "Nothing like that around here. I'd have heard if there was. People want to drink, they go into town."

We drove back into Northmont after that. If the Apple Orchard existed, no one knew of it. Jack Tober and his wife were more disturbed than ever. "We were there!" Becky insisted. "We saw it."

"We spoke with the man in the peaked cap!"

"Phantoms," I told them. "You're part of a murder investigation now, and you'll need hard facts to back up your story. Right now there's nothing to back it up."

"Did you search his pockets? Maybe he had matches from that Apple Orchard place."

"No matches," I told them, though I hadn't looked personally. I remembered something else that had been on the autopsy report when I read it. "And no alcohol."

"What?"

"Lenny Blue hadn't had a drink before he died. Don't you think that's odd if you really did run over him outside a roadhouse late at night? Why else would he have gone there except to drink?"

Jack Tober seemed deflated. "I don't know," he admitted.

* * *

For all of my debunking, I didn't find the Tobers' story completely unbelievable. My years in Northmont had taught me that a murder can often be surrounded by the most bizarre circumstances. It seemed to me that the victim was the only lead we had at the moment, the largest and only clue to what had happened on Turk Hill Road the previous night.

I couldn't find Sheriff Lens to discover what he'd learned from the victim's landlady, so after dropping off Tober and his wife I decided to call on Mrs. Goutski myself. She was one of the relative newcomers to Northmont, having moved from Boston about five years earlier. Despite her Eastern European origins she spoke English quite well. I guessed her age to be in the early forties and she was still attractive, even in the somewhat plain dresses she usually wore. I'd never heard her first name, nor did I know anything about her husband. She'd been simply Mrs. Goutski since she came to Northmont and bought the house where Lenny Blue had rented a room.

"I already spoke to the sheriff," she said when she responded to my knock. "Now I got to speak to the doctor?"

"You don't have to speak to anyone, Mrs. Goutski," I said. "I'm just helping out Sheriff Lens. Did you know Lenny Blue well?"

"What's to know? He was quiet and he paid his rent on time."

"Did the sheriff look at his room."

"I showed him, yes."

"Do you think I could see it too?"

She hesitated and then stepped aside, allowing me to enter the sparsely furnished downstairs. "I'll get the key."

She returned clutching a slender key of the most common sort and led the way upstairs. Perhaps from force of habit, she knocked gently at the dead man's door before inserting the key. The furniture here was as sparse as downstairs—a single bed, a faded couch, a straight-backed wooden chair, and a small table.

"You rented it furnished?" I guessed.

"Yes. He had nothing but that suitcase and some clothes in the closet. The sheriff said he'd send a deputy to pick everything up and hold it for the next of kin."

I walked around, casually opening drawers and trying to seem as if I wasn't searching the place. There was nothing unusual or out of place until I lifted a set of underwear in the bottom drawer and found a framed photograph face down beneath it. The picture showed the Nazi leader Adolf Hitler addressing a large open-air rally of the sort that was becoming increasingly common in Germany.

"What's that?" Mrs. Goutski asked.

"Just a picture." I returned it to the drawer. "I guess there's nothing much here."

"He didn't have much. He was a lonely man nobody cared about."

"Somebody cared enough to kill him," I reminded her.

* * *

Later, back at my office, I told Mary Best what I'd found. "He had a framed picture of Hitler hidden in his dresser drawer. That struck me as a bit unusual."

"I've read in the papers that the Bund is very active these days—the German-American Volksbund. With Germany mobilizing for possible war, they want to keep America out of it."

I thought about that. Lenny Blue hardly seemed a typical Bund member, but I'd never met any of them personally, so how would I know? "Bund or not, what was he doing at a roadhouse that doesn't exist, and why was he killed in such a way as to frame the Tobers for it?"

"They just happened along," Mary suggested. "It couldn't have been planned in advance."

"Then where is this roadhouse? We went over every inch of Turk Hill Road—"

"Then it's not on Turk Hill Road. It's somewhere else."

"His wife saw the sign."

"Signs can be changed. Let's drive out there and look at that signpost right now."

It seemed like a good idea, especially since I was at a dead end. It was not the first time that Mary had put me on the right track. We drove out Fairfax Road in my car and pulled onto the grass to park near the sign with the arrow pointing up Turk Hill Road.

Mary tried to shake the signpost without success. It wouldn't budge. Then she got down on her knees and poked around in the tall grass surrounding it. "This hasn't been moved," she decided finally. "The dirt hasn't been disturbed anytime recently."

"So much for that theory."

But Mary Best didn't give up that easily. "They could have used a fake signpost at one of the other roads. As long as we're here, let's check."

We spent the next half-hour carefully inspecting the ground opposite North Road and South Road. There was no hole, no evidence of tampering. "There was no signpost recently at either of these locations. If they saw the sign for Turk Hill Road, that's what it was."

So we drove over the road once more, slowing to a stop at the driveway into the Tober farm. "They seem to think it was almost across the street from their place," I said. "I saw nothing from the car but let's walk around over there."

We strolled around for another twenty minutes, but there was nothing. Where the roadhouse parking lot would have been there was only a strip of grass, then a field of fir trees standing in stately lines. In another year they'd probably be cut and sold for Christmas trees in the city.

"No roadhouse here," I said. "If it wasn't for the body, I'd say the Tobers were both drunk last night."

"But there is that inconvenient body."

We drove back to the office and I phoned Sheriff Lens. "Any new developments, Sheriff?"

"I tried to call you, Doc. The D.A.'s not satisfied with Jack Tober's story. He thinks Tober and Lenny Blue got into a fight and Tober shot him, then made up the story about the accident in hopes that the bullet wound wouldn't be noticed with the other injuries."

"Tober's wife backs his story."

"Wives do that, don't they?"

"How well did you search Lenny Blue's room?"

"I didn't search it at all, just looked around. I told Mrs. Goutski we'd send for his things."

"I looked around too. Blue had a picture of Hitler in one of his drawers."

"You think the killing was political? In his story about last night Tober mentioned arguing with Dave Foster about the Spanish Civil War."

I'd remembered that too. "Maybe I should talk with Foster. You're not going to arrest Jack Tober today, are you?"

"Well—"

"Hold off a bit, will you? I want to find the Apple Orchard first."

"Doc, there is no Apple Orchard. This isn't one of your impossible crimes. It's just a killer telling a lie."

"Maybe, maybe not. Give me till morning before you do anything."

"All right," he agreed reluctantly. We'd been through a lot together and he respected my opinions. "But I'll have to move on this tomorrow."

Dave Foster worked at the gas station across from the town square. I found him just sending a satisfied customer on his way with one of the red fireman's helmets they were giving away that month. He was a pleasant fellow in his late thirties and I had no idea what his politics were.

"Dr. Hawthorne! Shall I fill 'er up?"

I emerged from the Buick. "Do that, Dave. I wanted to ask you something while I'm here."

"What's that?"

"You saw Jack Tober and his wife at the Grange dance last night, didn't you?"

"Sure. We had a couple of beers, talked about things."

"The Spanish Civil War?"

A slow smile spread across his face. "I didn't think he'd remember. See, I was chatting with that lady who runs the fruit stand, Aunt Peachy, and the Tobers came over. She'd just said something about Franco, seemed pleased that he'd captured Vinaroz back in April. I was talking about it and Jack had just enough beer in him to make an argument of it. He's like that when he drinks. We left the women and the table and went outside to cool off. I thought for a minute he was going to fight me, but he was all right." He pushed the nozzle of the gasoline hose into the car's tank and squeezed the handle. I watched the fuel bubbling past the little window on the pump. "Pretty soon he went back to join the ladies and he bought beers all around."

"What time was all this?"

"Around ten-thirty, I think. Becky wanted to get going and they left soon after that."

I nodded. Jack Tober had said they left just after eleven. "Did you know Lenny Blue well?"

"He came by the station and we talked sometimes. Can't say I knew him well. He was a bit weird."

"Did he ever go to the Grange dances?"

Foster snickered and finished filling my tank. "Can't say I ever saw Lenny with a girl."

I paid for the gas and drove back toward the hospital and my adjoining office. I'd collected lots of information about the previous night, but I still didn't know what had really happened. I still didn't know how a roadhouse could appear for a brief time and then vanish, leaving no trace except a dead man with a bullet in his head.

As I entered the office I was surprised to find Jack Tober waiting for me. "Hello, Jack. Any messages, Mary?"

She shook her head. "Just Mr. Tober. He phoned earlier and then came in to wait for you."

"Come into my office, Jack. Is Becky with you?"

"She's at the sheriff's office, waiting for them to release our car. I told her I'd see her at home. This business has lost me a whole day of work."

It was almost five o'clock, later than I'd realized, and I told Mary, "You go on home. I'll lock up." Then I turned my attention back to Jack. "How can I help you? Is it a medical problem?"

"It's just this damned killing. I know Sheriff Lens doesn't believe me. I'm afraid he's going to charge me with murder. He's been talking to people at the Grange Hall and some of the bars about how I get belligerent after a few beers."

"Do you?"

"Not often. I've had one or two fistfights, but never anything with a gun. I don't even own a gun except for a hunting rifle I use during deer season."

"What do you want me to do, Jack?"

"I read about how doctors can determine the time of death with a fair amount of accuracy. Maybe the autopsy can show Blue was dead hours before we got to the roadhouse."

I shook my head. "I've read the entire report. Time of death was estimated at somewhere around eleven o'clock—maybe a half-hour before you reached the hospital with him."

"Doesn't Becky's word count for anything?"

"The person you really need is the mysterious man in the peaked cap. He must know more than he admitted at the time." I thought of something else. "These fistfights you mentioned—were any of them with Lenny Blue?"

"Of course not! I didn't even know him."

"But you know Sy Holden."

"Sure, I know Sy. What about it?"

"It just seems like a coincidence that his barn burned to the ground the same night as the killing."

"A barn's not a roadhouse."

"No, it isn't," I agreed. "I'm leaving now. Want a ride home?"

"It's out of your way."

"I don't mind. Maybe we can get an idea on the way."

We headed up Fairfax Road, once more retracing the route Tober had taken the previous night. It was when we'd reached the corner of Turk Hill Road, as I was about to turn left, that a green roadster came down the hill fast and Jack Tober gripped my shoulder. "It's him! It's the man from the roadhouse!"

I saw the face in profile, saw the peaked yachting cap, and spun my car around in pursuit, laying on the horn. The car ahead turned right toward town, increasing its speed rather than stopping. He was hogging the middle of the road, making it impossible for me to pull alongside or cut him off. Suddenly he swerved to the right, onto South Road. I went past and hit my brakes, losing precious seconds. By the time I was on the road after him the car had disappeared in a cloud of dust.

"He's up ahead," Tober said, stating the obvious. "He knows we've spotted him!"

"I don't know that I can catch him on these roads. I'm no race driver."

"Let me take the wheel. I'll catch him."

"No thanks," I said, visions of my overturned car making me cautious. At the same time, my refusal to let him drive seemed to obligate me to try harder. I knew my car could win on a paved highway, and it should do it on a dirt road as well. Finally we caught up with the cloud of dust and I knew I was close—so close that I seemed to drive right through him. The dust cleared and he was nowhere in sight!

"He turned off somewhere," Tober shouted.

"There's not even a driveway on this stretch."

But I was wrong, of course. I'd forgotten the little weed-grown path to the ruins of Sy Holden's barn. I'd passed the spot in the cloud of dust without even realizing it. Backing up now, I spotted the car parked behind some bushes. "Hang on!" I told him, barreling through the weeds.

"There he is!" Tober pointed, and I saw the man in the cap leave the car and run into a field of corn.

We were both out of the car and after him in an instant. We seemed to know it was our last best hope of solving the mystery. But August corn is high in this part of the state, and the summer weather had encouraged its growth. The man in the cap had vanished in a maze of corn stalks. We searched for twenty minutes before admitting we'd lost him.

I'd been careful to prevent him from circling around to his car, but apparently he'd made no attempt at that. The dark green roadster had a rumble seat which I discovered was unlocked. I pulled it open and looked inside, but there was only a large black cloth and a hand-painted sign which read Private Party—Closed to the Public.

"Anything there?" Jack Tober asked.

"Not much, but maybe it's enough."

* * *

I dropped Tober off at his farm and drove back into town, heading directly for the sheriff's office. He seemed pleased to see me. "You got anything on the Tober case?"

"I might have. Let's look at your map of the county."

"What's a map gonna tell us, Doc?"

"We'll see." I went to the wall behind his desk and studied the roads I'd been driving on all day. It was a large-scale map and Sheriff Lens, with industrious foresight, had at some past time marked off the various farms with colored pencils. I traced my finger over the properties, trying to imagine each one.

"What are you after?" he asked.

"Sy Holden had a barn fire early this morning."

"Hobos have been sleeping there. I chased some out a couple of weeks back."

"Sy's farmhouse and main barn are on the highway, but the farm runs all the way through to South Road. That's where he had the extra barn that burned."

"All those farms run through. See, Tober's place goes all the way through to North Road. This is all his property, except for this green rectangle where Aunt Peachy has her big fruit stand."

"Did you ever think of that fruit stand as a roadhouse, Sheriff?"

"What? That's crazy, Doc. Tober told us they had a neon sign, and there was music and voices coming from inside. And six or eight cars in the lot. The stand is big, but not that big."

"Let's take a ride out there and see. Do you have a couple of deputies who could follow in a second car?"

He grinned at me. "You want a show of force, is that it?"

"Something like that."

I left my car at the sheriff's office and went in his car with the deputies following. It was after six when we reached Aunt Peachy's fruit stand. Most of her bins were virtually empty and she was beginning to close down the glass windows along the front of the building. "I just got a few plums and cherries left," she told us. "You should have come earlier."

Sheriff Lens stepped up to her. "We want to ask you a few questions, Aunt Peachy."

"Questions?"

"About the Bund meetings you've been holding here," I said.

I'd thought she would deny it, but she stood up to us and said quite calmly, "This is a free country, isn't it? We're not violating any law in expressing our friendship with Germany."

"Then why keep the meetings such a secret?" I wanted to know. "Why disguise the place to look like a roadhouse, complete with music? I think if we look around under your counters we'll find the neon sign for the Apple Orchard and a phonograph for playing the music Jack Tober heard. Maybe the voices too. All those cars at a fruit stand in the middle of the night would have attracted attention, so on Bund nights the stand was transformed into an ersatz road-house."

I strolled into the place as I spoke, and she tried to block my way. "You got a search warrant?"

"I don't need one. I'm not a police officer."

She thought about that, her sharp eyes studying each of us, taking in the other two deputies who'd emerged from their car. "Search all you want," she decided finally. "You won't find anything."

She was almost right. There was nothing behind the counters but empty boxes and wooden crates. The low building, about thirty feet long and ten feet deep, hardly afforded any other hiding places. There was a closed door at the rear, though, and when I made for that Aunt Peachy squealed with fright. The door opened suddenly and the man we'd pursued earlier, minus his cap, came through it holding a gun. That was when I knew we had them.

"This is my nephew Otto," she said. "He's visiting from New York. Otto, put down that gun."

He hadn't seen the other troopers till then. There were three guns on him in an instant and he decided to follow his aunt's suggestion.

"Now suppose you tell us about killing Lenny Blue," the sheriff said.

We phoned Jack and Becky Tober that evening to tell them what happened, but it wasn't until the following morning that Sheriff Lens and I drove out to their farm to explain in detail. Becky brought coffee and donuts to the kitchen table while we talked about the missing roadhouse.

I showed them the hand-painted sign I'd found in Otto's roadster. "*Private Party*. This was in case some strangers happened by during their meetings. It was enough to make me believe your story—that and the tire tracks on Lenny's body. They showed he wasn't hit by the car but was already lying down when you ran over him. So I started looking for this phantom road-house. Holden's barn was an unlikely candidate even before it was burned, probably by hobos. A barn is taller than a two-story house. It could hardly be mistaken for the low building you described."

"What's that black cloth?" Tober asked.

"Since it was in Otto's rumble seat with the party sign, I think it was used to cover up the sign pointing to Turk Hill Road. Covered up like that, you'd easily miss it on a cloudy night. Now there'd be no point in covering the sign if the roadhouse was on South Road or Turk Hill. If you were being lured further along, it had to be beyond Turk Hill, on North Road. What was on North Road? Aunt Peachy's fruit stand, and we'd heard that Aunt Peachy herself supported Franco, as does Hitler. If there was a Bund involved, she could have knowledge of it."

"Why didn't I notice it wasn't my road?"

"You'd been drinking, as you admitted yourself. But in a way you did notice. You said the road seemed narrower every time you drove it, and North Road is a bit narrower and rougher than Turk Hill."

Sheriff Lens took over at this point. "Aunt Peachy and Otto haven't made a full statement yet, but it appears that Lenny Blue was acting unstable and threatening to report some of their activities to the police. One day he was a big Hitler backer and the next day he wanted nothing to do with the Bund."

I nodded. "The picture in the drawer."

"Exactly. They lured you two up there by covering over the sign-post point-ing to your road. You missed the road and took the next one, ending up at the supposed roadhouse. In the dark, with the neon sign temporarily in place and a hidden phonograph furnishing the proper music, you never rec-ognized Aunt Peachy's fruit stand. After all, the front of the stand is usually open when people see it in the summer."

"What did they have to fear from someone like Lenny Blue?" Jack asked. "They weren't violating the law."

"Not yet, but they had plans for the future. The fruit stand could only hold twenty or so people for meetings," the sheriff continued. "They wanted hundreds, thousands. They wanted to hold the biggest German-American Bund rally in the state."

"Amazing," was all that Tober could say.

"Blue was shot to death, probably by Otto, shortly before you arrived. One of his men placed the body under your rear tires while Otto distracted you. They figured when the bullet was found no one would believe your story."

"I should feed the chickens," Becky said, glancing at the clock. "There are always chores for a farm wife."

I smiled and said I'd go with her. "I've never really seen your place."

"There's nothing to see but a few chickens and a lot of apple trees."

She picked up a pail of feed and we strolled out to the backyard while the sheriff continued talking to Jack. "I still can't believe all of this really happened," she said.

"I had trouble believing it too," I told her. We'd reached the hen-house and Becky threw a few handfuls of feed as the chickens came running out for it. "I had trouble believing Otto and Aunt Peachy could ever be sure of luring you up there. And I had trouble believing that Aunt Peachy would miss an important Bund meeting just to attend a Grange dance. She was not only there, but Dave Foster told me you two sat with her."

She stared at me blankly. "Did we?"

"Becky, you engineered this thing from start to finish, didn't you? It was your idea to frame Jack for Lenny Blue's murder. You've been a member of the Bund from the start."

"That's crazy! I'm his only witness!"

"And when his case came to trial you'd conveniently fail to testify. Since a wife can't be forced to testify against her husband, the jury would draw the conclusion that you were absent because you knew he was guilty."

"Why would I be working with those two? What could I gain?"

"This farm. I was looking at a county map yesterday, seeing how your orchard runs through to North Road where the fruit stand is. With Jack in prison and the farm in your possession, you were going to turn it over to Aunt Peachy and Otto for the giant rally they always wanted. Your orchard would be alive with the songs and chants and speeches of Nazi Germany."

"How do you hope to prove any of this?"

"You were alone with Aunt Peachy for a time at the Grange, working out the details. When you two started home, she phoned Otto at the fruit stand. He took Lenny outside and shot him, then watched for your car. You tried to drive home, to be certain you turned into North Road. He wouldn't let you, but that was still all right. He missed the covered-over sign, of course, and you simply told him the sign was at the next corner. It couldn't have been, though, because we examined the ground in that area. You simply lied about it. At the roadhouse you told Jack to back up the car, which was when he hit Lenny. You overcame Jack's reluctance to drive Lenny to the hospital. You guided him every step of the way, Becky. None of it could have happened without you. When I studied that map I realized it had something to do with the farm. You were using Aunt Peachy and Otto just as they were using you—each for your own ends. You'd be rid of Jack and they'd have a real home for the Bund at last."

"You actually expect Sheriff Lens to believe this?"

I threw a final handful of feed to the chickens. "He believes it. I told him on the way out here. Now let's go in and see if Jack believes it too."

THE PROBLEM OF
THE COUNTRY MAILBOX

THE autumn of '38 (Dr. Sam Hawthorne told his visitor) was a time when the national press was full of Chamberlain and the Munich Pact with Hitler. War was on the horizon, and if it retreated for a time most people realized that was only temporary. It would come, sooner or later, and the streets of Europe would run with blood.

Back home in Northmont, I was concerned with more prosaic matters that autumn. There were vaccinations to give and allergies to treat. We had more doctors practicing in town and there was a steadily growing population. We had not yet seen the boom that would come in the postwar years, but there were signs of change everywhere. A small private college was being built in a neighboring town, with plans to open its doors for the fall semester of 1939. Though that was still a year away, it had encouraged a man named Josh Vernon to open a bookstore in our town.

Josh's Books was a small store just off the town square. The previous tenant had been a shop selling penny candy out of large glass jars, and I imagined I could still smell the chocolate and licorice when I entered. Josh Vernon was a slender man with a graying moustache and pince-nez glasses that gave him a scholarly demeanor. I couldn't have imagined him as a butcher or baker, but he looked right at home among the bookshelves.

Though he carried a large stock of used books, Vernon also stocked the newest titles from New York and Boston publishers. If he had little space for Faulkner's *The Unvanquished* or Dinesen's *Out of Africa*, it was a place where one could find *Gone With the Wind*, *The Late George Apley*, and *The Yearling*. He knew what the market wanted and he supplied it.

"It'll be different next year when the college kids start coming around," he told me one day, puffing on his pipe. "If business goes well, I might be able to enlarge the place and carry more literary titles."

I took down a copy of Cronin's *The Citadel* and thumbed through it. I was naturally intrigued by novels about small-town doctors, even if the towns were an ocean away. "Is this any good?" I asked Josh.

"It's popular. I've sold three or four copies."

"I'll take it." I put down a few dollar bills and he wrapped it in his distinctive green paper and twine.

131

"I been hearing you're pretty good at solving mysteries, Doc. Some say you're better than Sheriff Lens."

"I've been lucky a few times," I admitted.

"I have a mystery that would baffle even you." He tapped his pipe on the ashtray to empty it, then opened his pouch of tobacco. "One of my regular customers is Aaron DeVille out on the Old Ridge Road. You know him, don't you?"

"Slightly. He's not a patient and he rarely comes to town."

The bookseller relit his pipe. "That's certainly true since his wife died. But he loves books. He subscribes to *The Saturday Review of Literature* and every week he phones to order something he's seen in there. I've been open two months and I've probably sold him a dozen books. Says he used to order them from Boston, but I'm a lot closer. Of course, sometimes I don't have the books he wants and I have to order them myself, but quite often I can stop by on my way home and drop them in his mailbox."

"That's what I call service."

"But here is where the mystery comes in, Doc. Three times now I have left books in his mailbox and they disappeared!"

"Perhaps the postman takes them," I suggested. "They get fussy when mailboxes are used for things other than mail."

"That was my first thought, but the mail is always delivered on that route around one in the afternoon. Kenny Diggins drives along the Old Ridge right after lunch and fills the boxes from his car. I don't close the store till six and it's usually closer to six-thirty when I drop off the books. DeVille is sometimes watching for me. One time he even waved from the front porch. Then he walked out to the box and it was empty."

"Are there any mischievous children who might be sneaking up and stealing the books?" DeVille had a twelve-year-old son.

"I can't see how, at least not in the most recent instance where he was watching the box all the time."

"Maybe you'd better start pulling into the driveway and handing him the books."

"Isn't this the sort of puzzle you like to solve?"

"Well, yes," I admitted. "But I don't see where any serious crime has been committed. If someone is stealing the books—"

"They certainly are!" he insisted. "Could I call you the next time I make a delivery out there? I'd appreciate it if you could figure out what's happening."

"Sure, you can me. If I'm not involved with a patient I'll try to help."

That seemed to satisfy him and I departed with my book. In the evening when I left the office I detoured on my way home and drove out the Old Ridge Road past Aaron DeVille's house. The mailbox sat on a raised wooden board with three others, inches apart. Each family's name was painted in small neat letters on the side of the box. DeVille's, one of the middle boxes, looked just like all the others.

* * *

Sylvia Grant was a bright young woman who worked part-time in Vernon's bookstore. She was in her twenties, with curly blond hair and eyeglasses with thin black frames that gave her face the appealing look of a studious pixie. Two days after my conversation with Josh Vernon I saw her crossing the town square near the bandstand.

"On your way to the bookstore?" I asked.

"Sure am! Want anything today, Dr. Sam?"

"I might walk over with you." I fell in beside her, though until that moment I hadn't thought about going there. "How's business at the store?"

"Fair. Josh thinks Christmas will be good, if we're not in a war by then."

"We won't be," I said with an assurance I didn't really feel. "Josh was telling me the other day that he's been having trouble delivering books out to Aaron DeVille's place. They keep disappearing out of the mailbox."

"That's what he says. Hard to believe, isn't it?"

"You mean you don't believe it?"

Sylvia shrugged. "DeVille's son is probably taking them somehow."

"Damon?"

"He's a bit precocious. He loves to baffle his dad with some sort of mystery."

"Whatever happened certainly seems to have bothered Josh."

"Well, he's the one who's had to replace the missing books. It's costing him money, a few dollars anyway."

"Do you think Aaron DeVille is lying about the books disappearing from his mailbox?"

"What would be his motive? To get a second copy? That doesn't seem likely."

We'd reached the bookstore and Sylvia Grant turned in. I said goodbye and continued on my way. I hadn't given any thought to Josh Vernon's problem since driving past DeVille's mailbox. Whatever the explanation, it wasn't one that particularly concerned me.

Josh phoned the office the following afternoon while I was with a patient. My nurse Mary told him I'd return the call and I felt obliged to do so. "How are you, Josh?" I asked when he answered. "How's the book business today?"

"I've had another order from Aaron DeVille. He wants a copy of *War and Peace*."

"Do you have one?"

"Yes, in the Modern Library edition. I told him I'd bring it out tonight on the way home. He suggested I bring it right to the door, but I want to leave it in the mailbox while you watch and see what happens."

I was convinced nothing would happen while I was watching, but I reluctantly agreed. "I'll stop by the store a little before six," I promised, "when I finish up here."

At five, when I'd seen my last patient, Mary Best came into my office to say she was going home. "You're going over to Josh's bookstore now?"

"I guess so. Sometimes I think I'm too nice to say no to people."

"Sylvia Grant thinks you're nice."

I chuckled. "You know Sylvia?"

"We go to the movies occasionally. She's very friendly."

"Has she mentioned this book business with Aaron DeVille?"

Mary became occupied with the patient files on her desk. "You mean the books disappearing out of the mailbox? She mentioned it."

"You probably know more about DeVille than I do. Wasn't his wife killed by a truck?"

Mark Best nodded. "Two years ago next week. She was driving Aaron's Ford down the Old Ridge Road when she was broadsided by a truck loaded with pumpkins."

"I remember now. People were talking about the pumpkins rolling all over the road."

"It was funny to some, I suppose, but not to Aaron DeVille and Damon."

"The boy's twelve now. I see him in town sometimes. He would have been ten when it happened."

"That's right. He's a smart lad, very personable for his age."

"What was his mother's name?"

"Rachel. Rachel DeVille."

"A biblical name, like Aaron." I said good night to Mary and went out to my car.

It was only a five-minute drive from my office at the hospital to the center of town. At that time of day I could park right in front of Josh's Books. He was waiting for me by the door, ready to close for the night. "Thanks for coming, Doc."

"Ready to go?"

"I just have to wrap the book."

I followed him over to the counter and thumbed through the pages of Tolstoy's massive novel. "Haven't had to read this since college."

"It hasn't changed much," the bookseller said with a smile. He pulled a couple of feet of his trademark green paper down from the roll, ripped it off, and placed the book in the center. The wrapping took only seconds and he finished it off with a length of matching green twine. "All set!" He handed the book to me. "You bring that, Doc, and we'll be on our way."

"Is DeVille always this classical in his choices of reading matter?"

"No. In fact, the three books that disappeared were all modern novels— Steinbeck's *Of Mice and Men*, Graham Greene's *Brighton Rock*, and *Rebecca* by Daphne de Maurier."

"Maybe you'll have better luck with this one."

I held the book on my lap during the journey out to the DeVille house. Like many of the homes along that stretch of Old Ridge Road, it had once been a farm. As neighboring farms expanded and bought up property, only the old farmhouses remained. The barn on the DeVille property had been torn down long ago, and a storage shed was now used as a garage. The house itself, some two hundred feet back from the road, was in need of painting, but otherwise it seemed in good shape.

Josh Vernon pulled up by the line of mailboxes. As I'd observed before, each name was painted on the side of a box: Chesnut, Millars, DeVille, Breen. "Put it right in the box, Doc. This is your show."

I opened the mailbox and slid the book in. "Shall I put up the little red flag?"

"Better not. The post office could get really upset about that."

I turned to watch the boxes out the rear window as we drove on about fifty feet. Then Vernon stopped the car just beyond a clump of bushes. "Get out and watch. I'll drive on."

"Do you think I'll see someone?"

"DeVille will be out in a minute. I'm sure he saw us."

I got out quickly, still keeping an eye on the mailboxes. No one had approached them. Then, crouching down so I was partly hidden, I waited.

It didn't take long. A stocky man in his late thirties, whom I recognized as Aaron DeVille, came ambling down the driveway from the direction of the house. As he approached the mailbox I had to admit that I would be the most surprised man in the country if that book wasn't still inside.

DeVille paused before his box and opened it. From my viewing angle down the road I saw him pull the green-wrapped book out of the box and slip it into the pocket of his leather jacket. I almost sighed with relief. Josh Vernon had been wrong. This time, at least, the book hadn't vanished.

As he started back up the driveway DeVille seemed to have second thoughts about the book. He removed it from his pocket, untied the string, and ripped off the paper. I saw him start to open the cover. There was a terrible flash and a sound like a clap of thunder.

I broke from the cover of the bush and ran toward him, knowing even as I ran that Aaron DeVille was beyond the help of a doctor.

* * *

Sheriff Lens had been trying to lose weight that autumn, and it hadn't improved his disposition. He left it to his deputies to clean up what was left of Aaron DeVille while he questioned Josh Vernon and me. "You're telling me, Doc, that you were watchin' that mailbox the whole time and nobody came near it?"

"That's what I'm telling you, Sheriff."

He turned to Vernon, who was standing there pale and shaken. "There was a bomb inside that book you delivered, Josh. Looks to me like you're the only one who coulda put it there."

"But I couldn't have, Sheriff! Dr. Sam was with me when I wrapped it. I think he even flipped through the pages."

"That's right," I confirmed with some reluctance.

"He even held the book on his lap during the ride out here. It was never out of his sight."

Sheriff Lens looked at me with a sour expression. "That right, Doc?"

"I'm afraid so."

A few neighbors had been attracted by the explosion, and it was Marta Chesnut from across the road who said suddenly, "What about young Damon? He must still be at his piano lessons!"

Sheriff Lens scowled at her. "Could you go pick him up, Marta? I'll have my deputy drive you."

"Of course," she replied without hesitation.

While we waited for Damon's return the sheriff questioned the other neighbors, Millars and Breen, without learning anything. The three families occupied a trio of small cottage-type houses across the road from the DeVille home. The plots of land had been carved out of another piece of the DeVille farm when it was sold off by Aaron's father. They'd been having dinner when they heard the sound of the explosion and came running.

Sheriff Lens finished with them and came back to me. "What do you think, Doc?"

"I don't want to say, not quite yet."

"There was that case a few years back, the Fourth of July murder, when a firecracker had a stick of dynamite in it—"

"A different thing entirely. In that case the killer was nearby. No one was anywhere near Aaron DeVille. No one but me."

Our conversation was interrupted by the return of the sheriff's car carrying Mrs. Chesnut and the DeVille boy. It was obvious that she'd broken the news to him en route. He emerged crying from the car, clinging to her as she hurried him across the road to her house. "I think it's better if he stays with us tonight," Marta Chesnut explained to the sheriff. "He says there's an aunt in Hartford who should be contacted."

"We'll take care of it," Sheriff Lens assured her. "Could I just have a few words with him?"

"I think later would be better. He's had a terrible shock." Her husband had taken young Damon inside and she followed him.

"We'd better have a look inside the house," the sheriff said. "DeVille left the door open when he came out for the book."

I glanced at Josh Vernon, who'd been standing off to one side without speaking through all of this. "If you want to go along home, I'm sure the sheriff would give me a ride back."

He seemed reluctant to leave without permission from Sheriff Lens, who quickly gave it. "I know where to find you, Josh. Get along now and I'll drop by the store in the morning."

"Thanks, Sheriff." He trotted off to where he'd left the car, down the road.

"What do you think, Doc?" Lens asked again, patting his belly as if gauging the success of his weight reduction.

"Honestly?" I watched Josh's car drive away. "I think he suckered me somehow into delivering a book with a bomb in it, but for the life of me I can't figure out how he could have done it."

* * *

The inside of the house had the look of a bachelor's quarters. There was a bottle of bourbon on the coffee table along with a half-empty glass. A wall rack held three hunting rifles. And on either side of the stone fireplace were shelves of books, filled to overflowing. A pair of reading glasses was on the table next to the whiskey glass. The shelves were dusty and the windows dirty. The grass in the yard had been recently cut, but that only proved DeVille had a son to cut it. My eyes ranged over fiction, poetry, and books on building, hunting, guns, and explosives.

"What did DeVille do for a living?" I asked.

"Construction work, but lately he's been off. He got a settlement from the trucking company that killed his wife. He's been living off that."

I could see evidence of Rachel DeVille still present in the framed picture of smiling mother, father, and son on the mantel, and books like *Little Women* that still found a place on the shelves. I took it down and found her maiden name still on the leaflet—Rachel March. No wonder she was attracted to the Alcott novel, sharing the same last name as the book's family.

The kitchen showed signs of meal preparation, and the beds upstairs were unmade. The basement had the typical dirt floor of most farmhouses, with shelves holding a few jars of peaches and tomatoes no doubt left over from Rachel's time. Aaron had a work table in one corner with equipment for loading his own hunting cartridges. Sheriff Lens ran his finger over a container of gunpowder. "Everything's dusty. He hasn't been down here in a long time."

"Two years," I suggested, pointing out the hunting licenses tacked to the wall above the table. "The last one's thirty-six, the year his wife was killed. Looks like he lost interest in hunting after that." There were some old newspapers at the bottom of the stairs, dating back just a few months, that he or the boy must have brought down. A mousetrap sat under the steps, its bait moldy and its trap un-sprung. I wondered if anyone, even a mouse, had spent time down there in the last two years.

We went back outside where the deputies were cleaning away the last evidence of the explosion. "We want to have it decent before the kid comes back," the sheriff said.

"What about the book and the wrapping?" I asked.

"All burned up except for a few charred pieces for the lab to check."

I bent to retrieve a piece of burned newspaper. ". . . *sevelt Nominated by Acclaim* . . ." The rest of it was gone, blown away like Aaron DeVille.

"Before I can take you home, Doc, I'd like you to come with me and see if we can speak with young Damon."

"Of course."

It was starting to get dark as we crossed the road to the Chesnut house. Marta Chesnut answered the door. She glanced over her shoulder and said, "Come in. He's pretty good now."

Damon was a sandy-haired boy who seemed a bit thin and short for his age. Not surprisingly, his eyes were red from crying and he faced us now with a trembling lip. Sheriff Lens said a few words to relax him and then asked, "When did you last see your father, Damon?"

"This—this afternoon. I left for school at my usual time, about eight-thirty. I came home around three-thirty to pick up my music, and later my dad drove me to the piano lesson. He was supposed to pick me up at six-thirty but he never came. Mrs. Chesnut—"

"We know, son. That's all right."

I sat down next to him. "Damon, you know me, don't you? I'm Dr. Hawthorne. I know these questions are difficult, but we're just trying to learn what happened to your dad." He'd lost both his mother and father within two years and in his eyes I could see a desperate plea for help.

"Did someone kill him?" Damon asked.

"We think so. Was anyone at the house this afternoon when you came home? Anyone who might have fooled with the books?"

"No. When Mom was alive I could never touch the books, and Dad was still fussy about people handling them."

"Were there any recent visitors?"

He glanced away. "Not while I was there."

I wondered what that meant but decided not to pursue it at the moment. "What about the mail?" I asked instead. "Did your dad bring it in every day?"

"I guess so, yeah. I always looked in the box when I got home but it was usually empty."

"You looked even if the flag wasn't up?"

"Sure," he said with a shrug.

I looked up at Marta Chesnut. "You can take care of him overnight?"

"Of course." Her blue eyes sparkled. "We're planning to."

"I'll be out again in the morning," I promised.

Riding back to town with Sheriff Lens, I pondered the mailbox problem. "I think I should talk with Kenny Diggins tomorrow."

"The postman?"

"Yeah. There was a bomb in that book. Either Vernon switched packages on me somehow or it was done in the mailbox."

"You told me you were watching it the whole time."

"I was. Right now I don't know which of my alternatives is the more impossible."

* * *

I went out to the Chesnut house in the morning and talked to Damon again. He was doing pretty well and Marta told me his aunt and uncle would be arriving later that afternoon. They would stay for the funeral and then take the boy back to Hartford with them.

"Did he sleep all right?" I asked Marta when we were alone.

"I don't know. He was up roaming around some. I heard him go outside once, over to his house, but he wasn't gone long. I suppose he wanted to convince himself it wasn't all a terrible dream."

I went outside and crossed the road myself, stopping to examine the mailboxes closely for the first time. All four had been bolted to the stout board that supported them. The boxes on either end, for Chesnut and Breen, were beginning to work loose, but the middle two, for DeVille and Millars, were tightly bolted in place. Since three of the boxes were for houses across the road I wondered why DeVille's box was the second in line rather than being at one end or the other. It was already afternoon, so I decided to wait for Kenny to bring the day's mail.

Just before one I spotted his Chevy coming over the hill, stopping at each roadside mailbox to make a delivery and lift the flag. I walked out and hailed him as he reached the boxes in front of the DeVille house. "Hi, Doc," he greeted me. "What's this I heard about Aaron DeVille?"

"Someone put a bomb in his mailbox."

The postman stared at the box as if unable to believe such a thing, then gradually opened it to peer carefully inside. "It's against the law to put anything but mail into these boxes."

"Especially bombs," I pointed out.

"Yeah." He scratched his head. "I heard Josh Vernon was delivering a book to him. You know, that Vernon is always putting things in the mailboxes that he's not supposed to."

"Ever see anyone else doing it?"

He thought about it. "Just kids once in a while. If I catch them I give 'em a good scolding." As he spoke he was slipping mail into the boxes. He put a few bills and *The Saturday Review of Literature* in DeVille's box.

"He's dead," I reminded him.

"I go by the book, Doc. Nobody's notified the post office to stop delivery."

"Tell me something, Kenny. How come the DeVille mailbox is second in the row instead of at the end? The other houses are all across the street."

"That's easy. DeVille was always here. Then they built the Chesnut house and their box went next to his. When the other two families moved in a few years later, their boxes went on the other side of DeVille. I guess they just put 'em there for no special reason."

As he drove on I noticed another car coming over the hill. It was traveling fast, raising a cloud of dust behind it. When the driver saw me he pulled to a stop. "You Sheriff Lens?" he asked. He was in his mid-thirties, dressed for the city in suit and tie and hat. The woman next to him wore a plain black dress and hat.

"No, I'm Dr. Sam Hawthorne. You'd be the DeVille family from Hartford?"

"That's correct. They phoned about my brother—"

"A terrible tragedy. I can't tell you how sorry I am."

"The boy—Damon?"

"Staying with neighbors across the street. Pull into the driveway and we'll walk over."

It was the woman, Florence, who hurried to the boy. Zach DeVille hung back as if unsure of himself. "We'll give him a good home, of course," he tried to reassure me.

"Were you close to your brother?"

"Not really. He was five years older: the first, as you probably gathered from his name. I was the last. Our folks did things like that."

He said a few words to his nephew and then left him in his wife's care. "Would you like to see the house?" I asked.

"I suppose I should. Florence and I will get the job of cleaning it out and selling it. And we'll be staying there till the funeral."

"Aaron had no other relatives?"

"None."

I went back to the Chestnut house and got the key from Marta. Then Zach DeVille and I went in. "Sorry about the liquor bottle. The deputies didn't bother cleaning up."

"I've seen plenty of them before around Aaron."

"What was he like when he drank?"

"Miserable to Rachel when she was alive. Gave her a black eye once. She called me long distance that night and I had to talk to him."

"What about the night she died?"

"I think she was running away from him, but what difference does it make? Her death was clearly an accident. There was nothing anyone could do to Aaron."

"Somebody did something to him. They blew him away."

Zach DeVille glanced around the room and shrugged. "Maybe he found another woman, one who didn't like being pushed around."

I thought about that as we walked back over to the Chestnut house. When Zach and Florence took Damon back home I asked Marta if I could have a word with her outside. "What is it?" she asked.

"Your front window is right across the road from the DeVille house. You must have noticed his comings and goings, things like visitors."

"He didn't have many visitors."

"Young Damon hinted there might have been someone."

"Oh, there was that woman from town. She came out occasionally. Damon probably didn't like her."

"What woman from town?"

"The one who works at Vernon's bookstore. I think her name is Sylvia."

* * *

I had no patients scheduled the following morning so I dropped by the sheriff's office early. Sheriff Lens was pondering the report from the state police laboratory, where he'd sent the charred remains of the bomb. "You might find this interesting, Doc," he said as he passed the report to me. "It's only preliminary. They got more tests to run."

I glanced over the pages, "A mousetrap?"

"A mousetrap set to go off when the book's cover was opened. That in turn set off a detonator and exploded a charge of gunpowder. The whole thing was packed in with newspaper to keep the gunpowder from spilling out."

I remembered finding a piece of charred newspaper. But the most interesting part of the report proved to be about the book itself. The center had been hollowed out to make room for the mousetrap and gunpowder, but it was not a copy of *War and Peace*. It was Pearl Buck's *The Good Earth*. "Josh couldn't have switched books on me," I insisted.

"Someone did, and you claim no one else approached the mailbox until Aaron DeVille removed the book. He sure didn't kill himself."

"Maybe he did." I was grasping at straws now. "He slipped the book into the pocket of his jacket and then took it out again and unwrapped it. Maybe he switched packages."

But Sheriff Lens shook his head. "He had three rifles hanging over the fireplace, and it's not as awkward as you might think to kill yourself with one. A lot easier than buildin' a bomb and hollowing out a book to put it in. Besides, what happened to *War and Peace?*"

I had to agree he was right. "Did the wrapping match the paper Josh uses?"

"Identical, though I suppose anyone could have gotten it by simply buying a book."

I shook my head. I still came back to Josh. And now I thought I might have his motive. I left the sheriff's office and walked down the street to Josh's Books.

Sylvia Grant was working behind the counter. There was no sign of Josh. "He's gone over to the funeral parlor to pay his respects. It's a closed coffin, of course. Mr. DeVille is being buried tomorrow."

"Did you know him well?" I asked casually, thumbing through Van Doren's impressive biography of Benjamin Franklin.

"Hardly at all, just as a voice on the telephone."

"That's odd, because one of the neighbors told me you used to go out to his house occasionally."

Sylvia took off her glasses and stared at me. Maybe she could see me better without them. "I might have gone there once or twice to deliver books."

"No, I got the impression these visits were more personal. They were usually when Damon was away, but he knew about them."

Her pretty face froze into a noncommittal mask. "What are you trying to do to me, Dr. Sam?"

"Just get at the truth."

"My God, do you think I killed him?"

"No, but you might have supplied the motive. I'm sorry to ask you these personal questions, Sylvia, but they've become important. I need to know about your relations with Josh—and with Aaron DeVille.

She shook her head, laughing now. "My relations with Josh are strictly employee-employer. I've never even had a drink with the man. Frankly, I doubt if he cares too much about women."

"All right. What about DeVille?"

"He was almost twice my age but we liked each other. I won't deny it. I think it had pretty much run its course, though. He was looking for a wife and I didn't see him as a husband for me."

"Thank you for being honest with me," I said. "I was thinking Josh might be jealous about—"

The door opened and he walked in, cutting short our conversation. "I'm glad you stopped by, Doc. I have another book here that might interest you."

I winked at Sylvia and turned my attention to Josh. "Were you over at the funeral parlor?"

"Yes. A terrible thing, really. The more I think about it the more it seems he must have killed himself. How else could it have happened?"

"I've been talking to Sheriff Lens. The bomb was in a copy of *The Good Earth*. If he killed himself, Josh, what happened to *War and Peace*?"

He thought about that. "Damned if I know."

Sylvia had moved away, tactfully, to arrange the window display.

"It's a mighty thick book to just disappear," I said, and even as I spoke the words I knew how it was done, and who had done it.

* * *

The funeral was scheduled for the following morning, and I needed to consult with Sheriff Lens about how to proceed. It was going to be difficult, either way. When I told him my suspicions, and went over it all bit by bit, he could only shake his head.

"You're bringing this to me, Doc?"

"I'm just asking, would it be better to make an arrest now, or wait till after the funeral in the morning?"

"After the funeral," he decided grimly. "I'll do it then."

There was a typical autumn chill in the air the following morning as the mourners gathered about the gravesite. Aaron DeVille was buried alongside his wife Rachel as the minister intoned words of final rest. I heard a few murmurs about the shortness of the wake, but most people seemed glad to have it over with. All of DeVille's neighbors were present, along with his brother and sister-in-law and Damon. Josh Vernon and Sylvia Grant had come too, apparently locking the bookstore for a few hours. Even Kenny Diggins was there, watching from the road where he'd parked his car before resuming his mail route.

Most everyone went back to the DeVille house afterwards. The neighbors had brought food, a country custom, and most people sat outside eating despite the chilly breeze. Sheriff Lens and I walked around the back of the house, where I spotted young Damon attacking some dead flowers with a stick.

"Come here, boy," I said kindly. "I want to talk to you." The sheriff stood off to one side as I put my arm around his shoulders. "I know it's a bum day when they bury your dad."

He muttered something, head down. I went on, gripping his shoulders just tightly enough so he couldn't break away. "It's an especially bad day when you know it was you who caused his death."

"Me? I didn't—" He tried to jerk away but I held him fast.

"Sylvia Grant told me you liked to baffle your dad with mysteries. This was just the sort of thing to appeal to you, making books disappear out of mailboxes. Then you decided to carry it one step further, causing a copy of *War and Peace* to turn into *The Good Earth*, all while the mailbox was being watched. It took me awhile to figure out how you did it, but I should have guessed it a lot sooner. I put a thick copy of *War and Peace* in that box, but a moment later your dad removed a book slim enough to slip into his jacket pocket, slim enough that even he must have realized it was a mistake. He unwrapped it on the spot, there in the yard, setting off the bomb you'd carefully planted."

"*No!*" the boy screamed. "I didn't mean to kill him. I didn't mean to! I didn't—"

"It took me the longest time to realize that you switched the books, Damon, in the same way that you caused the earlier ones to vanish. You did it simply by switching mailboxes."

He was breathing heavily, trying to break away, and Sheriff Lens moved in on his other side. "Just calm down, son. We'll let you make a statement after we talk to your aunt and uncle."

"I noticed yesterday that the boxes for your house and the Millars's place were tightly bolted down while the end ones were loose. That told me something when I thought about it later. It told me they'd been tampered with, loosened, removed—and transposed. Kenny delivered the mail around one. You got home at three-thirty and simply switched your mailbox with the

Millars, putting them back in their correct positions after dark. Josh Vernon would drive up, look at the names, and deliver his books to the third box from the left, just as I did the day your father died. Naturally your dad, used to the position of the box, second from the left, opened it without bothering with the names. He came out that day without his reading glasses, so the names on the boxes were probably a blur to him anyway. The first three times the Millars' box—the one he opened by mistake—was empty. The last time, the bomb was in it, made from material you found around your own basement—a mousetrap, gunpowder from your father's cartridge reloading. When you put the boxes back in position the other night—Marta Chesnut heard you go across to your house—you made the mistake of tightening the nuts and bolts too much. They were different from the others."

Sheriff Lens had one question. "Why didn't any of the neighbors see him making the switch in the afternoons, Doc?"

"He probably loosened the bolts earlier, so he only had to give them a quick turn and lift the boxes. His body would have shielded the action from across the street. They'd think he was just checking for mail, if they noticed it at all."

Damon was crying now, heavy gasping sobs that seemed to shake his entire body. "I didn't do it, I didn't kill him!"

"You had the paper from Josh's store because you'd stolen the earlier books. Why'd you pick *The Good Earth?* Just because it was the right size to fit the wrapping for one of the earlier books?"

"That's enough, Doc," Sheriff Lens decided. He took the sobbing boy and led him away.

I was breathing hard myself, trying to calm my emotions. It was a terrible thing to accuse a twelve-year-old boy of killing his father. Had he done it because of the cruelty to his mother years earlier, or because he felt that Sylvia Grant was gradually taking his mother's place? I walked away from the DeVille house, through the tall weeds, because I hadn't really come to grips with the motive yet. If he resented the beating of his mother he would have acted much earlier than this, wouldn't he? Sylvia had said he liked to baffle his dad. That implied trickery. Any one of the tricks could have been deadly before this. And if he resented Sylvia he would have acted against her and not his father.

I went over the reasoning again in my own mind, remembering the position of the mailboxes clearly. I'd placed the book in the third box in line, the one with DeVille's name on it. Later the second box had carried his name. The boxes had been switched, and only Damon DeVille could have done it. He was trying to baffle his father with another mystery. Everything fit. The material for the bomb had come from the DeVille basement, where the killer must have had access to it. Therefore the killer had to live in the house. Certainly DeVille wouldn't have left Sylvia alone in the house long enough for her to fashion a bomb, even if she'd had a motive. No, it had to be a member of the household. There were only the two of them, Aaron and Damon. I'd shown it couldn't be suicide, so that only left Damon—

"Damon!"

How could I have been so wrong?"

I ran through the grass and weeds, calling his name as I reached the house. It was Sheriff Lens who told me he was in the sheriff's car with his Uncle Zach. He'd admitted switching the mailboxes and the books, but denied any knowledge of the bomb.

I ran out to the car and yanked open the rear door where the boy sat with his uncle. "Damon, you'll have to forgive me. I had it all wrong. Because it had to be you who switched the boxes, I jumped to the conclusion you assembled the bomb. It wasn't you. It was never you."

"Then who was it?" Zach DeVille demanded.

"Rachel DeVille killed her husband, even though she's been dead nearly two years."

* * *

Sheriff Lens was shaking his head sadly. "You almost made a terrible mistake, Doc. We all did."

I was staring out the window of his car as we drove back to town. "The motive didn't work out for Damon, but it did for his mother, who'd been beaten and abused by Aaron DeVille. I said the makings of the bomb were in the basement, but there were no detonators there. A detonator isn't the sort of thing a boy comes up with. And what about the other things? I saw a mousetrap in the DeVille basement that probably hadn't been touched in a couple of years. And there was a thick layer of dust on the containers of gunpowder. More than that, a charred bit of newspaper used as packing for the bomb had a headline about Roosevelt's renomination, dating it from late June of 1936—more than two years ago. Yet the old newspapers in the basement only went back a few months."

"She made the bomb back then?" Sheriff Lens asked. "Before she died in that accident? How'd she even know how to assemble it?"

"Probably from one of her husband's books. I saw one there on guns and explosives. She probably did it in a moment of controlled rage, then put *The Good Earth* back on the shelf and waited. The ten-year-old Damon was forbidden to touch the books, so she knew only her husband would be likely to open it. If he didn't, I'm sure she had another scheme. She might phone him and say, 'I'm leaving you. There's a letter in *The Good Earth* explaining everything.' As fate would have it, she died before she could complete her plan."

"How do you know Damon didn't find the bomb in the books and follow through with his mother's plan?"

"Because if he'd opened that book he'd be dead now instead of Aaron."

As we drove back to town I remembered that photograph of the happy family at the DeVille house. I remembered Rachel's smiling face—a woman already punished for a crime she'd only now committed.

THE PROBLEM OF
THE CROWDED CEMETERY

I used to picnic in Spring Glen Cemetery in my younger days [Dr. Sam Hawthorne told his visitor over a suitable libation]. That was when the place was more like a park than a cemetery, bisected by a creek that flowed gently through it most of the year. It was only in the spring, with the snow melting on Cobble Mountain, that the creek sometimes overflowed and flooded part of the graveyard.

That was what happened following the especially harsh winter of '36. The flooded creek had so eroded the soil on its banks that several acres of cemetery land had been lost. I was a member of the cemetery's board of trustees at that time and when we met in the spring of 1939 it was obvious something had to be done.

"It's just been getting worse for the past three years," Dalton Swan was saying as he showed us photographs of the damage done by the flooded stream. He was the tall, balding president of the board, a rotating responsibility each of the five members had assumed at one time or another. Swan, a fiftyish bank president, was in the second year of his two-year term.

I shuffled the pictures in my hands before passing them to Virginia Taylor on my right. Aware of the cemetery's shaky financial underpinnings, I asked, "Couldn't this go another year?"

"Look at these pictures, Sam," Dalton Swan argued, "The Brewster family gravesite is almost washed away! Here, you can actually see the corner of a coffin among these tree roots,"

"Those coffins need to be dug up and moved," Virginia Taylor agreed. She was a tall, athletic woman in her thirties whom I often glimpsed on the tennis courts around town. The Taylor family had made their money growing tobacco all over the state of Connecticut but all it had earned them was the largest family plot in Spring Glen Cemetery.

We discussed it awhile longer, with Randy Freed, a trustee and the cemetery's legal counsel, suggesting we give it another month. "We simply can't justify this expense if there's another way out."

Dalton Swan scoffed at that, "The only other way is to let the Brewster coffins float down Spring Glen Creek. That what you want?"

Freed bristled, more at Swan's tone of voice than at the words. "Do what you want," he grumbled.

Swan called for a vote on the motion to move the endangered coffins. "I've already spoken with the Brewster family. They'll sign the necessary papers."

Miss Taylor, Swan, and I voted yes, along with Hiram Mullins, a retired real-estate developer who rarely spoke at our meetings. He sat there now with a sad smile on his face, perhaps remembering better days when creeks did not overflow their banks. The only negative vote came from Randy Freed.

"We'll proceed, then, as quickly as possible," Dalton Swan said. "Gunther can have the workmen and equipment here in the morning." Earl Gunther was the cemetery's superintendent, in charge of its day-to-day operation.

"You're making a mistake rushing into it like this," Freed told us. "A truck-load of dirt tamped down along the bank of the creek would be a lot easier than relocating those coffins."

"Until it washed away with the next heavy rain," Swan argued. "Be practical, for God's sake!"

It did seem to me that the lawyer was being a bit unreasonable and I wondered why. "If it'll help matters any," I volunteered, "I can be out here in the morning when the workmen arrive, just to make certain nothing is touched but the Brewster plot."

"That would help a great deal, Dr. Hawthorne," Virginia Taylor agreed. "We'd all feel better if there was some supervision on this besides Earl Gunther."

The superintendent had not been a special favorite of the trustees since a pair of his day laborers had been found drunk one morning, finishing off a quart of rye whiskey on the back of a toppled tombstone. Sheriff Lens had been called by some horrified mourners and he'd given the two a choice of thirty days in jail or a quick trip out of town. They'd chosen the latter, but the matter had come to the board's attention. Earl Gunther had been warned to stay on top of things if he wanted to keep his job.

After the meeting we sought him out in the house near the cemetery gate. It went with the job, though his office was in the building where we met. Earl's wife Linda ushered us in. "Dear, Dr. Hawthorne and Mr. Swan are here to see you."

Earl Gunther was a burly man with a black moustache and thinning hair. He'd been a gravedigger at Spring Glen for years before taking on the job of superintendent. None of the board had been too excited at the prospect, but he seemed to be the best man available. He was newly married to Linda at the time and somehow we felt she might help straighten him out. She had, but not quite enough.

The Spring Glen board of trustees only met quarterly. This April meeting would be our last till the traditional July outing at Dalton Swan's farm. It wasn't something that took a great deal of my time, and until now it had never involved anything other than the perfunctory board meetings. All that was about to change. "Dr. Hawthorne will be out in the morning to oversee the disinterment and reburial," Swan told the superintendent. "We don't foresee any problem."

Earl Gunther rubbed his chin. "I'll get a crew lined up, with shovels and a block and tackle. There are six coffins in the Brewster plot. That's gonna be an all-day job."

"It can't be helped. Someone from the family will be here for the reburial, probably with the minister."

"We'll do the best we can," the superintendent informed us.

Dalton Swan nodded. "I'm sure you will."

I drove back to the office where I had a couple of early afternoon appointments. "Any excitement at the meeting?" Mary Best asked, knowing there never was.

"Nothing much. I have to go out there in the morning while they move the Brewster plot. The creek's just eating away at the banks."

She glanced at my appointment book. "Shall I reschedule Mrs. Winston for the afternoon?"

"Better make it Friday morning if you can. There's no telling how long I'll be out there."

While I waited for my first patient I glanced at the newspaper headlines. Hitler was insisting on the return of Danzig and a war between Germany and Poland seemed a distinct possibility. Up here in Northmont such concerns were still far away.

Late that afternoon, as I was leaving my office, I saw Virginia Taylor coming out of the adjoining Pilgrim Memorial Hospital. She paused by her car, waiting till I reached her. "Will you be at Spring Glen in the morning?"

"I'm planning on it."

"That's good. The Brewster family is very concerned that the remains be moved in a dignified manner."

"I'm sure there'll be no problems. Whatever his other faults, Gunther is a good worker."

She nodded and motioned back toward the hospital building. "I do some volunteer work here on Tuesdays. It makes for a full day when there's also a board meeting." She belonged to one of Northmont's older families and spent much of her time with charitable causes. A few years back she'd been engaged to a young lawyer from Providence but they'd broken up, leaving her still unmarried. As often happened with unmarried women, her tennis and travel and volunteer work had managed to fill her life. The family tobacco business had long since been sold to others.

We chatted awhile longer and then she went off in the sporty little convertible she drove around town. I'd had a car something like it in my younger days.

In the morning I drove out to the cemetery, arriving before nine. Earl Gunther had a flatbed truck parked by the Brewster plot, its back loaded with shovels and picks, a block and tackle, and a bulky tarpaulin folded into a heap, A half-dozen workmen were just arriving on the scene, walking over from the main gate.

"Good to see you, Doc," Gunther greeted me with a handshake. "I'm using two crews of three men each. One will work on the creek side, digging into the bank. The other will dig in from the top to reach the other coffins. It'll probably take all morning and maybe longer."

I watched the crew by the creek as they shoveled away the soft dirt and cut through some of the tree roots with axes. The tombstones up above told me that the most recent of these graves was over fifteen years old, and a couple dated back to before the turn of the century. As one coffin finally came free an hour later the workmen hoisted it out with the block and tackle, guiding it onto the flatbed truck. After that the pace seemed to pick up. Before I knew it a second and third coffin had appeared on the flatbed, with a fourth being lifted from its resting place.

I'd wandered around the cemetery while the work was in progress, reading the names off the tombstones, remembering a few old patients whose lives I'd briefly prolonged. Finally, around noon, the last of the six coffins was pulled free of the tough oak roots that encircled it. I walked over to the truck as it was slid into place.

"Good work, Earl," I told him. "It looks like just one or two of the corners were damaged." These burials had been in the days before coffins were enclosed in metal vaults, and the older ones were showing evidence of their decades in the earth, even before the recent ravages of the flooded creek.

Still, all six seemed to be reasonably sound. Or at least I thought so before my probing fingers encountered something wet and sticky at the damaged corner of one coffin.

"What's this?" I asked Gunther. My hand had come away moistened by blood and for a moment I thought I'd cut myself.

"You bleeding?"

"I'm not, but this coffin is."

"Coffins don't bleed, Doc, especially after twenty or thirty years."

"I think we better open this one up." The lid was still firmly screwed down and my fingers were useless. "Do you have a tool of some sort?"

"It's just bones," the superintendent argued.

"We'd better have a look."

He sighed and went to get some tools. The lid was unscrewed and easily pried open. I lifted it myself, prepared for the sight of decay. I wasn't prepared for the bloody corpse that confronted me, jammed in on top of the stark white bones.

Impossibly, irrationally, it was the body of Hiram Mullins, who'd sat next to me at the board meeting not twenty-four hours earlier.

It was Sheriff Lens who offered the best commentary when he arrived to view the body less than an hour later. "You've really outdone yourself this time, Doc. How could a man who was alive yesterday end up murdered inside a coffin that's been buried for twenty years?"

"I don't know, Sheriff, but I damn well intend to find out." I'd been questioning Earl Gunther and the workmen while we waited for the sheriff's arrival, but they professed to know nothing. Earl seemed especially upset, nervously wiping the sweat from his brow though the temperature was barely sixty.

"How's the board goin' to react to this, Doc? Will I lose my job?"

"Not if we can show you weren't responsible. But you have to be completely honest with me, Earl. Had any of those graves been dug up during the night?"

"You saw the ground yourself, Doc, before they started digging. It hadn't been touched in years. There's no way a coffin could have been dug up and reburied without leaving traces."

"Did you know Hiram Mullins well?"

"Hardly at all. I saw him when he came to your board meetings, that was it. He seemed like a nice man. Never said much."

That was certainly true, and I used virtually the same words to describe Mullins to the sheriff when he arrived. Sheriff Lens peered distastefully at the body in the coffin and asked, "What do you think caused the wound?"

"Some sharp instrument like a knife, only the blade seems to have been longer and thicker. There's a great deal of chest damage and so much blood that it actually leaked out of this rotted corner of the coffin."

"Good thing it did, or the Brewsters would have been reburied and Mullins along with them." The sheriff had brought a camera with him and was taking some photographs of the crime scene. He'd been doing this recently, following techniques outlined in crime investigation handbooks. He might have been a small-town sheriff but he was willing to learn new things. "What do you know about Mullins?"

I shrugged. "No more than you, I imagine. He was around seventy, I suppose, retired from his own real-estate business. I never saw him except at the cemetery board meetings, every three months."

"His wife is dead and they had no children," the sheriff said. "But how do you think he got into that coffin, Doc?"

"I have no idea."

When I got back to my office I looked through my bookshelves until I found an Ellery Queen mystery I remembered from seven years earlier. It was called *The Greek Coffin Mystery* and it dealt with two bodies discovered in a single coffin. But the second body had been added before the original burial. It didn't help a bit with Hiram Mullins's killing. His body had been added to a coffin already buried for two decades.

Before long my telephone started ringing. The word was getting around. First to call was Randy Freed, the lawyer who served as legal counsel for Spring Glen. "Sam, what's this I hear about old Mullins?"

"It's true. We found his body in one of the coffins Gunther's crew dug up."

"How is that possible?"

"It's not."

"Look here, Sam—you're the last one I'd expect to believe in any sort of supernatural business. Maybe Earl Gunther's crew added the body after they dug up the coffin."

"I was there all the time, Randy, never more than a hundred feet away."

"Do you think Spring Glen could face any sort of liability from the Mullins family?"

"I don't know how much of a family there is, and he was clearly murdered. We just have to figure out how."

"I'll be in touch," Freed told me as he hung up.

The next call came from Dalton Swan, advising me that he was calling an emergency meeting of the cemetery board for the following day. "We have to get to the bottom of this. The board has to issue a statement of some sort and we have to pick someone to fill his place."

The latter didn't seem that urgent to me, since we only met quarterly. "Whatever you say, Dalton. I have some hospital visits in the morning but after that I'm free till afternoon."

"Let's say eleven o'clock, then. I've spoken with Virginia and that time is good for her."

"Fine."

Mary Best came in as I hung up, returning from a late lunch. "What's this business of two bodies in one coffin?" she asked immediately. "Is Spring Glen getting that crowded?"

"I suppose the news is all over town."

She sat down at her reception desk. "All I know is, it's another impossible murder with you right in the center of things again."

"Believe me, I didn't plan it that way. Until now, being a cemetery trustee was about the easiest position I ever held."

"The creek's the problem there. Maybe they should have gone in with Shinn Corners after all." The nearby town had wanted to develop a new regional cemetery serving both communities, but before anything could be decided the land was sold to a private college now under construction for a September opening.

"I never knew a thing about that till it was over," I admitted. "I don't know that anyone on the board did."

Mary had a way of thinking things through to their basics. "Would Earl Gunther have any reason for killing Mullins?" she asked.

"I can't imagine what it would be. The old man just sat there at the meetings, never said a word about Gunther or anyone else."

"Still, you don't think Gunther could be involved?"

"Maybe. But I don't picture Mullins going out to the cemetery to meet him at the crack of dawn. And even if he did, how would Gunther have gotten the body into a coffin buried six feet deep in firm, undisturbed earth?"

"Let me think about that while I type up the bills," she said. Mary was never one to admit defeat.

* * *

I waited around the hospital that afternoon until Doc Prouty completed the autopsy on old Hiram. There were no surprises. "Fully dressed except for collar and tie," he said as he washed up in the autopsy room. "It was a large, deep wound that encompassed the chest and heart. Went in under the rib cage, slanting up."

"What could make a wound like that? A broadsword?"

He chuckled. "Northmont isn't quite that far behind the times. There must be a lot of gardening tools around at the cemetery. I suppose a hedge trimmer could have done it."

"Can you estimate the time of death?"

"He'd eaten breakfast maybe an hour before he died."

"Breakfast?"

"Looks like toast and scrambled eggs."

"I was out there before nine."

A shrug. "People the age of Mullins, living alone, sometimes eat breakfast at four in the morning. I'd say he could have been killed anywhere between five and nine A.M. judging by the body temperature and such."

"Thanks, Doc."

I was halfway out the door when he said, "One more thing."

"What's that?"

"With a wound like this, there's no way the killer could have moved the body without getting blood on his clothes."

* * *

I phoned Sheriff Lens with the advance word on the autopsy results. I also told him about the blood. "Didn't notice blood on Gunther or any of his workmen," was his comment.

"Of course not. The killing couldn't have happened while I was there."

"Hiram Mullins drove a fancy Lincoln. Had one long as I can remember. We found it parked in his driveway."

"Well?"

"How'd he get out to the cemetery, Doc? He sure didn't walk at his age. Not in the dark."

It was only a couple of miles, and certainly walkable, but I admitted it was unlikely for someone like Mullins. That meant he'd probably been driven to the spot by his killer. It had been someone he knew and trusted to get him out that early in the morning. Would Earl Gunther have called him? One of the board members?

I finished talking to the sheriff and told Mary she could go home. I stayed awhile longer, puzzling over the life and death of a man I'd barely known, a silent man I'd seen four times a year and barely nodded to. I wondered if that ignorance was his fault or mine.

"Dr. Hawthorne?"

I looked up at the sound of my name and saw a young woman standing in the doorway. The light from the hall was at her back and it took me an instant to recognize Linda Gunther, Earl's wife. "Can I help you?" I asked, certain the reason for her visit must be medical.

"I just wanted to speak with you about Earl, and about what happened this morning. I hear there's a meeting—"

"Sit down. I was just closing for the day."

"I know my husband has been in trouble with the cemetery board before. He was worried about losing his job. Now, with what happened this morning, he's afraid of being arrested."

"We have no reason to believe Earl is implicated in the killing. I was there the whole time the coffins were being disinterred. If he'd done anything unusual, I'd have noticed."

"But some of the others have never liked him."

"I don't know that that's true. He's always done his job."

"Is there anything I can do to help him?"

"Just tell the truth if Sheriff Lens has any questions. Did anything unusual happen this morning, for instance?"

"Nothing. Earl got up around seven and I fixed him breakfast. Then he walked over to the Brewster gravesite."

"What did you two have for breakfast?"

"Juice, cereal, toast, coffee. He has the same thing every morning."

"No eggs?"

"No. Why do you ask?"

"Just wondered. You didn't hear any unusual noises during the night or early morning?"

"No. Should I have?"

"If Hiram Mullins was murdered in the cemetery he might have screamed or cried out."

"We didn't hear anything."

I remembered what Doc Prouty had said about the blood. "What was your husband wearing when he went out?"

"His work overalls, like always."

"Did he have more than one pair?"

"He keeps an extra down at the tool shed."

I tried to reassure her. "Don't worry, Mrs. Gunther. We're having a special meeting of the cemetery board in the morning, but it's not to take any action against your husband. We'll be talking about a replacement for Mullins."

"And Earl—?"

"—has nothing to worry about if he isn't involved in the killing. He won't be blamed just because it happened in the cemetery."

Linda Gunther allowed herself a cautious smile. "Thank you, Dr. Hawthorne, I appreciate that."

After she'd gone I decided for the first time that she was a fairly attractive woman. Surely she could have done better than Earl Gunther for a husband, but then the ways of love and marriage are sometimes strange.

I had two hospital patients to visit in the morning, both recovering nicely from mild heart attacks. Then I checked in with Mary at the office and told her I'd be driving out to the cemetery for the board meeting. "I thought that wasn't till eleven o'clock," she said.

"I want to get there early and nose around, especially in the tool shed."

"Do you know how it was done?"

"Pure magic," I told her with a grin.

When I arrived at Spring Glen the morning sun was filtering through the spring leaves, bathing the place in a soft, inviting glow. I was an hour early for the meeting and I was surprised to find I wasn't the first to arrive. Virginia Taylor's sporty convertible occupied one of the parking spaces, though she was nowhere in sight.

I avoided the red-brick superintendent's house where Gunther and his wife lived and headed down the gently curving road toward the tool shed. Off in the distance I could see a couple of workmen removing some limbs from a tree ravaged by winter storms. The shed was unlocked, as it usually was when there were workmen about. I searched around among the tools for Earl's extra pair of overalls but found nothing.

Just as I was about to give up my search I spotted a large pair of hedge trimmers that seemed to be hiding behind a piece of canvas. I pulled them out, not thinking about fingerprints, and examined the blades for bloodstains. They appeared to have been wiped clean, but near the juncture of the blades were rust-colored spots that would be worth examining. I wrapped them in an oily cloth, trying not to damage fingerprints any more than I already had.

I was leaving the shed with my find when I saw Virginia Taylor walking toward me. "What have you got there?"

"Hedge trimmers. Could be the murder weapon."

"I always forget that you're something of a detective."

"Just an amateur."

"I wanted to see the spot where Hiram's body was found," she explained. "They seem to have removed all the Brewster coffins now."

"Did you know Hiram well? I only saw him at the meetings."

"He handled some real-estate transactions for my family years ago. He was good at making deals."

"A man of few words."

She smiled. "He could keep his mouth shut. Sometimes that's a valuable asset."

"Did he still work?"

She shook her head. "He's been retired for a year or so, ever since he put together the parcels of land for the new college in Shinn Corners."

"He was probably an interesting man. I'm sorry I never got to know him better. I remember last summer's party at Swan's place. Even out there I never saw him without a stiff collar and tie." It was still the era of highly starched detachable collars and men like Mullins and Swan wore them regularly. I preferred a shirt with an attached collar, as did younger men like Randy Freed.

We strolled back toward the small office building where the board held its meetings, A part-time secretary helped Gunther with the bookwork when she was needed, but most days he was there alone unless he was supervising a work crew. Today, as always, he gathered up his papers to leave us in privacy.

"Stay a few minutes, Earl," I suggested. "We'll want to talk with you about what happened."

"Sure, whatever you say." He stayed at his desk rather than join us at the board table. Almost at once two more cars pulled up outside and I saw that Swan and Freed were arriving.

The lawyer was first through the door, all business. "We've got a serious problem here, Gunther. I'm worried about the cemetery's liability."

Dalton Swan took his seat at the head of the table, running a hand through his thinning hair. "We'll get to that later, Randy. Let's everyone sit down and go over what we know. Have you been able to learn anything, Sam?"

"Not much," I admitted. I ran through the autopsy report for them and then turned to Gunther. "Earl, you usually keep a clean set of overalls in the tool shed, don't you?"

"That's right."

"I was just looking for them. They're not to be found. I did find this hedge trimmer, though, with what looks like traces of blood."

Virginia Taylor made a face. "Sam thinks it could be the murder weapon."

"It's possible."

Dalton Swan now shifted his gaze to the cemetery superintendent. "Isn't that tool shed kept locked, Earl?"

"Sure, most of the time."

"Was it locked night before last?"

"Well—" Gunther looked uneasy, "See, we had all this work to do in the morning, digging up those coffins for reburial. I thought some of the workmen might arrive early so I left the shed unlocked for them. Nobody dug up the graves before we got there, though. Doc saw that for himself."

"That's right," I agreed reluctantly. "The coffins were still underground when I got there."

"Do you have any idea how Mullins's body could have gotten in there?" Swan asked.

"None. It's like a miracle."

"All right." Swan waved him away. "Leave us alone for a few minutes."

Earl left the office and walked across the driveway to his house.

"Who do you have in mind as Hiram's replacement?" Virginia asked.

It was Randy Freed who answered. "I spoke to Dalton on the phone and made a suggestion. Milton Doyle is—"

"Not another lawyer!" Virginia exploded. "Cemeteries are about families, not lawsuits, for God's sake! How about another woman?"

"We have a woman," Swan answered quietly.

"Then how about *two* women? You men could still outvote us."

"It's worth considering," I agreed. "I suggest we adjourn until after the funeral. In the meantime maybe we can come up with some good women nominees."

Virginia Taylor gave me a smile of thanks and Swan agreed to adjourn until the following Monday. As we were leaving, Freed said, "It doesn't seem the same without old Mullins."

"He never said anything."

"But he was there, right in that chair! With those popping eyes and that bull neck he always looked as if his collar was strangling him."

Something occurred to me. "Randy, where would the records of real-estate transactions for the new college be kept?"

"Shinn Corners, At the courthouse."

It was just a hunch, but it was worth a drive to Shinn Corners. On the way over I started putting the pieces together in my mind. There was a way it could have been done. I saw it clearly now. Sometimes killers set out to create impossible situations but that hadn't been the case here. The killer had only wanted a safe way to dispose of the body, a way that would keep it hidden for another twenty years.

The courthouse was a big old building dating from the turn of the century with a stone fence already grown dark and weathered. In a big room I found maps and deeds, records stretching back a hundred years and longer. A girl in her late teens, a part-time clerk, came to my assistance at once. "The new college? We're very excited about it. I'm already enrolled for September."

"That's great," I said, meaning it. "I need to see the deeds on the various pieces of property that make up the college land. Would that be difficult?"

"No, not at all. It's a matter of public record."

There were so many individual parcels of land involved that the task seemed hopeless at first. Then I spotted Hiram Mullins's name and started concentrating on the deals he'd handled. I turned over the page of one deed and found the name I'd been seeking. After that it was easy.

I phoned Mary at the office and told her to postpone my afternoon appointments till the following day. "That's easy," she said. "There's only the Kane boy, and his mother says he's feeling fine now. The spots are all gone."

"Tell her to keep him out of school the rest of the week. He can go back on Monday."

"Sheriff Lens has been looking for you."

"I'll call him."

A moment later I had the sheriff's familiar voice on the other end of the line. "Where are you, Doc?"

"Over in Shinn Corners, checking the real-estate transactions regarding the new college."

"Why the college?" he wondered.

"It was the last deal Hiram Mullins worked on before his full retirement."

"Find anything?"

"A motive, I think."

"We've got something too. My deputies came up with a pair of blood-stained overalls. Earl Gunther admits they're his. Had his initials inside."

"Where were they found?"

"On the bank of the creek. Looks like Earl rolled them up and tossed them into the water, only they fell about a foot short. There's a collar and tie with bloodstains, too. Remember, they were missing from Hiram's body."

"I remember. What are you going to do now?"

"Arrest Earl Gunther for the murder, of course. Those overalls are the proof we need."

"Look, Sheriff, you can bring him in for questioning but don't charge him yet. I'll be at your office in an hour."

I covered the back country roads in record time and arrived at the sheriff's office just as he was starting to question the cemetery superintendent. Linda Gunther was outside in the waiting room, looking nervous, and I tried to comfort her.

"Earl's in trouble, isn't he?"

"Yes, but he could be in lots worse trouble. Try to relax until we finish talking to him."

Inside the office Sheriff Lens was talking with Gunther while a deputy made notes. "I never wore those overalls to kill Mullins," the superintendent was saying. "Someone found them in the tool shed."

"Come on, Earl—you expect us to believe that?"

"I'm innocent!" He turned to me for help. "You believe me, don't you, Dr. Hawthorne?"

I sat down across the table and chose my words carefully. "You didn't kill Mullins, but you're hardly innocent, Earl. You'd better tell us the whole truth if you expect to get out of this with your hide."

"What do you mean?"

"You know how the body got into the Brewster coffin."

"I—"

"What you gettin' at, Doc?" the sheriff asked.

"We've been saying all along that the ground over those coffins was solid and undisturbed, and that's perfectly true. But the ground on the creek side was a different story. The coffins were being moved, remember, because the waters of the flooded creek had so eroded the banks of the creek that some coffins were actually visible, held only by the tree roots that enveloped them.

The morning of the murder I watched your crews shovel away the soft dirt and chop out those roots."

"Then you saw that I didn't—"

"I saw what you wanted me to see, Earl. That dirt was soft because it had been removed and replaced the night before. You went down there and saw one coffin virtually free of the earth, its corner badly damaged. You were afraid I, or one of the other trustees, would raise a fuss if we saw that, so you removed it yourself, using the block and tackle on your flatbed truck. You placed the coffin on the truck, carefully hiding it beneath a bulky folded tarpaulin and some tools. You had two crews digging, concentrating on their own efforts, not paying much attention to each other. At some point when I'd strolled off examining tombstones it was easy enough for you to yank off the tarp and reveal one more coffin. I remember thinking that the second and third coffins appeared on the truck before I knew it."

"If he pulled that trick he must have killed Mullins," the sheriff argued.

"Not at all. Earl had been in trouble with the trustees before and he was afraid we'd fire him for sure if we saw how bad he'd allowed that Brewster plot to get. He was only worried about his job. He had no way of knowing a murderer would find the coffin in the early morning hours and decide it was the perfect place to hide a body."

Sheriff Lens was still skeptical. "Who'd have a motive for killing the old guy?"

"Someone who'd used him to assemble parcels of land for the new college. Someone in a position to hear the talk about a possible new community cemetery with Shinn Corners and use that information to buy up property, then derail that project and sell the land to the private college for a huge profit."

"You talkin' about one of the trustees, Doc?"

"Exactly. No one else would have had the knowledge and the position to bring it off. No one else could have enlisted Mullins's help when he was in virtual retirement. I found the name I expected on those deeds over in Shinn Corners this afternoon. Mullins must have threatened to talk, or maybe tried a little blackmail. It's doubtful that anyone but another board member could have lured him to the cemetery early that morning, probably on the pretext of checking the erosion, and then killed him. The killer had to know about the tool shed, and the extra overalls, to protect his clothing from bloodstains. The killer might even have had a key, in case the shed was locked. The trustee put on the overalls, picked up the hedge trimmers, and went out to meet Mullins when he arrived. A quick thrust beneath the rib cage and it was over.

The coffin lid was unscrewed and Mullins was added to those long-dead bones. Only there was too much blood, and a damaged coffin that allowed it to seep through and be seen."

"Which one, Doc?"

"Even without the name on those courthouse records I would have known. The overalls covered everything except the killer's collar and the top of the tie. Why were the dead man's collar and tie missing? Certainly he'd worn them. Mullins even wore them to summer picnics. No, the blood didn't get on the victim's collar and tie but on the killer's! A few drops splattered above the protective overalls. So the killer discarded his and replaced them with the victim's. The bull-necked Mullins would have had a collar big enough to fit any of the other trustees."

"Which one, Doc?" Sheriff Lens asked again.

"There was only one possibility. Miss Taylor is a woman, after all, with no need for male attire. Randy Freed and I wear shirts with attached collars. Only the dead man and Dalton Swan still wore the detachable collars. Dalton Swan, president of the board of trustees, whose term began before the land deal was closed, who was in the best position to hush up any proposal for a community cemetery and buy the land for himself, who could have gotten Mullins to front for him with the college people, who knew about the tool shed and could have killed Mullins and hidden the body without difficulty, who would have needed to replace his own bloodstained collar and tie before appearing that morning at his bank. The collar and tie you found can be traced to Swan. That and the land deal should be all the evidence you need."

"Dalton Swan. . . ."

"That's your killer. Go get him, Sheriff."

THE PROBLEM OF
THE ENORMOUS OWL

T HE summer of '39 was a tumultuous one [Dr. Sam Hawthorne was tell-ing his guest over a small libation]. War was in the air, and every day the newspaper headlines told of troop movements and preparations in Europe. Still, in a small New England town like Northmont life went on pretty much as it always had. Certainly there were more automobiles now than when I'd moved here in 1922, a newly licensed M.D. with my folks' gift of a yellow Pierce-Arrow Runabout. The car attracted more attention than I did during those early years.

Already by the late thirties cars were changing the way we lived and worked, broadening our horizons. No one had been particularly surprised when the old Duffy farm sold to a New York City playwright who'd won a Pulitzer Prize back in the twenties. His name was Gordon Cole and he did most of his writing on the farm, driving into Manhattan only when it was necessary to consult his agent or producers. The surprising thing was that Cole and his wife Maggie were actually farming the land, which was more than a hundred acres and quite a chore, even with help.

I'd treated Maggie Cole for a minor complaint earlier in the year, though I barely knew her husband. Still, when Maggie phoned the office that Tuesday morning in late August to tell me something had happened to Gordon, I told her I'd be right over.

"What is it?" my nurse Mary Best asked as I picked up my black bag and headed for the door.

"Maggie Cole's husband, our famous playwright. She found him out in the field and she's practically hysterical. Mrs. Philips has an eleven o'clock appointment. Better tell her I've been called out on an emergency and reschedule her for later in the week."

I drove out to the Duffy farm, as the local people still thought of it, and saw Maggie waiting for me in the cinder driveway. From her medical records I knew that she was forty-seven years old, though she seemed much younger. Her husband was fifty. The local paper had done a story on him when they moved to Northmont a couple of years back, and one of their columnists, Polly Ketchum, had interviewed him recently.

"He's way back in the field," she told me, getting into the car. "We can drive part of the way."

"Is he conscious?"

"I think he's dead," she sobbed. "He's not moving at all."

Maggie's hair was long and blond, with only a few streaks of gray beginning to appear. Her blue eyes now were red and puffy. She wore a pair of old slacks and a man's plaid shirt, apparently her work clothes on the farm. She was a small woman, barely coming to my shoulders.

"What time did he go out this morning?" I asked as I drove along the rutted driveway toward the barn and other outbuildings behind the house.

"I don't really know. He has a studio out back where he does his writing. Sometimes when he's deep into a new play he sleeps out there. I hadn't seen him since last night after dinner."

We left the car out behind the barn and walked about a hundred yards back through the field. There was only grass growing here. Maggie explained that they practiced crop rotation. Next year they'd planned to plant corn here.

I knew Gordon Cole was dead even before we reached the body. There were flies buzzing around him in the morning sunshine, attracted by subtle odors we could not yet detect. As I bent over the body I saw a trickle of dried blood on his mouth and chin, indicating internal bleeding. Though I'd never examined Cole in his lifetime, it looked to me as if his chest had caved in. I put my hand on his rib cage and could feel the broken bones. "What's this?" I asked, indicating a pair of greasy feathers stuck to his shirt.

"I don't know. Bird feathers, I guess. They were there when I found him. Is he—?"

"I'm sorry, Mrs. Cole. It appears he died of internal injuries, but we won't be certain until after the autopsy."

"But—but what happened to him?"

"Sometimes a tractor accident—"

She shook her head. "The tractor's back in its shed by the barn. I looked there after breakfast because he was going to plow a field this morning. When I saw the tractor still there I headed back to his studio to see if he'd overslept. He sometimes did that if he worked half the night on a play."

I straightened up. "We're going to have to notify Sheriff Lens."

"Of course."

"Is there anyone else here with you on the place?"

"We have a farm manager, Jud Duffy."

"I know Jud."

"We bought the land from his family after his folks died. We needed someone to manage the farm and he knew more about it than anyone else. We hire seasonal workers to help with the planting and harvesting."

"Is Jud here now?"

She shook her head as we headed back to the house. "On Tuesday morning he usually goes shopping for supplies. He'll be back around noon."

I phoned Sheriff Lens and told him what we had. "Does it look like murder, Doc?" he asked.

I glanced at Maggie Cole, cleaning up the breakfast dishes. "I can't say. You'd better have a look."

* * *

The end of summer was always a slow time at the hospital. People were vacationing, the weather was good, and the schools hadn't yet reopened to a new season of childhood diseases. Mary Best had the autopsy report for me by the end of the afternoon, and I phoned Sheriff Lens at once.

"Sheriff, as I suspected, Gordon Cole's chest was crushed. He died within minutes from massive internal bleeding. Dr. Miller, who did the autopsy at the hospital, is also a bird watcher in his spare time. The feathers found on Cole's shirt are from a great horned owl."

I could hear the sheriff's sigh at the other end of the line.

"Doc, you gonna tell me Gordon Cole was killed by an owl? That would look great in the New York papers!"

"It would have taken an enormous owl to inflict those injuries. Still, something killed him. I think we'd better go back out there in the morning. We can have another talk with Mrs. Cole and look around the place."

Mary was grinning when I hung up the phone. "An enormous owl? Are you going off on one of your crazy murder investigations again, Sam? Do you think the owl ran into him in the dark, or maybe picked him up in its claws and dropped him from the sky?"

"I don't know what killed him, Mary, but at this point it hardly seems to have been a natural death."

The sheriff and I drove out there the following morning. He was in a rare contemplative mood as he maneuvered the official car around a herd of cows being led out to pasture. "You know, Doc, all this war news is upsetting my wife. She's afraid they might start drafting people into the army."

The thought of it made me chuckle. "We're too old for them, Sheriff. I'll be forty-three pretty soon."

"If there's a war in Europe it could change a lot of things."

I couldn't argue with that. Mary and I had talked about it in the office, too.

Maggie Cole was waiting for us at the farmhouse and Jud Duffy was with her. "I have to go to the funeral parlor with Gordon's clothes," she said dispassionately. "Jud can answer any questions you have."

Jud was a muscular young man with dark hair and a port-wine birthmark on his left cheek. Possibly because of the birthmark, he'd grown up somewhat shy and withdrawn. The farm could have been his after his parents died, but he'd shown no interest in the responsibilities that entailed. He seemed quite content working as a manager for the Coles. After Mrs. Cole went off to the funeral parlor he turned his attention to us. "What is it you need to know?"

"Well, mostly about Gordon Cole's movements during the hours before his death," the sheriff said. "We understand he spent the night in his studio. We'd like to see that."

"I'll get the key."

"He kept it locked?" I asked.

"Sure. His manuscripts are all out there, including the current one." He took a key from a pegboard in the kitchen and we followed him out the back door. "This is the spare," he explained. "He carried his own key with him."

There was little point in driving to the barn, so we left the sheriff's car where it was and walked the entire distance. "Mrs. Cole mentioned that her husband was planning to do some plowing yesterday morning," I said. "What was that about?"

"They recently bought a five-acre lot from Pete Antwerp on the next farm. The lot's cut off from the rest of his place by the creek and he wanted to sell it. Gordon Cole figured he might as well add it to his land. He was planning to take the tractor out yesterday morning and harrow it."

"Isn't that something you'd have done?" Sheriff Lens asked.

"He often sought relaxation from his writing by performing various chores around the farm. Since it was my morning to buy supplies, he figured it was a perfect time for him to harrow the field."

The place where Maggie had found her husband's body was about halfway between the barn and the studio, across the open field. When I saw where Duffy was leading us I said at once, "That's the old sugarhouse!"

"Sure," he agreed. "When I was a kid we made maple syrup there. My brother an' me hauled small trees and helped cut the wood for the fire. After Cole bought the place, he converted it into a studio for his writing. Had to put a new roof on and fix the floor, but he didn't mind. Place still smells of maple syrup to me."

He unlocked the door and we went inside. If I'd expected to find signs of a struggle, I was disappointed. Cole's big Underwood typewriter still had a page of his script in it and the narrow bed was unmade. Otherwise the place was neat and clean. "He never ate here," Jud Duffy explained. "Always went back to the house for meals."

"What about breakfast?"

"If he had a chore, he'd do that first and then eat."

"So he was working on his play and then slept here till early morning when he left to get the tractor from the shed by the barn. And something killed him as he walked across that field."

Duffy looked at me and shrugged. "I guess that's what happened."

Sheriff Lens had been looking around while we talked. "Any owls around here?"

"There might be some barn owls."

"Great horned owls. Big ones."

"You see them occasionally."

"Ever hear of one attacking a human?"

He shook his head. "Sometimes if you're out at night walking through the brush you might scare one up and he'll fly at you, but they're not really attacking." His eyes had turned away.

I had another thought. "Is there any farm equipment here that might have killed him? His chest was pretty badly crushed."

"Everything is put away at night, and I wasn't here yesterday morning to take any of it out. Mrs. Cole never touches that stuff, and if her husband took out the tractor or the truck it would have been by the body, wouldn't it? Besides, it's been a fairly wet August. The ground is soft. Any heavy machinery would have left tracks."

"The tractor?"

"It weighs two and a half tons. It would have left all sorts of tracks."

"Let's go look at it," I suggested. There was nothing more to be learned at the studio. Then, as we started for the door, I went over to read the page in the typewriter. It wasn't a suicide note, just page four of a play about a couple of fishermen.

When we reached the spot where Maggie Cole had found her husband's body, the sheriff and I went over the ground carefully, searching in an ever-widening circle. Except for some trampled grass, there was nothing to be found.

We moved on to what would have been Gordon Cole's destination, the large shed where the tractor was stored. Jud Duffy opened the unlocked double doors and we went in. There were no windows and the place was dim, with daylight entering only through the doors and an opening for ventilation near the ceiling. "Nice machine," the sheriff said, patting the oversized tires. The harrow was already in place behind it.

"Could you start it up for us?" I asked Duffy.

"Sure thing," He climbed up behind the wheel and turned on the ignition switch, then came down, got out the crank, and inserted it into the hole at the bottom of the grille. Working in the cramped space between the tractor and the back wall of the shed, he cranked the engine until it turned over, then got back up behind the wheel and shifted from neutral to reverse. He had no trouble backing the tractor out of the shed and lowering the harrow. Obviously he'd done it many times before.

"Just to complete this reenactment of Cole's planned route, could you show us how he would have reached the field he was going to harrow?" You don't have to bring the tractor. We can walk over."

"It's pretty far."

That was all right with me, but Sheriff Lens chose to remain behind looking over the shed and other outbuildings. As we walked across the field, at about a right angle to the route we'd followed to the studio, Jud Duffy said, "The sheriff should lose some weight. He gets out of breath when he walks a lot."

"I've been telling him that for years." I shaded my eyes against the sun. "Is that where we're headed? Over by that big oak?"

"Right there! That's a marker tree, for the boundary between the farms. But the creek finally got so wide that it wasn't practical for Antwerp to farm these acres anymore. He'd have had to go all the way out to the road and then get permission to cross the Cole property. It was easier to sell off the five acres."

"Isn't that Pete Antwerp now?"

He followed my gaze toward a slender man with graying hair and a moustache who'd waded through a shallower portion of the creek and headed our way. He wore work boots and overalls with just an undershirt visible beneath. "Doc Hawthorne, isn't it?" he called out as he drew closer.

"That's right. Haven't seen you around lately, Pete."

"Been healthy. Don't need the likes of you." He glanced in Jud's direction. "Hello, Duffy."

Jud grunted something and turned away, showing only the good side of his face. "Of course you heard about Gordon Cole," I said.

Antwerp nodded. "What was it, a heart attack?"

"His chest was crushed. We don't know how."

He frowned and moved closer. "You mean it could have been foul play? Do you think he was beaten to death?"

"There was no other evidence of it, just the massive blow to the chest. Do you know if he had any enemies?"

"We all have enemies, don't we?"

"Was there any problem about his purchase of your property?"

"No, I was glad to get rid of it. He paid me a fair price."

While we chatted, Jud Duffy had moved away. When Antwerp finally turned to go I had to jog over to catch up with Jud. "You don't much care for him, do you?"

"He used to pick on me when I was growing up, on account of my face."

As we walked around the five-acre plot I saw that the field was rough and uneven. It had been plowed in the spring but neither planted nor cultivated. Weeds had sprung up all over. I could see why Cole would have wanted to smooth it out. But he hadn't gotten that far. Something, an owl or a human, had been waiting for him.

* * *

I stopped by the funeral parlor that afternoon, the first of the three days Gordon Cole would be shown prior to his funeral on Saturday morning. The Coles had no children, but an aunt was coming down from Boston and a couple of nephews were also planning to attend. Maggie seemed to be holding up as well as could be expected. When I returned to the office around four, Mary Best said Pete Antwerp had phoned and asked me to call him back.

"This is Dr. Hawthorne, Pete. What can I do for you?"

"I didn't want to mention anything in front of Jud Duffy this morning, but you know, there was something funny going on with Cole."

"Going on? What do you mean?"

"He wasn't just writing back in that studio. Sometimes late at night, if I was walking the dog, I'd see a car parked on my road, down near the path leading across the fields to his studio."

"What sort of car?"

"A blue roadster."

"Any idea whose it is?"

He hesitated. "I'd rather not say. I've told you enough."

"This is a murder investigation, Mr. Antwerp," I reminded him.

"I've told you everything I know," he said and hung up.

I thought about phoning the sheriff but then decided maybe I'd overlooked something during our brief search of the studio. I knew Maggie would be at the funeral parlor from seven to nine and decided to drive out to her place for another look around.

When I got there, I pulled the car back by the barn, sitting there for a moment to make certain no one else was around. I figured Jud Duffy would probably be at the funeral parlor too, and it appeared I was right about that. I'd waited till nearly eight o'clock, when it was past sunset and night was settling over the countryside. There was barely enough light for me to see where I was going, and I'd brought along a flashlight to guide me.

As I was passing the tractor shed, something made me open the doors and peer inside. The tractor was there, in near-total darkness, and as I stepped inside I heard a sudden flutter of wings. Something large seemed to fly directly at my head. I ducked down, imagining a bat, then realized it was a great horned owl. It flew out the doors and up into the evening sky. Probably it had entered the shed through the ventilator near the ceiling.

I circled the shed and followed the path through the field I'd taken with Duffy earlier in the day. When I was perhaps halfway across, at about the spot where the body had been found, I suddenly saw a car's headlights on Pete Antwerp's road off to my left. The car slowed to a stop and the lights went out. It was too far from Antwerp's house to be a visitor for him. Perhaps, if I was lucky, it was the blue roadster he'd told me about.

I moved cautiously forward. The darkness was almost complete now, but. I was on a line with the studio and could still make out its shape against the western sky. As I drew closer, I saw the glow of a small flashlight approaching from the direction of the side road. I figured the driver must have walked about the same distance as I had, but faster. It was someone familiar with the terrain—and someone with a key to the studio, I realized a moment later when the light reappeared inside the old sugarhouse. Well, that would save me the trouble of breaking in.

I turned the knob of the door as quietly as I could and slipped inside. The intruder was near the cot, shining a flashlight on the floor "Who's there?" I asked suddenly, turning on my own flashlight.

The figure whirled as my light hit her full in the face. I recognized Polly Ketchum at once. She was a strikingly pretty young woman who did book reviews and an arts column for our weekly newspaper. "My God—who is it?" she gasped, blinded by the light.

"Polly, it's Sam Hawthorne. What are you doing here?"

She sat down hard on the cot, as if the wind had been knocked out of her. I found a kerosene lamp I'd remembered seeing earlier and lit it. "What have I done?" she said, not expecting an answer.

"You were searching for something, Polly. Something you lost on a previous visit?"

"An earring. Isn't that the worst cliché, Dr. Sam? If I read it in a book I was reviewing I'd groan aloud."

I sat down at Cole's work table and she took a chair next to it. The flickering light glistened off her yellow hair, making her seem like an innocent teenager caught stealing a cookie. "Tell me about it," I said in a kindly voice.

Polly took a deep breath. "I interviewed him about six months ago for the paper. That's when it started"

"He must have been fifty years old."

"Fifty-one next month. That didn't matter to me. I thought. I loved him."

"You were here with him two nights ago?"

"Yes."

"How did he die?"

In the lamplight her face suddenly stiffened. "I have no idea. We left here before dawn. I hurried back to my car because I wanted to be gone before Pete Antwerp was up and around. The last time I saw Gordon, he was starting across the field to get out his tractor."

"He never made it," I said. "Something killed him on the way—crushed his chest like an eggshell."

She recoiled at my words as if I'd struck her. "You can't believe I had anything to do with it."

"I couldn't have believed any of this until about ten minutes ago."

She tried to think of some response, then finally asked, "Will you help me search for my earring? I don't want it found here."

"Did you lose it Monday night?"

She shook her head. "Probably one night last week. I meant to look for it Monday, but we got talking and I forgot. Gordon was a brilliant conversationalist."

"Sure." I lowered the lamp to the floor and we searched together but found nothing. She felt around the bedclothes too but it was fruitless. After ten minutes we gave up.

"I had to try finding it," she said, somewhat apologetically.

I stood up and brushed off the knees of my trousers. "Ever see any owls around her, Polly?"

"I never did. Once we heard a noise at night and Gordon said it was an owl. Why?"

"There were owl feathers on his shirt." I didn't bother to repeat any theories about enormous owls.

"My earring—" she began but then stopped.

"What?"

"I have to be going," she decided. Then, hesitating, she asked, "You won't tell anyone—?"

"That you were here? Certainly not, unless it becomes important to the investigation."

We left the studio together and after locking the door she handed me her key. "I won't be coming here again. You'd better keep this."

"All right."

Then she was gone into the darkness, pursuing a path she probably knew by heart. I wasn't worried about her. She was smart enough to profit from her mistakes.

I was back in my car before nine and on the road before Maggie Cole returned to her lonely farmhouse.

* * *

By Thursday afternoon Sheriff Lens was about ready to admit defeat. "If we knew what killed him, maybe we'd know who did it," he speculated.

"You haven't turned up any enormous owls?" I asked.

"You know, Doc, that's not as crazy a question as you might think. I've got a big owl somewhere in my memory if I can just dig it out. Were you at the Grange Halloween party last year?"

I shook my head. "I avoid costume parties like a plague."

"Maybe it was the year before," he mused. "I'll have to ask Vera." The sheriff had married in middle age, less than ten years earlier, and his young wife, Vera, had a reputation for remembering every date and place.

I'd thought about my conversation with Polly Ketchum and its implications, but for the present I was keeping to my promise to say nothing. Another question had occurred to me, though, and later in the day I found an opportunity to phone Polly from my office.

"This is Sam Hawthorne. How are you?"

"All right," she answered warily.

"I have a quick question about that earring you lost."

"Has it turned up?"

"No. I was just wondering what it looked like, in case it does. You started to say something about it last night."

"It has a small gold owl on it. I bought them in Boston last year. When you mentioned the feathers it made me shiver."

I thanked her and hung up. For a time I stared at the phone, thinking about owls.

It was raining when I awoke on Friday, and the weather had turned cooler. I had no reason to complain. It had been a pleasant summer and this was, after all, the first of September. The Northmont paper where Polly worked was only a weekly, not given to international reporting, so many of us had a nearby daily paper delivered to our doors. When I picked it off the porch and unrolled it I saw the headline that would change everyone's life. Germany had invaded Poland in a move almost certain to mean widespread war in Europe.

I went to the phone and called Sheriff Lens. "It looks like war," I said.

"Just heard about it on the radio, Doc. They say the British are mobilizing and they've started evacuating women and children from their cities."

"God help us all."

"Doc, I was going to phone you. Vera's been going through some snapshots she took at the Grange Halloween parties. I think she found our owl."

"I'll stop on my way to the office."

I phoned Mary Best at her apartment, knowing she wouldn't yet be in the office at eight o'clock. "They say there's going to be a war, Sam. Will America get into it?"

"We might, if it lasts awhile. Hitler is crazy enough to try anything. Look, Mary, I'm still helping the sheriff on the Gordon Cole case. Do I have anything urgent this morning?"

"Only your hospital rounds. Mrs. Sydney had her baby during the night and all's well. Dr. Fitzpatrick delivered it."

"Fine. I'll stop by to see her later this morning." More and more of my patients were going to specialists—in this case, an obstetrician who'd recently set up a practice in Northmont. I could see the changing face of medicine and had nothing but praise for the better care my patients were receiving. I felt just a bit envious though, when I heard of specialists with annual incomes twice as much as mine.

Vera Lens greeted me at the door when I arrived an hour later. "The sheriff remembered an owl and so did I. Come in and I'll show you my pictures."

Vera was forever snapping away with a Kodak box camera, and sometimes even took flashbulb photographs at indoor parties. I followed her into the parlor where Sheriff Lens was sifting through piles of her black-and-white snapshots. I glanced through some of them, recognizing the sheriff himself as an overweight cowboy and even Mary Best daringly costumed as a harem girl. She never told me she'd gone to any of the Grange Halloween affairs.

"Who's this?" I asked, holding up a picture of someone costumed as a shapely black cat. It was dated 1938.

"Polly Ketchum from the newspaper," Vera answered.

"Was Gordon Cole there?"

She thought for a moment before replying. "I don't believe so, unless I failed to recognize him in his costume."

The sheriff had been holding out one of the pictures. "This is the one I wanted you to see." It was a photograph of someone in a long feathery cape, wearing an owl's mask rimmed with more feathers. "There's your enormous owl, Doc."

"Who is it?"

Vera answered. "The owl? That's Jud Duffy."

* * *

We drove over to Duffy's place in the rain and I went in with the sheriff. He stared at us, as if knowing we'd come to interrupt his routine. "I have work to do at the Cole place," he said. "I gotta be going."

"Sit down, Duffy," the sheriff ordered. "I want to tell you how you killed Gordon Cole."

"Killed him! I never—"

"You'd had the tractor out on Monday. You knew Cole planned to use it first thing Tuesday morning on that field he'd bought from Antwerp. You also knew it was quite dark in that shed. When you put the tractor away, instead of leaving it in neutral you shifted it into high gear after you turned off the ignition. When Gordon Cole entered the shed the following morning, just around dawn, he couldn't see the gear shift clearly and assumed it was in neutral as it always was. He turned on the ignition and got out to crank the engine. When the engine started, the tractor lurched forward, crushing Cole against the rear wall before it stalled."

He was right, of course, but I had to ask, "How did the body get into the field?"

"The death in the shed would have pointed to Jud here as the one who'd left the tractor in gear. He could claim it was an accident, but it was much better to come by Tuesday morning, make sure the deed was done, and carry the body to some other location. Maybe he wanted it out in the middle of the field, maybe he was headed somewhere else and his burden got too heavy." Turning back to the slender young man he asked, "Can you tell us that, Jud?"

He started speaking, turning half away from us as he'd done earlier. "You've got it right about the tractor, Sheriff, but it was an accident, not murder. I'll tell you what happened, and what I should have told you from the beginning. I needed some spark plugs for the tractor and I stopped by the farm on my way to the John Deere dealer in Shinn Corners. The shed doors were closed when I got there a little before seven. I unlatched them and looked inside, figuring Mr. Cole was already out in the field. I was surprised when I saw the tractor, and then I saw him, pinned against the wall with the tractor hood against his chest. I quick backed it up, thinkin' he might still be alive, but I was too late to save him. I don't know why I did what I did next. I musta figured I'd be blamed. I wanted to get the body out of there, away from the tractor. That's why I carried him out in the field and left him on the ground."

Sheriff Lens stared at him intently. "If it was like you say, Jud, why were you wearing your owl mask when you carried the body out to the field?"

"I wasn't—"

"There were owl feathers caught in his shirt." He stood up. "You got a raincoat? I'm going to have to take you down to the office for further questioning. You can have a lawyer present if you want."

Jud Duffy faced us now, and the will to resist seemed drained out of him. "I'll get a coat," he said.

When he reappeared a moment later he was wearing a raincoat and the owl mask I'd seen in the snapshot. The sheriff's hand dropped to his revolver but my hand was on top of his. "No, Sheriff," I whispered. "It's all right."

"I thought you'd want this too," Duffy said, "so you could compare the feathers. I wasn't wearing it Tuesday."

Sheriff Lens lifted his hand from the gun. "Come along," he said.

* * *

I wasn't satisfied and in truth neither was Sheriff Lens. When I spoke with him later on Friday he still didn't have a confession to the murder. Jud Duffy admitted only to moving the body.

"I'm beginning to think it was an accident," the sheriff told me. "At least there'd be enough of a reasonable doubt in a jury's mind to win him an acquittal."

"What about the feathers?"

"He's right. The feathers on the mask had been treated with some sort of preservative. The ones caught on Gordon Cole's shirt are fresh from the owl."

"I suspected as much. An owl flew at me in the shed Wednesday evening."

"What were you doin' there Wednesday, Doc?"

"Just looking around. Those feathers were no doubt on the hood of the tractor when it rammed into Cole's chest. There was enough grease on them to make them adhere to his shirt."

"So you think I missed out on Duffy as the killer. I didn't solve it after all."

"You solved the *how* very nicely, Sheriff—how a man could die of a crushed chest in the middle of an empty field. It was the *who* that tripped you up, and I didn't know the answer to that myself until I thought about what Jud Duffy told us this morning."

"Then it wasn't an accident?"

"No."

"Did he kill himself?"

I smiled at this. "It would be a bizarre method of suicide. Let's wait till tomorrow, after the funeral. Then I'll explain everything."

"Suppose the killer gets away?"

"That won't happen."

The intermittent rain had ended by Saturday morning and the sun actually appeared as Gordon Cole's body was laid to rest. Some of us returned to Maggie's house afterwards. The neighbors had stocked it with food during the service and I knew many of those in attendance. Jud Duffy was still being held for questioning and Polly Ketchum was nowhere to be seen, but Pete Antwerp from the adjoining farm stopped by a few minutes. No one stayed much beyond noon, and finally when the last of the mourners had departed only Sheriff Lens and I remained.

"Take some food with you," Maggie suggested. "There's plenty left over."

"No thanks," I said. "We have to talk to you about Jud Duffy."

"I can't believe he had anything to do with my husband's death. Jud wouldn't hurt a fly. You must know that. He's such a shy person because of that birthmark."

"He's admitted moving the body," the sheriff told her.

"From where?"

"Gordon was crushed to death by his tractor. It happened in the shed. Duffy removed the body, carried it to the field. He was afraid he'd be blamed for leaving the tractor in gear the night before."

"Did he?" she asked.

I shook my head. "You see, once we established how he died, the question remained as to whether it was accident or murder—or even suicide, remote as that might sound. Jud cleared up that point for us. Once he started talking we could pretty much trust what he said. When he told us he came by here before seven on Tuesday morning and found the shed doors closed we believed him because he gained nothing by lying about such a point."

"The doors were closed?" she repeated.

I nodded. "Odd that Gordon would close the doors if he was planning to back the tractor out. Odd—but the next thing Duffy told us was downright impossible. He said he unlatched the doors! Since Gordon could not have latched them from the inside, it meant that someone else closed and latched them after he was dead. Someone saw the body, then closed and latched the doors out of habit. If they saw the body, why not phone for help, raise the alarm? There could be only one reason. The door-latcher *expected* to see the body. The door-latcher wanted to see the body because this was the person who shifted the tractor gears into high the night before and prepared a deathtrap for Gordon Cole. The only reason for visiting the shed Tuesday morning was to make certain he was really dead."

Maggie moistened her lips with her tongue. "Go on."

"Only a handful of people close to Gordon could have known he planned to take the tractor out early Tuesday morning. Whoever it was had to know about Antwerp's field and Gordon's habits and the fact that Jud Duffy would be off shopping Tuesday morning. That narrowed it to Jud and Antwerp and you and perhaps one other person close to Gordon. Of these people, only you and Jud had a legitimate reason for checking on that shed early in the morning. He worked here and you lived here. He's admitted being here and finding the doors latched. Maggie, it had to be you who unthinkingly latched those doors after finding Gordon's body. It had to be you who set the trap that killed him."

"Why?" Sheriff Lens asked. "Why would you want to kill him?"

She made a sudden movement for the pocket of her black dress, and for a moment I feared the sheriff would go for his gun again. But Maggie Cole had no weapon when her hand reappeared. She held only a small gold earring with an owl on it. In Maggie's life this had been the enormous owl.

THE PROBLEM OF
THE MIRACULOUS JAR

T HE war was still a long way from Northmont in November of 1939 [Dr. Sam Hawthorne told his visitor after the drinks had been poured], and to tell the truth there were those who never thought it would amount to much, at least in the beginning. Life went on pretty much as it had before Hitler's invasion of Poland, even though the entry of England and France into the conflict had caused some in the press to start referring to "World War II." Most folks around the country were more stirred up about the president's attempt to break with tradition and move Thanksgiving Day ahead a week on the calendar.

Two of our more prominent citizens, Proctor Hall and his wife Mildred, had spent the months of September and October touring the Mediterranean region, a trip planned before the outbreak of European hostilities. There was some concern for their safety but they were far from the region of conflict. Hall, a man still in his forties, had inherited one of the big tobacco farms near Northmont, though he left its daily operations to Jason Sennick, a lumbering hulk of a man who managed the place. Hall seemed only too happy to be a gentleman farmer, and when he and Mildred weren't traveling, they were active in community and church affairs.

I'd treated her for some minor female ailments over the years so it wasn't too surprising that my nurse Mary Best and I were invited to a welcoming party their friend Rita Perkins threw for their return. Rita was director of the church choir and also a patient of mine. Mildred sang with them when she was at home, and she and Rita had become close friends. They were both in their late thirties, both attractive in their own way. Mildred was the traveler, the sophisticate, while Rita was the girl next door who'd never left home. This was quite literally true since she still lived in the family homestead following the deaths of both parents.

The party was on a Sunday afternoon in early November, when the temperature had dropped unexpectedly into the low thirties and brief flurries of snow were in the air. Because Rita's house just off the town square was relatively small, there were only ten people invited. Besides Mary and me, there were the Halls, Rita, Jason Sennick, the minister and his wife, and Bud and Doris Clark, a young couple who'd become friendly with the Halls. When we walked in everyone was chattering and I saw we were the last arrivals. While Mary Best hurried over to welcome Mildred back, I said hello to Proctor. He was just lighting a cigar so I avoided the seat next to him and settled into an empty chair next to the Reverend Mooney. He was Episcopalian, but his faint Northern Irish brogue made some strangers take him for Catholic.

"How are you, Dr. Hawthorne?" he asked, his cheeks as ruddy as if he'd been out in the wind.

"I got through the summer."

"Haven't seen you lately."

I knew he meant he hadn't seen me in church lately. We often passed each other in the corridors of Pilgrim Memorial Hospital, going about our separate callings. "It's been a busy time."

"Eliza was just saying the other day we should have you for dinner."

Eliza Mooney had always seemed a bit daring for a small-town minister's wife. She prided herself on keeping up with the latest fashions and probably didn't approve of the tight sweater and skirt Mildred Hall was wearing. Now, as she bent across her husband to join in the conversation, I couldn't help looking down the front of her low-cut dress. "By all means, Dr. Sam! You must join us at the rectory," she gushed. "Perhaps some night later this week? You may bring Mary Best if you wish."

For many in the town, an invitation extended to me had come to include my nurse. I viewed the whole thing with amusement and had been startled to see Mary blush the one time I'd attempted to kid her about it. "I'll check my schedule and phone you tomorrow," I promised.

We became aware that the others had ceased talking to listen to the world travelers, and as Rita Perkins went around pouring tea and passing cookies Mildred Hall was answering Bud Clark's questions about the impact of the war. Clark and his pretty blond wife were in their mid twenties, two decades younger than most of the others. "On our ship we had very little knowledge of what was happening in Europe," Mildred said. "We had just left port on September first, when Hitler invaded Poland, and we heard virtually no news." She took a sip of tea and complimented their hostess. "We did find in Palestine that Jewish immigration has swelled in the past decade because of the threat from Hitler. As we traveled around the country on our tour bus we found many of the Jewish shopkeepers to be deeply concerned about the effects of war on their relatives still in Poland."

Reverend Mooney smiled, trying to shift the conversation into a more uplifting channel. "Did you visit any Christian shrines in the Holy Land?"

"We did indeed," her husband took over. Proctor Hall had close-cropped steely gray hair and wore thin-rimmed glasses that went well with his face. He was a handsome man with a face almost the color of the tobacco others grew for him. "We saw Bethlehem, Jerusalem and Nazareth, and even took a side trip to Cana where Jesus performed the first miracle at the wedding feast."

"What sort of place is that?" Rita wanted to know, having finished her hostess chores for the moment. "I've always been intrigued by the story of the water being changed into wine."

"It's a small town, merely a suburb of Nazareth. They are quite close." He reached beneath his chair and produced a small package wrapped in fancy paper. "In fact, Rita, Mildred and I brought you back a special gift from Cana. I'm sorry we couldn't bring them for everyone."

"What is it?" the choir director wondered, carefully unwrapping it. Inside was a stoneware jar about six inches high, resembling in miniature those familiar Biblical receptacles for carrying oil, wine, and water. "Oh, how lovely!"

"It's a water jar from Cana," Mildred Hall explained. "The little shop girl who sold it to us insisted it was identical to those used in the miracle. They had large ones too, holding fifteen to twenty-five gallons like the originals, but she assured us these smaller ones were just as authentic."

"You can fill it with water, Rita, and turn it into wine," Proctor told her with a chuckle, opening a pack of cigarettes.

"Oh, I wouldn't," she insisted. "That would be a sacrilege, wouldn't it?"

Everyone laughed and Rita placed the Cana water jar on the tray with the teapot. It was Jason Sennick, the farm manager, who'd been silent till now, who broke the mood of the moment. "You sure you didn't buy that at some gift shop in New York City?"

Sennick was a large, crusty man whose occasional disrespect seemed to mask a feeling of insecurity. But Mildred Hall had come prepared for doubters. She opened her purse and produced a copy of their customs declaration. "There! See for yourself!" She pointed to a line that read *Cana stoneware, weight 28 oz., value $25.00.*

"Twenty-five dollars!" Rita Perkins exclaimed. "You shouldn't have spent so much! I'll treasure it always."

"Try filling it with water," Sennick suggested. "We'll have the reverend say a prayer over it and see if it changes into wine."

Reverend Mooney scowled to show his displeasure with the farm manager's words but he did reach out to examine the Cana relic. The reddish brown stoneware jar, hard and opaque, bulged at the sides and had a fairly wide mouth. I guessed it might hold nearly a quart of water. Mooney's wife Eliza leaned over to examine it with him. She sang in the church choir too, and was forever organizing the Northmont ladies to aid in one good cause or another. On occasion she'd even been known to give them fashion tips, which brought a silent smirk from Mary Best.

"Well," Doris Clark said, jumping to her feet, "if no one's going to fill it with water, I will!" The minister smiled indulgently and passed it to her. Doris had a youthful verve that seemed to please Proctor Hall. I'd noticed when they were together that his eyes were often on her face, even when she wasn't speaking.

She went into the kitchen and filled the stoneware jar with tap water, then brought it in and set it on the table in front of Rita Perkins. "Your wine, miss."

Everyone laughed, but Rita decided she'd wait before savoring it. "How long did it take at Cana?" she asked nervously. "We don't know, do we?"

It was Mary Best who said, quite innocently, "This is almost like a wedding. All we need are the bride and groom."

That was when Rita Perkins fainted.

* * *

She was revived quickly enough with some smelling salts I always carried with me. "I—I must be coming down with something," she stammered. "Please forgive me."

Everyone was talking at once, assuring her she should lie down and rest. The Clarks were already on their feet, preparing to leave. "It's the change of seasons," Bud assured her. "Doris always gets a cold this time of year."

"Perhaps the wine will help you," Jason Sennick suggested, offering her the stoneware jar with a touch of his ironic humor.

She seemed to play along and took a sip, then shook her head. "It's only water. Please don't go yet, people. Here, I'll make a fresh pot of tea."

Out of politeness we stayed another twenty minutes, listening to Mildred and Proctor relate their adventures on the Greek islands and some of their other stops. Then the Clarks insisted they really had to go, and the rest quickly followed. Rita saw them to the door and made arrangements for choir practice the following afternoon with Mildred and Eliza. Proctor took Rita aside to thank her for the party, and then he and Mildred departed. Mary and I lingered till last so I could determine how Rita was feeling.

"It was nothing," she insisted. "Just a passing lightheadedness."

"People don't faint for no reason," I told her. "Was it something someone said?"

"No, no. I'm fine."

"Something you ate?" I persisted.

"No." She smiled at me. "You're too much the doctor, Sam."

"All right," I said with a sigh. "But promise me you'll phone if you have any pains or dizziness. I'll come right over."

"I'll remember that, but I'm sure I'll be all right."

As we were leaving I paused and picked up the stoneware jar. "I wonder if the water has turned into wine yet." I took a sip, but it was still water.

She showed us out and I heard her bolt the front door behind us. Obviously Rita was planning to stay in for the rest of the day, which was probably wise. A light snow with big flakes had started to fall more steadily.

"What do you think?" Mary asked as we got into my Buick. "Will she be all right?"

"I hope so. She seems better."

The afternoon's outing had proven shorter than planned, but Mary pleaded work to do at home so I dropped her at the double house she rented near the hospital. Watching her walk up the steps to her porch, I noticed the shapely legs that were usually hidden by her white uniform and stockings. Mary had been with me four years and I'd never regretted hiring her.

When I drove up to my own house I had a surprise waiting. Burly Jason Sennick was seated out front in his truck, ignoring the falling snowflakes which were coating the vehicle. My first thought was that he'd come for some sort of medical attention, though he wasn't one of my patients. "Hello, Jason. What can I do for you?"

A good workman, he tended to be clumsy at conversation and social intercourse. "Can I come in, Doc?"

"Certainly." I led him into the house and offered him a chair.

"I was a bit outta line this afternoon, pokin' fun at the reverend and suggesting he could pray over that jar of water."

"I think we all took it in the right way," I assured him, "as a little joke."

"You don't think that upset Rita and made her faint?"

"No, it was some minutes later when she was taken ill, after my nurse Mary mentioned a wedding and needing a bride and groom." As I spoke the words I was remembering the sudden draining of color from Rita's face, wondering if Mary's words had somehow caused the reaction.

"What I really came to you about was Reverend Mooney's wife Eliza. I swear, Doc, the woman is tryin' to seduce me! She leans over with those low-cut dresses and shows her breasts every chance she gets."

I had to laugh at that. "Believe me, Jason, you're not alone. That's just the way she behaves with men. I don't even know if she's conscious of the effect she has."

"I hate being around her because of the thoughts I have."

"You should talk to your minister or priest about it, not to me."

"Reverend Mooney is my minister."

"Oh."

"What am I gonna do, tell him his wife is seducing me?"

That this burly man whom I hardly knew had come to me with his confession left me at a momentary loss for words. Finally I suggested, "Try not being in her company, Jason. I know you have to see her during the church service when she signs in the choir, but you should be able to avoid her at other times." I gave a little shrug. "That's all I can tell you."

"There's no kind of pill I could take?"

"You don't need a pill, just some willpower."

He didn't seem completely satisfied but he accepted it. "Thanks for your time, Doc."

"I hope I did some good. Feel free to call me anytime."

After he left I thought about it some more. It was hard to believe his problem was so great as to prompt this unannounced visit, but we never know what goes on in someone else's mind.

About twenty minutes later the telephone rang, and when I picked it up I heard a gasping voice speak my name. "Who is this?" I asked.

"It's Rita Perkins, Sam. I'm terribly dizzy. I drank—" Her voice broke off in a choke.

"I'll be right over!"

I drove fast across town, ignoring the drifting snowflakes still blanketing the road. In ten minutes I was at Rita's house. It was less than an hour since Mary and I had left, and there were no footprints in the fresh dusting of snow. I rang the bell but no one answered. I tried the door but of course it was locked. There was a light burning toward the rear, in the kitchen, and I walked back along the side of the house to the other door, treading on the unmarked snow. That door was locked too, but at least I could see into the kitchen. On the table was the telephone and an empty glass. In the center stood the stoneware jar the Halls had brought home from Cana.

On the floor by the chair was Rita's body.

I smashed the glass in the back-door window, reached through to turn the bolt, and entered the kitchen. Though I knew she was dead, I felt for a pulse, then walked through to the front door to make sure it was still locked and bolted. Turning on lights as I went, I established that all the downstairs windows were latched too. Then I saw a car pulling up out front behind my own. Proctor and Mildred Hall got quickly out and I opened the front door for them. Both wore topcoats against the snow and chill. Proctor kept his on but his wife removed her coat and tossed it over a chair. She still had on the tight sweater and skirt she'd worn earlier.

"Sam," Proctor asked, "did she call you too?"

I nodded. "We're too late. She's dead."

Mildred staggered as if from a blow. "Oh my God! I answered the phone and she sounded so sick. I said we'd be right over."

"She's on the kitchen floor," I told them. "Please don't touch anything. I have to call Sheriff Lens."

"The sheriff?" Hall asked, frowning.

"I can detect a faint odor of cyanide. I think she was poisoned."

"You mean she killed herself?" Mildred asked.

I shook my head. "It's doubtful that she'd take poison and then phone you and me for help. I think she was murdered."

We went into the kitchen together and I took the phone off the table and gave the operator Sheriff Lens's home number. When he answered I turned away and said quietly, "Sheriff, this is Sam. Could you get over to Rita Perkins's home right away?"

"What's up, Doc?"

"She's dead. She may have been poisoned."

I hung up and returned the phone to the table. Mildred had gone into the living room but Proctor stood by the body. "This is terrible, Sam. She was like a sister to my wife."

I bent to sniff at the empty glass but there was no trace of the familiar bitter odor. Next I tried the jar from Cana and thought I detected something.

"What is it?" Hall asked, seeing my frown.

I lifted the jar from the edge of the table and brought it to my nostrils, being careful to hold it with my handkerchief and avoid smudging fingerprints. "A definite bouquet, but something else too. It could be cyanide."

"Do you mean—?"

I carefully poured a few drops into the empty glass. "Your stoneware jar has done its job. It's converted water into wine, and poisoned wine at that!"

* * *

Sheriff Lens arrived just seconds before his photographer and fingerprint expert. As one who remembered the sheriff's investigative techniques from the 1920s, I was constantly surprised at how much he'd adapted to the changing times. Though some years older than me, he was still under fifty, and with his wife's help he'd even managed to slim down a bit.

"What's it look like, Doc?" he asked, moving around the table for a better view of the victim.

"If I had to guess, I'd say cyanide in the wine. It wasn't full strength or she wouldn't have lived long enough to make two phone calls."

"When did you last see her?"

"This afternoon. There were ten of us here, counting Rita." I told him about the gathering and the stoneware gift from Cana.

"You mean people pay money for this junk?" he asked. "They probably make 'em by the hundreds for the tourists."

"Of course, but it's something unique to Cana and they try to cash in on it."

"You say she filled it with water?"

"Actually it was Doris Clark, Bud's wife, who held it under the tap."

"Could she have slipped wine or cyanide into it then?"

I shook my head. "Rita tasted it right away, and I had a swallow as we were leaving. It was water, all right. Not a drop of wine or poison."

Sheriff Lens stepped aside while his fingerprint expert brushed the jar with dark powder. "Who did you see handle this earlier?" he asked me.

"Rita, Doris Clark, and myself. And Reverend Mooney, I think. I handled it again after I found the body, but I was careful to use a handkerchief. I suppose you might find the Halls' prints too, since they gave it to her."

The fingerprint man, a young fellow named Frank whom I'd once treated for whooping cough, spoke up. "Looks like there are no prints at all on this, Sheriff. It's been wiped clean."

I frowned, puzzled by the news. "You'd better have it analyzed, along with the dregs in that empty glass. I did pour a few drops of the wine in there."

I went into the living room where Proctor and Mildred waited in silence. "What can I do?" she asked immediately, getting to her feet. "We feel so helpless."

"You'd better notify Reverend Mooney and the rest who were here today—the Clarks and your farm manager. Sheriff Lens will want to question them all."

"Of course." She turned to her husband. "We'd better make those calls from home."

On his way out Proctor shook hands with me. "Keep us advised, Sam. This is a terrible thing."

Other deputies were arriving, along with the county coroner. The sheriff came into the living room and said, "Nothing seems to have been taken. It doesn't look like a burglary."

"Burglars don't use poison, Sheriff. And they do leave footprints in the snow. No one entered or left this house after the party guests departed."

At that point I was just beginning to realize how baffling and complex the death of Rita Perkins was becoming.

* * *

Sheriff Lens showed up at my office at eleven on Monday morning, carrying lab findings and the coroner's autopsy report. "So soon! It makes me think Northmont is finally part of the twentieth century!"

"These are just preliminary, Doc, but there's something I thought you should know about."

"You found the poison?"

"In the wine, just as you thought," he said, slumping down in the chair opposite my desk.

"Was there any other wine in the house?"

"Not a drop, and we even checked the rubbish for empty bottles. Mildred Hall and Eliza Mooney both insist she never drank."

"So the killer had to bring it."

"Unless it was a miracle, Doc."

"Did the coroner have any guess as to how long she might have lived after ingesting the poison?"

"He thinks it was diluted somewhat. And cyanide salts are slightly slower acting than the liquid form. She could have lived five or ten minutes. Dizziness and convulsions would have been the first symptoms. Certainly she had time enough to make those phone calls. There's something else in his report, though, that's really the interesting part."

"What is it?"

"Rita Perkins was almost three months pregnant."

I sat and stared at Sheriff Lens. "There must be some mistake."

He grinned a little. "Why's that, Doc? 'Cause she wasn't married?"

"Rita sang in the church choir."

"Yeah. Well, I guess there was another side to her."

"She invited four men to that party yesterday. Maybe she used the occasion to break the news to the father."

"Tell me again who was there besides Proctor Hall."

I counted them off on my fingers. "Jason Sennick, Bud Clark, and Reverend Mooeny."

"I guess we can rule out the Reverend."

I let that pass for the moment. "Of course, if one of their wives discovered this affair with Rita, she'd have had a motive too."

He nodded. "They say poison is a woman's weapon. I guess I'd better start questioning all of them."

"While you're at it, Sheriff, find out how any of them could change water into poisoned wine inside a locked house surrounded by unmarked snow."

* * *

By afternoon the sun had melted the remains of the previous day's snow and the weather was a bit more seasonable. I drove over to Saint George's, Reverend Mooney's church to the town square. It was an impressive building for a town our size and Mooney himself was playing the organ as I slipped in the rear door. I'd remembered about the scheduled choir practice, not knowing if Rita's death might have postponed it. But a handful of women were clustered near the front of the sanctuary, talking in low tones. I spotted Eliza Mooney at once, and as I walked nearer I realized that the minister's wife had been appointed to replace Rita as the choir leader.

"Mildred," she said to Proctor's wife, "I want you to handle printing the song sheets for Sunday's service. Rita used to do most of these things herself, but it's time we spread the work around."

"I'll be glad to help out."

They both saw me and Eliza said, "Hello, Sam. We're trying to carry on here."

Reverend Mooney ceased his organ practice and came down to join u. "Do you have any news?"

"Sheriff Lens is investigating several angles." I thought it best not to mention the pregnancy quite yet.

It was Mildred Hall who seemed the most concerned. "I suppose Proctor and I are the chief suspects because we brought her that stoneware jar from Cana."

"There are other possibilities," I said, trying to reassure her. Certainly I'd considered the idea of some slow-dissolving inner coating that released the poisoned wine into the water after Rita and I had tasted it. The entire scenario seemed a bit fantastic, but I'd asked the sheriff to have his lab run special tests on the jar.

"I hope Sheriff Lens doesn't seriously consider any of us," Mooney said, brushing back his graying hair and passing a protective arm around his wife's waist. The gesture may have been reassuring to her, but he seemed to be calling attention to Eliza as a suspect.

"I wonder if I could speak to you alone, Reverend," I asked.

"Certainly." He released his wife and motioned toward the rear of the church. "These ladies want to get on with their choir practice anyway. Of course they'll be singing at Rita's funeral on Wednesday."

I followed him into the little oak-paneled office around back. There was a traditional print of Jesus behind his desk, and bookshelves crammed with concordances and collections of sermons. I sat down and came right to the point. "Rita Perkins was one of your flock, Reverend. Did she ever tell you she was pregnant?"

He blinked once but did not change his expression. If my words surprised him he hid it well. "You know I can't answer that question, Sam. We don't have a seal of confession like the Catholics, but I regard any conversation about my parishioners' problems to be privileged. I'm sure you feel the same way about your patients."

"You're telling me she did speak with you."

"Not at all. You've jumped to that conclusion."

"Did she name the father?"

He studied my face for almost a minute before replying. Then his answer was the briefest shake of his head. I could take it for what I wanted—a refusal to answer or a negative reply.

"One more thing," I said. "Does Jason Sennick attend your church?"

"He comes occasionally. I wouldn't call him a loyal parishioner."

"And Bud and Doris Clark?"

"They're Catholic. Talk to Father Brewster about them."

I stood up. "Thank you for your time."

We shook hands at the door and he said, "One other thing. I'm lining up pallbearers for the funeral. Could you be one?"

"Certainly."

When I went back out through the church the choir was singing "O God, Our Help in Ages Past."

* * *

Bud Clark was employed by a company that purchased the bulk of Proctor Hall's tobacco output, which was how the two couples had become friendly. Hall had his tobacco grown under great canopies of cheesecloth which covered entire fields, producing the large thin leaves used for cigar wrappers. Our southern New England climate was perfect for such a product, and Hall had become wealthy growing it. I found Bud the following morning in one of the remote fields at the Hall farm, inspecting tobacco leaves damaged by the weekend's unexpected cold and snow.

"I'm afraid this field is lost," Bud was telling Jason Sennick as I walked up to join them. "You stretched the growing season too far this year."

"Well, we got most of it in a few weeks ago. I thought we'd make it with this batch too, based on the weather forecasts."

Bud turned to greet me, extending his hand. "What brings you out in the middle of a tobacco field, Sam?"

"Wanted to chat with you, Bud. They told me at the office you were out here." I turned to acknowledge Sennick's presence. "Tough luck with this field, Jason."

The big man shrugged. "Guess I needed more than luck. I shoulda asked Mooney for some prayers. Hope it doesn't cost me my job."

"Is Proctor upset about it?"

"You might say that. He got back from his trip and never asked me about this field. Figured the leaf was all harvested. I had to break the news to him yesterday."

He and Bud Clark exchanged a few more words and then separated. I stuck with Bud because he was the one I'd come to see. "What's up, Sam?" he asked when we were alone. "Is it about Rita's death?"

"That's right. I'm trying to help Sheriff Lens if I can."

"I don't know a thing about it. Doris and I didn't even know she was dead until yesterday morning."

"How did you find out?"

"Proctor called to tell us."

"The autopsy showed Rita was nearly three months pregnant, Bud."

He seemed truly surprised. "That can't be! Not Rita Perkins. Hell, she was Mooney's choir director, wasn't she?"

"That's no protection against pregnancy."

"Do they know who the father was?"

"Not yet." I looked him in the eye. "It wasn't you, was it?"

"Me? Sam, the woman was twelve, thirteen years older than me! I hate to speak ill of the dead, but she couldn't hold a candle to my Doris in the looks department. You're barkin' up the wrong tree with that question."

"I had to ask it. Remember Rita's fainting spell at Sunday afternoon's tea party? She fainted just after my nurse Mary said the Cana jar reminded her of the Biblical wedding and all we needed was the bride and groom. I think the baby's father was at the party, and that Rita's sudden thoughts of him, and the strain of her secret pregnancy, caused her to faint."

"That means me or Proctor or Jason, unless you want to include Reverend Mooney too."

"For the moment I'm not leaving anyone out."

"Maybe the pregnancy was too much for a religious woman like her and she took her own life."

"I doubt it,' I replied. "She lived long enough to phone the Halls and me, trying to get help. That's not the sort of thing a suicide does. There was no note and she said nothing on the phone about killing herself."

He shook his head. "Sorry I can't help you, Sam. Believe me, I never had any sort of relationship with Rita Perkins. We were only invited to the party on Sunday because we're friends of the Halls." Clark and I walked back to our cars together and parted. I could see Jason Sennick watching from the barn, but happily he didn't approach me for any more advice.

It was late that afternoon when Sheriff Lens stopped by my office in the doctors' wing of Pilgrim Memorial Hospital. The lab that did tests for the county was located there too, and he brought me the report on the water jar from Cana. "I had it tested every which way, just like you wanted, Doc. They even x-rayed it."

I could tell from his tone of voice that they'd found nothing, but I still took the report and looked it over: *One stoneware water jar, height 6 in., weight 14 oz., capacity 27 fluid oz. Word "Cana" scratched on bottom. X-ray and chemical analyses reveal no irregularities or foreign substances.* I handed it back to him. "Got any ideas?"

"Maybe we should consider suicide again."

"You're the second one who's suggested suicide. Bud Clark was telling me that just this morning."

"Look at it this way, Doc. There was no wine in the house. No one poisoned that jar before you all left, because you tasted it yourself and it was still water. The killer didn't return with the poisoned wine because there were no footprints in the snow that started falling as you and Mary left. Where does that leave us? Suicide, right?"

'Where'd she get the wine?"

"Maybe a little cooking wine somewhere. My men might have missed it."

"Why put it in that Cana jar when there was a perfectly good glass on the table right next to—?"

I stopped speaking and saw again in my mind that empty glass standing next to the poisoned jar at the center of the kitchen table. "My God, Sheriff, it just came to me! Come along. I'm going to show you how water changed into wine and who poisoned Rita Perkins."

* * *

Jason Sennick was working on his truck in the front yard of the Hall farmhouse when we drove up. He stared at me, as he had done earlier, and then went back to his task. It was Mildred who answered when we rang and showed us to the big living room. "Is your husband here, too?" I asked.

"He's in the study. What is this about?"

"I have a question to ask you, and I'm sure he'll want to hear the answer."

The color drained from her face. "I'll get him."

Proctor Hall came in smoking one of his long cigars, dressed in a plaid shirt and jeans. "Hello, Sam, Sheriff. Good to see you. What's this all about?"

"I just have a question for your wife, Proctor."

"What's that?"

"Mildred, how many stoneware jars did you buy in Cana?"

"How many?" She glanced at her husband.

Proctor answered the question. "You bought two, Mildred. Don't you remember? We kept the other one for ourselves."

"That's right," she said, moistening her lips.

"Could I see it?" I asked.

She went out and returned in a moment carrying a brown jar that seemed the exact duplicate of the one they'd given Rita. "Here it is. They're both the same."

I turned it over and saw the Cana marking scratched on the bottom. "How did you know there were two, Doc?" the sheriff asked.

"Because the customs declaration gave the weight of the stoneware as twenty-eight ounces, while your lab report listed it as fourteen ounces. Obvious deduction: There were two jars."

"What does that tell us?"

"How Rita Perkins was poisoned in a locked house surrounded by unmarked snow."

"Look here," Proctor Hall spoke up, "if you're accusing my wife of anything, you'd better watch your step!"

"The autopsy shows Rita was three months pregnant," I went on. "The pregnancy began in August, Proctor, and I think you were the cause of it. When you returned from your cruise she threatened to name you as the father."

His expression had turned angry. "You don't have an ounce of evidence to back up any of this."

"I think I have. When I first saw Rita's body and entered her kitchen on Sunday, the jar and the empty glass were at the center of the table. You two arrived almost at once, and moments later, when I went to examine the contents of the jar, it was at the edge of the table. Only one of you could have moved it, could have substituted Rita's original jar for the second one you'd brought with you."

"The poisoned wine?" Mildred asked. "But she was already dead then! You're accusing us of bringing poisoned wine and substituting it for the water jar after she was dead?"

"Exactly," I told her. "But I'm only accusing one of you."

"Which one?" Sheriff Lens asked, shifting his gaze between them.

"When I let them into Rita's house they were both wearing top-coats as protection against the weather. Mildred took hers off and left it over a chair in the living room, but Proctor kept his on. She could hardly have hidden the substitute jar under the tight sweater and skirt she was wearing, so it had to be you, Proctor. A large cork or a piece of rubber, held in place with a rubber band, would have kept the wine from spilling while it was hidden under your coat. You switched jars while I turned away to phone the sheriff. That's why there were no fingerprints on it. You knew from Rita's phone call, of course, that she had swallowed the poison and was dying."

His smile was hard and cold. "You're accusing me of getting Rita pregnant and then bringing a jar of poisoned wine into her house after she was already dead. What purpose could I possibly have had for substituting those jars?"

"You had to introduce poison into the house in some manner, so the police wouldn't realize the true source of it. The water jar from Cana provided a perfect opportunity. It left us puzzling over a miracle while obscuring the truth."

"What truth was that?" he asked.

"I think you slipped Rita a packet of poison when you took her aside to thank her for the party. Later, after everyone had gone, she went into the kitchen and mixed it with water in that glass. She drank it down and then washed out the glass before the first symptoms started. You gave her the poison and that's why she tried to phone you first when the convulsions began."

"Why would she take poison that I gave her?"

I took a deep breath. "Because you told her it would induce a miscarriage."

* * *

Proctor Hall was tried and convicted early the following year. A supply of cyanide salts and some letters from Rita were found hidden in a closet of his home, and Mildred testified that it had been his idea to keep secret the purchase of two water jars in Cana. She divorced him soon afterward and moved out of state. By that time the Germans were in Denmark, and the world was changing faster than anyone could have imagined.

THE PROBLEM OF
THE ENCHANTED TERRACE

THE war was a terrible thing [Dr. Sam Hawthorne was saying as he refilled his visitor's glass], but in the autumn of 1939 America still hadn't felt its full fury. Though the president had declared our neutrality in the European war on September fifth, he proclaimed a state of limited national emergency three days later. German U-boats were active in the North Atlantic all through those early months, and the British liner Athenia, bound for Canada, became the first of many ships to be sunk.

In Northmont, life went on pretty much as it always had. My nurse Mary Best and I had been invited by friends to accompany them on a drive through southern New England to view the fall foliage. When a new young doctor named Harry Gilbert offered to look after my patients for a few days, such a trip began to seem practical. I'd never been a great one for vacations, but Mary convinced me we could drive up to Cape Cod and back without being missed. "Sam, a year from now we might be in a war," she argued. "Let's get away while we can."

So we set out with Winston and Ellen Vance in their new sedan, heading southeast across Connecticut and Rhode Island so that they could stop at New Bedford to visit a friend of Ellen's who'd just opened a Melville museum there. Winston Vance was an art dealer from Hartford who had a small farm in Northmont. He and his wife spent their vacations and most summer weekends at the farm. I'd become his country doctor when he suffered a mild case of heart palpitations during one such visit, and after Mary Best became friendly with Ellen, the four of us ended up having dinner together once a month or so. This was the first time we'd gone on an overnight trip with them. They had a son in high school and were starting to think of a college for him. I hoped the war in Europe wouldn't interfere with those plans.

Ellen was younger than her husband, and younger than me, for that matter. I guessed her to be in her mid thirties; she still had a girlish figure and a giddy manner left over from the Roaring Twenties. Sometimes I would kid her about being the only flapper left alive, but I did enjoy her company. "Too bad she's happily married," Mary would chide me following her occasional office visits, when I sat grinning behind my desk.

"She cheers me up," I answered defensively. "Nothing wrong with that."

"I'll have to take lessons from her," Mary said, retreating to her desk.

On our auto tour through an autumn wonderland of golden leaves, Winston did all the driving. He seemed to enjoy the outdoors, and we stopped frequently to gaze off at some particularly splendid view. "I know an artist in New York who could paint that magnificently," he told us.

"I know just who you're thinking of," Ellen joined in. "Archie Quain."

He nodded. "But the future of art doesn't belong to the realists. Nothing can be more real than photography. Ten, twenty years from now the great paintings will be abstracts. Surrealists like Dali will reign supreme."

"Maybe," I answered a bit uncertainly. Arguing modern art was not one of my strong points and I was glad later in the day when we crossed over into Massachusetts and spotted the first sign directing us to Fall River and then on to New Bedford. The road was bumpy here and the autumn rains had left puddles of water for Winston to splash through.

"Let's get our rooms first," he suggested. 'Then we'll locate the museum and go see your friend, Ellen." We found suitable lodging at a motel near the shore and then headed for the museum.

New Bedford had been an important whaling port from about 1820 until the beginning of the Civil War. It was here that Herman Melville had boarded his first whaling ship, the Acushnet, in January of 1841. It didn't matter that he and a friend had deserted the ship in the South Pacific eighteen months later. The seeds of *Moby Dick* had been planted in his mind. I learned all this later that afternoon when we arrived at the Melville Museum on Dartmouth Street. It was an old two-story house with a traditional widow's walk on top, and I imagined a lonely nineteenth-century wife pacing up there for the first sighting of her husband's incoming ship. As we entered I caught the musty odor of an old building, not quite covered by the fresh paint job.

We were welcomed by Ellen's friend, who proved to be an old school chum named Martin Faulk. He was tall and muscular, with a few strands of gray in his otherwise coal-black hair. I wondered if the gray was premature or if I'd guessed too low in estimating Ellen Vance's age. "God, Ellen," he said, giving her a hug; "you look just like you did the day we graduated from high school!"

She laughed appreciatively. "Thanks for the fib, Martin. This is my husband, Winston Vance."

Winston shook hands, already sizing up the place. "Glad to meet you, Martin, after all my wife has told me about her school days. How long have you been open here?"

"About three months. We opened the Fourth of July weekend."

"Do you live here too?"

"No, it's all museum. I have a small place a few blocks away. You'll find lots of material on whaling here, but we try not to compete with the city's Whaling Museum. Our true focus is on Herman Melville and his writings."

While Martin Faulk and Ellen got caught up on each other's lives, I looked around at the various exhibits. There were first editions of several of Melville's books, plus photographs of him at various stages of his adult life, all with a full beard. There were paintings and photographs of whales, of course, and actual examples of the gear used to hunt them. There were harpoons and whaling pikes and gaffs, long cylinders dating from the early 1800s called California Whaling Rockets that a seaman could fire from his shoulder, and pulleys for lifting dead whales onto the ship. There was even a cat-o'-ninetails, used for shipboard floggings. I tried to remember one in a Melville novel. *Billy Budd,* first published years after Melville's death, not long after I graduated from college, seemed the most likely, but I was pretty certain the title character had been hanged, not flogged.

"I want you to see the view from our widow's walk," Faulk was saying. "Perhaps if we're lucky we'll see Melville's ghost." He grinned and led the way upstairs.

"I didn't realize you were bringing us on a ghost hunt," Mary Best told Ellen.

"I don't know a thing about it!" Ellen pleaded. "I think he's pulling our leg. He was always something of a jokester in high school."

But we followed him up to the second floor where there was more Melville memorabilia, including a sketch of the author's birthplace in New York City and woodcuts of early whaling ships. There was even a portion of a sail from an actual whaler. "Just one more flight," our guide told us with a smile.

Living in New England for most of my life, I'd observed many widow's walks on the tops of houses, especially those situated near the shore. However, this was my first view from one that actually faced the ocean, with a perfect view of the distant horizon. When we'd all had time to appreciate the view, Faulk pointed in the other direction, toward a more modern house that backed up to his museum. It was more than a hundred feet away, with a semicircular flagstone terrace on the back, facing us. It came out about ten feet from the rear of the house and had a low stone wall around the edge. There were no steps down to the yard, but a door at the corner of the house provided access.

"I tried to buy that property and the nineteenth-century inn that was on it," he explained, "because it was where Melville is believed to have stayed the night before he boarded the Acushnet in 1841 for the Pacific whaling waters. But this fellow Ainscott outbid me and built that house two years ago. I can't complain, because he keeps the property in perfect condition. He grows roses all along the terrace wall in the summer. There are those who say Melville's ghost has been seen on the terrace, and it's been hit by lightning during thunderstorms."

"A haunted terrace!" Winston Vance remarked. "Just the thing for you, Sam!"

Martin Faulk turned to me with renewed interest. "Are you a student of the paranormal?"

"Not really. Occasionally in Northmont we've had some crimes of a seemingly impossible nature. I've helped Sheriff Lens get to the bottom of them. But they rarely involve ghosts or the supernatural. The folks in Northmont are more down-to-earth. Perhaps it's your nearness to the sea that brings about these ghostly manifestations."

We went back downstairs while Winston questioned Faulk about the economics of the Melville Museum. "I see you have a nominal admission charge. That hardly seems enough to support the place."

"My father left me a little money when he passed away," Faulk explained, "and I have a backer here in town."

While we were up on the widow's walk admiring the view, some other customers had come in down below. Faulk hurried to greet them and collect the admission fee. I could see that Ellen wanted to remain and chat about the old days, so I suggested that Mary and I stroll around the neighborhood and return in an hour. That was how we came to meet Ken Ainscott.

* * *

The museum building was at the top of a hill running almost to the harbor. Mary Best peered at the slope and decided a stroll down the hill would necessarily mean a stroll back up it. "Not in these shoes," she decided. "Let's walk around the other way, Sam."

The wind had come up a little as the early autumn darkness approached, sending gray clouds racing across the sky. We'd walked around to the new house that backed up to the museum before we encountered a middle-aged man coming quickly along the sidewalk. As he passed us, the dim streetlight's glow barely reaching my face, he recoiled slightly and reached up to adjust his glasses. "Gallagher? Is that you?"

"No," I assured him. "Hawthorne's the name."

He seemed to realize his mistake. "Hawthorne! A fine New England name. Not related to Nathaniel, are you?"

"Afraid not."

"For a moment I mistook you for someone else." He turned in at the sidewalk of the new house and I realized he must be the owner.

"Mr. Ainscott?" I asked, remembering the name Faulk had mentioned.

He paused and smiled. "Do you know me?"

"No, we're visitors to New Bedford. I'm Dr. Sam Hawthorne and this is my nurse, Mary Best," I said, making the introduction more formal. "An acquaintance was describing your house and its unusual terrace."

Ainscott snorted. "Nothing unusual about it." He studied Mary and me a bit more closely, then added, "I'll show it to you if you like, Dr. Hawthorne."

We followed him up the front steps, waiting while he unlocked the door. With a flip of the switch, the downstairs seemed flooded with light. "I understand this was once the site of a country inn where Herman Melville spent his last night ashore before setting sail on a whaling voyage," I said.

"That's the story, but who knows what really happened a century ago?"

The interior of the house seemed pleasant enough, its dining room windows at the rear looking out onto the flagstone terrace we'd heard about. The furnishings were Early American, and when I noticed a wall of framed pictures facing the terrace windows I assumed they were portraits of Ainscott relatives and family gatherings. It was Mary who went over to inspect them more closely, and I heard her sharp intake of breath. "Is this Hitler?" she asked.

Ainscott came up behind her. "Yes, the Führer himself. I took those when I was in Germany last year. The rally in this picture was attended by one hundred thousand people."

"What are your feelings about the war?" she asked.

"I think we should stay out of it. What Hitler is doing so far is good for Europe. Believe me, I am not the only one who feels that way."

"Tell me about your terrace," I said, trying to shift to a less controversial topic. "Is it really enchanted? Does Melville's ghost really walk there?"

"I have never seen him. I believe the stories were started by neighborhood children last Halloween. Sometimes they come around on rainy nights and I have to chase them away."

"Someone said the terrace has been struck by lightning."

Ainscott nodded. "At least twice that I've seen, though it didn't do any damage." He'd opened the terrace doors while he spoke and we followed him outside. Even in the twilight we could see the fine workmanship of the flagstones and the low wall at their edge.

"Was this done by local workmen?" I asked.

"Fellow named Roddy Gallagher. I thought you were him for a moment outside. Fine workman when he's sober, but there were days when I had to track him down at the bar to get any work out of him."

I smiled. "That's the first time I've been mistaken for a drunken Irishman."

"I meant no offense."

A gust of wind blew some dead leaves from the overhanging trees and Mary shivered slightly. We went back inside. There was no sign of Melville's ghost.

* * *

Winston and Ellen Vance had enjoyed a nice visit with Martin Faulk, but they were ready to leave by the time we returned to the Melville Museum. "Good meeting you," Faulk said, shaking my hand. "I wish I could dine with you tonight but I have to see my backer. How long with you be here, Ellen?"

"Just overnight," she told him. "We're on our way to Cape Cod."

He shook his head. "The Cape in October can be a chilly place. You really feel that wind off the ocean. And you know what happened with that hurricane last year. Why not stay here tomorrow instead, and I'll take you all to dinner in the evening."

We exchanged glances, and since the Vances were driving I left the decision to them. "We don't have reservations on the Cape," Ellen said. "Why don't we stay here? We could drive over to the college tomorrow and see the campus. The University of Massachusetts is one of the places our son is interested in."

So it was decided. Ellen promised to phone Faulk the following afternoon and we went off to a seafood restaurant he recommended. Over cocktails I asked, "Is he like you remembered him, Ellen?"

"Pretty much. Of course it's been nearly twenty years since we were in school together. Everyone grows up."

Mary told them about our meeting with Ken Ainscott, about his house and the pictures of Hitler on the wall. "Can you imagine? I feel like I should report him or something!"

"I guess there's no law against having a picture of Hitler on your wall," Winston said. "It's a free country and it's not our war."

It wasn't our war, and even though the following morning's newspaper carried a story about another British ship sunk by U-boats in the North Atlantic, it still seemed a long way away. Winston drove us to the college and we spent a few hours roaming the campus, experiencing the same sights and sounds their son might experience in two years' time. If it still wasn't our war.

When we returned to New Bedford in midafternoon the streets were shiny from a recent to Faulk's place. The museum was open till six and he'd be there at least that long. We decided on a drink at a neighborhood tavern a few blocks away. A tall, slender man with graying hair was entertaining some of the bar patrons with simple card tricks as we entered. Ellen Vance studied his face and movements and suddenly said, "That man looks like you, Sam."

Even though we see our faces in the mirror each day, I don't believe a person can easily spot someone who looks like them. For one thing, appearances have as much to do with gestures and expressions as with the structure of one's face. In a mirror the face is generally at rest, and we rarely see ourselves as others see us. But Ellen's words did focus my attention on the man, and I had to agree there was a passing similarity. I hadn't attempted a card trick since my youth, but I walked over to observe the man with the fleet fingers while the others took seats in a booth.

As he finished a trick involving four aces, I asked, "Your name wouldn't be Gallagher, would it?"

Closer up, he was probably ten years older than me, but perhaps in the twilight it wasn't too surprising that Ainscott had confused us. "Do I know you?" he countered.

"I was visiting Ken Ainscott and I admired his flagstone terrace. He said a local fellow named Roddy Gallagher had done it."

"That's me. I do fireplaces too. Any sort of stonework. Ainscott's was a special job. Did he show you the trick to ti?"

"No."

"Here, let me buy you a beer."

"Sorry, I'm with those other people. I really must get back. Just wanted to see if you were Gallagher."

He fanned the deck of cards with one hand and gave a little bow. "That's me!"

I returned to our booth. "He's the man who built Ainscott's enchanted terrace."

Mary's face brightened. "The person Ainscott mistook you for!"

"They do look something alike," Winston agreed.

"Does he know anything about the ghost?" Ellen asked.

"I didn't ask him." But I was remembering his remark about some sort of trick.

* * *

Ellen phoned Faulk from the tavern and he invited us to stop at the museum for a cocktail before we went off to dinner. We went back to the motel to freshen up, and when we arrived at the Melville Museum about seven I noticed a sporty roadster parked outside. "Looks as if the place is still open," I commented.

But the door was locked and Faulk had to come in answer to our knocking. "You're just in time. Come in and meet my backer."

He ushered us into the main display room where a broad-shouldered woman in a flowered dress stood holding a half-empty cocktail glass. "Hello," she said with a smile. "I'm Ann Percy. Martin likes to describe me as his backer, but it's his hard work that is making this museum a success."

She was older than the rest of us, probably in her late forties, and her bright blond hair had obviously been touched up. There was a middle-aged spread about her that I often saw in female patients of her age. "Ann is a professor of American literature at the college," Faulk explained. "She's always been interested in Melville. Despite what she says, this place wouldn't exist without her."

We exchanged some pleasantries while Faulk poured more cocktails. "Will you be joining us for dinner, Miss Percy?" Winston asked.

"Martin already invited me but I'm afraid I can't. I have a meeting with his neighbor, Ken Ainscott. He beat us out on that piece of property, but we're hoping he'll give us an easement for an outdoor fair we want to hold in the spring."

I was still interested in the so-called Melville ghost and the flagstone terrace. "Are you going over there now?"

"Right now."

"I have a quick question for Ainscott if you don't mind me tagging along." I turned to the others. "I'll be back in five minutes."

Ann Percy put down her glass and slipped into a raincoat. "This time of year you never know what the weather's doing."

I'd been wearing mine all afternoon, more for warmth than rain protection, but as we stepped out the door I felt a few drops. "It's starting to drizzle," I called back to the others.

"Damn!" Faulk grumbled. "I'll have to go up and close the windows before we leave for dinner."

The streets were dark, lit only by occasional streetlights that seemed too far apart. "Is this your first visit to New Bedford?" Ann Percy asked between raindrops.

"The first in many years. I came here with my parents once."

The rain was increasing and I wished I'd brought an umbrella from the car. But Ken Ainscott's house was not that far and we were ringing his bell before either of us was seriously wet. Ainscott greeted Ann Percy warmly, but he was obviously surprised to see me again. "Hawthorne? I didn't know you were acquainted with Professor Percy."

"We're new friends," I explained. "I just walked over with her to ask you a question about the terrace."

"That again! Still looking for ghosts?" He turned to Ann Percy. "And what's this about an easement?"

"We just need a portion of your backyard for two weeks in the spring. We have some large outdoor exhibits we'd like to display. Of course we'd pay you something for your trouble."

He nodded. "Let me take care of Dr. Hawthorne first and we'll talk about it. Now what's this about my terrace?"

"I happened to run into Roddy Gallagher this afternoon."

"At a bar, I'll bet!"

"Well, yes," I admitted. "He mentioned there was some trick about your terrace. I wondered if—"

"What's that?" Ann Percy asked suddenly. She was pointing toward the dining room windows that looked out on the terrace. A strange greenish light seemed to have appeared for an instant and then vanished. In the distance there was a rumble of thunder.

Ainscott grunted. When the flash of greenish light came again he muttered, "Kids playing tricks. Getting close to Halloween. I'll settle them!"

He picked up a flashlight, hurried to the glass doors, and threw them open, ignoring the rain as he stepped outside. There was a sudden clap of thunder and a flash of lightning from the sky. Ainscott gave a brief scream and then there was darkness. I was right behind him, out the door within seconds, grabbing up the flashlight from where it had fallen on the terrace. I turned it on, scanning the terrace and the surrounding yard.

Ken Ainscott was nowhere to be seen.

"Where is he?" Ann Percy asked.

"I don't know. He was here and then he was gone."

"Was he hit by lightning?"

I ignored the question, walking all along the low stone wall of the terrace, shining the flashlight on the yard below. It was about three feet lower than the terrace itself, maybe six feet below the top of the wall. All along the edge of the yard had been rosebushes, now cut back for winter. The brown soil was wet and unmarked. Ainscott had neither jumped nor been pulled from that railing. I turned to shine my light up at the house itself, but the second-story windows were well out of reach. There was no rope, no flagpole for him to have grabbed onto. And no terrace windows except those in the dining room.

"You'd better go get the others," I decided. "I'll phone the police."

"Do you think that's necessary? He might come back. He's only been missing a few minutes."

"He's not coming back," I said, "because there's no place he could have gone."

* * *

She hurried down the block to the Melville Museum and returned with Mary, the Vances, and Faulk, all carrying umbrellas against the steady rain. "What is it?" Martin Faulk demanded. "What happened to him?"

"I don't know. The police are on the way. He stepped out on the terrace and disappeared." I told them exactly what had happened, complete with the eerie green light.

Mary and Ellen suggested we search the house, and they set out to do that. Before they returned, a police car with two officers had pulled up. One of them knew Professor Percy and she told them what has happened. "We've been called here before," the officer said. "He claimed he was having trouble with neighborhood kids, but he never had any evidence to show us."

Mary and Ellen came downstairs to report that the house was empty. One of the officers went up to look for himself and the other, the friend of Ann Percy whose name was Jenks, went outside with his flashlight to inspect the terrace. I followed him out and showed him the unmarked dirt of the flower bed that bordered the terrace wall. "He couldn't have jumped down," I said, "even if there'd been time. As it was, there were only seconds. And you can see for yourself there's not another building or even a tree within a hundred feet of here."

Officer Jenks grunted. "I read a mystery story once where a killer lassoed his victim from an upper window of the house and pulled him up there."

"The rest of the house was empty. There's no one upstairs now and no one could have slipped by me to escape, especially not with a body. I've been here since it happened."

"What about Professor Percy?"

"She's been here too, except for going to get the others."

Jenks seemed puzzled. "Why send her out in the rain? Why didn't you phone them?"

"I guess I never thought of it. The museum is just down at the next corner and I was thinking I'd phone the police while she was gone."

"You heard the talk about ghosts and haunting out here?"

"I doubt if Herman Melville's ghost had anything to do with Ainscott's disappearance."

Finally, after speaking with the others, Officer Jenks made a few notes on his pad and said, "There's no evidence of a crime here, and none of you are family members. If he doesn't turn up in twenty-four hours, get one of his family to file a missing persons report."

"He has no family," Martin Faulk informed them. "I got to know him pretty well two years ago when I was trying to buy that old inn. He was always a loner, even when he traveled around Europe."

Finally, after the house had been locked up and the police had departed, Winston asked if we were still going to dinner.

"I certainly am!" Faulk said. "I could eat a horse."

We walked back to the museum for the Vances' car. Mary had left her purse in the museum so Faulk and I went in for it while the others waited. "If it's not downstairs, look in the upstairs bathroom," she called after me.

That's where we found it, with Faulk taking the opportunity to turn out a few lights and close some windows against the rain. With the purse restored to her, Mary was as hungry as the rest of us. Faulk took us to a steak and seafood place not far from where we'd eaten the previous night. I was seated facing the bar and immediately had a memory of the previous evening when I'd encountered Roddy Gallagher.

A special job. Did he show you the trick to it?

Yes, Roddy. He showed me the trick to it.

* * *

We should have been gone in the morning. We should have been heading back home to Northmont. Instead, Mary and I borrowed the Vances' car and went searching the city of New Bedford for Roddy Gallagher, the man who looked something like me.

We quickly established that he hadn't been home, and his wife seemed to know nothing of his whereabouts. She was a thin, shy woman who answered the door with some hesitation. "He hasn't done anything wrong, has he? You're not police, are you?"

"We're not police," I assured her. "I'm a doctor just visiting the city. I wanted to talk to him about the terrace he built for Mr. Ainscott."

"That was over a year ago."

"I know."

She sighed and brushed a stray hair from her eyes. "Sometimes when he's been drinking he stays over with a bartender friend of his. I can give you the address."

"It would be a big help."

Mary and I were both aware that the Vances wanted to be on the road as soon as possible. Still, I didn't feel I could leave Ainscott among the missing, especially with the police showing so little interest in the case. Armed with the bartender's address, I thanked Mrs. Gallagher and we headed across town. When we finally located Roddy he was having a late breakfast at his friend's apartment.

"I know you," he said when he saw me. "But where from?"

"Yesterday in the bar. You were doing card tricks."

He smiled, remembering it. "So I was! You asked about the stonework I did for Ken Ainscott."

I nodded. "Ainscott has disappeared. We're trying to find him."

"Can't help you there. Haven't seen him lately." His eyes strayed to Mary Best. "This your wife?"

I felt my face flush. "She's my nurse. I'm a doctor visiting the city."

"We fear Ainscott may have come to some harm," Mary told him. "Does he have any enemies?"

"I don't know him that well."

"But you built that terrace," I said, "and you mentioned there was a trick to it."

"Well, a trick to the construction."

"We need to see what it is."

"Sure, I'll show you. He's pretty proud of it."

"Let's go. We'll drive you over and bring you back."

We arrived at the Ainscott house around eleven o'clock. I'd left the front door unlocked the night before, and it was still unlocked. Apparently Ainscott hadn't returned. I led the way through the dining room and out onto the terrace. The sun was just beginning to appear after the rain, sucking the moisture from the damp flagstones in little wisps of mist.

"It's still one of the best jobs I ever did," Gallagher said, marveling at his own craftsmanship.

"Show us the trick."

"Sure."

He walked over to the center of the terrace, at the point where the low semicircular wall was farthest from the house, and lifted his right foot to push against the top of the wall. It started to move, and as Mary and I watched, the stones gave a slight grinding sound and pivoted down until the top came to rest in the rose garden. "You see? It forms a couple of steps so you can reach the yard without going back inside and out the other door. It was Ainscott's idea but I worked out the mechanics of it. After you step off, the balance causes it to rise up and close by itself. You can pull it down from the garden side too."

The demonstration, interesting as it was, disappointed me. There was nothing in this so-called trick to explain Ainscott's disappearance the previous night. I could see even now that the lowered steps had left an indentation in the soft garden earth that hadn't been there before. And Ainscott would have had no time to use the steps in the few seconds before I followed him outside.

"This is it?" I asked. "There's no built-in hiding place or anything like that?"

"Why should there be a hiding place? I built him a terrace with hidden steps to the garden and yard. Isn't that good enough?"

"It's very clear," Mary complimented him. "Sam and I will drive you back home now."

After we dropped him off, not at home but at his friend's bar, I headed back to the motel where Ellen and Winston were waiting for us. "I hate to admit I'm baffled," I told Mary. "Ainscott pulled off that stunt right before my eyes and I don't know how he did it."

"You think he's alive?"

"I'm beginning to think he must be. Imagining him dead is even more impossible."

Winston and Ellen were sympathetic but could offer little help. I sat in their room, ready to check out but not quite able to leave this business behind me. "What about that Percy woman?" Ellen asked. "She was with you at his house. Could she have done something?"

"I don't see how. Or why. Apparently her dealings with him had been friendly enough. But you people were with Faulk. Did he indicate any troubles with his neighbor?"

Winston Vance shook his head. "I don't remember him saying anything. After you and Professor Percy left he just went upstairs to close the windows and then poured us some drinks."

Finally Mary got me moving. "You can't sit here all day, Sam. It's time to go. Ainscott is probably alive and well, having a good laugh. It might be just some magic trick that Gallagher fellow taught him."

We checked out of the motel and climbed back into Winston and Ellen's car for the return trip. As we were passing the Melville Museum I glanced up at the widow's walk at the top and suddenly I knew what had happened to Ken Ainscott.

"Stop the car," I said. "We haven't bid goodbye to your friend Martin."

* * *

He saw us coming and somehow he must have known the purpose of our visit. "We're closed for a while, or I'd invite you in," he told me at the door. "I'm busy rearranging some exhibits."

"We just wanted to say goodbye again, Martin," Ellen told him.

He tried to relax and be gracious. "Of course. Come in, but just for a minute. This is a busy day for me."

I wasted no time coming to the point. "I'd like to take another look at your widow's walk before we go."

"That's impossible. I'm doing some work up there right now."

"I'm afraid I'll have to insist. Otherwise the police will be called."

Martin Faulk smiled slightly. "I see. Of course. Follow me."

I turned to the others. "Stay down here."

"You're not going up without me," Mary insisted, trailing along.

"Keep back, then."

On the second floor Faulk paused to pick up a tube about six feet long with a barbed tip projecting from it and a coil of stout rope hanging down. We'd seen it on our first visit. I was on him in an instant, pushing him off balance as we wrestled over the device. I ended up on top.

"What is it, Sam?" Mary called from behind me.

"Just what I feared. The California Whaling Rocket we saw on display when we first came here. Will you show us Ainscott's body now, Martin, or do we need to search the place?"

"You have to realize why I did it," he pleaded as Ellen and Winston came up the stairs to join us.

But there was no fight left in him. He took us to the attic stairway and showed us the body of Ken Ainscott wrapped in sailcloth, a gaping wound in his chest. Ellen Vance simply stared at Faulk, unbelieving, unable to focus on the body before her.

"I remembered he said he was going to close the upstairs windows when the rain started," I told them. "And you confirmed that he went up to do just that. But when we came back here later last night he was closing the windows then. When I remembered that, I wondered what he had done earlier. We'd seen the California Whaling Rocket, of course along with the pulleys for lifting dead whales onto a ship. The rocket was actually a rocket-powered harpoon, easily capable of covering the hundred feet between this house and Ainscott's terrace."

Vance stared at his wife's old friend. "You're telling me Faulk harpooned him and hauled him up to the widow's walk on this roof?"

"Exactly. When I thought back to that flash of lightning I'd seen just as Ainscott vanished, I realized the crack I took for thunder came a split second before the flash, contrary to the laws of nature. It wasn't lightning and thunder at all, but the firing of the rocket and its streaking trail from the widow's walk down to the terrace. The eerie green light was simply a flashlight shining through green cellophane to attract Ainscott's attention and lure him onto the terrace. And the previous lightning strikes Ainscott reported were Faulk's testing of the rocket harpoon to see if it would carry that far. He had the end of the rope attached to the pulley for raising dead whales, and he contrived it to yank Ainscott's body into the air as soon as the harpoon struck him. Any traces of blood were washed away by the rain. When I got out there, seconds later, the body was up on the widow's walk, invisible in the darkness and rain. He needed a rainy night, of course, so the rocket's trail would be mistaken for lightning."

Ellen was shaking her head, still trying to comprehend. "But why, Martin? I thought you were getting along well with him. You couldn't still be angry because he outbid you for that old inn."

"It wasn't the inn, Ellen. Don't you understand? The man was a Nazi! His whole attitude, the pictures on his walls! He admired Adolf Hitler, and here we are almost at war with Germany. I had to do something. If war broke out who knows what damage the man might have done? I tested the rocket harpoon a couple of times and it seemed to work well. Then you came, Ellen, and you even mentioned your son who'd be off to college if war didn't break out. I thought of him and all our country's other sons, and knew I had to go through with my plan. I wished it was Hitler himself down there. It was only Ken Ainscott, but that was a beginning."

Vance said, very quietly, "We'll have to tell the police, Martin."

"I was going to bury his body in the basement. No one would ever have found it there."

Once, a year or so later, I thought of Martin Faulk and asked Ellen if a trial had ever been held. She told me he'd been ruled insane and sent to an institution. By that time the Battle of Britain was under way and the first peacetime draft had been approved. The entire world seemed to be drifting toward insanity.

Remembering that view from the widow's walk, I wondered if Martin Faulk might have looked down on Ainscott's terrace far below and seen Hitler there, and imagined himself to be like God, hurling not a harpoon but a thunderbolt.

THE PROBLEM OF
THE UNFOUND DOOR

I T was the summer of 1940 [Dr. Sam Hawthorne was telling his guest], and the war in Europe was heating up. More than three hundred thousand British and French troops had been evacuated from Dunkirk in late May and early June as the German army invaded the Low Countries and France. The *Luftwaffe* was regularly attacking convoys in the English Channel and several cities, ports, and airfields in southeast England had been bombed by midsummer.

The war was still a long way from Northmont, though the mayor and town council were reminded of it when a small community of Anglican nuns who'd settled in our town asked permission to bring over some British children. The south of London had already been hit by a few stray bombs and the evacuation of women and children had begun.

I had firsthand knowledge of the Sisters of Saint George because they'd chosen me as their doctor. Sister Simeon had explained it to me on my first visit. "Hawthorne is such a literary name. We knew you must be a good man."

"He wrote *The Scarlet Letter*," I reminded her with a smile.

The small congregation had come to Northmont two years earlier, purchasing the old Bates estate out on Town Line Road. There were only eight of them in the beginning. Sister Simeon had come later, as abbess of the convent, when the original abbess, Sister Luke, fell ill. That was when I first entered the life of the Sisters of Saint George. Sadly, there was little I or anyone could do for Sister Luke in her eighty-fifth year. She died before Christmas of '39 and was buried on the convent grounds.

Shortly after the nuns arrived in the summer of '38 they had a high brick wall built around their entire yard, leaving only the front of the convent accessible to visitors. It was an expensive project that took months of labor by three masons and an apprentice. The wall was twelve feet high, topped with barbed wire, and the first time I saw it I wondered if the purpose was to keep intruders out or the nuns in. "Back in England we are a cloistered order," Sister Simeon explained. "The strict rules have been relaxed over here, but still we must follow the dictates of our mother superior back home."

Sister Simeon, was a commanding presence. She was a woman around fifty, though the starched white wimple she and the other nuns wore made it difficult to determine age with any degree of accuracy. They dressed all in white, unlike the black-and-white habits of most Catholic nuns. All of them spoke with refined British accents which were a pleasure to hear. Of the seven besides Sister Simeon, all but two seemed younger. Sister Faith was seventy-two, as I learned when I treated her for a throat infection on one of my calls, and Sister Hope was probably in her mid sixties.

It was on my first visit to the convent of the Sisters of Saint George that I was introduced to the full congregation. "Sisters, this is Dr. Sam Hawthorne," Sister Simeon announced in the common room where they took their meals. It had been a simple dining room when old Bates lived there, and like the rest of the convent it was dimly lit.

"I'm pleased to be here," I told them with a smile. "Welcome to Northmont."

Sister Luke was upstairs in bed at the time, waiting out her final illness. It was Sister Simeon who introduced the others. "They have their more formal religious names, but since there are seven they have taken the names of the seven virtues during their stay here. This is the eldest, Sister Faith, then Sisters Hope, Charity and Fortitude. Over here are Sisters Temperance, Prudence, and Justice." She smiled and added, "Sister Justice is the tallest. She can reach all the top shelves." A couple of the others giggled at what was obviously a familiar joke.

"That makes it easy to remember," I said.

Little Sister Temperance, perhaps the most attractive of them, gave me a glowing smile and commented, "I pray you can keep us all in the best of health."

Except for the unavoidable death of Sister Luke, I did fairly well. When Sister Simeon phoned me on that August morning I assumed she was calling about a medical problem. "How's Sister Charity's allergy?" I asked. "We're into the hay-fever season now."

"It doesn't seem to be bothering her too much as yet," Sister Simeon assured me. "Actually, Doctor, I called about a different matter entirely. I've been pressing Mayor Stokes to let us bring a dozen or so children over from London to live at the convent. He seems reluctant for some reason. I was wondering if you could speak to him."

"Well, I can try. Tell me a little about this."

"They're starting to evacuate some women and children from the city, especially children. There's a feeling the bombing will only get worse. Our convent is large enough so we could easily accommodate twelve or fifteen girls, but we need some sort of zoning permission from the town. Mayor Stokes is afraid we might try to make nuns out of them."

"I'll speak to him," I promised.

"Thank you so much, Doctor."

The town council only held one meeting during the summer months, and it was just two days away. I knew I'd better present Sister Simeon's case to the mayor before that. Being mayor of a town like Northmont was only a part-time job at best, and Doug Stokes earned his living selling Ford automobiles. After I'd seen the day's last patient I told my nurse Mary Best that I was leaving early. Then I drove over to the local Ford dealership.

The dog days of August had settled over the automobile business and I found Northmont's mayor seated in his office with his feet up on the desk, enjoying one of his fine Havana cigars. "What brings you to this neck o' the woods, Doc? Thinking of trading in that Buick on a shiny new 1940 Ford?" He was a big man in his late thirties who'd played football in high school and never let anyone forget it. He always wore one of those hard straw hats during the summer months, the kind that started to yellow by Labor Day and had to be discarded, to be replaced the following spring.

I dropped into the only other chair in the tiny office. "Sister Simeon phoned me from the convent, Doug. She's concerned that you're trying to block her from bringing some English children over here."

His feet came off the desk and he took the cigar out of his mouth. "That's a tough one, Doc. The land is zoned for. agriculture out there. We made an exception when the nuns came here two years ago, but now they're trying to turn it into a boarding school."

"They're doing no such thing! London and the other cities in the south of England have already been bombed. The nuns are trying to save at least a handful of children by evacuating them while there's still time."

Mayor Stokes looked unhappy. "I don't know, Doc. I talked to a few of the council members and they were against it. If the nuns don't teach them, they have to go to our schools. They're not like us here. They talk different, they act different."

"Perhaps more intelligent and civilized," I responded with a smile. "Maybe if they stay long enough to grow up in Northmont they'll even become customers of yours."

He thought about that. "Look, come to the council meeting on Thursday and tell it to the rest of them."

I readily agreed. "I will. And maybe I'll bring Sister Simeon along."

* * *

Summer meetings of the town council were never very crowded, and this one was no exception. Sheriff Lens was there, seated in the back row. I knew he often dropped in on the meetings if he had no pressing business. I was greeting Mavis Baker, one of the two women council members, as Mayor Stokes called the session to order and went quickly through some routine agenda items. Then he took up the request of the Convent of Saint George to house up to fifteen teenage and preteen girls at the convent, said girls to be evacuees from London and other British cities. Someone mentioned zoning and asked if this was to be a school. I raised my hand and announced that Sister Simeon, the abbess of the convent, was present to address that issue. Though she'd been seated by my side in her white habit through the entire session, Mayor Stokes seemed taken by surprise.

"Ah, Sister Simeon! It's a pleasure to have you here! I know so little about your order. Are you Catholic nuns?"

"Anglican," she replied, remaining seated. "There are eight of us at the convent since the death of Sister Luke. We are all British, which is why we feel a special kinship with the children. We do not wish to convert any of them to our faith, though it is quite likely they are Church England already. A certain amount of instruction in basic subjects would be given, of course, on an informal basis."

"But the space, Sister Simeon—"

"It is quite adequate. If you have your doubts, I would invite you and the other council members to tour our facilities."

There was a whispered conversation among the half-dozen men and two women who made up the town council. I could see that Mavis Baker, the only teacher on the council, especially supported the nuns, and finally it was agreed that Mayor Stokes would get his first look at the convent the following day, reporting back to the council for a final decision. Because I knew both parties quite well, Mrs. Baker suggested that I accompany Stokes and Sister Simeon on the following day's tour.

It seemed like a harmless enough request at the time.

* * *

Friday morning was warm and sunny, a perfect late summer's day in New England. A house call that took longer than expected made me late arriving at the convent on Town Line Road. It was a little after ten o'clock and Doug Stokes had already arrived. Going up the circular cinder driveway, I saw his car near the front door, its rear speckled by falling samara wings, seed spinners from a towering maple overhead. I parked right behind it as Sister Hope came out to meet me. She was a tall thin woman one of the older nuns, who walked with a slight limp left over from a fall on the convent staircase. "You're just in time, Dr. Hawthorne," she said with a pleasant voice. "Sister Simeon and the others are just starting to show Mayor Stokes around. They're in the yard but the gate is locked so we'll have to go in through the house."

I followed her through the dim corridors and down the narrow, ill-lit steps to the back door. Out in the sunlit backyard, surrounded by the high wall, I could see the cluster of nuns surrounding Mayor Stokes, his familiar straw hat visible above their heads. He must have seen me too because I saw a flash of his blue suit as he raised a hand above his head and motioned for me to join them over by the wall.

I walked slowly so the limping Sister Hope could keep up with me, and I took her hand to guide her over the rougher parts of the yard. "You should have this rolled in the spring," I suggested, not unkindly. "It's quite bumpy."

"Oh, we're used to it."

As we approached the other nuns I became aware that Doug Stokes seemed no longer among them. "Where's the mayor?" I asked Sister Simeon.

"He's gone," she replied simply, and the others nodded in agreement.

"Gone? I saw him with you just seconds ago! Where could he have gone? The grounds are walled in!"

It was little Sister Temperance who seemed to answer for them. *"The lost lane-end into heaven, a stone, a leaf, an unfound door."*

Something had happened to Mayor Stokes and I had no idea what or how or why.

* * *

An hour later, as Sheriff Lens and his deputies searched the grounds of the convent, he brought me news of the first results. "We found Doug's skimmer, Doc. Want to take a look?"

The straw hat was there, all right, on the other side of the high wall. It lay upside down in some tall grass. There was no doubt it was the mayor's hat.

The sweatband had his initials stamped in gold: *D. S.* for Douglas Stokes. "Looks like he climbed over the wall," the sheriff commented. "Or walked through it."

There was no other sign of him, and the rest of the grass seemed undisturbed. "I won't consider walking through it," I told him. "And climbing over it is an impossibility. Even with a boost from the good sisters he could barely have gotten a finger-hold on the top. There's barbed wire up there, and the grass around his straw hat seems undisturbed by the impact of a body landing. Remember, I saw him wave to me. I was walking right toward him and he never left that circle of nuns."

"But he did leave, Doc," Sheriff Lens insisted, "if we're to believe your story."

"You can believe it, every word of it."

The sheriff let out a sigh. "Where are the sisters?"

"Praying in their chapel."

"Let's go see."

The seven virtues, as we thought of them, were in two pews of the tiny chapel, added to the main house when the nuns moved there. An altar up front was available for visiting ecclesiastics, but at the moment it was serving Sister Simeon as she led them in prayer. The sheriff waited until she came to a pause and then he joined hex at the front of the chapel. "Sisters, we have an unusual problem here. Doc says he saw Mayor Stokes with you in the convent yard, and then he just disappeared. My men found his straw hat on the other side of the wall but he couldn't have climbed over or walked through it. His car is still parked out front but he's nowhere to be found. I gotta have an explanation for all this."

Sister Simeon had bowed her head as if still in prayer, and it was Sister Charity who responded from the front pew. Her wrinkled face seemed painfully squeezed in the white wimple and I wondered fleetingly if the tight habit might somehow contribute to her allergy problems. "It was not the mayor who was with us," she said, "but only his spirit. What Dr. Hawthorne saw was but a shadow of a man already passed from us."

It was my turn to speak. "Are you trying to tell us the mayor is dead? I've never believed in ghosts, and I don't think a ghost drove his car out here."

Sister Simeon raised her head. "Mayor Stokes himself will tell us what happened, when the time comes."

Sheriff Lens laid a hand on my shoulder. "Come on, Doc. We won't learn anything here. Let's go check that wall again."

He was right, of course, and I followed him out of the little chapel. The Sisters of Saint George, if they knew anything, were not about to tell us until they were good and ready. Outside, we walked over to one of the deputies and listened to his negative report. Then we walked to the spot where the twelve-foot-high wall joined a front corner of the house, near the driveway where the mayor's car was still parked. There was a narrow iron gate in the wall at this point, allowing entry into the grounds without passing through the convent itself. The gate had been locked when the sheriff arrived, but Sister Simeon had quickly provided the key from the ring attached to her belt.

From this point Sheriff Lens and I walked along every inch of the lengthy wall, running our hands over the whitewashed bricks, pausing to examine every slight irregularity. "They know what happened to him," the sheriff said as we walked.

"Of course they know," I agreed. "But that only makes the problem all the more intriguing. What happened to him and why are they hiding the truth?"

He grunted, and we covered the rest of the wall in silence Finally, satisfied there were no hidden doorways or secret exits, we gave it up. We'd circled the house to the front again and I walked over to peer into the mayor's coupe. The keys were still in the ignition. No one would lock their car while visiting a convent. I tried the motor and it turned over. Then I removed the keys and walked around to the rear of the coupe.

"What you gonna do, Doc?"

"Look in the rumble seat." I inserted the key and turned the handle, pulling it open. A small collection of maple spinners slid off the lid to the ground.

Whatever I'd expected or feared to find, it wasn't there. The compartment was empty. I relocked it and returned the key to the ignition.

"Let's go back into town," the sheriff decided. "I'll leave a couple of deputies here to search the fields, but Doug Stokes is probably sittin' in his office having a good laugh at all of us."

* * *

But Stokes wasn't at the dealership or his town-hall office. No one had seen him all day. The councilwoman, Mavis Baker, walked by as we were asking for him. "Wasn't he going out to inspect that convent today?" she asked.

"He was there," I confirmed, "but then he left."

"It's very important that we find him," Sheriff Lens told her. "If you see him, tell him to call Doc or me right away."

She gave him her sternest teacher's gaze. "I have a right to know what's going on."

I took over the conversation. Mavis and the sheriff had never gotten along. "Doug disappeared somehow out at the convent. I saw him in the yard near the wall. Then he was gone. There was no door, and he couldn't very well have walked through the wall."

Mavis Baker snorted. "If this is another of your locked-room things—"

"No locks, no rooms. Just a wall with an unfound door." I remembered the passage Sister Temperance had quoted.

"People do walk through walls," she said. "When I was in high school my parents took me to see the great Houdini perform in Boston. He walked through a wall."

"Onstage they can do it with trap doors," the sheriff told us. Mrs. Baker ignored him.

I still wasn't willing to believe that anything serious had happened to our missing mayor. The idea of the Sisters of Saint George conspiring to harm him in any way seemed out of the question. Yet when I remembered the cryptic words spoken by good Sister Temperance I wasn't so sure.

As we left the town hall Sheriff Lens said, "He'll turn up." But his voice lacked conviction.

"Your men searched the grounds, Sheriff. I think we'll have to search the convent itself."

"You mean go into their rooms?"

I nodded. "I'll drive back out there and speak with Sister Simeon. Give me a half-hour and then follow along. I think she'll let us do it without a search warrant."

* * *

It was Sister Fortitude, one of the younger nuns, whom I found in the front yard of the convent. She was watering the grass with a garden hose and when she saw me she spoke with a wonderful Scottish brogue. "The Lord has been stingy with water this summer, Dr. Hawthorne."

"It's been a dry one," I agreed. "Is Sister Simeon around?"

"She may still be in the chapel."

I couldn't help noticing that Doug Stokes's car remained in the curving driveway by the front door. "Someone should call the mayor's brother about his car."

"Perhaps he will return and wonder where it is."

"Unless he's gone to that undiscovered country from whose bourn no traveler returns."

Sister Fortitude smiled slightly. "Ah, Hamlet! It is good to speak with educated people. Do you really believe your mayor is dead?"

"I hope to find out. Right now I must speak with Sister Simeon." I left her and entered the convent.

Sister Prudence was on her hands and knees, scrubbing the staircase to the second floor. She gave me a weak smile, perhaps surprised to see an unescorted man in the building. "I'm looking for Sister Simeon. I was told she might be in the chapel."

The stocky Sister Prudence placed the scrub brush in her pail and came down to join me. "I'll show you the way."

"I hate to take you from your work. I know where it is."

"A break is good for me. Come."

Sister Simeon was just leaving the chapel as we approached. Perhaps she'd heard our voices. "Your second visit today, Dr. Hawthorne."

"There's still no sign of the mayor," I explained. "Sheriff Lens is coming back with a request to search your convent. I just wanted to inform you before he arrives."

"We have nothing to hide."

The sheriff arrived with five deputies and Mavis Baker, much to his dismay. Each was assigned a different portion of the convent to be searched, with one of the nuns acting as guide. When I returned to the walled-in yard where Doug Stokes had last been seen, I found that little Sister Temperance had been assigned to accompany me.

As we returned to the whitewashed wall, I said, "I've been wanting to ask you, Sister, about what you said earlier. About that unfound door."

She blushed a little. "It's from Thomas Wolfe. I found it at the beginning of his novel Look Homeward, Angel. Perhaps the unfound door leads to the afterlife. Since we were seeking a door in the wall that wasn't there, it seemed appropriate at the moment."

"You were out here with the mayor when it happened."

"We all were, except for Sister Hope. She was with you."

"Yes. But you must have seen something."

"He was here, and then he was gone," she said simply.

Sheriff Lens had come out of the convent, accompanied by Sister Simeon. "There's nothing in my section, Doc. Not a trace of Doug Stokes."

Sister Simeon spoke then. "I am quite concerned about this entire matter. As you know, Mayor Stokes came out here this morning to inspect our facilities before supporting our attempt to bring evacuated girls over from England. I believe he liked what he saw. I would hate to think our entire project might founder because he has disappeared."

"You were with him when it happened," Sheriff Lens reminded her.

"So was Dr. Hawthorne. He was within fifty feet of us."

"Sister, you must know what happened to him. There's no other possibility."

She smiled benevolently and said nothing.

The deputies and Mrs. Baker returned one by one, joining us with nothing to report. Mayor Stokes was not in the convent, alive or dead, and he was nowhere on the grounds. "He had plenty of time to get away," Mavis Baker pointed out, "while you were coming back to town looking for him."

"His car never left," Sheriff Lens replied, and of course he was right. The car still sat there, collecting its harvest of maple spinners from the overhead tree. Only the lid of the rumble seat that I'd opened earlier was free of the falling seeds.

"Mavis," I said, "you mentioned earlier that you saw Houdini walk through a wall once when you were young. Any idea how he did it?"

"Not the slightest," she admitted. "I was never good at figuring out magic tricks. I only remember he was surrounded by assistants wearing white smocks, caps, and eyeglasses. A screen was put up around him and when it was taken away he'd vanished. The group of assistants put up the screen on the other side of the wall and he reappeared. I never forgot it."

I remembered Stokes waving to me from that group of nuns. Perhaps he'd been beckoning me to join him on the other side of the wall.

I felt he was beckoning me once again as I walked to the driver's side of his car and removed the key from the ignition, just as I'd done earlier. "You looked in there already," Sheriff Lens reminded, me as I walked to the rear and inserted the key in the rumble-seat lock.

It was Sister Simeon who saw me from the convent doorway and came running out to stop me. "No!" she warned. "Don't open it!"

But I already had, far enough to show us the crumpled body of Mayor Doug Stokes, a terrible deadly gash visible on his forehead.

* * *

"All right," Sheriff Lens demanded of Sister Simeon. "Which one of you killed him?"

She was staring at me as if she hadn't even heard his question. "You looked in there once," she said. "Why did you look again?"

"I looked a couple of hours ago. Those seeds are still spinning off the maple tree but there aren't any on the rumble-seat lid as there were before. I knew it had been opened again, quite recently."

Sheriff Lens moved to her side as if ready to grab her if she tried to escape. "How did he get through that wall, and which one of you killed him?"

"We'd better go inside," I suggested. "We can talk better there."

We sat in the parlor and as we talked the other Sisters of Saint George drifted in. Mavis Baker sat at the side of Sheriff Lens as I began to speak. "It was Mrs. Baker's account of Houdini's stage illusion of walking through a wall that told me how Doug Stokes disappeared. On-stage the white-coated assistants are the key to the trick. With so many of them milling around, one person more or less passes unnoticed. Houdini simply stepped behind that screen by the wall, pulled a white smock, cap, and glasses from a hidden pocket in the screen, and put them on. Then he mingled with the other identically dressed assistants."

Mavis Baker's mouth had dropped open as I spoke. "You mean Doug disguised himself as one of these nuns?"

I turned my attention to Sister Justice. "Do you want to tell us about it, Sister?"

The tall nun retreated a step under my gaze. "What do you mean?"

"Mayor Stokes had no possible motive for disguising himself as a nun, but you had a very good motive for disguising yourself as Mayor Stokes. I only caught the briefest glimpse of his straw hat and blue jacket and upraised arm, surrounded by all of you. As the tallest nun here, Sister Justice, it must have been you wearing that hat and jacket. In an instant the straw hat and the jacket came off and you were back to your true self. The jacket was easily hidden beneath one of the Sisters' habits."

"You wouldn't have noticed the quick change from fifty feet away?" the sheriff questioned.

"I was helping Sister Hope over the rough ground, because of her limp. When you're helping someone like that, you naturally look down several times. That's when the change took place."

"But why?"

"I think the plan was for Sister Justice, wearing the mayor's straw hat and jacket, to exit the grounds through the gate and go directly to the car. They hoped I would arrive late enough to see him driving away. I came late, but not late enough."

Sheriff Lens was frowning. "You're telling us the mayor was already dead at that time?"

"That's exactly what I'm telling you. Doug's body was hidden somewhere, perhaps behind the chapel altar, and then moved to the rumble seat of his car while we were gone and the deputies were searching elsewhere. The nuns had seen us check the rumble seat earlier."

"Which one of them killed him, Doc?"

I sighed and shook my head. "Nobody killed Doug Stokes, Sheriff. I think while they were showing him around the convent, the worst thing that could possibly have happened to them did happen. He accidentally fell down the dimly lit convent stairs and killed himself. The Sisters were only trying to hide that fact."

It was Sister Simeon who came forward then. "You seem to know everything, Dr. Hawthorne. Your magic is greater than Houdini's."

"Anyone who's been here knows that the place is dimly lit, especially the staircases. Sister Hope got her limp from falling down your stairs. For Mayor Stokes, who'd never been here before, it became a dangerous place. I'd guess that he fell on the front staircase to the second floor, perhaps on the way down, and cracked his head open on the first landing. That was where Sister Prudence was scrubbing this afternoon, no doubt trying to remove the last traces of blood."

"Why couldn't they have pushed him?" the sheriff wanted to know.

"For what purpose? He was here to pass judgment on the convent as a temporary home for girls evacuated from England, a project very dear to these nuns' hearts. No matter what he might have said, they would want no harm to come to him. If he fell on the stairs, it was an accident. They certainly wouldn't have gone through this elaborate charade if one of them had killed him."

"It was an accident," Sister Simeon confirmed. "He was leading the way down, and turned to speak with Sister Fortitude and me. He missed the step and couldn't grab the railing in time. When I heard his head hit, my body turned to ice."

I could almost feel it happening, and I knew what they must have gone through. "You saw the end of your dream then, shattered like his head. With the mayor accidentally killed while touring your convent you'd never be allowed to bring the children here."

"We thought of them in the rubble of a bombed-out city," she said. "We knew we must do anything to hide how and where he'd died. I suppose we were a little crazy even to try this, but you were late arriving and we had to take the chance. We wanted to get the car away until you'd left, then bring it back for the body. We would have run it off the road to make it appear he'd died in a car accident." She raised her eyes to look at me. "It never would have worked."

"No."

"What will happen now?" old Sister Faith wanted to know.

"I guess that's up to the sheriff," I told her.

I wasn't a party to what followed, but no charges were brought against the nuns. Mavis Baker arranged for them to put the convent up for sale and move to a new home near Saratoga Springs in New York State. I heard later that they'd been successful in caring for a number of British girls there during the war years. And I suspect they never forgot Mayor Stokes in their prayers.

It was some days later, after Doug Stokes's funeral, when Sheriff Lens said to me, "There's one loose end in all of this business, Doc. How did Doug's straw hat get on the other side of that twelve-foot wall?"

"They don't call them skimmers for nothing, Sheriff. While I had my eyes on Sister Hope's feet, they just skimmed it over the wall."

THE SECOND PROBLEM OF
THE COVERED BRIDGE

A visit from Sheriff Lens on a snowy Sunday morning was more than unusual [Dr. Sam Hawthorne was telling his guest over brandy]. It was downright strange. When I saw him at my door at ten o'clock on that January morning in 1940 I thought there'd been some startling overnight development in the European War or else a brutal slaying right here in Northmont.

"Can I come in, Doc?" he asked. "I want to talk to you about something important."

"Of course." I opened the door, not knowing what grim message he might be bearing. "I hope it's not bad news."

His face relaxed into a grin. "No, no nothing like that. I didn't mean to scare you." Never a small man, Sheriff Lens had been putting on weight lately. He moved a bit slower these days because of age and weight, but he was still my oldest and closest friend in town.

He joined me at the kitchen table and I poured him a cup of coffee. "What can I do for you?"

"Not keeping you from church, am I?"

I shrugged. "We've got Dr. Brewster from Shinn Corners filling in this week. It's no great loss if I miss his sermon."

"We had a meeting last night about the Northmont centennial. It's this year. The town was founded in eighteen forty, you know."

"Time flies," I told him with a smile. "I guess I was never too big on centennials or birthdays."

"Doc." He was serious now. "We want you to take part in the celebration in a special way. Vera and I worked it out." Vera was his wife of ten years, a wonderful woman who'd made him delighted that he'd waited till past fifty to remarry after the death of his first wife.

"I'm not much at speeches, Sheriff. You know that."

"Who said anything about a speech? We're going to dramatize the four most memorable events in Northmont history, one for each season. Vera wanted to do one each month, but no one could think of twelve events that memorable." He gave a little chuckle. "I guess Northmont's not New York, or even Boston."

I still couldn't get what he was driving at. "What does all this have to do with me?"

"Well, Doc, I know it would make more sense to dramatize these events in the order they happened, but we have to tie them in with the seasons, you see. For winter we want to memorialize the first mystery you ever solved in Northmont."

"What?" I wasn't sure I'd heard him right.

"You know, the horse and buggy that vanished going through the covered bridge."

"That's crazy, Sheriff. Surely something more important than that must have happened here during the winter."

"It was a big event, Doc. People hereabouts really took notice of you."

"That was eighteen years ago!" I argued.

"Sure! The other three events are lots older than that."

I poured myself another cup of morning coffee. "Just tell me what you have in mind before I decide."

"We want to have a horse and buggy like the one Hank Bringlow was driving the day he disappeared. Vera was thinking maybe one of his relatives could fill in for him, but they've all moved away. So Mayor Sumerset said he'd ride in it."

"For what purpose, Sheriff? Do you think he'll disappear like Hank did?"

"There won't be any disappearance this time because folks'll be on both sides of the bridge. But we gotta do it this month or next, Doc, while there's snow on the ground. You see that, don't you?"

"Yes." The disappearance and murder of Hank Bringlow eighteen years earlier had been accomplished by some clever trickery involving tracks in the snow. Obviously the event could never be commemorated without snow on the ground. "But I just don't like the idea. I'm no hero, to be honored for something I just stumbled upon. . . . Sometimes I think those first months here were more a curse than a blessing. People started thinking of me as the doctor detective rather than the doctor."

"Would it help any if Vera talked to you?" Sheriff Lens asked.

I gave him my Sunday sigh, usually reserved for patients who telephoned me with inane questions on my supposed day of rest. "I really don't want to get involved with this, Sheriff."

He finished his coffee and stood up. "I'll have Vera speak with you."

* * *

I'd expected that Vera Lens would phone me or stop by the office in a day or two. Instead, she was at my door two hours later, just at noon, brushing wet snowflakes from her coat. "Hello, Sam," she greeted me. "I hate to bother you on a Sunday like this, but our time is running out."

"Come in out of the snow, Vera." The sheriff's wife was a spunky, solid woman of around fifty who'd served as our postmistress for as long as I'd been in Northmont. The first Mrs. Lens had died during the influenza outbreak after the war and the sheriff had waited until December of '29 to marry again. "I haven't seen you since your tenth- anniversary party before Christmas."

She took my hand and smiled broadly. "You know, my husband was of two minds about inviting you. He was afraid there might be a murder if you were there."

I laughed. "Happily, it was a festive occasion with not a crime in sight."

I helped her off with her coat and she draped it over a chair. "I know my husband spoke with you about the centennial celebration, and I can understand your reluctance to take part in it. But I promise you won't be embarrassed, and I can guarantee Mayor Sumerset won't present you with a key to the city or anything like that. We just want you present when the mayor rides through the covered bridge like Hank Bringlow did back in nineteen twenty-two."

"And disappears."

She laughed at my reluctance. "That sort of thing only happens once in a lifetime. Come on! If you won't do it for Northmont, do it for me."

"Exactly what would be expected of me?"

"You simply stand there at the other end of the bridge with the sheriff and me. Shake hands with the mayor and that's it! Everyone will be there and we'll have an afternoon of ice skating and sledding for the kids."

"It sounds harmless enough," I admitted.

"Then you'll do it?"

It wasn't the first or last time in my life I was won over by a woman's wiles. "Sure. For you, Vera, I'll do it."

* * *

The first event of Northmont's centennial year was scheduled for the last Sunday in January. I was awakened by the sun sneaking through my bedroom curtains and glanced at the outdoor thermometer by the window. It was just over freezing at thirty-four degrees, not yet warm enough to make a significant dent in January's snowfall, but a perfect day for outdoor activities.

I phoned my nurse, Mary Best, as soon as I'd finished breakfast. "Hi, Mary. Ready for the big centennial celebration?"

"Sure, I guess so."

"The sheriff and Vera want me there by two o'clock. Should I pick you up around one-thirty?"

"I'll be ready."

Since I'd passed my fortieth birthday a few years back, I'd been viewed by friends and patients as a confirmed bachelor. There were both advantages and disadvantages to the label. One advantage was that I could escort Mary Best to social functions without anyone viewing it as a serious romance. One disadvantage was that she never viewed it as a serious romance either.

The Buick I drove that day would never erase memories of the Pierce-Arrow Runabout that was my first car, but Mary hadn't been my nurse in those early days and she thought the Buick was just great. "The sunshine should bring out a crowd," she said as I helped her into the car. "I brought sandwiches in case we get hungry."

"Good idea." Mary Best was a fine nurse and a good woman. She'd been with me for nearly five years and I never regretted hiring her. About ten years younger than me, she was a city girl who ended up in Northmont purely by chance. When I hired her she'd worn her dark blond hair in a stylish bob, but I'd been glad to see the end of that passing fad. She was much more attractive now.

"You must feel honored." she said as we drove along the road to the covered bridge where it had all happened. "You took part in one of the four most memorable events in Northmont's history."

"I can't help feeling I'm the butt of some elaborate joke. I guess they wanted something from recent times and I was the best they could do. Mayor Sumerset made the final decision, I understand. He spent months poring over old newspapers and journals kept by the town historians."

"Everyone wanted you, Sam. The sheriff and mayor and even Joe Sweeney."

"Sweeney! Clipper Sweeney!" He was the first barber I'd gone to in Northmont after I set up practice in '22. He hadn't done any barbering in years but folks still called him Clipper because of the shrewd and shady business deals he was noted for.

North Road had been paved since that fateful day eighteen years earlier, but the covered bridge was still there. During the depression years the government had sent a crew from the Civilian Conservation Corps to repair and strengthen it. Now there was talk of making it a town landmark, not because of that long-ago mystery but simply because covered bridges were becoming something of a rarity. I hoped they did something before the government decided to tear it down.

We rounded the next curve in the road and I said, "It looks like there's a crowd already." Several cars were parked off the road, allowing a clear path for the horse and buggy that stood waiting for Mayor Sumerset. They were owned by Doug Tanner, a local horseman who had a collection of old buggies in his barn. We drove through the bridge and I pulled up behind the buggy.

Will Sumerset stood off to one side, wearing a frock coat and top hat more reminiscent of the turn of the century than the 1920s. It certainly was nothing like the farm clothes young Hank Bringlow had been wearing on the day he vanished. But then the mayor wasn't planning to vanish, only to memorialize the event. He'd been a saddle and harness maker by trade, and lived to see his business die in the early 1920s with the growing popularity of the automobile. Luckily for him, he'd made a good profit in a real-estate partnership with Clipper Sweeney and gone on to enter politics.

"Ah," Sumerset said, walking over to shake my hand. "Here's my favorite sleuth now." He was a tall man with a ruddy complexion, and his gaunt features were sometimes called Lincolnesque by members of his own party.

"I'd rather be called your favorite doctor," I replied with a smile. "You know my nurse, Mary Best, don't you?"

"I've had the pleasure," he said, bowing slightly. For all his cordial demeanor, he seemed nervous.

Anna Nagle from the library came running over. "The band has arrived. We're almost ready to begin, Mayor." She was an ambitious young woman, a bit overweight but very vigorous, who'd become the unofficial town historian. Everyone liked Anna, and Northmont's wives were forever trying to find a suitable young man for her.

"Then I guess I'd better climb into my carriage," the mayor said, giving his horse an affectionate pat on the neck. "I'll see you on the other side, Sam."

He took the reins in his left hand and flicked the horse lightly with the buggy whip. At the other end of the bridge the band was tuning up.

"All this because a man disappeared here eighteen years ago," I grumbled to Mary.

"But you figured out what happened to him, Sam. Just go along with it and behave yourself."

"Hey, you're starting to sound like a wife."

"Huh!" was her only reply to that.

Joe Sweeney, barber-turned-real-estate-tycoon, appeared from the crowd to take me in hand. "Come on, Sam, I have to escort you to the other side of the bridge."

"I know."

We headed back across the covered bridge with Mary following along, and I wondered how many times I'd driven through it. Certainly close to a hundred, though this was the first time I'd walked it since the disappearance all those years ago. "I have to say the CCC did a good job of rebuilding this," I remarked, making conversation.

"It'll last another fifty years," Clipper Sweeney agreed.

Vera and the sheriff came through the covered bridge to meet us, and suddenly I heard the Shinn Corners high-school band launch into a lively medley of winter songs. Everyone was crowding around me and I heard Vera saying, "Sam, I want you to meet Dr. Brewster. He's filling in at the church."

I had the impression of thick glasses and a balding head. "I've heard nothing but good things about you," I told him, lying just a bit. "I'm sorry you won't be here longer."

"Actually, I might be. Your pastor may be facing surgery. I've lived around the area most of my life, so I'm a natural replacement."

Before I could pursue the conversation there was someone else to greet. Sheriff Lens had wandered over with the mayor's wife in tow. "Doc, you know Gretchen Sumerset, don't you?"

"Of course, Gretchen! You came to me once when you had the flu."

"I remember," she said with a laugh. "You prescribed some sort of powder. It had a foul taste going down but it did the job." She was a rosy-cheeked woman about my age, a good decade younger than the mayor. I remembered hearing that their daughter was away at college.

The band had stopped playing and the mayor's buggy paused at the other end of the covered bridge so he could say a few words into a microphone. The crowd, numbering perhaps two hundred people at our end, fell silent. "My fellow citizens of Northmont," he said, speaking through the crackling of the sound system. "Thank you for this fine turnout! As you know, we have come together here to celebrate the first of four seasonal events marking the founding of our town one hundred years ago. Later this year you will learn valuable lessons about Northmont in its early days, during the Civil War, and at the turn of the century. Today we commemorate a more recent event, that day eighteen years ago when Hank Bringlow disappeared from this very bridge along with his horse and buggy. It was the first of many local mysteries solved by a man who has become one of our leading citizens, Dr. Sam Hawthorne."

A wave of applause swept through the crowd and I felt Mary squeeze my arm. Somehow the whole thing embarrassed me, but there was no way out now. I saw that the band from Shinn Corners had come up behind the horse and buggy. Mayor Sumerset was going to lead a small parade through the covered bridge.

The band struck up "Yankee Doodle," our state's song, with the afternoon sun flashing off their shiny instruments, and the mayor urged his horse forward with the buggy whip, holding it high as he clutched the reins in his left hand. He was halfway through the bridge, with the band's music swelling up from behind, when something happened. The mayor's body seemed to jerk on its seat and toppled to the left. His top hat fell off and rolled a few inches back and forth on the bridge's flooring.

I was the first to move, dashing forward onto the bridge while the rest of the spectators seemed frozen in position. The band was still playing, but one by one the instruments were losing the melody and dropping out. When I reached the buggy Mayor Sumerset was lying on his left side with blood seeping from a small wound in his right temple. There were powder burns around the wound and he was dead.

It appeared that he'd been shot at close range while alone at the center of the covered bridge, with more than two hundred people watching.

* * *

The next few minutes were a confusing blur, though I remember Sheriff Lens by my side, ordering everyone to stay back. There were uniformed band members clustered around, and Dr. Brewster from the church trying to fight his way through the crowd. I caught sight of Gretchen Sumerset, her face drained of blood, and immediately went to her. The living always took precedence over the dead.

"What—what happened?" she wondered, unable to comprehend.

"Your husband's been shot."

"Is he—?"

"I'm sorry. I'm afraid he's dead."

She started to topple and I managed to catch her, shouting, "Give us air!" to the crowd pressing in on us.

"Is she all right?" Mary Best asked, materializing at my side.

"I think so. Can you get her away from here?"

"I'll try."

A band kid with red hair and a tuba was in my way and I told him, "Look, get the rest of your band and regroup back where you were, okay?" He retreated and I turned my attention once more to the dead man. "Sheriff, can we get something to cover the body, just to keep the gawkers away?"

"I've got a blanket in my car. I already radioed for deputies and an ambulance."

"Good."

"How did it happen, Doc?"

"I wish I knew."

The ambulance was already arriving and the crowd cleared a path for it. Clipper Sweeney was acting as a traffic director, guiding it onto the bridge. "We'll want some pictures before they move the body," Sheriff Lens said.

"Of course." I turned and studied the bridge's wooden wall directly opposite where Mayor Sumerset had been riding when he was hit. The planks were tightly fitted, with no sign of a bullet hole.

"Remember the powder burns," the sheriff reminded me. "The gun had to be fired close up."

"I know, but there was no one here. There has to be some other explanation."

A couple of deputies had arrived to take snapshots of the scene before the body was removed. Sheriff Lens gave them instructions and then walked back over to me. "The only explanation I see is that some killer has given you a second impossible crime on this same covered bridge."

* * *

The winter afternoon continued sunny and most of the townspeople remained in the area of the bridge, talking in small groups about what they'd seen or hadn't seen. Mary Best and Vera were with Gretchen Sumerset, trying to comfort her, and I walked with Sheriff Lens, scanning the snow-covered ground for possible clues as we talked. "First we have to consider suicide," I said.

"There was no gun," he pointed out.

"You may remember during the previous covered-bridge mystery I had occasion to refer to the Sherlock Holmes story about Thor Bridge. In that one, a weight attached to the gun pulled it over a bridge railing and into the water after it was fired."

Sheriff Lens sighed in exasperation. "Doc, we don't have the time for any useless speculation. It's the mayor who's been killed and I have to get to the bottom of it or they'll have my head. We were all watching Sumerset ride through that bridge and he never had a gun in his hand. Even if he had, it couldn't have been yanked into the water by a weight because the sides and top of the bridge are enclosed. You couldn't even find space for a bullet hole."

"All right," I agreed. "I just wanted to eliminate the possibility of suicide. With that out of the way, the covered bridge becomes a locked-room murder."

"How do you figure that? It's a bridge, not a room."

"But there are only two ways in or out of that room, or bridge. The band was behind him and we were in front of him, some two hundred of us. You should know from past experience, Sheriff, that for any locked room there are only three possible solutions in a general sense. Either he was shot before he entered the bridge, or while he was on the bridge, or after he left the bridge."

"He never left the bridge," the sheriff reminded me. "Not alive."

"So we can rule that out. Could he have been shot as he entered the bridge, and kept on driving the buggy?"

"I don't see how. That shot would have killed him instantly. He was still alive as he rode through. He was urging the horse on. He had the reins in one hand and the whip in the other."

"I agree, Sheriff. So where does that leave us? He had to be shot and killed while inside the covered bridge, yet he couldn't have been."

Mary Best came along to interrupt us then. "Gretchen Sumerset is near collapse, Sam. I want to get her home and into bed. Do you have anything we could give her?"

"My bag's in the car. I'll get back to you, Sheriff."

I followed Mary to the car, unlocked it, and snapped open the black bag that was every doctor's talisman. "Give her two of these. They'll help her sleep. Here's a prescription in case she needs more."

"Thanks. I'll call you later." She headed toward Vera Lens's car, and I could see Mrs. Sumerset in the front passenger seat.

I stood for a moment studying the crowd, beginning to thin out now that the body had been removed. Anna Nagle, the librarian, was talking with Clipper Sweeney and I headed toward them. "What has the sheriff found out?" Anna asked me immediately.

"Very little, so far."

Her face, usually so serene, had a drawn and pasty look. "You know, I was helping the mayor on his research for these centennial events. He spent many an evening at my library digging through old newspaper clippings. I can't believe he's dead."

"None of us can believe it, Anna," I told her.

Clipper was shaking his head sadly. "Old Will was a one-time business partner of mine. He didn't deserve such a terrible end. When I had the barbershop he used to come in for a shave every morning on his way to the saddlery. It was a dying business even then, and I finally talked him into investing in real estate."

"When would this have been?" I asked.

"I think it was nineteen twenty-two, about the time you set up practice here, Sam."

"I may want to talk about that later," I told him. Just then I'd spotted Sheriff Lens and I wanted to continue our interrupted conversation.

The sheriff was questioning some of the kids in the high-school band as they prepared to board the bus back to Shinn Corners. None of them had noticed anything unusual, though one thought he might have seen a flash near the mayor's head. "Did you hear anything that sounded like a shot?" Sheriff Lens asked. No one had.

"Did you get their names?" I asked as the bus pulled away.

"My deputy did. Damn it, Doc, why didn't they see or hear anything?"

"They were playing 'Yankee Doodle' pretty loud. We were at the other end, further away from the music, and we didn't hear anything."

"Why didn't they see anything, then?"

"One thought he saw a flash. The sun was reflecting off their instruments so we can't be certain what anyone saw."

"We sure didn't see a gunman—or woman—walk or ride up to Will Sumerset and shoot him in the head!"

We walked over to where Doug Tanner was holding onto his horse and buggy, waiting for the sheriff's consent to take them back home. Doug was a bit younger than me and wore jodhpurs most of the time. He owned a couple of prize-winning horses and had ridden them at horse shows in Providence and Boston.

"Are you finished with the buggy?" he asked the sheriff.

"Let me just look it over first," I told Tanner. The horse was standing there quite contentedly. I patted him and turned my attention to the buggy.

Its top was down, so no part of it had been close to the mayor's head. The killer had a clean shot at his target. I ran my hands over the frame and the upholstery but found nothing except a few drops of blood. "Nothing here," I told Sheriff Lens.

He motioned to Tanner. "Take it away. If we need anything else we'll be in touch."

I noticed what looked like the mayor's frock coat and buggy whip lying over against one wall of the bridge. "What's this?" I asked.

"The ambulance attendants took off his coat when they were working on him. I already checked the pockets. They're empty."

I went through them anyway, hoping the sheriff wouldn't be offended. After eighteen years I figured he knew all my little quirks Then I picked up the buggy whip with its braided leather handle. It was carefully made and I wondered if Sumerset had done it himself. "Something's missing," I said, scanning the floor of the bridge.

"What's that?"

"His top hat. Where is his hat?"

* * *

While the sheriff and one of his deputies searched around the bridge for the missing hat, I went back over to Anna Nagle. Clipper Sweeney was gone but now she was talking with Dr. Brewster. "I could arrange a service," he was saying.

"Well, you'd have to speak with Mrs. Sumerset about that. I don't think the mayor was too much of a churchgoer."

She obviously knew more about him than I did. She turned to me with a sad smile and asked if she could help me. "I was wondering about those newspaper clippings the mayor was checking out at the library. Do you remember anything about them?"

She thought about that. "I know he was interested in nineteen twenty-two. Come by the library tomorrow and I'll see if I can find something."

Sheriff Lens returned empty-handed from his search for the mayor's hat. "I don't know what could have happened to it," he said. "Think it's important?"

"It could be very important. The man was shot in the right temple. That would have been just below the brim of the hat."

"I'll ask folks if they saw what happened to it."

I drove home alone, wondering how Mary Best was making out with Mrs. Sumerset. Before I'd been in the house twenty minutes the phone rang. It was Mary with her report. "She's resting comfortably now. I told her tomorrow would be time enough to think about funeral arrangements. She has a brother in Providence and I phoned him. He and his wife are driving here tonight, and her daughter should get home from college tomorrow."

"Good. I'm going to the library first thing in the morning. I want to speak with Anna Nagle about the historical material Mayor Sumerset was researching. I think I'm clear of patients in the morning but if an emergency develops you can reach me there. After that I'll probably check on Mrs. Sumerset."

Monday morning turned quickly into a January thaw, with temperatures climbing into the low forties and the snow receding to springtime puddles. I drove to the small square building that housed the Northmont Free Library. Only a few years old, the library prided itself on stocking nearly ten thousand books and a complete file of local publications. It was the logical place for the mayor to have begun his research into the town's history, especially with Anna acting as historian.

I slipped off my coat as she directed me to a large table and immediately began pulling out large bound volumes of our weekly newspaper. I had to dampen her vigor a bit and explain that what I really wanted was material from 1922, the year of the first covered-bridge mystery. "He must have been working on that first, wasn't he?"

"Well, yes," she admitted. "I think he got sidetracked a bit because that was the year of the big land deal, when the mayor and Joe Sweeney went in together to buy the Pascel and Oates farms. I think he was bothered by a certain date and he wanted that day's newspaper. Of course, we only have the weekly and he couldn't find what he was looking for."

"What was the date that interested him?" I asked.

"August fourth, nineteen twenty-two, a day on which nothing at all happened, so far as I can tell."

"Something happens every day, Anna. What day of the week was it?"

"A Friday."

"I'd only been here about six months then, and I was busy building a practice. Tell me about this land deal."

Anna Nagle smiled. "I was only in high school myself, but I was already interested in the town's history. It seems the Pascel and Oates farms adjoined, and both men died within a month of each other in early summer. Mayor Sumerset was a saddle maker then, and he used to get his hair cut at Joe Sweeney's barbershop."

"Clipper Sweeney."

"Yes, they still call him that. Anyway, one day the two of them got talking about those parcels of land, totaling more than six hundred acres in all, and decided that between them they might have enough money to buy both parcels for some sort of real-estate development. Because he knew the heirs, Mayor Sumerset handled the deal. Since those land parcels later became the successful Jennings Tobacco Company, I suggested the land deal be memorialized as one of Northmont's centenary events."

"The mayor wouldn't have wanted to honor himself."

"That's exactly what he said," she agreed, opening another bound volume for me. "That's why he chose your covered-bridge mystery in the same year. See, here's the Northmont paper for the week covering August fourth. The land deal isn't reported, though the parties seem to have reached an informal agreement that week. The mayor told me that Joe Sweeney telephoned the Oates nephew in Boston at the end of business that week and worked out the deal over the phone. It's a good thing he did because the nephew was hit by a car and killed that same weekend."

"Oh?"

Anna shook her head. "Nothing mysterious. A little old lady drove her new automobile out of the showroom and hit him a block away. In those days people didn't need a driver's test to get a license."

I wanted to get this clear. "You're telling me that the sale was completed on the word of a dead man, without any signed contract?"

"Well, of course there was a signed contract with the other heirs. But they had no reason to doubt Sweeney's account of the deal worked out over the telephone. He had detailed notes of the entire conversation."

I could only sigh for the good old days. "I guess people trusted each other a lot more back then. But there's the solution to your mystery involving Mayor Sumerset's interest in that date. You said the call was made at the close of business that week, which would have been Friday."

But Anna Nagle shook her head. "It wasn't that. Mayor Sumerset and I had already discussed the phone call. No, it was something else that he saw."

"Where? In this newspaper?"

"Or in one of the books we were looking through. I can't be sure."

"If anything occurs to you, call me at once." I put on my coat and went out into the sunshine.

* * *

Though it was after ten when I reached the Sumerset house, the shades on the first-floor windows were all drawn. It was as if the big house itself was in mourning. I saw the black Ford in the driveway with Rhode Island plates, and I knew the Providence relatives had arrived. Gretchen Sumerset herself opened the door to admit me. "Thank you for coming, Doctor. Mary Best said you might be stopping by."

"I'm so sorry about what happened, Gretchen. Sheriff Lens and I are working on every angle."

"I appreciate that," she said quietly, leading me into her sitting room. She introduced me to her brother and sister-in-law, who quickly excused themselves so we could talk privately.

"Did your husband have a special enemy who may have wanted him dead?" I asked when we were alone.

"People in politics always have enemies. There was no one special."

"No recent threats, nothing like that?"

"No."

"Did he have an office or study here at home?"

She nodded. "He's had one since we moved in twenty years ago, when he was still making saddles and harnesses."

"I wonder if I could see it. He may have made some notes on the centennial celebration."

"Of course." She led the way down a long, narrow hall to a small room at the back. "I love this house. Our daughter grew up here."

The study was in some disarray, but right on top of the desk I found what I was looking for. It was a pad with the date August 4, 1922 underlined at the top. The word *Bell* had been written beneath it and circled. Further down the page he'd written the name of Joe Sweeney. I tapped the pad with my finger. "Was this the date your husband and Sweeney completed the purchase of that farmland?"

"Where they grow tobacco now? Yes, it was around that time."

"Will and Sweeney had a falling-out about the deal later, didn't they?"

"That was business. It didn't involve me. My husband kept a file on it, if you wish to see it." She dug it out for me and I glanced through it, paying special attention to handwritten notes of a telephone conversation with the Oates nephew.

"Did Sweeney feel he was cheated?" I asked.

"He had nothing to complain about. He made a handsome profit. They both did."

"May I have this top sheet off the pad? It might help, though I don't know how."

She waved her hand. "Take it."

I picked up a slender length of leather. "Is this a thong of some sort?"

"It's to be braided into a buggy whip. Will still made bridles and whips for people in his basement workshop. He was pretty much out of the saddle business, though."

"Could I ask about your current relations with Joe Sweeney?"

"Oh, we were both cordial when we saw him. It wasn't frequently, though."

I turned to go and then remembered something else. "Your husband's top hat seems to have disappeared after he was shot. Do you have any knowledge of its whereabouts?"

She looked blank. "None at all. I told him he was foolish to wear that thing, but he insisted on getting that and the coat down from the attic. He thought it would add to the celebration if he drove the buggy across the bridge wearing an outfit from the past."

* * *

Sheriff Lens was at his office when I arrived. It was a toss-up which of us was in the glummer mood. "I feel bad for Vera," he said, shaking his head. "All the time she spent working on this centennial project and it ends up with another murder on the covered bridge."

"The first time, eighteen years ago, was just a disappearance at first," I reminded him. "The two cases aren't anything alike, except for the bridge. Do you have the autopsy report yet?"

Sheriff Lens nodded. "Killed with a single thirty-two-caliber bullet, fired at close range. Is there any way that top hat could have been rigged to fire a bullet?"

"Exactly what I was thinking. We have to find it."

"If the killer picked it up in all the excitement, it'll never turn up now."

I took out the sheet of paper from the mayor's pad. Unfolding it, I asked, "Does this date mean anything to you, Sheriff? And *Bell* and *Joe Sweeney?*"

"Not a thing. Where'd you find it?"

"In Mayor Sumerset's study at home."

"Clipper Sweeney was always involved in shady deals. That's how he earned that nickname. He's always prided himself on being a shrewd operator."

"He's supposed to have closed that land deal with the Oates and Pascel families in August of twenty-two. Know anything about it?"

"Hell, Doc, my business has always been crime, not real-estate deals. I'll tell you who to ask about it, though. The Reverend Dr. Brewster. He was the Pascels' pastor and advised both families on the transaction. After the nephew died in that accident he said they should honor the verbal commitment to sell."

"All right," I agreed. "Dr. Brewster is my next stop."

I found him at the little church facing the town square. When I walked in he was standing in the center aisle staring up at the church organ. "Hello, Doctor. I was just wondering where I could get enough money for a new organ."

"Well, times are getting better."

"They always do when there's a war on. It's good for everyone except the people who are being bombed out of their homes." He smiled sadly. "What can I do for you today."

"I'm still working on the killing of Mayor Sumerset." I showed him the sheet of paper. "Does this date mean anything to you?"

"August fourth, nineteen twenty-two? Should it?"

"I believe it was the date of a land transaction by which the mayor and Joe Sweeney acquired the property which later became the Jennings Tobacco Company."

"I remember that," he said with a nod. "I thought they were crazy at first, growing tobacco leaf this far north under big white sheets. That deal made Will Sumerset's fortune. And Sweeney's, too. The Pascels attended my church so I helped the family in their decision about the land."

"What was there about a phone call to the Oates nephew that day?"

Dr. Brewster nodded. "He lived in Boston, and he was negotiating for both families. That weekend he was hit by a car and killed. Sweeney said they'd talked to him on the phone for over an hour Friday evening and clinched the deal. There was no signed contract, of course, and the families asked me what they should do. The selling price seemed fair to me, so I told them to accept it. I had no idea Sweeney and Sumerset would make a huge profit by reselling the land to a tobacco company."

"But there was nothing illegal about it?"

"No. Sweeney had all the notes he'd made during their conversation. I believe they talked from just after six until nearly seven-fifteen."

"You have quite a memory."

Brewster smiled, obviously proud of it. "Names and dates are my specialty." He frowned at the paper he still held in his hand. "This word Bell, for instance. I'll bet I know what it means. Alexander Graham Bell died in Canada on August second of that year, and he was buried on the fourth."

"What a memory!"

"In fact, I can tell you something else." He was staring at the paper now. "But it's strange. It makes no sense."

"What is it?"

We were interrupted by his housekeeper coming over from the rectory. Sheriff Lens was phoning me, and it was important. I followed her to the phone and picked it up. "Yes, Sheriff?"

"Doc, I'm on my way over to Shinn Corners. They've found the missing top hat at the school."

"I'll meet you there."

* * *

Though Shinn Corners was the next town from us, it had its own doctors and I rarely found cause to go there. The high school served the entire county, though, and Sheriff Lens's jurisdiction extended there. When one of the boys from the band showed up at school with a top hat, the principal had phoned the sheriff at once.

"I feel terrible about what happened," he told us in his office, on the way in to see the boy. "Mayor Sumerset phoned me on Friday and invited the band to play at the centennial event. He was excited about it and so was I. Who could have imagined it would end like it did?"

The boy's name was Michael and I recognized him at once. He was the red-haired tuba player to whom I'd spoken the previous day, right after the shooting. "It fell off his head and rolled right over to me," he told us in the principal's office, obviously frightened. "I collapsed it and slid it under the jacket of my band uniform. Nobody noticed. They were all looking at the body."

"Didn't you know that was stealing?" Sheriff Lens asked.

"The mayor was dead. He didn't need it anymore. I just wanted to bring it to class today and show everyone."

I turned the top hat over in my hands, but there was nothing inside. On the portion of the brim that would have been closest to the wound, there was a bit of scorching from the powder burns. It was the mayor's hat, all right, but it told us nothing.

"Just a dead end," Sheriff Lens grumbled as we left the school. A lecture to the boy about stealing evidence from a crime scene had put a proper amount of fear in him. "We're no closer to a solution than we were before."

"I wouldn't say that, Sheriff. I was having a very interesting chat with Dr. Brewster when you phoned me. It was all about the death of Alexander Graham Bell."

"Was he shot on a covered bridge too?"

"No, he died in Nova Scotia of diabetes, at the age of seventy-five."

"Then what does it have to do with—?"

"We both should have remembered it, even though it happened nearly eighteen years ago. Follow me back to Northmont, and I'll take you to meet our number-one suspect."

I led the way over the back roads, where the melting snow was fast turning everything to mud. When we reached our destination it was the big brick home of Clipper Sweeney, who'd come a long way since his early days as the barber of Northmont.

"You cracked the case yet?" he asked as he opened the door.

"Pretty much, Joe. Can we come in and tell you about it?"

"Sure." He led the way into the sitting room. "Is it too early for an afternoon drink, Sheriff? Doc?"

We both passed, but waited while he poured one for himself. "I think we have a motive," I began. "That's important in a murder investigation."

Sweeney laughed. "It's always sex or money, isn't it?"

"This is money," I agreed, "in a sense. It dates back to nineteen twenty-two, the same year as the original covered-bridge mystery. Mayor Sumerset was researching facts for the centennial celebration and somehow he stumbled on this. We were all around at the time, of course, but only Dr. Brewster seems to have remembered that far back, to August fourth, nineteen twenty-two. It was the day you worked out the land deal with the Oates nephew on the telephone."

Clipper Sweeney closed his eyes for just an instant, as if he could see what was coming. "I think you've got it all wrong," he said.

"Not this time. Your notes indicate that you spoke with young Oates at his Boston office from just after six until seven-fifteen. The notes of the conversation are very complete. It's too bad it never took place."

"What?" Sheriff Lens said, his mouth open in surprise.

"It was the day of Alexander Graham Bell's funeral in Nova Scotia. As a tribute to Bell's invention of the telephone, on that day all telephone communication in the United States was shut down for one minute, at exactly six twenty-five P.M. Eastern Time."

"Yeah," the sheriff said. "Seems I do remember something, now that you mention it."

"Surely you would have noted a one-minute interruption in your conversation with the Oates nephew, Joe. The reason it wasn't mentioned was that you didn't make those notes on Friday but several days later, after you heard about Oates's death in that car accident. There never was any conversation. You relied on their believing you and going along with a deal that never happened. And by the time you'd made those notes you'd forgotten about the one-minute telephone interruption. All this centennial research brought it to light again. You knew Anna Nagle or someone else would realize the conversation couldn't have taken place as reported. Oates never agreed to anything before he died, and you closed the land deal under false pretenses. Your partner Sumerset had already discovered it, and I think you killed him rather than have the truth come out."

Joe Sweeney smiled sadly. "There's only one thing wrong with that theory. I didn't write up the notes of that telephone conversation because I never made it. Will Sumerset phoned young Oates in Boston on that Friday evening, or said he did. It was Will who wrote up the notes the following week, after we learned of Oates's death. Check the handwriting if you don't believe me."

But I believed him. It was suddenly all clear, everything from Joe Sweeney's nickname to the Shinn Corners high-school band. It all fitted together. "Come on, Sheriff," I told him. "We have to stop at your office for something and then I'm paying another call on Gretchen Sumerset."

* * *

This time she was alone in the big house when I arrived with Sheriff Lens, carrying a large paper bag in one hand. "They're doing some grocery shopping for me, and then they're picking up my daughter at the train station," she said, replying to my question about her brother and sister-in-law.

"Perhaps it's just as well we can talk alone," I said. "You understand that I had to bring the sheriff along with me."

"Yes." Her eyes met mine and she knew that I knew.

I sat down opposite her and began to talk. "Nearly eighteen years ago your husband and Joe Sweeney lied about a phone call to a man named Oates who had the misfortune to be killed by an automobile. It enabled them to purchase some valuable land at a lower price. No actual crime was committed, and the truth wouldn't have mattered to a man like Sweeney, whose shrewd business deals had already earned him the nickname of Clipper. But it was different for your husband, who was now the mayor of Northmont. The notes about that phone call were in his handwriting. It was his lie even more than Sweeney's, and if no crime was committed, it could still ruin his reputation. Perhaps he thought about you and his daughter, about this house and his election as mayor. It was all based on that lie, and I don't think he could have lived the rest of his life under that shadow."

Her expression hadn't changed. "Are you saying—?"

"I think you know what I'm saying, Gretchen. Your husband killed himself in such a way that it would appear he was murdered." I opened the paper bag we'd brought from the sheriffs office, and extracted the coiled buggy whip Will Sumerset had been using when he died. "He made this himself, of course. You told us he still made things like reins and buggy whips."

"Yes." Her voice was barely a whisper.

I held up the handle of the buggy whip and carefully lifted the piece of leather that covered a slender metal tube. "It was only made to be fired once. The thirty-two-caliber cartridge is still at the bottom of the tube, with a primitive firing mechanism. I remembered him holding the whip in his right hand, raising it to urge his horse forward. He raised it toward his temple, squeezed this firing mechanism, and fired the fatal bullet into his head."

"I still don't see why we didn't hear it, or see the flash of the powder," Sheriff Lens said.

"There were flashes all over, from the winter sunlight reflecting off those shiny brass band instruments. As for the sound of the shot, it was muffled by the horns and drums of the band marching toward us. The whole thing wouldn't have worked without the band playing. It was Mayor Sumerset who phoned the school on Friday and made a last-minute request for the band. I think that was the day he decided to kill himself, but in such a way that his reputation and his family name wouldn't be damaged."

"I suppose it's the only explanation," Sheriff Lens agreed, "especially with this buggy whip." He lifted the leather covering, then watched it drop back in position over the open metal tube. "But what if Clipper Sweeney or someone else had been blamed for the crime? Was that what he wanted?"

Surprisingly, it was Gretchen Sumerset who answered. "That wouldn't have happened," she said. She reached into her pocket and brought out a folded envelope which she handed to me. On the envelope was written, *To be opened only in the event that someone is arrested and charged with my murder.*

"It's been opened," I noted, turning over the envelope.

"I had to see what it said, of course. He left it in my sewing basket. Will was a good man. He tells the whole story here, from the phone call he never made back in nineteen twenty-two to his planned suicide with the pistol barrel he built into the handle of this buggy whip. He wanted to save his family from the pain of it, but not at the expense of an innocent person who might be falsely accused. You can use this any way you wish."

No official announcement was ever made about the death of Mayor Sumerset, but I guess the truth worked itself around town by word of mouth. In any event, it was the last mystery involving our covered bridge. After the war, in a burst of highway improvements, the road was widened to four lanes and the old bridge replaced with a new steel and concrete one. It was never quite the same.

THE PROBLEM OF
THE SCARECROW CONGRESS

B Y the summer of 1940 the war in Europe was heating up. Dunkirk had been evacuated and Paris had fallen to the Germans on June fourteenth. The RAF was bombing German cities while Englishmen kept a nervous eye on their own skies. In America there was more and more talk that we would be drawn into the war. [Feeling just a bit like a history professor, old Dr. Sam Hawthorne left his chair to pour his visitor another glass of brandy. Then he resumed his seat and continued the story.] But in Northmont that summer, folks were more interested in the festivities planned for the redesigned town square, now christened Congress Park.

The name was actually in honor of the Continental Congress, because a citizen of our area had attended its first session in 1774, to petition the British government for a redress of grievances. It was our main claim to fame during the nation's colonial period, and in the face of impending war the town fathers decided a redesigned and renamed town square would be a patriotic gesture. The new square was more of a park, with a small fountain at the center surrounded by benches. The bandstand which had dominated the old square was gone now, and the entire two-acre park was ringed by thirteen lampposts commemorating the thirteen original states.

It was the lampposts that gave Mayor Cutler the idea for the Scarecrow Congress. He was a friendly, generous man, owner of the town hardware store and our first mayor to be younger than me. I'd just turned forty-four at the time and he had celebrated his forty-first birthday soon after being chosen mayor by the town council, following Mayor Sumerset's untimely death the previous January. In turn, I'd been appointed to fill Cutler's seat on the council pending the November election, so I was present on that June evening when he proposed his plan.

"I suggest a contest for the thirteen best scarecrows—a symbol of the summer harvest—with the winners to be attached to the thirteen lampposts in Congress Park. We could put them up sometime in July and leave them until Halloween if people wanted."

"We could call it the Scarecrow Congress," Wayne Braddick suggested, and several voices around the table seconded the suggestion. I thought it was a harmless but silly idea, and abstained on the final vote.

247

In my office the next morning my nurse, Mary Best, asked me how the council meeting had gone. I hadn't been on it long and she still expected me to return after each gathering filled with earthshaking news. "They're going to build a baseball stadium," I told her, "and try for a major league team."

"Sam!"

I tried again. "They're going to put up scarecrows around Congress Park and call it a Scarecrow Congress."

"Be serious for one!"

"Believe it or not, I am being serious. That's the resolution they passed last night. It'll be in tomorrow's paper."

"Whose idea was that?"

"Doug Cutler's. He's taking this mayoring business seriously."

"You call that serious?"

I shrugged. "Maybe making scarecrows will take folks' minds off the war news."

* * *

It was late July before the thirteen scarecrows had been selected and tied to the lampposts in Congress Park. Earlier in the month, on July tenth, seventy German planes had bombed the docks in South Wales and the Battle of Britain had officially begun. Perhaps the scarecrows were becoming a symbol for our town, trying to frighten away the thickening clouds of war.

Mayor Cutler, all smiles, was at the park to cut the ribbon for the official dedication at high noon, announcing a whole series of concert and contests to be held there during the rest of the summer. Most everyone knew these were designed to replace the former mayor's ill-fated reenactments of famous events marking Northmont's centennial year, a plan that had come to a sudden, tragic conclusion with the first reenactment.

Early Winters, a dairy farmer with an improbable name, was one of the first entrants in the contest, and his overstuffed scarecrow earned a place of honor out by the street. Towering more than six feet high, it was a favorite from the beginning with its bib overalls, checked shirt, and red bandanna. A smiling face painted on a feedbag stuffed with straw served as the head, topped by a soft and shapeless straw hat, not a hard straw skimmer like I wore myself. A broomstick through the shirtsleeves held its arms outstretched, and tufts of straw served as its hands.

"He's someone I'd like to know," Mary confided as we inspected Early's scarecrow in Congress Park. "He's certainly more appealing than some of the boyfriends I've had."

"I hope you're not including me."

She blushed just a bit. "You're not a boyfriend, Sam. You're my employer."

Wayne Braddick's daughter Jessica had demonstrated her individuality by creating a female scarecrow, complete with breasts, a skirt, and long hair. "Jessica was always a bit different," I commented. The twenty-year old was an occasional patient of mine, but I'd seen little of her since she went off to college. "She must be home for the summer."

As we reached the last of the scarecrows, a virtual duplicate of the one in 1939's hit movie *The Wizard of Oz*, we came upon Sheriff Lens tugging at the straw man with both hands. "Are you trying to steal it, Sheriff?" Mary wondered.

"What?" He jumped back, startled. "Oh, hello, Mary. Hi there, Doc."

"What are you up to?" I asked.

"Mayor Cutler's afraid some wild kids will steal the scarecrows, or even set them afire. He wants me to station a deputy here all night for the next few months. Hell, I got better things to do with the county budget than guard a bunch of straw! I been tugging at these wires and they all seem secure enough to me. Nobody's gonna make off with them, and the fire department has a volunteer on duty all night right across the street. Even if one of these did get damaged, the mayor had the winners keep duplicates at home to bring in if necessary."

I'd known Sheriff Lens since virtually my first day in Northmont. He was a bit unimaginative and set in his ways, but that didn't mean he was always wrong. "It sounds to me as if they're safe enough. Like you say, you've got more important things to worry about."

As we strolled further along we found Jessica Braddick at her female scarecrow, checking it over for any damage. "Hello, Dr. Sam!" she called out, "Did you see mine?"

We walked over to join her. "That's very clever, Jessica," Mary told her. "How was college this year?"

"Pretty good," she told us. Jessica was very much her father's daughter, though I doubted she'd ever serve on the Northmont town council. She was bound for Boston or New York, with the looks and personality to suit life in the big city.

"Any boyfriends?" I asked her, making conversation as one does with the young.

"Oh, no one serious. The boys at college all seem so immature."

"I've heard that before," I told her as we parted.

That night there was an inaugural concert for the new park, followed by a few skyrockets left over from the Fourth of July. Mary was at a meeting of her library circle so I attended by myself. It was good seeing old friends and patients away from the usual office setting.

Because of the fireworks, Mayor Cutler had Seth Sterne standing by with his ambulance in case of an accident. Seth's ambulance was the only one in town, carefully equipped and upgraded by Seth himself. He was paid to transport patients to and from Pilgrim Memorial Hospital, and rumor had it that he often romanced the nurses on the side. A local kid named McGuire, whom everyone called Sonny, often rode in the ambulance with him and helped to carry the stretchers.

McGuire was with him now, smoking a cigarette with nicotine-stained fingers while he lolled against the side of the ambulance. He was a reedy young man with flaxen hair that always seemed to be in his eyes. "Hello, Seth," I said, walking up to them. "Hi, Sonny."

Sonny grunted a greeting, his eyes on the circulating crowd, but Seth Sterne was as friendly as ever. "Whenever there are fireworks, Doug Cutler wants me out here. Waste of money if you ask me. More likely to need the first truck than my ambulance."

There were always a few volunteer firemen at functions like this. "There's Early Winters now," I pointed out. "He's a volunteer. And Wayne Braddick with his wife and daughter." Sonny McGuire perked up at this and followed our gaze. He tossed the cigarette butt away and made a beeline for Jessica Braddick. I remembered then that they'd graduated from high school together.

"Do you think Early's scarecrow is the best?" I asked Sterne.

"Who knows? There's no prize riding on it. Early made a good traditional scarecrow. That Braddick girl made a lady scarecrow." He snickered as he said it.

"Sonny probably likes that."

Seth snorted. "Sonny was lucky to make it out of high school. If he thinks he's gonna make time with young Jessica Braddick he's dead wrong. She's busy driving those college boys wild."

"How come you know so much about it?"

"Kids talk. I sit around down at the soda fountain and hear things."

Seth Sterne remained by his vehicle while I walked across the park to speak with Early Winters. He was a small but muscular man with the weathered face of a farmer. His wife had died a few years back in a tractor accident but he'd carried on without her, hiring what help he needed from neighboring farms to keep his place going. "That's a great scarecrow, Early."

"I spent hours on the thing, getting it just right. But then, I have nothing better to do with my evenings since Evangeline passed away."

A skyrocket took off and burst above the park, signaling that the evening's festivities were nearing an end. Two more followed, lighting the sky briefly. I caught a glimpse of Mary across the park talking with Jessica Braddick. The library circle had finished early. I wandered over to one of the nearby lampposts and was surprised to see the name of Constance Cutler attached to scarecrow number seven. She was Mayor Cutler's wife and I had no idea she'd entered the great scarecrow contest. Her straw man was cleverly concocted of familiar household implements, with a rolling pin for a hand and a strainer covering the face. The hair was a stringy mop, the straw feet two brooms.

"Admiring my handiwork?" Constance asked, startling me as she came out of the shadows. She was a formidable woman, a bit taller than the mayor, with a slim body and an unlined face that almost seemed Oriental at times.

"It's very clever," I answered truthfully.

"Doug didn't want me to enter because of being the mayor's wife, but why not? There's no cash prize or anything. It's just the idea of having my scarecrow displayed here for a few months." She fluffed up its moppy hair. "Think it'll last till Halloween?"

"I doubt it. That's a long way off."

Mary Best joined us, and I was a bit surprised that she and Constance Cutler seemed to know each other so well. They chattered awhile and then we parted. "She volunteers at the Red Cross," Mary explained. "I see her there occasionally." As the county seat, Northmont had a small Red Cross chapter.

"What do they need volunteers for?" I asked.

"Not much right now, but we've been talking about the future. If we do get pulled into the war, Red Cross chapters around the country will be rolling bandages, among other things."

We headed back toward my car. "I saw you with Jessica Braddick. What did she have to say?"

"Oh, girl talk. You know. Actually, I was rescuing her from Sonny McGuire."

"I saw him bearing down on her, I guess they graduated from high school together."

"Sure, but now she's in college trying to make something of herself. Sonny just hangs around and rides the ambulance with Seth Sterne. He told her he's worried about getting drafted. There's talk that Congress will pass a Selective Service bill by the end of summer and Sonny will be twenty-one in September."

"In that happens, they'll probably want me too," I told her.

She shook her head as we reached by Buick. "What they're talking about is only drafting men twenty-one to thirty-five right now. Of course, there's always a need for able-bodied doctors."

I knew she was kidding me just a bit, but it was a thought that hadn't occurred to me before.

* * *

Two days later, I was just finishing with a woman patient when Mary told me Early Winters was in the waiting room in a highly agitated state. I had a light schedule that morning, and it was almost lunchtime, so I told her to send him in. Early had never been a patient of mine, and I wondered what was ailing him.

He entered my office quickly. In his overalls and plaid shirt he looked a bit like a smaller version of his own scarecrow. "Doc, you've got to help me. I think someone's trying to kill me."

"Sit down, Early. Tell me what's happened."

He took the chair opposite my desk. "I got up this morning and discovered someone had broken into my house overnight. They left this on my kitchen floor." It was a straw doll, like an Indian child's toy, with a straight pin driven through its heart. "Is it some sort of voodoo curse?"

I smiled at the idea, though I couldn't come up with any immediate explanation for the doll. "Was anything taken from your house?" I asked.

"Not that I noticed. The window in the kitchen door had been broken and whoever it was simply reached in and turned the knob from inside. The door was still slightly ajar when I came down for breakfast."

"But you heard nothing?"

Winters shook his head. "I'm a pretty heavy sleeper. My wife always said I could sleep through an earthquake."

I sighed and shook my head. "Early, I'm a doctor. You need Sheriff Lens for this."

"He wasn't in his office, and I thought you might help. You've solved a good many mysteries around these parts."

"I don't think I can help. It was probably just a prank by someone who resents all the attention your scarecrow is getting. I don't think this straw doll is meant to be a person. It's meant to be your scarecrow."

"I hadn't thought of that," he admitted, calming down a bit. He returned the straw doll to his overalls pocket.

I rose from my chair, a gentle signal that the conversation was ending. "It's just about lunchtime. If I see Sheriff Lens, I'll tell him you're looking for him."

Mary Best joined me for lunch, as she often did when neither of us had other engagements. We ate at the new Sweet Shoppe across the street from Congress Park, and I could see a small but steady stream of folks strolling around to the various scarecrows mounted on their lampposts. Seth Sterne's ambulance came by and stopped while Sonny McGuire ran into the Sweet Shoppe for a couple of chocolate ice cream cones.

We lingered over lunch, and as we were leaving I saw Sonny bearing down on Jessica Braddick once more. They were across the street from us, at the entrance to the park, and Mary saw them too. "I guess I'd better go rescue her again." She left my side and hurried across the street.

I watched the whole thing with some amusement, but Sonny seemed alarmed about something. He kept gesturing at Early Winter's scarecrow until Jessica and Mary went over to look at it. Just then Seth Sterne pulled up in his ambulance. "What's the trouble?" I heard him ask, but I couldn't catch their replies.

Seth was at the scarecrow now, trying to reach under the bib overalls the straw man wore. "Get the stretcher, Sonny," he called out, a hint of alarm in his voice as he tried to free the scarecrow from its post with a pair of wire cutters.

I started across the street to join them. "What's going on there?" I called out.

Seth and Sonny McGuire had freed the scarecrow now and were carrying it on the stretcher to the ambulance. It seemed like a sight out of some bizarre version of The Wizard of Oz. Seth poked his head around the ambulance door to answer me. "Sonny noticed the scarecrow was bleeding. I think there's a person inside."

I pushed the door aside and joined them. Seth was unhooking the buttons of the bib overalls, pulling the top down to reveal more blood. "Out of my way," I said, pushing them unceremoniously aside. Mary and Jessica were crowding in behind me, and others were joining the group. "Keep the crowd back."

It was a small man's body inside the scarecrow, and it appeared he'd been shot through the heart. Working within the confines of the ambulance, I tore away the painted feedbag face of the scarecrow and looked upon the dead face of Early Winters.

He'd been in my office, alive and well, just an hour earlier. Sheriff Lens arrived within minutes, summoned by the cashier at the Sweet Shoppe who saw the excitement. "What's going on here, Doc?" he asked.

"Early Winters has been murdered," I told him. "His body is inside the scarecrow."

"I'll be damned! You mean someone managed to get the body in there during the night?"

I shook my head. "Winters was in my office an hour ago. He wanted to report a break-in at his house and couldn't find you. Besides, the body's still warm. He hasn't been dead long."

"Then how'd he get in the scarecrow?"

"I don't know," I admitted. "We'll take him to the hospital in case there's any chance of reviving him, but I'm sure he's gone. Follow along and we'll question Sonny McGuire there. He's the one who noticed the blood."

At Pilgrim Memorial they pronounced Early Winters dead on arrival and quickly confirmed that he'd been killed by a single shot to the heart. Mary and Jessica had followed along took, and Sheriff Lens herded us all into a small conference room while he questioned Sonny. "Just tell us what happened," he urged the young man.

Sonny McGuire, nervously biting his lower lip, began to speak. "I was with Seth in the ambulance and we stopped at the Sweet Shoppe so I could run in for a couple of ice cream cones. They taste good on a warm day."

"What about the scarecrow?" Sheriff Lens prodded.

"Well, we'd finished our cones and Seth wanted to drive back to the garage, but I spotted Jessica here across the street. I hopped out of the ambulance and ran across to say hello." Jessica's face had turned red at his words. "That was when I noticed that Winters's scarecrow was bleeding."

"You actually saw the blood flowing?" I asked.

"That's right," he replied. "It was running down the front of those bib overalls."

"I saw it too," Mary confirmed. "When I crossed the street to join then, they were both looking at it."

"Yes," Jessica said softly. "I never saw a dead man before. When Dr. Sam pulled that sack off his head and I recognized Mr. Winters, I felt like I was going to faint."

"All right," the sheriff said. "Let's not get ahead of the story. What happened after you all saw the blood?"

"Seth pulled the ambulance around to see what was going on," Sonny continued.

Seth Sterne took up the story then. "Sonny pointed out the fresh blood on the scarecrow's bib overalls and I put my hand under them to feel around. I got inside the shirt and I could feel skin, and a wound. That's when I told him to get the stretcher out of the ambulance. I cut the wires, and Sonny helped me lower the body onto the stretcher. I didn't want to examine it further with Mary and Jessica there, and others were coming up too. We got it into the ambulance and by that time Dr. Sam had come over."

I nodded. "I opened the shirt and saw the wound. I was pretty sure he was dead. Then I pulled off the feed sack with its painted face and saw that it was Early Winters."

"The same Early Winters who was in your office an hour before that."

"The same," I said with a sigh. "I know it's impossible."

Sheriff Lens just shook his head. "Even by your standards this one is impossible, Doc. It's unlikely Winters's body could have been put in there during the night without someone seeing something, and it's downright impossible during the day. There're always people around the park. It's the center of town!"

Sonny McGuire looked at me and suggested, "Maybe it was his ghost that came visiting you."

"It was no ghost. He brought along a straw doll with a pin stuck in its heart. Someone broke into his house during the night and left it on the floor."

The sheriff's questioning was interrupted by the arrival of Mayor Cutler. "What's happened here?" he demanded. "Folks are telling me Early Winters was shot and his body put into the scarecrow."

"That's what happened," I confirmed. "But we don't know exactly how."

"I won't let something like this ruin our new Congress Park," Cutler sputtered. "Sheriff, I want the murderer in custody by nightfall. We can't have people afraid to walk the streets of Northmont!"

"A man is dead," I reminded him. "I'm sure Sheriff Lens is doing his best to get to the bottom of it."

"He'd better, or the town will be looking for a new sheriff! I'm not as easygoing as my predecessors."

Cutler stormed out of the room, leaving us speechless for a moment. We'd never seen him like that before. Sheriff Lens was the first to recover his voice. "I guess that's all for now. I'll probably have more questions later."

* * *

Between patients, Mary and I spent much of the afternoon discussing the murder of Early Winters. "What we need is a motive," I told her. "If we can figure out who wanted Early dead maybe we can determine how it was done."

She thought about it. "I don't think he had a close friend or an enemy in recent years. Since his wife's accident he's stayed pretty much to himself."

"What about that accident? Didn't a tractor tip over while she was driving it up a hill?"

Mary Best nodded. "Her leg was trapped underneath and broken. But it was a broken neck that killed her."

"I remember there was some uproar over it at the time."

"A close woman friend claimed Evangeline had been beaten by her husband on occasion. She wanted Sheriff Lens to investigate the death as suspicious, but nothing ever came of it."

"You've got a good memory for these things, Mary. Who was the woman friend?"

"Constance Cutler, the mayor's wife."

I decided it was time to call on Mrs. Cutler, whom I knew only slightly. Our brief conversation about her scarecrow was probably the longest talk I'd ever had with her. I left the office early and drove out to the large house on Maple Street. It was one of the handsomest homes in town, with a wide front porch that circled around both sides. She'd decorated it with all sorts of blossoming flowers in just the right shades to add color to the grayness of the house itself.

When I drove up, she was watering the flowers with a metal sprinkling can, squinting into the late afternoon sun to identify her visitor. Her frown of uncertainty changed to a smile when she recognized me. "Dr. Hawthorne, this is indeed a pleasure! I heard about the terrible tragedy at Congress Park."

"That's what I wanted to talk about," I admitted, removing my straw hat as I stood at the bottom of the steps awaiting an invitation to proceed further. "I'm trying to help out a bit by searching for a motive for the killing. Do you happen to know anyone who disliked Early Winters enough to kill him?"

She shook her head. "Not really."

"His wife died in a terrible accident a couple of summers ago."

"Evangeline, yes."

"You knew her?"

"Very well."

"Could there be any connection between her death and his?"

"Oh, I doubt that."

"I saw him this morning before he was killed. Someone broke into his house last night and left a little straw doll on the floor. It had a pin through the heart, like a voodoo doll."

"Who would do a thing like that?" she asked, the shock of it reflected in her face.

"Probably the killer, since Winters was shot through the heart."

"Could I see this straw doll?"

I didn't have it with me, and I realized I wasn't sure just where it was. "I'll try to get it and show it to you. In the meantime, is there anything you can tell me? Is it possible that Early might have killed Evangeline two years ago?"

"I don't know," she answered simply. "That's something we'll never know now."

I thanked her and returned to my car, aware that she hadn't invited me up onto the porch.

* * *

After throwing together a quick dinner for myself, I went out again, this time back to Pilgrim Memorial Hospital. I didn't stop at my office in the darkened physicians' wing but went instead to the admitting desk. I was looking for the clothing Early Winters had been wearing when Sterne delivered his body to the hospital.

"We've got two sets of clothing here," the admitting nurse told me. "We're waiting for a family member to claim them."

"Two sets?"

"One from the scarecrow and one from the body inside it."

"I'm interested in the body's clothing."

She took out a cardboard box and placed it on the counter. I remembered Early putting the straw doll in his overalls pocket and that was the first place I looked, but it wasn't there. Both the overalls and the plaid shirt were stained with blood around the bullet hole, but there was no sign of the doll. "Could I see the other box?" I asked.

But there was nothing in the scarecrow's overalls pockets either. I ran my fingers over the smooth unmarked fabric of the bib and tried to make sense of it all. One other place the straw doll might be was in Seth Sterne's ambulance. I hadn't thought to look there.

I thanked the nurse and went back to my car. Seth parked his ambulance in a garage behind his house so he could go out on night calls if necessary. It was dark by the time I reached his street, but though the lights were on in his living room, I didn't stop at his house first. Seth was unmarried but had a reputation with women. I didn't want to intrude on something that might prove embarrassing. I went around the barrel used for burning trash in his backyard and headed for the garage. The side door was standing slightly ajar.

I entered that way and used the street light from outside to guide myself to the back doors of the ambulance. I searched around, mostly by hand, and found nothing. The empty stretcher was in place and nothing else seemed disturbed. Suddenly, I heard the door behind me squeak as it swung open. Desperate for a hiding place, I pulled myself onto a long narrow supply shelf beneath the one on which the stretcher rested. Sterne had designed it for first-aid equipment or for an extra stretcher if needed. Lying there with the ambulance door ajar, I heard footsteps cross the floor. The ambulance doors swung shut without quite latching.

Almost at once I heard the side door squeak again and a voice I recognized said, "Hello there, Sonny. I thought I might find you around here."

Sonny's voice answered a bit uncertainly. "What? Mr. Braddick! What are you doing here?"

"I came to have a word with you," the councilman replied. "About my daughter."

I remained where I was, hardly daring to breathe.

"What about her?" Sonny whined. "I didn't do anything to her."

"I want to make sure you don't. Jessica is going into her third year of college now. I don't want anything to interfere with that. Whatever might have been between you in high school is over and done with. Understand?"

"There was nothing between us."

"I've been watching how you follow her around. Just keep this in mind, boy. If you ever lay a finger on my daughter, I'll come after you with my deer rifle. It makes a pretty big hole!"

A sound that might have been another whine came out of Sonny. Wayne Braddick said nothing more, and I couldn't be sure if he was still there or not. Then suddenly I heard a shot.

I kicked open the ambulance doors and pushed myself out, a foolish move that might have cost me my life. But there was only Sonny McGuire on the garage floor now, lying in a widening pool of blood. I ran to him and felt for a pulse, but I was already too late. The bullet had taken him in the heart, just like the one that killed Early Winters.

* * *

I roused Seth, who was, fortunately, alone in his house, and put in a call to Sheriff Lens. Two murders in one day were a bit too much for Northmont to handle, and I wasn't too surprised to see Mayor Cutler drive up just behind the sheriff's car.

"Were you're here when this happened?" the mayor asked me while Sheriff Lens was examining the body on the garage floor.

"I was. I heard Sonny talking with someone and then I heard a shot."

"Did you recognize the voice?"

"Pardon me, Mayor, but I'd rather the questioning came from Sheriff Lens."

He glowered at me and walked away. One of Lens's deputies had arrived and was photographing the scene before the body was removed. In Sonny's pocket he found what looked like a gun, but it was only a water pistol. The sheriff studied it, shrugged, and strolled over to ask me what the trouble with the mayor was all about.

"Nothing serious. I just thought you should be handling the questioning."

"Do you know who shot him, Doc?"

"Wayne Braddick was in here just before the shooting, telling Sonny to stay away from his daughter. He made a threat."

"Where were you?"

"Hiding in the ambulance. I came here searching for that straw doll."

"You should have asked me," he said. "It's back at my office. I picked it up as evidence."

Mayor Cutler would not be kept away. "Is this killing connected with the murder of Early Winters?" he demanded to know.

"We won't be sure until we compare the bullets," Sheriff Lens told him. "We may have to send them to the FBI lab in Washington. There's no one around here with the equipment for that sort of work."

Seth Sterne shook his head sadly. "I'm certain I locked that side door tonight."

"It was unlocked when I arrived, and Sonny followed me in within minutes," I said. "Did he have a key for it?"

"Well, yes, in case the ambulance was needed when I was away from the house. I suppose he might have come out here for something."

I turned to look at Sheriff Lens. "We'd better go talk to Wayne Braddick," he said.

The mayor was on that remark in an instant. "Braddick? What's he got to do with it?"

"Dr. Sam heard him threatening Sonny just before the shooting."

"I can't believe that. Why would he threaten a kid like Sonny?"

"To warn him away from Jessica," I said. I left the mayor standing there and followed Sheriff Lens out of the garage.

* * *

Wayne Braddick saw us arriving and met us at the door, switching on the porch light as we approached. "I just heard on the radio that there's been another killing. Somebody shot that McGuire boy."

"That's right," the sheriff confirmed. "We want to talk with you about it."

Braddick glanced around nervously. "We can talk here where we won't disturb my wife and daughter."

I didn't want to entrap him into making a false statement so I laid our cards on the table. "Wayne, I was in Seth's garage tonight. I heard you threaten Sonny just before he was shot."

"You—? I didn't see you."

"I was in the ambulance. I heard a shot not a minute after you stopped talking."

"Then you must have heard me drive away before that shot."

I hadn't, but I couldn't swear that he'd still been there when Sonny was killed. "Did you have a gun with you?" the sheriff asked him.

"Of course not! That was just a threat I made. You must know I'm not a violent man."

"A threat to one's family can turn many peaceful men violent," I pointed out.

Jessica came downstairs then, attracted by our voices. "What is it, Daddy? What's happened?"

"Sonny McGuire has been killed," he told her. "Go back upstairs. I'll be up in a minute."

"Sonny? Dead?" Her face seemed to mirror more surprise than shock at the news. She looked from one face to another, waiting for more information. Then she turned and ran up the stairs.

"She'll be all right," her father said.

"Who would have wanted both Early Winters and Sonny dead?" I asked.

"I have no idea."

I glanced toward the kitchen and suddenly froze. Propped up against the refrigerator was Jessica's female scarecrow with its breasts and long hair. "What—?"

Braddick managed a soft chuckle. "I told her she can't leave it there till fall."

Then I remembered. Mayor Cutler had wanted duplicates made in case of vandalism. "Of course," I muttered, grabbing onto Sheriff Lens. "Come on, Sheriff. We have another call to make."

We spent twenty minutes searching Early Winters's house, concentrating on the basement and the garage. Then we checked the barn and outbuildings, the glow from the lights illuminating only empty stalls. His neighbors had taken in the livestock.

"It's not here." I decided finally.

Sheriff Lens scratched his head. "Maybe he didn't make one, Doc."

"Of course he made one."

"I don't see why that's important."

"Remember the straw doll?"

"Sure, but I—"

"Come on, Sheriff."

The last of the deputies' cars had left Seth Sterne's house by the time we returned. There were still lights on in the house, and in the darkness I didn't see him in the backyard until there was a sudden flare of a match at the burning barrel. Then I was out of the car and running toward it. "Don't do it, Seth!"

"Doc! He's got a gun!" Sheriff Lens shouted as flames shot up from the burning barrel.

Seth Sterne fired and I dropped to the ground. There was an answering shot from the sheriff, aimed at the flash of the gun. Seth gasped and I saw him go down. We both reached him at the same time and I kicked the gun away. The bullet had caught him in the side and he was trying to stanch the flow of blood. "You killed me!" he cried out.

"No such luck," I told him. "You'll live to stand trial for two murders. Sheriff, stamp out that fire while we still have some evidence left."

"What was he trying to burn?"

"Early Winters's scarecrow from Congress Park."

* * *

We took Seth to the hospital in the sheriff's car, with the siren shrieking. While they wheeled him into the operating room to probe for the bullet, we talked about the murders in the waiting room.

"You'll still have to work on the motive," I said, "but with Seth's reputation as a ladies' man, you may come up with evidence that he was friendly with Evangeline Winters. Whether true or not, I think Seth suspected Early of killing his wife or at least contributing to her death. When Early's scarecrow was chosen to be shown in Congress Park, Seth found a way of getting revenge by committing the perfect crime, or so the thought."

"The perfect impossible crime?"

"It wasn't meant to be impossible," I told him. "Seth had no way of knowing that Early would come to me when he found that straw doll on his kitchen floor. If I hadn't seen him alive an hour before his body was found, it might have appeared he'd been killed during the night, at least until an autopsy was performed and the time of death established."

"Why was the straw doll left on his kitchen floor?"

"That's what I asked myself, Sheriff. Why risk breaking into the house when the doll would have served the same purpose if left outside on the steps? The answer came to me almost at once. The doll was left for misdirection, to hide the fact that the house had been broken into for another purpose. Yet nothing seemed to have been taken. It wasn't till this evening at Jessica's house when I saw her duplicate scarecrow that it came to me. The person who broke into Early's farmhouse left the straw doll but stole the duplicate scarecrow."

"Seth?"

"More likely his accomplice Sonny. If Seth had broken into the house, he probably would have gone upstairs and killed Early then and there. But Sonny brought back the scarecrow as ordered and Seth used some excuse to lure Early to his house. Seth shot him through the heart and then Sonny helped put the body inside the duplicate scarecrow. Early was a small man, remember, so it wasn't too difficult. Then they put that scarecrow on the stretcher in the ambulance and drove to the park, not knowing that I'd seen the dead man just before lunch."

"How'd they get the scarecrow onto the lamppost without anybody noticing?"

"They never did, Sheriff. Early's body was never inside the scarecrow on the lamppost."

"The blood—"

"Sonny squirted it, or a reasonable facsimile, from his water pistol as he walked by the scarecrow. Then he called attention to the blood and Seth swung his ambulance around right on schedule. Seth confirmed there was a body in the scarecrow and immediately produced a pair of wire cutters to snip it free. That should have told us something. How many ambulance drivers carry wire cutters in their pocket?"

"So he and Sonny carried the scarecrow on the stretcher to the ambulance. Then what?"

"While the ambulance doors partially blocked our view, they slid the empty scarecrow onto the bottom storage shelf and hid it from view. Then Seth started working on the duplicate scarecrow with Early's body inside. I even helped him uncover the body and declared Early dead, never realizing a substitution had been made."

"How can you be so sure that's what happened?"

"When I came here to the hospital earlier searching for that missing straw doll, I checked Early's coverall pockets and the scarecrow's too. They'd forgotten to squirt blood on the scarecrow's bib overalls, and it hadn't soaked through from inside. There was blood on Early's shirt and overalls, but not on the scarecrow's bib. It didn't match the one they removed from the lamppost. When I remembered that, I knew there'd been a substitution."

"Why did he kill Sonny?"

"The young man had to be his accomplice, of course. Even though Early Winters was small, he had muscles and weighed well over a hundred pounds. Sonny would have known there was no body inside the scarecrow they carried to the ambulance. And he would have seen Seth hide the scarecrow on the lower shelf below the duplicate containing the body. Seth was probably looking for an opportunity to get rid of a dangerous accomplice. When he overheard Wayne Braddick threatening Sonny in the garage tonight he had the perfect opportunity. He may have brought the gun with him when he heard voices in his garage. As soon as Wayne left, Seth shot Sonny. He might have testified later that he saw Wayne's car leaving the scene."

The sheriff nodded. "That gun should be enough to make our case."

A surgeon had come out of the operating room. He was a young man I barely knew. "I've got good news," he said with a smile. "We were able to remove the bullet and Mr. Sterne should stage a full recovery."

"Now the county has to pay for a trial," Sheriff Lens grumbled.

A DR. SAM HAWTHORNE CHECKLIST

BOOKS:

Diagnosis: Impossible, The Problems of Dr. Sam Hawthorne. Norfolk: Crippen & Landru Publishers, 1996. Contains Dr. Sam's first twelve cases.

More Things Impossible, The Second Casebook of Dr. Sam Hawthorne. Norfolk: Crippen & Landru Publishers, 2006. Contains Dr. Sam's next 15 problems.

Nothing Is Impossible, Further Problems of Dr. Sam Hwthorne. Norfolk: Crippen & Landru Publishers, 2013. Contains 15 more problems.

All But Impossible, The Impossible Files of Dr. Sam Hawthorne. Norfolk: Crippen & Landru Publishers, 2017. Contains 15 more problems.

INDIVIDUAL STORIES:

All of Dr. Sam Hawthorne's reminiscences were first published in *Ellery Queen's Mystery Magazine* [EQMM]. Dates when the events took place are recorded below in brackets.

"The Problem of the Covered Bridge" [March 1922]. EQMM, December 1974.

"The Problem of the Old Gristmill" [July 1923]. EQMM, March 1975.

"The Problem of the Lobster Shack" [June 1924]. EQMM, September 1975.

"The Problem of the Haunted Bandstand" [July 1924]. EQMM, January 1976.

"The Problem of the Locked Caboose" [Spring 1925]. EQMM, May 1976.

"The Problem of the Little Red Schoolhouse" [Fall 1925]. EQMM, September 1976.

"The Problem of the Christmas Steeple" [December 25, 1925]. EQMM, January 1977.

"The Problem of Cell 16" [Spring 1926]. EQMM, March 1977.

"The Problem of the Country Inn" [Summer 1926]. EQMM, September 1977.

"The Problem of the Voting Booth" [November 1926]. EQMM, December 1977.

"The Problem of the County Fair" [Summer 1927]. EQMM, February 1978.

"The Problem of the Old Oak Tree" [September 1927]. EQMM, July 1978.

"The Problem of the Revival Tent" [Fall 1927]. EQMM, November 1978.

"The Problem of the Whispering House" [February 1928]. EQMM, April 1979.

"The Problem of the Boston Common" [Spring 1928]. EQMM, August 1979.

"The Problem of the General Store" [Summer 1928]. EQMM, November 1979.

"The Problem of the Courthouse Gargoyle" [September 1928]. EQMM, June 30, 1980.

"The Problem of the Pilgrims' Windmill" [March 1929]. EQMM, September 10, 1980.

"The Problem of the Gingerbread Houseboat" [Summer 1929]. EQMM, January 28, 1981.

"The Problem of the Pink Post Office" [October 1929]. EQMM, June 17, 1981.

"The Problem of the Octagon Room" [December 1929]. EQMM, October 7, 1981.

"The Problem of the Gypsy Camp" [January 1930]. EQMM, January 1, 1982.

"The Problem of the Bootleggers' Car" [May 1930]. EQMM, July 1982.

"The Problem of the Tin Goose" [July 1930]. EQMM, December 1982.

"The Problem of the Hunting Lodge" [Fall 1930]. EQMM, May 1983.

"The Problem of the Body in the Haystack" [July 1931]. EQMM, August 1983.

"The Problem of Santa's Lighthouse" [December 1931]. EQMM, December 1983.

"The Problem of the Graveyard Picnic" [Spring 1932]. EQMM, June 1984.

"The Problem of the Crying Room" [June 1932]. EQMM, November 1984.

"The Problem of the Fatal Fireworks" [July 4, 1932]. EQMM, May 1985.

"The Problem of the Unfinished Painting" [Fall 1932]. EQMM, February 1986.

"The Problem of the Sealed Bottle" [December 5, 1933]. EQMM, September 1986.

"The Problem of the Invisible Acrobat" [July 1933]. EQMM, Mid-December 1986.

"The Problem of the Curing Barn" [September 1934]. EQMM, August 1987.

"The Problem of the Snowbound Cabin" [January 1935]. EQMM, December 1987.

"The Problem of the Thunder Room" [March 1935]. EQMM, April 1988.

"The Problem of the Black Roadster" [April 1935]. EQMM, November 1988.

"The Problem of the Two Birthmarks" [May 1935]. EQMM, May 1989.

"The Problem of the Dying Patient" [June 1935]. EQMM, December 1989.

"The Problem of the Protected Farmhouse" [August or September 1935]. EQMM, May 1990.

"The Problem of the Haunted Tepee" [September 1935]. EQMM, December 1990. Also featuring Ben Snow.

"The Problem of the Blue Bicycle" [September 1936]. EQMM, April 1991.

"The Problem of the Country Church" [November 1936]. EQMM, August 1991.

"The Problem of the Grange Hall" [March 1937]. EQMM, Mid-December 1991.

"The Problem of the Vanishing Salesman" [May 1937]. EQMM, August 1992.

"The Problem of the Leather Man" [August 1937]. EQMM, December 1992.

"The Problem of the Phantom Parlor" [August 1937]. EQMM, June 1993.

"The Problem of the Poisoned Pool" [September 1937]. EQMM, December 1993.

"The Problem of the Missing Roadhouse" [August 1938]. EQMM, June 1994.

"The Problem of the Country Mailbox" [Fall 1938]. EQMM, Mid-December 1994.

"The Problem of the Crowded Cemetery" [Spring 1939]. EQMM, May 1995.

"The Problem of the Enormous Owl" [August-September 1939]. EQMM, January 1996.

"The Problem of the Miraculous Jar" [November 1939]. EQMM, August 1996.

"The Problem of the Enchanted Terrace" [October 1939]. EQMM, April 1997.

"The Problem of the Unfound Door" [Midsummer 1940]. EQMM, June 1998.

"The Second Problem of the Covered Bridge" [January 1940]. EQMM, December 1998.

"The Problem of the Scarecrow Congress" [late July 1940]. EQMM, June 1999.

"The Problem of Annabel's Ark" [September 1940]. EQMM, March 2000.

"The Problem of the Potting Shed" [October 1940]. EQMM, July 2000.

"The Problem of the Yellow Wallpaper" [November 1940]. EQMM, March 2001.

"The Problem of the Haunted Hospital" [March 1941]. EQMM, August 2001.

"The Problem of the Traveler's Tale" [August 1941]. EQMM, June 2002.

"The Problem of Bailey's Buzzard" [December 1941]. EQMM, December 2002.

"The Problem of the Interrupted Séance" [June 1942]. EQMM, September/ October 2003.

"The Problem of the Candidate's Cabin" [October-November 1942]. EQMM, July 2004.

"The Problem of the Black Cloister" [April 1943]. EQMM, December 2004.

"The Problem of the Secret Passage" [May 1943]. EQMM July 2005.

"The Problem of the Devil's Orchard" [September 1943]. EQMM, January 2006.

"The Problem of the Shepherd's Ring" [December 1943]. EQMM, September/ October 2006.

"The Problem of the Suicide Cottage" [July 1944]. EQMM, July 2007.

"The Problem of the Summer Snowman" [August 1944]. EQMM, November 2007.

"The Problem of the Secret Patient" [December 1944]. EQMM, May 2008.

All But Impossible

All But Impossible, The Impossible Files of Dr. Sam Hawthorne, by Edward D. Hoch, is set in Goudy Old Style, with one small bit in Arial. It is printed on sixty-pound Natures acid-free, recycled paper. The cover design is by Gail Cross. The first edition was published in two forms: trade softcover, notch-bound; and one hundred fifty copies sewn in cloth, numbered and signed by the author of the introduction. Each of the clothbound copies includes a separate pamphlet, *The Long Way Down*, an impossible crime story by Edward D. Hoch. *All But Impossible* was typeset by G.E. Satheesh, Pondicherry, India, and printed and bound by Thomson-Shore, Inc., Dexter, Michigan. It was published in June 2017 by Crippen & Landru Publishers, Inc., Norfolk, Virginia.

CRIPPEN & LANDRU, PUBLISHERS
P. O. Box 9315
Norfolk, VA 23505
Web: www.crippenlandru.com
E-mail: info@crippenlandru.com

Since 1994, Crippen & Landru has published more than 100 first editions of short-story collections by important detective and mystery writers. Please check our website for in-print books.

☞This is the best edited, most attractively packaged line of mystery books introduced in this decade. The books are equally valuable to collectors and readers. [*Mystery Scene Magazine*]

☞The specialty publisher with the most star-studded list is Crippen & Landru, which has produced short story collections by some of the biggest names in contemporary crime fiction. [*Ellery Queen's Mystery Magazine*]

☞God Bless Crippen & Landru. [*The Strand Magazine*]

☞A monument in the making is appearing year by year from Crippen & Landru, a small press devoted exclusively to publishing the criminous short story. [*Alfred Hitchcock's Mystery Magazine*]